Praise for William Gay

The Lost Country

"If you fancy a blast of full-on Americana, it's hard to think of anything published recently that blasts in such a brilliantly sustained way—or that makes much of contemporary fiction suddenly seem so bloodless by comparison."
—*The Times*

"Gay's style was fully formed: sinister and lovely, dark and atmospheric, blood-soaked and word-drunk. He fit squarely in the Southern Gothic tradition, but the languid, unrolling richness of his language made the stories and novels that followed feel fresh, a rebirth of a genre prone to pale imitations."
—*The Wall Street Journal*

"An eerie, stream-of-consciousness drift through storms, death, and mystery in midcentury Tennessee."
—*Garden & Gun*

"Gay's great abilities in character building, richness of language and storytelling are on full display in this posthumous novel."
—Charles Frazier, National Book Award-winning author of *Varina*

Little Sister Death

"Chilling, beautiful, quietly shocking...a study of the writer: his temperament, his torment, and his devil's pact for the price of a good story."
—*The Independent*

"*Little Sister Death* is not a glib meta-commentary on horror...but a personal glimpse at Gay's own life, at the way a dedicated artist does not exorcise his demons—but seeks them out, and invites them in."
—*Electric Lit*

"Gay's signature muscular prose, authentic dialogue, and vivid setting combine to make this posthumous novel a worthwhile read."
—*Publishers Weekly*

"Cannily crafted, exceptional in its storytelling and doubly seductive in its sultry Southern setting…*Little Sister Death* is literary horror of the highest order." —*Tor.com*

"Gay takes the familiar trope of the haunted house and imbues it with a slow-burning melancholy and a sense of the inescapability of fate." —*Big Issue*

"If you mix Stephen King with William Faulkner, the result would be the posthumous novel *Little Sister Death* by William Gay…a great read for a quiet night at home, in an empty house, with the lights off except for a lone reading lamp." —*The Knoxville News Sentinel*

THE LONG HOME

"Gay has created a novel of great emotional power." —*Denver Post*

"It'll leave you breathless…" —*Rocky Mountain News*

PROVINCES OF NIGHT

"Earthily idiosyncratic, spookily Gothic…an author with a powerful vision." —*The New York Times*

"An extremely seductive read." —*Washington Post Book World*

"Southern writing at its very finest, soaked through with the words and images of rural Tennessee, packed full of that which really matters, the problems of the human heart." —*Booklist*

"A writer of striking talent." —*Chicago Tribune*

"This is a novel from the old school. The characters are truly characters. The prose is Gothic. And the charm is big." —*The San Diego Union-Tribune*

"Writers like Flannery O'Connor or William Faulkner would welcome Gay as their peer for getting characters so entangled in the roots of a family tree." —*Star Tribune* (Minneapolis)

"[A novel] about the preciousness of hope, the fragility of dreams, interwoven with a good-sized dollop of Biblical justice and the belief that a Southern family can be cursed." —*The Miami Herald*

"An old-fashioned barrel-aged shot of Tennessee storytelling. Gay's tale of ancient wrongs and men with guns is high-proof stuff." —Elwood Reid, author of *Midnight Sun* and *What Salmon Know*

"A finely wrought, moving story with a plot as old as Homer. Sometimes the old ones are the best ones." —*The Atlanta Journal Constitution*

"William Gay is the big new name to include in the storied annals of Southern lit." —*Esquire*

"Gay is a terrific writer." —*The Plain Dealer*

TWILIGHT

"Think *No Country for Old Men* by Cormac McCarthy and *Deliverance* by James Dickey…then double the impact." —Stephen King

"There is much to admire here: breathtaking, evocative writing and a dark, sardonic humor." —*USA Today*

"William Gay brings the daring of Flannery O'Connor and William Gaddis to his lush and violent surrealist yarns." —*The Irish Times*
"This is Southern Gothic of the very darkest hue, dripping with atmosphere, sparkling with loquacity, and with occasional gleams of horrible humor. To be read in the broadest daylight." —*The Times*

I Hate to See that Evening Sun Go Down

"William Gay is richly gifted: a seemingly effortless storyteller…a writer of prose that's fiercely wrought, pungent in detail yet poetic in the most welcome sense."   —*The New York Times Book Review*

"One perfect tale follows another, leaving you in little doubt that Gay is a genuine poet of the ornery, the estranged, the disenfranchised, crafting stories built to last."   —*Seattle Times*

"Gay confirms his place in the Southern fiction pantheon."
     —*Publishers Weekly*

"Every story is a masterpiece…in the Southern tradition of Carson McCullers, Flannery O'Connor, and William Faulkner."   —*USA Today*

"As charming as it is wise. Hellfire—in all the right ways."
     —*Kirkus Reviews*

"[Gay] brings to these stories the same astounding talent that earned his two novels…a devoted following."   —*Booklist*

"Supple and beautifully told tales…saturated with an intense sense of place, their vividness and authenticity are impossible to fake."
     —*The San Diego Union-Tribune*

"Gay writes about old folks marvelously.…[His] words ring like crystal."
     —*Washington Post Book World*

"Even Faulkner would have been proud to call these words his own."
     —*The Atlanta Journal Constitution*

Stories from the Attic

William Gay

DZANC
BOOKS

DZANC
BOOKS

2580 Craig Rd.
Ann Arbor, MI 48103
www.dzancbooks.org

Library of Congress Cataloging-in-Publication Data Available on Request

First paperback edition: July 2024
Jacket design by Steven Seighman
Interior design by Michelle Dotter
ISBN 9781950539963

Printed in the United States of America

10   9   8   7   6   5   4   3   2   1

Contents

FRAGMENTS

POSTSCRIPT

The world will take care of you if you'll let it....if you go in the same direction nature wants to go. Cross it and it will destroy you. Fight it and it'll break you like a prisoner on the wheel and rack.

—William Gay

PREFACE

This collection of short stories is taken from the William Gay archive found after his death in February 2012. His family quickly discovered that he left a huge horde of unpublished writing including four novels and this collection of short stories. The bulk of these stories were found among the handwritten manuscripts which were stored in the attic of the house where he raised his kids. In addition to these short stories, this collection includes four memoirs about his life as a writer and four fragments from unpublished works in progress.

William started writing as a teenager and never stopped. Remarkably he managed to hang onto much of the material, even during his frequent moves. He was constantly watching for stories he could use and characters to populate them. There are notebooks with stories from each decade, starting with the fifties and continuing up to his death. By the late seventies he had perfected his style and some of the stories in this collection date from that time. By then he was writing stories and working on the novels that would bring him literary fame. He was submitting stories constantly and found, to his dismay, that sending out his work was a thankless and discouraging endeavor. He eventually found an agent in New York and got one of his novels typed into a suitable manuscript to shop around Manhattan. During this time, if he got any feedback at all, it was typically his agent or a potential publisher saying they liked the story, but he would have to get rid of the flowery language. He read William Faulkner and Thomas Wolfe as literary role models and he studied their styles intensely. By the late seventies he had been writing for over twenty years and he was not about to back off the lyrical realism that he had worked so hard to create. Yet it would be another twenty years before he saw anything accepted for publication. It is a measure of his determination and of his destiny as a writer that he wrote for over forty years before being published.

This book represents the unpublished short stories from the archive along with a few pieces that were published in the last few years of his life but never appeared in any of his books. All the short stories in this collection except two are previously unpublished. The story, "Homecoming," was published in *Blue Moon Café II*, and "The Dream" was published, posthumously, in *The James Dickey Review*.

The four memoirs published here read like fiction and, while he was clearly writing about his own life, he was doing it in the form of a short story. Two of the memoirs are accounts of his interior life finding Southern fiction and its inspiration in his life. "Wreck on the Highway" is thinly veiled fiction, William changed the names of the characters in the story, naming himself Vestal and giving his son a different name but the story is a very straight forward re-telling of a terrible incident in his life. The piece "Fumbling for the Keys to the Doors of Perception" is more lighthearted. It was published by Sonny Brewer who requested that William give him a story to include in one of his *Blue Moon Café* anthologies, so William came up with this piece which is a story of one of the factory jobs he had as a young man. He would work at a job for a few weeks or months and then, when all the bills were paid, he would quit and sit home and write. It drove his wife crazy as she had to make ends meet for four kids. Then, when the wolves were at the door, William would stop writing and go out and find another job and make some money until they were caught up and then do it again. This story is an account of one of those episodes.

The Faulkner piece was commissioned by the Great Books Company. When they decided to do a folio edition of *As I Lay Dying,* they commissioned William to write the preface. He was flattered and delighted with the hefty payment they gave him. In it he described the impact the book had on his life and his writing. The other piece about reading Southern literature was the last thing he published, which came out shortly after his death.

The first of the two unfinished novels, titled *The Trace,* was about the early days on the Natchez Trace, and the second, *The Wreck of the Tennessee Gravy Train,* is the piece he was working on when he died. The first was from a novel he was writing in 1990. While he was working on it, he went off to a literary conference and came back to discover someone had broken into his trailer and stolen his CDs, DVDs, and all the notebooks that had his current work in progress. The Natchez Trace goes through Lewis County and was only a mile from where he was living. It intrigued him, and he started a novel about people traveling on the Trace. I remember him remarking that he thought the scene about the flooded river was some of his best writings. He never knew, but always suspected, who broke into the trailer. He found some of the music and movies but never found the manuscript. However, about 2018 I had a call from Hohenwald offering to sell me one of William's paintings. When I went to pick up the painting, I saw a stack of yellow pads and quickly recognized they were covered with William's distinctive handwriting. I bought them, along with the painting, and there was the stolen manuscript.

We see a number of characters in these stories who reappear in the novels: Winer from *The Long Home*, Stoneburner from the novel by the same name. Sheriff Bellwether will be familiar to many of William's readers. William created a literary landscape and many of the characters who inhabit that landscape appear and reappear in different books and stories, all set in the countryside around Ackerman's Field and the Harrikin. He was fond of the name "Yates", and we see different members of the Yates family in a variety of stories. Some of the characters in these short stories were fleshed out and given major roles in later, more substantive works. Now that we have the complete oeuvre of William's work, we can get the full picture of these characters and their inter-relationships. William was always questioned at literary conferences about how he wrote. One of the things he said was that he would often start with a short story and then the theme of the story would develop, and it would become a novel. I believe the Stoneburner story is the first inspiration for the novel of that name.

William seldom dated his work, though there are occasional clues and indications that date the stories. By the late 1970s he had come into his own and was writing in the style that would define him. In the unfinished story, "My Brother's Keeper," he was still using quotation marks around the "voices" of the characters. At some point in his evolution as a writer, following the style of one of his favorite popular authors, Davis Grubb, he stopped using quotation marks and let the reader figure out when the characters are speaking by indenting each line of dialogue. Consequently, it is easy to assume that this story, where he still retained the quotation marks, was earlier than those that don't have the quotation marks. But for uniformity of style the decision was made to cut the quotation marks since he clearly didn't consider them necessary, and it was a characteristic of his style not to use them. However, this is probably the earliest piece of writing in this collection.

Finally, in the last year of his life, William started talking about a novel he was writing titled *The Wreck of the Tennessee Gravy Train*. However, it was a bad year for him, he had a severe heart attack and had to wear a pacemaker. Then his youngest daughter got cancer and it looked like she wasn't going to make it, and it really distracted him. Consequently, he wasn't doing a lot of writing, but he did work on this story and had a couple of chapters worked out in his notebooks. Then he had another heart attack, and there was no coming back from this one. His daughter died of cancer a month later.

These four fragments all have the characteristic lyrical realism of his poetic prose, so it seemed fitting to include them in the collection. Clearly unfinished, they are offered to the readers as the works in progress of a literary genius who, for various reasons, was never able to complete them. Nonetheless, they deserve a place in his literary legacy.

—JMW

SHORT STORIES

THE ASCENSION OF PEPPER YATES

Yates had caught two already today and was waiting for a third. He was lounging in the begarbed Cadillac in the sideroad where the sumac both shaded and concealed him, his eyes fixed on the blacktop like a predator's. Cars passed, trucks, one by one he discounted them, just anyone would not do. He prided himself on his knowledge, knowing the selection process. Finally, a ten-year-old Plymouth station wagon with Florida plates drove into view, an old purple-haired woman was crouched over the wheel and beside her a wizened old man with a golf cap drooped over his shrunken skull. Yates was instantly out of the sideroad upon them, riding their rear bumper, red light winding and siren wailing and his intent little fox face fixing the wildeyed old woman's reflection in the rearview mirror with the stern authority of the law.

The Plymouth veered to the shoulder of the road, sat idling. Yates eased the Cadillac in behind it and got out, taking a notepad out of his pocket and wearing his most official expression. The woman had started rolling down the glass. Yates had shut off the siren but he left the red light revolving.

Hidy, he said. For a while she didn't speak, sat regarding his approach apprehensively.

Officer? she finally said, the question mark audible, for there was little about him or the car that inspired confidence and surely even in his too big khaki garb he was clearly no officer of even so warped and blasted a backwoods as this, just something conjured up by the morning August heat, a familiar of this lonesome backroad.

Yates was tipping his cop's cap with a studious deference. His hair beneath it a motley of fine gold curls Rapunzel might have spun. His wily fox's face cunning beneath the transparent innocence, his demented child's demeanor caught ever between arrogance and obsequiousness.

You about to run a wheel off there, he called sternly.

Do what?

You about to lose a wheel, that right rear. Didn't you feel it wobblin and carryin on?

No, she said, looking past him to study the car, a car unlike any police car that ever was, a madman's dream of a police car, a police car that had grown warped and mutant and alien, garbed and bedecked with fish pole antennae and foglights and mudflaps studded with ruby glass reflectors and any fancy car part imaginable that could be mail ordered out of anywhere.

Lord, I don't know how you held in the road. Must have mighty good shocks.

Who are you?

I'm the Law, Yates said. I'm a duly deputized deputy in Flatwoods.

The old man was punching the woman on the arm. What is it? He demanded. She was ignoring him. He quit pummeling her and began to fiddle with an enormous turnip-shaped hearing aid.

What can we do? the old woman was saying. Can you fix it?

They Lord, Yates said. I'm the law, not no licensed mechanic. Where was you goin?

Gatlinburg. Do you suppose we could make it that far?

I doubt you'll make it on that wheel to the next bend in the road, Yates said.

Then what can we do? Is there a mechanic around here?

Yates looked all about, as if there might be one crouched in concealment somewhere. His face wrinkled in concentration, trying to think of one.

The old man had taken off the hearing aid and was slapping it viciously against the palm of his hand. What's the matter? What's the matter? he kept saying. The woman continued to ignore him.

Well, what can we do then?

Yates pondered, scratched his fair head, hair like spun gold. You might make it to Duckbutter's.

To where?

Old Jess Duckbutter got a garage right up the road from here. About a mile and a half. Just take the next exit, the Flatwoods road. It'll be the first building you see, a big old white one. Right next to the Belly Stretcher Café.

The woman nodded, looked slightly dazed, as if either the heat or Yates or this blighted place had rendered her insensate. Well, we appreciate you stopping us. Lots of folks would have just drove on and went about their business.

Helpin folks is my business, Yates said. I'll follow you a piece, make sure you get there all right. You drive careful, now. We proud to have ye in Tennessee.

He retraced his steps, got into the old Cadillac, watched her inch cautiously onto the blacktop, as if it were made of eggs. He withdrew a small notebook from his shirt pocket, made a note of the license number, then eased into gear, flipped the red light off and followed them sedately. The woman was driving about ten miles an hour.

At the exit she turned onto the Flatwoods road. Below in the valley he could see Duckbutter's garage; it was a white stucco building completely surrounded by a vast ochre field of derelict car bodies, cars of every make and model and degree of decomposition. In the wavering heat the white building was a buoy rocking on a rusty sea.

When he saw the Plymouth pull into the service station he

turned laboriously with much backing up and pulling forward and squealing of tires, returned to his rounds. Eyes alert for more prospects, ever wary for speeders and DWIs.

Pepper Yates had always wanted to be a policeman; it was an obsession, he literally ached with a sexual intensity to be a law. It was just another part of the curse that seemed to have dogged him all his life. His father had been an itinerant preacher, travelling from town to town with his old guitar strapped to his back, preaching in the streets for pennies or playing in the beer joints for nickels. He pretended to be blind, and generally was if he had met with any degree of success and there was a bootlegger available. Followed by a ragtag covey of jeering children, sleeping wherever chance decreed or night overtook him; usually at the stockbarn, ranting drunken salvation at hogs and cows already doomed to the meatpacker's mallet and long past any feeble absolution he might offer.

His mother had disappeared one Saturday night as finally as if she had stepped through a fault in the earth and was seen no more. But he had no doubt that wherever she was her mouth would still be painted in a drunken cupid's bow, and she would still be cadging beer and juke-box quarters off sawmill hands.

But if his parents had been hard to take, his brother had been the worst. His brother Clyde had been an idiot. He was older than Pepper and even at nineteen he had gone around with a steering wheel he had replevied from some dump or other, steering himself everywhere he went, making slobbery chugging noises and gearing himself up and down hills. When he stopped he always screeched his brakes and set his emergency brake so he would not fall away. But the worst thing about him was that he would not leave. He did not have enough sense to go anywhere else, did not even know that anywhere else existed.

He would follow Pepper as far as he could, gearing vainly into second on the straights, at last dropping behind, lost in dog days dust while Pepper went on his rounds selling Watkins products from his old bicycle he had constructed from cast-off parts.

Then after his mother had disappeared and his father had been sent to prison for crimes against nature (the cow had not been charged), people in suits and ties had come at last and taken Clyde away. It had been hard to take. Pepper had denied his heritage, claimed that he had been a foundling, ending by unfortuitous circumstances on old Cy Yates's uninviting hearth. Duckbutter had told him once, I'll be goddamned if I'd deny my own people. Two things I won't do is pimp for my sister and lie about my people.

You ain't got no sister, Yates pointed out.

No, but I got brothers and a daddy and a mama.

Well, I ain't.

The law had been his salvation, Henry Garrison his hero. Garrison in his khaki uniform, patrolling the back roads, blackjacking miscreants and keeping the country safe for Pepper Yates and his ilk. Stopping suspicious-looking attractive women on dusty roads, standing with his enormous khaki butt cocked up in the air and his head stuck inside their car, mouth going a mile a minute. The .38 on his hip as lethal as a cancer.

He had passed Garrison in just such a manner one summer. As he pedaled by, the basket on his bicycle full of Watkins liniment and vanilla flavoring, Garrison had called after him: You better hold her down, Lightin. Catch you speedin again I'll run that ass in.

The woman's laughter had arisen, raucous and sharp as broken bottles. He had become suddenly aware of how he looked, skinny ribs showing, soda-straw arms and a pale chest like an undernourished pigeon. He had flushed from head to toe, vowed to someday redeem himself in Garrison's eyes.

Pepper had gotten his nickname in a similarly grotesque manner. His name had always been Junior, not anything Junior just Junior, until he and Jeannine, the fat nurse, had been two years married. What Yates liked to call a piece of stray had drifted through and Jeannine had caught him in the act. She had not done anything right then. She had waited, laying for him. That night she had thrown him against the side of their trailer. Then she had sat on him, tore his pants down and pulled his thing out. She had skinned it back and rubbed the head of it all over with a pod of cayenne pepper, blind to his writhing legs and deaf to his cries of agony.

She had also bragged about it in the pool hall, so that from then on Yates could not walk down the street without men calling after him, Hey, Pepper. How's ye pod hanging? The name had adhered to him like some vast sheet of flypaper that was slowly smothering him.

The only redemption in sight had been the Law. As soon as he was old enough he had begun running for constable every year, always in vain. He had put in unnumbered applications for city policeman. He had begged to be a deputy, traffic policeman, process server, anything. Finally they told him they could not hire him until someone retired. Then, when he got in the Civil Defense, he had begaudied his car with revolving lights and sirens and fishpole antennas that were connected to nothing capable of snatching a signal out of the air and worked all the parades, guiding ungrateful children across the streets, the butt of any slurring remark anyone cared to make.

The day was almost gone, the sun had begun to sink. Telephone pole shadows fell long and black and slanted. Yates could see only local traffic, had given up on another prospect for today. Prospects had to be selected carefully. He judged it to be near quitting time anyway. He drove back to the road, exited there. Flatwoods, the sign said. Home of Old South Charm. Jesus Christ is Coming, Be Ready, the next sign warned, but it did not say for what.

Duckbutter laid two tens on the counter, smoothed the wrinkles out of them, tenderly slid them toward Yates. Yates set his Double-Cola down, regarded them with malice. He made no move to pick them up.

You short one, ain't ye?

I don't reckon, Duckbutter said. Two is all I counted, and two ain't that far to count to.

Two hell. They was three. That old whiteheaded preacher and them two schoolteachers and then that old man and woman.

Man and woman? Duckbutter picked up a menu, used it to smash a blue-bottle fly. I don't believe I recall no man and woman.

Goddamn right man and woman. Yates withdrew his notebook, cited vital statistics, license plate numbers.

I must of missed them, Duckbutter said easily.

Well, shitfire. You couldn't of missed em. It was a purple-headed fat lady and a dried-up lil' old man had a hearin aid the size of a goddamn pork chop.

Oh, them, Duckbutter said. They just bought a dollar's worth of gas and went on. I guess they wan't sold as hard as you thought.

Oh, they was sold all right. They was sold one forty dollar wheel bearin job, and you give'm one, too. You cheatin bootleggin old bastard. You been beatin me out of my rightful wages God knows how many years. If they was any law in this goddamned town you'd be coughin up that other ten right this minute.

Duckbutter smiled, placating. Oh, well, there'll be others. Maybe tomorrow will be better.

Tomorrow's ass, Yates said. He grabbed the two tens, stuffed them into the pocket of his khaki city policeman's shirt. Gimme them Fat Boys.

Duckbutter slid him a sack containing a dozen Fat Boy hamburgers, turned to carton six cold Double-Colas. You comin out here tonight and help me? We'll get us a six-pack or two and lay for them kids been stealin them carburetors off of me.

I ain't studyin no shittin carburetors, Yates said viciously, jerking up the sack of Fat Boys, reaching for the Double-Colas. Don't you know this is Mule Day? I got a goddamn parade to run.

Yates's trailer sat in a shadeless field bare of tree or flower, a decrepit silver box canted on its concrete blocks as if it had been dropped from some great height, landing by happenstance upright in this scorching field. About it lay strewn the dismembered corpses of Detroit's larger models, parts scattered at random like tidbits dropped by some hasty metallic carnivore. Yates moved through this debris carrying the Fat Boys and cold drinks and a plastic bag from the dry cleaners.

Jeannine had the fan on and was sitting in front of it with her legs spread. She was sweating anyway. The trailer was sweltering, the heat seemed some satanic presence that hovered about them.

Jeannine arose with some effort, reached for the poke. Gimme them Fat Boys, she said. Yates handed them to her, set the drinks on the dining table, began to look for an opener.

Jeannine's whine began over the hum of the fan. She had a slow, aggravating way of talking, as if all her words came out stuck together with molasses. I've nearly foundered in this heat, she said. After ridin that old bus all the way from Memphis. All them old people sniggering at me. Looks like you could have took a day off from your precious job and drove me down there. Wouldn't hurt you to ever visit my people.

What was they sniggerin about, baby? Yates asked innocently.

I guess cause they suspected I was married to a skinny dried-up thing like you, she told him.

He ignored her. He had taken the plastic cover off his Civil Defense uniform, regarded with satisfaction the knife-edge creases, the crispy starched collar and cuffs. The gleaming lustrous buttons. He hung it carefully on a nail, began to wash his hands in the sink.

Where you think you're headed, Jeannine asked, her mouth full of Fat Boy.

Town, he said, beginning to pull his shirt off.

Town? You just come from town, Daddy. She finished the last Fat Boy, wadded its waxed paper wrapper and threw it in the corner. Why you goin back to town? I thought we might go to bed awhile, pass some time.

Hellfire, Yates said, knotting his tie. I ain't studyin no passin time. Don't you know this is Mule Day? I got a parade to run. Yates put on his pants, went to regard himself in the mirror. I just wisht I was a law, he said.

You and your old law. Bein a law don't mean nothing to anybody ever was a register nurse.

You wasn't no register nurse. All you ever done was empty bedpans and hold old folk's hands while they died.

A law ain't nothing alongside a register nurse, she said unperturbed.

A register nurse can't tote no pistol, he told her.

What was perhaps Yates's worst humiliation took place that night, the final indignity that forced him to nightshade deeds darker than any he had ever known.

He had his Cadillac parked at the intersection in front of the funeral home, directing traffic while the parade passed. It was the best Mule Day parade in anyone's memory. Championship mules went by on trucks, low-boys, on foot. Behind them came dancing girls and baton twirlers and majorettes, strutting past him with sequins sparkling, white thighs winking at him secrets he would never know. Marching band after marching band passed, the metallic airs strident in the summer night. All Flatwoods was one sweating throng of humanity with fireworks breaking high overhead, bathing them in the phosphorescent glare of skyrockets and roman candles, rocking them with heavenly blasts.

At the height of this celebration came the nadir of Yates's life. He was motioning traffic across the intersection with his brand-new twelve cell flashlight when old Mary Hinson and her gangling pair of teenage boys came by. Move it along, Yates told them in his official voice. As they passed even with him one of the boys jabbed his brother in the ribs and sniggered. You better straighten up, he said. There's the law. Mary Hinson was just an old whore anyway and Yates did not care what he said in front of her. I said move it, you little turds, he said out of the side of his mouth.

You little duck-legged son of a bitch, Mary said. She hit him alongside the head with her pocket book, erupting a strange Fortean rain of rouge jars and hair brushes and earrings and even a spare pair of shoes. He was knocked completely down. He fell backward on two little girls, spilling their popcorn and causing them to break into screams of rage and to commence pummeling him with their fists.

Talk about my boys thataway, Mary was saying, drawing back the pocket book again. Yates's ears were ringing like deathbells. He could barely hear her and his impaired vision cloned her into multiple threatening images, each bearing down upon him with the purse.

Laughter had broken out all around him, people were pointing at him and pounding each other on the back in near-delirious hilarity. He struggled to his hands and knees, began to crawl about and look for his flashlight. Mary and the boys went on down the street. Then he found the light, it had rolled or been kicked against the curb and it was broken. He picked it up tenderly. It had come by mail-order out of Chicago and he had given $19.95 for it. $19.95 would buy a lot of Fat Boy hamburgers.

Even though the parade was not over, Yates limped back to his car. As he was getting in Henry Garrison pulled parallel with him and rolled down the glass. What's the trouble, Slick?

None I know of, Yates said bitterly, turning off his red light and cranking the Cadillac.

I heard there was, Garrison sniggered. Listen, Slick. Handlin these parades is a lot of responsibility. If you can't handle it we gonna have to get somebody that can.

Yates made no reply. Garrison eased the car into gear, flipped on his lights and drove slowly up to the crossing. Yates watched with bleak eyes as Garrison began to guide the traffic effortlessly. Garrison was greyheaded and old now and should have been retired off the force long ago. Yates had tried in various ways to encourage him along, but so far it had all been fruitless. Now he sat hunched behind the wheel, engine idling and forgotten, wondering what sort of dark gods guided his fate. Struck down by a common whore. It would not have been so bad if she had been of the country club class.

It was still stifling in the trailer, the fan hummed ineffectually. The mindless round screen of the TV threw flickering gray images about. Yates moved through these images, pulling off his uniform, kicking his disgusted way through sacks of garbage and Fat Boy wrappers and Double-Cola bottles.

In the tiny bathroom he stared at his reflection, washed his face with cold water. He took down a pint bottle of bootleg whiskey from the top shelf of the medicine cabinet, dumped the toothbrushes out of their glass and half-filled it. He drank, gagged, and drank again.

He sat on the commode and drank, thinking about Mary Hinson. She wouldn't of done the law thataway, he said aloud. The law would of booted that wore-out ass for her. He imagined himself kicking her, his foot fairly tingling with anticipation. My time's coming, he told the walls, Jeannine asleep beyond the cardboard perimeter of light. It's been a long time comin but, by God, they'll know when it gets here.

He finished the whiskey, drank water from the tap, set the glass aside and went out. He got his shotgun from the hall closet and filled it with shells. He laughed softly to himself and went out the door, letting it fall to behind him.

Garrison lived out of town in a little white frame house isolated from any neighbors. It was a neat house with green shutters and a good-sized picture window. Pepper Yates stared at the window down the barrel of his shotgun. He was spread-eagled wet with dew in the high grass across from Garrison's driveway, peering above the jagged myopic horizon the grass made for any sign of light.

It was three o'clock in the morning and the house was still and dark, the only light the moon reflecting off the window and falling pale on the yard. Yates was no stranger to this high grass; he had crouched here on two other occasions, rising to dart bent and gnomic and wraithlike to the dark side of Garrison's squad car, spinning off the gas cap, unleashing a hushed snowfall of sugar, fading back into the shadows the way he had come. Yates had locked up the motors of the last two squad cars Garrison had had and the last time he had left a note, laboriously cut from a newspaper and pasted onto a grocery sack. RETIRE OR DIE, the note had said, signed cryptically, AN ENEMY YOU MADE ALONG THE WAY.

As if to leave no doubt of this enmity, Yates shot out the picture window. It was the loudest sound he had ever heard. There was an appalled hush from the nightbirds and into the deep ringing stillness came only a final tinkling of falling glass from inside the house, the tardy echo of the shot rolling back from the timbered hills. Yates swung the gun to the front door and cocked the hammer of the remaining barrel. He shut one eye and sighted, waited with held breath for the door to slowly open, Garrison's image to appear there like a developing photographic plate. He expelled his breath. You'd have just the sense to try it, he said. Wouldn't you?

Garrison did not appear. At last Yates lowered the gun, unbreeched it and reloaded the first barrel. As a cloud scudded over the moon and momentary dark fell Yates arose, faded watchfully backward until thickening timber enveloped him, began the trek back to the old log road where he had left his car.

When Yates got the phone call from Mayor Rittenberry he was seized by a feeling of apprehension, thought perhaps he'd been seen. He went into City Hall like a prisoner approaching the bench. But when he came back out into the blinding dog day sun, he was a man transformed. His step was light and airy, and he did not seem to know where he was, nor did he seem to care. He moved with jerky high steps as if he were jiggled along on strings by some careless puppeteer and his face had the stunned beatific smirk of one who has been called aside by God and had secrets whispered in his ear.

He was carrying a plastic bag containing a city policeman's uniform as reverently as if it were the Shroud of Turin and every few feet he would stop and look at it. He passed his car twice, once in each direction.

When he was finally ensconced behind the wheel he sat watching the passersby, felt a lofty pity for them; each luckless and each mortal, not yet privy to what he knew. All in all, he looked like a man for whom the dice had come round at last.

It was Sunday, and it was still hot. Yates and his fellow deputy, Doughgut, drove through a countryside blighted by dog days, past churchgoers strung out along dusty roads, past old lost Churches of God. One with a big handpainted sign caught Doughgut's attention.

DECIDE THIS MOMENT, it said: ROCK IN SWEET JESUS'S ARMS OR ROAST IN HELL.

I don't know why they had to send me, Doughgut said. I'm a valuable man. I been to fingerprint school and everything.

Just stick with me and you'll be all right. Pepper told him.

Doughgut did not even consider this worthy of reply. He gave Yates a withering look of contempt.

Scrappy Waters would have been put away years ago if juries wasn't afraid to convict him, Doughgut said. He's burnt people's houses, killed men and throwed them in old wells. Does juries convict him? Hell no, they turn him right aloose to do the same things over again. Put it off on us so we have to go get our asses shot off.

Waters lived in a shack made of scraps of lumber and RC Cola and Bull Durham tobacco signs and billboards with the faces of smiling political candidates on them. There was one tiny window and a face briefly there as the car spun onto the bare earth yard. The face was gone instantly. An old hound walked toward the car, urinated on the wheel, did not even deign to bark.

Git out and read him the warrant, Yates said.

Doughgut stared at him in disbelief. This is your show, he said. I don't even know what I'm doing here in the first place. I got a wife and a little bitty baby.

I'll see that this goes on your record, Yates told him. I'll do it my damn self. He got out with the warrant in his hand, made to approach the door.

When the gun barrel appeared in the window he whirled to run. The blast blew the heel completely off his right boot and spun him around sideways so that even as he drew the .38 he was falling. He rolled onto his stomach in the dust and steadied his shaking right hand with his left and fired four times very rapidly through the window. The air was filled with splintered glass and noise and a figure sprinted out the side door like a broken-field runner and made for the woods. Yates's eyes followed the fleeing figure above the pistol sights but it was only a girl in cut-off jeans.

He leapt up and ran to the police cruiser, scrambled in and put it in gear and pressed the accelerator to the floor. The cruiser slammed into the shack with the sounds of splintering wood and scraping metal, rent the smiling face of a long-forgotten candidate, halted bouncing on its springs with the wall caved and the joists dropped. Yates leapt out into a rain of rat manure and dirt-dauber nests.

I'm runnin that ass in, he screamed.

But the invincible Waters was past running anywhere, he was pinned between the hood of the cruiser and the other broken opposite wall where the car had halted. He had his arms thrown up as if he'd fight the strange metal beast hand to hand, but his fierce little eyes were glaring at nothing and he had vomited blood all down his front. Nobody had the presence of mind to take the cruiser out of gear and the rear wheels kept spinning on the edge of the sill and the hood bouncing impotently against Waters's chest. After a while Doughgut got out raking pebbles of safety glass out of his hair. He looked at Waters and then at Yates with his eyes round and white and his mouth opened as if he'd speak but he couldn't think of anything to say.

Yates lived in a constant state of exultation. His life carried him from one exhilarating peak to the next one. It was a wonder that his heart sustained him, that his blood pressure did not precipitate a stroke. He began to see his past life as some sort of bookkeeper's error. He had been denied even an existence, then when the mistake was discovered, whoever was in charge had begun to bestow reparation so lavishly that he did not know what to expect next.

The Nashville paper had printed his picture under a headline that said, FRONTIER STYLE SHOOTOUT LEAVES ONE DEAD.

Then the very next day he had arrested Log Chain Norton. Nobody had ever been able to arrest him before, but Yates caught him drunk and off-balance at the same time and blackjacked him right down to the floor and drug him off to jail. I'm runnin his ass in, he had said. Law had come to Flatwoods whether it wanted it or not.

Then on Saturday morning he had been parked in front of the Belly Stretcher Café trying to catch Duckbutter in the act of selling an untaxed half pint of whiskey when Scrappy Waters's daughter Charlene came out and walked slowly up the street. He watched her go.

Charlene...

She turned and he watched her undulate away, turning once to wave at him. He watched her out of sight with a kind of hunger. She was every cheerleader and high school sweetheart who ever dismissed him contemptuously with her eyes. He was not going to let her get away.

Now we're comin up in the world we need to do some inprovin ourselves, Jeannine told him that night. I aim to lose me a bunch of this ole weight and I need me some teeth. I seen some in a book just exactly like I want.

Teeth costs money, Pepper said. You ain't but thirty-five year old and you comin all to pieces.

We need to be thinkin of us a house, too.

Pepper remained silent. He had in fact been thinking of a house, had a picture of one in the back of his mind. It was a little white house with climbing roses almost covering one end of the porch. But it was located in a stand of trees on some land that until lately had belonged to Scrappy Waters, and the woman swinging right slow in the porch swing was not Jeannine.

You got your foot in the door now, her voice droned on. It sounded like a fingernail scraped endlessly across a blackboard and

Pepper had a headache. But secretly he thought her right. With a foot in the door there was no telling where a go-getter like himself might wind up. He saw himself as chief of police, even saw Mayor Rittenberry with Garrison on the sidelines.

They fell silent, sitting in the shade of the trailer, listening to the sound of whippoorwills calling from the distant woods.

Daddy, some man called out here today. A kind of funny phone call.

A faint tremor of unease coursed all through Pepper, like a flicker of summer lightning, the first beginnings of fear.

What kind of phone call?

Some man said you was foolin around with that old whore Charlene Waters.

People always got it in for the law, he said easily. They always tryin to make trouble for em.

Just so they don't think they the only ones can make trouble, she said darkly.

Pepper thought he would burst into flames, he felt completely engorged and congested, as if his entire body was tumescent. He and Charlene were parked on an old log road near the homesite he had picked out. She had her blouse off and had been letting him play with her breasts. They were the most fascinating things he had ever seen, he could not seem to get enough of fondling them and sucking on them and just looking at them. They were shaped like perfect cones and stood straight out with their nipples erect and were the softest things he had ever imagined.

It had not even been good dark when he had picked her up and it was now after nine o'clock. He had been going slowly mad. He was torn between a frenzy of desire for Charlene and a nagging fear of his wife. There was a six-pack of Double-Cola in the back floorboard already hot and a sack of Fat Boys already cold and what Jeannine was going through now and planning to do later was something he did not care to think about.

Charlene's cut-off jeans were shoved down around her thighs and her legs parted and she was cuddled against Pepper's shoulder.

You just a right-sized man, she told him, nibbling at this throat. No old gut like Henry has got.

I wish you'd forget that washed-up son of a bitch, Pepper said. That was another nagging thing. On his way into Charlene's he had met Garrison driving out and when he raised a hand in casual greeting Garrison had shot him a quick vicious look and stared stonily ahead. Pepper had been unable to avoid remembering worshipping Garrison and reflecting on what a long and winding road life was.

Come on, Charlene, he begged. His voice sounded strange to him. He had to make a constant effort to avoid breaking into a squeak. He would try to force Charlene down in the seat and she would just laugh and wrestle with him and tickle him. Come on Charlene. Give me a little.

Not till we start on our house, she told him, straightening her clothes and smoothing back her raven black hair, I can't live in that lil' old shack you knocked the front out of and besides, you got to start looking after me. I ain't aiming to be just a little something on the side.

Course I'll look after you, Pepper said. What else is the law for?

NIGHTTIME AWAKENING

At first there had been a cheap-looking woman named Roxanne and a little strawhaired girl with him but there was no woman now. No woman and no little girl either, just Clay scissoring his way through thigh-high grass and looking neither to the right or to the left.

Mrs. Tippitt set the dishpan of tomatoes down and straightened to rest her back for a moment and watched to see where he was going. He had no business anywhere except around the little tenant house where he lived. But you would not have known it to look at him. He looked like he owned the place. His sharp fox's face was thrust forward under the bill of his cap as if he were following a scent and there was a quick deliberation to his walk and no wasted effort, as he walked like a man who knew exactly where he was going. Not, Mrs. Tippitt noticed, like an ordinary man. An ordinary man would have a snakestick and be spreading the tall grass with caution and looking for snakes, for there were copperheads on this creek. Not Clay. Clay walked like a man above snakes, a man who had not been able to fit snakes into his schedule.

She picked the tomatoes up and started walking back toward the house with them. Mrs. Tippitt liked to stir early, and on this morning the dew had not yet dried on the grass. An obscure regret touched her. She felt in some way that Clay had ruined her morning. She liked to get out early on these last days of late summer, had done so even before Mr. Tippett passed away. She liked the hot dry smell of the garden and the song of the morning's first bird and the warm weight of the sun. She was fond of telling people that she did not know how many more summers she had left and that she had better enjoy them while she could. Now she was going to have to quit and go see what Clay wanted and see he did not pick anything up. She had been warned that Clay would steal anything that was not chained down or in flames, and she had been warned of things direr still.

Clay had stopped. He had stomped down the weeds all the way around the old '57 Buick Mr. Tippett had died in and stood with his hands in the hip pockets of his overall pants and was staring at the car as if he expected it to do something of great interest.

She set the tomatoes on the shady part of the porch and walked to within a few feet of Clay. He had not yet touched the automobile but now he walked all the way around it, as if he studied the way the sun caught it from different angles. Clay was a thin little dark knife-blade of a man who could have been anywhere between thirty and forty, and Mrs. Tippitt could not understand why people considered him dangerous. He did not look dangerous to her. Just trashy. He had got his bluff in on people. That was what she had told Tatum at his grocery store the day he had tried to warn her about letting Clay live on her place.

You've let him git his bluff in on you, she had said. Just like a bitin dog. No dog or man either gets up early enough in the morning to git its bluff in on me.

Tatum had been sacking up her groceries. Well. I ain't tryin to run your business for ye. It's just so far down on that creek where you live and they ain't hardly nobody lives down there.

That's the way I like it. It wouldn't surprise me if you sold him stuff on a ticket because you're afraid he'd burn you out if you didn't.

He has got a bad name. They say he's burnt enough people out to run two or three insurance companies into bankruptcy.

Mrs. Tippitt had begun to gather her purchases together. Well, none of that matters to me. I been handlin people all my life and I can handle him. Them old cows and Arabian horses are too much for me to take care of and that old house is just rottenin down. So it looks like it does us both a favor.

Clay turned toward her, acknowledging her presence only by his glance. He went back to staring at the old Buick.

Mrs. Tippitt had tomatoes to can and she wanted to get through with them before the stories came on. She could watch them only after she was through with all her work and her conscience clear and if she did not get about her work soon she would be running behind her schedule.

What was it you wanted?

I was just lookin at this old car. What you want for it?

It's not for sale. This was Mr. Tippitt's car. He died in it and it was his favorite out of all the cars he ever owned.

I never owned a car myself, Clay said, sounding somehow as if the blame for this could be laid squarely on Mrs. Tippitt.

This did not surprise Mrs. Tippitt. She admitted to a deep chasm between herself and her dead husband and people like Clay. Mr. and Mrs. Tippitt had owned a lot of cars. Mr. Tippitt had worked for the TVA right up until he died, and they had always lived well. When people were working for fifty cents and a dollar a day and glad to get it, Mr. Tippitt had been going to work with the TVA every morning and coming in every Friday with a good paycheck. While Clay's daddy had been making whiskey on other people's land and beating the bushes for ginseng, Mr. and Mrs. Tippitt had been building their brick house on the little rise it sat on and raising prize-winning Arabian horses.

It don't run anyway, she told him. They had to bring it home with a wrecker after they found Mr. Tippitt. Whatever makes it go is broke. They figured Mr. Tippitt was tryin to fix it when he had his heart attack.

I can fix them transmissions, Clay said.

You? Well. I didn't know you could even drive.

He showed his teeth briefly, perhaps he would have called it a smile. I said I never had a car. I didn't say I couldn't drive one. I could drive when I was twelve year old.

Anyway, it's company to me. Sometimes when I get to missin Mr. Tippitt I can look out here at this car and it's nearly like seein him. I can imagine him out here putterin around like he was always doin.

Clay looked away, as if all this was beneath his contempt. He stared at the treeline, at the absolute blue of the sky. The sun had begun its climb and already the heat seemed malefic. There was a hot brassy look to the air. Clay spat into the high grass. I don't know see how you seen it for the hog weeds, he told her. I heard you couldn't sell it. I heard he was dead in it three days before they found him and you never could get the scent out of it.

That's a blackguardin lie, Mrs. Tippitt said. I was offered five hundred dollars for this car.

You ort to've took it, Clay said. He seemed to lose interest in the car, glanced past the lot gate toward the barn. I got to have a car. But I guess I don't need a five-hundred-dollar one you can't get the scent out of.

Mrs. Tippett thought of several sharp things to say, held her tongue. She did not believe in lowering herself to Clay's level and besides this she had seldom been in a situation she could not turn to her advantage.

What do you need with a car?

I need me a way to work, Clay said. They's a pipeline job coming through here in a week or two and I aim to get me a job on it. They pay good money. I aim to get my little girl back.

In times past Mrs. Tippett had seen the three of them strung out along the highway going to town or coming from town and now she remembered that during the last two or three weeks she had seen only Clay.

Get her back from where? Did your wife go off somewheres with her?

Roxanne took off by herself, Clay said. She ain't got no use for a kid pullin at her, because she never could stay out of a honkytonk. But that ain't it. The county come and taken Rinney. I been out there but they ain't let me have her. They got some kind of paper bout a unfit home.

I'm sorry, Mrs. Tippitt said, although she wasn't. The woman named Roxanne was the kind of trash that made Mrs. Tippitt ashamed she lived in Tennessee and it came as no surprise that she held an affection for honkytonks. Her hair had been bleached a garish electric blonde and her eyebrows looked like they had been shaved off and then painted back on with a toothbrush dipped in stove black. The one time Mrs. Tippitt had been in the house she had tried to strike up a conversation with Roxanne but Roxanne did not even want to be friendly. Mrs. Tippitt had looked all about her and said, I see you ain't got ary television. I don't think I could live without seein my stories.

I ain't got time for no stories, Roxanne said, and laughed mirthlessly, as if at some joke Mrs. Tippitt had not heard. I'm a story all to myself. Them stories can't hold me a light.

Mrs. Tippitt had flown angry and it had been on the tip of her tongue to ask her how she spent her time. It had not been house cleaning, she had noticed that.

It ain't nothin to be sorry about, Clay said. It's my little girl and I aim to get her back or know the reason why. It's just kind of a mix-up is all. They said she was a gifted child.

A what?

A gifted child. They said she was. Give her all kinds of tests, took her clear to Nashville. They kept actin like they didn't believe it. She knows stuff grown people don't know. She can play songs on a piano and she ain't never even seen no piano. She can add up figgers fastern a machine can.

That's ridiculous, Mrs. Tippitt said.

Clay was not perturbed, as if his knowledge came by an authority she could not impeach. I seen it with my own eyes. They had a lady callin off figgers on a sheet of paper. When she got through callin em off, Rinney told em what the answer was and that machine was still clickin away. They all just looked at one another.

The day Mrs. Tippitt had seen her she had not appeared gifted. She had just appeared dirty and she had been playing with a rag doll with the stuffing coming out of it and she did not appear to be listening to anything that was said.

I don't see how this car can help you get your little girl, she said. Gifted or not. But we might work up a trade on it. I need some winter wood cut and I'd just as soon pay somebody with that car as in money.

How much wood?

A hundred dollars' worth, Mrs. Tippitt said. Seein as how it won't go I'll let it go cheap. When do you want to start?

Any time, I reckon. That seems like a sight in the world of wood.

Clay got an axe and the old crosscut saw from the woodshed and set to work. He began on three dead windfall pines for kindling. She watched him from the shade of the porch, peeling tomatoes and packing them into quart fruit jars. There were no children and no one at all to can for but some compulsion kept her canning and preserving year after year.

It was always pleasing to Mrs. Tippitt to sit on the porch and look to the south. As far as she could see the land had belonged to Mr. Tippitt and herself, now to her alone. The yard sloped gradually away from the shading cottonwoods to the creek and the wooden bridge that spanned it. The red chert road followed the meanderings of the creek as if it were in some manner its mirrored image. Beyond it lay fallow fields, their boundaries still kept by the good woven-wire fences Mr. Tippitt had hired put up, and the green tapestry of fields faded incrementally into distant hazy brush and thickening timber, to rows of hollows with cedar-hid mouths, hollows mysterious and deep, from whose dark interior doves called mournfully the live-long day.

The sound of the crosscut saw was pleasant as well, it hinted of work getting done, of time's passing not marked solely by the television schedule. Mrs. Tippitt had been hesitant about turning the money for winter wood loose and now Providence had stepped in, as it had often done before. It seemed good to hear the sounds of work being done; in another time she imagined she and Mr. Tippitt might have been slave owners, might have overseen some huge plantation; as it was, their brick house, unostentatious but still the only brick house on Sinking Creek, suited her quite well.

When she had finished packing the tomatoes she carried the jars into the house, after some consideration she took a tray of ice out of the refrigerator and made Clay a half gallon of ice water.

Clay's clothes had darkened with sweat and he paused, sitting by the fallen pine. He glanced once at the meager progress he had made, then, as if for sustenance, toward the green Buick. Mrs. Tippitt was thinking that she wished Tatum could see him now. She could hardly wait to tell about Clay cutting her winter wood.

The next day was Sunday but Clay was back anyway. Mrs. Tippitt was getting ready for church when she heard the axe commence, and when she peered through the kitchen window he had begun on the lightning-struck oak in the corner of the barn lot.

When she came out in the yard to wait for her ride to church, he was hard at it, white chips flying around him and the sun flashing off the axe-bit like a heliograph. The day was already hot and the air had the bright coppery smell of the pines. The idea of Clay cutting wood in this weather amused her. She told herself that she doubted if he had ever cut any winter wood without first having to kick the snow off it.

I don't believe I've ever seen you work so hard, she told him.

He paused, rested his weight on the axe handle. Well. I don't aim to get habited to it. It'd be a sight easier if I had a chainsaw. They ain't one about, is they?

No.

Where you headed all dolled up so?

I ain't missed a Sunday in twenty year, she told him. I'm going to church.

You a Church of Christ, ain't ye? Feller told me one time he heard a Church of Christ preacher stand right up and say ever other denomination was doomed to Hell. Is that a fact?

Yes, she told him. Don't you believe it?

I wouldn't give you a nickel for a boxcar load of none of it, Clay said. They can't be much to a outfit'd take in that bench-legged Shorty Wares. Ain't he Church of Christ?

Mr. Wares is one of our deacons, she said.

Well, I don't know. On Sunday he might be the big wheel that makes the little ones go around, but through the week he's just a self-made son of a bitch, and I wish you'd tell him I said that. He's the one signed them papers about Rinney. He better pray ever night I get her back, too.

Mr. Wares is in charge of the welfare department in this county, Mrs. Tippitt said stiffly. He has a job to do and he does it the best he knows how.

Clay spat into the grass. I imagine a grave-robber'd say the same thing, he said. He went back to notching the tree.

———

The morning he finally finished he racked wood along both sides of the house and across the front porch. Then without saying a word he walked to the car. He rolled all the glasses down and raised the hood, stood staring as if entranced into the workings of the motor. At last he got behind the wheel, tried to start it, got back out again and stood staring as if he would will it to life, would raise it from the dead like Lazarus by sheer concentration.

When he finally gave up and left he was carrying the battery on his shoulder, wending his way through the grown-up lot toward the tenant house where he lived.

On the morning he was back with the battery and a gallon jug Mrs. Tippitt judged to contain gasoline. She was putting up pickles and did not have time to watch him, though once when she did glance out, he appeared to be washing the plugs in gasoline. Then a little later a noise drew her back. He had it started. Blue smoke was rolling through the high weeds like some vitriolic fog and Clay was in the driver's seat holding onto the wheel with both hands as if he was going a hundred miles an hour.

She wiped the vinegar off her hands and walked into the edge of yard.

Clay had let off the gas now and gotten out, stood regarding the car.

I see you got it started.

I got the motor runnin. You put it in gear and it don't do nothin.

Well, I didn't misrepresent it. I told you it wouldn't go. You goin to have to work on it somewheres else anyway. The motor runnin tears up the television.

I don't aim to have the motor runnin while I work on the transmission, he said. But I didn't aim to work on it here noway. I need it up there at the house, where that washed-out place is by the bridge. That way I can get in under it and have room to work.

Well, I don't know how you'll get it there. But it's your car. You can do whatever you want with it.

I can get it there, he said. I have a car now. Gettin it there is the last of my worries.

On Saturday morning the cab came for her as it did every Saturday. Later she realized that that was what Clay had been waiting for.

She had planned on spending the entire day in town but about noon a dark cloud came up out of the west and sent her home early. There was a smell of distant rain, a smell of ozone. The cloud was ominous, dully metallic. Thunder rolled from it and faraway lightning flickered about its base. The world seemed to darken in measurable increments, the very air turned amber.

The cab rounded the last curve and carried Mrs. Tippitt onto a scene so surreal her mind refuted it even as her eyes showed it to her.

Bare to the waist and near black from the sun, Clay was hauling the Buick along the creek bank, through bracken and saplings and stumps and whatever came his way. He had Charlemagne and Princess, the two best Arabians, geared up in mule harness and chained to the bumper of the car. He was cursing the horses steadily and whipping them with a stick he had cut and they were hurling themselves against the chains, pulling against each other and rearing in panic.

Let me out! she said. The cab pulled to the shoulder of the road and she had the door open and briars slapping it and she was out even before the cab ceased rolling.

The wind had risen with the storm's approach and leant the willows with its weight, troubled through their branches, so that the pale undersides ran like quicksilver in the wind. The air was full of leaves.

Under the brunt of Clay's stick, or his invocation of some dark power, the car lurched free of whatever held it, raked a stump, came crashing sideways through the canes like some great metallic beast in pursuit of the horses.

Goddamn you, you better pull, Clay was saying.

Mrs. Tippitt hardly knew what she was doing. She stumbled through the grown-up ditch and into the field. She did not even feel the saw-briars ripping her stockings. Everything she saw was tinged with a red haze as if her rage had clotted like blood in her eyes, there was a far-off roaring like water in her ears.

When Clay's axe-bit face jerked toward her there was nothing there of fear or even guilt. He just looked aggravated. He looked sullen, as if her early homecoming was just one more annoyance, one more burdensome weight to carry. He went back to flailing blindly with the stick, trying to pull the horses along by the traces. The horses were streaked with foam and galled by the harness and she could see bloody scrapes and cuts from the unwrapped chains.

You stop that this minute! she screamed. The creek was shallow here, and by this time she was in it. It began to rain, huge slanted drops that roiled the water and fell about her like stones.

I want you off a my land. I want you gone now and I don't want a word about it.

Clay threw the stick into the creek, gestured toward the scraped and battered Buick. That's my car there.

You've ruint them horses, she said. You're through on this place. Her throat felt constricted, engorged with blood. She felt her heart would burst. I'll have you locked up. If you ain't got that mess off a them horses and headed out of my sight by the time I get to that bank I'll have you in jail.

Clay watched her approach. She climbed the bank, began to calm the horses. I meant ever word I said, she told him. As God is my witness, I'll law you if you ain't got your plunder off my place by night.

Law me, Clay said, as if he was darkly amused. He withdrew a plug of chewing tobacco and a knife from his pocket, dusted the plug off, and sliced him a chew. With the tobacco in his jaw the thin face was even more out of balance, a saturnine predator's face sliced through and improperly joined. He smiled. Lady, don't you know I could have you dead and in a shaller grave before the Law set down his coffee cup?

She was apoplectic with anger. Threatnin my life goes on the warrant, too, she said.

A warnt ain't shit to me, Clay told her. A warnt is tomorrow or next week or whenever you get into town to get one swore out. Me and you here right now is what you need to think about.

You're just lucky I didn't have a gun around, she told him.

Rain fell harder, rattling the leaves, turning the creek to a sluice of silver. His clothes were plastered wetly to him and rain coursed from beneath the bill of his cap and down his face. All right, he said, as if he had come to some decision. By God, I'll go get my stuff and go. But not on your sayso. I ain't stayin nowhere I ain't wanted.

I doubt if you ever been anywhere you *was* wanted, she said.

By dusk the only sign left from the storm was a thick shoal of fog rolling up from the creek as she watched him go. He came into her vision through a dark stain of cypress, edged into the field, a thin and angry figure bent gnomish beneath a great bundle of bedclothes wrapped in a blanket, like some tramp grossly overburdened. Dark was creeping up from the willows at the creek's banks and from the cedars at the far wood's edge to meet it, so that he traversed from dark to dark, attended by fireflies that lit his way to the hollow's mouth like fairy lanterns.

She watched until he was gone as finally as though the night had dissolved him and absorbed him into itself: he was there one moment dreamy through the blue light and then he was no more and she went back into the house to fix her supper. She decided tomorrow she would clean out the tenant house and that she would set the torch to it herself before the likes of Clay would enter its doors again.

She prowled through the rubbish he had left, seized by a dull righteous anger. Cracked dishes piled stacked and fouled together by spoiled food or by worse. Old curled and shapeless shoes that had been cast off who knew how many times. Clothes a dumpkeeper would but curl his lip at. Hot light fell slanted through the moted windowpanes, dirt daubers droned through it and plied their craft at will.

In the end she had a huge mound of refuse in the backyard. She burned it and when there were only ashes and broken glass it seemed to her that a life should come to more than this, a honkytonk wife and a gifted child, both gone, and this smoldering pile of ashes and melting glass now gone as well. But she did not dwell on it. Everybody starts the same in this world, hungry and naked and nothing except what his hands can latch onto, if Clay had chosen to latch onto this instead of what Mr. Tippitt had it was another's lookout than her own.

Yet still she was not shut of him. Fall became winter and the trees bared and as early evening fell she would see him, appearing at the edge of the woods, sometimes carrying a grocery sack or what looked like one. Once he was drunk. She saw him hold a bottle aloft, drink from it. He threw the bottle away, stood swaying like a graceless dancer, walked toward the hollow awkwardly, as if his feet would not do his will. He would stop, gesticulate with his arms as if he berated some invisible companions.

On the 28th of November the first skiff of snow fell, and he even managed to ruin that. He came scrawling across the snowy winter field, dark and graceless and unloved, an interloper, a petulant child's ink slash across a Currier and Ives winterscape.

Then one day when she came from the barn he was hunkered on the porch, sitting as she had seen the old and worthless sit about the courthouse square, spitting tobacco juice and whittling nothing recognizable out of cedar wood. Clay was wearing a beat up old black frockcoat that looked like it had been replevied from a shallow grave.

Hidy.

How do, she said.

Turned wintertime. He rubbed his hands together briskly, as if the statement needed further reinforcement than the bitter wind.

It generally does this time of a year. Where you livin?

I'm stayin in that old banded hotel back in there toward Flatwoods. Didn't you know it was there?

I'd forgot about it, she said.

It ain't on you.

I know it ain't. But you have to cross me to get to it.

Well. A man's gotta have a right-of-way, he said, as if in some queer manner he had fallen heir to it. It's a big old place. People used to come to them sulfur springs in there by the droves back in the twenties. Come from as far away as Memphis and Nashville in horses and buggies and stay there all summer. Got a big old high-ceilin dance hall in there. A man can sleep in a different room ever night if he's a mind to.

On the floor, I expect. What did you want with me?

Never one to inspire trust or warm the heart, he had now a look about him, stranger still, strange as the stories she had heard. People called him mad, said he lurked in the grove of pines behind the honkytonk at Flatwoods, going down needled paths as dark and silent as himself.

He had a closed, shut-up look about him, the look of a man too much to himself, a man on nodding terms with madness, who had only nightbirds and winter winds to keep him council. She wondered if he heard ghostly revels that were deader than yesterday, if spectral dancers moved beneath the high old ceilings still. She wondered what he thought about on winter nights before sleep came. She wondered if he thought of the gifted child.

Clay had drawn out a tablet and pencil from beneath the frock coat, proffered them.

What's that?

I need you to write me a little somethin. I need a reference. A character reference, they called it.

I don't know what you're talkin about. Who called it?

They's gonna be a hearin. I hired me a lawyer and he got me a hearin with a judge about Rinney. I need you to write down some things'll make the judge give her back to me.

She still had not taken the tablet he woodenly offered. She stared at him in a kind of awe.

What kind of things?

I don't know. That I worked for you, that you know me. I've got four or five already.

Lord God. Nothin I could write would make a judge even think about putting a child into your hands. Anything I'd write you'd be better off without. Besides, if you've already got four or five you don't need mine.

I need yourn the worst of all. You a big church member and all of that. You're a respectable citizen and anything you'd write would do me a lot of good.

Mrs. Tippitt was far from immune to flattery but she did not assess this as such, rather saw it as an accurate description of her character. The thought crossed her mind to reach for the tablet, but she had a momentary vision of the girl following Clay across the snow: the vision was so strong that it was like a photograph of a stark winter scene, Clay's long legs scissoring across the white waste of the field, behind him the girl unable to keep up, thin legs chilled and blue from the cold. All about and framing them, bleak winter trees, black brittle branches sheathed in ice.

She shook her head. It wouldn't do no good, she said. No matter what I wrote they're not goin to give you that little girl. You could carry letters in there by the bushel basketful and it won't change one thing. I ain't no lawyer but then I ain't chargin you to tell you neither.

I guess you know it all, he said. I reckon your old man learnt everything on that TVA you always talkin about while he wadn't condemnin people's farms and building lakes on top of em; I guess he was learnin all about how Christians like Shorty Wares takes people's kids away from em.

I don make the laws, she said. But the law's made to protect people that can't protect themselves.

The laws is made for people like you that's got the money to buy em, Clay said. I ain't no Church of Christ and I ain't never worked for no TVA but I got the sense to know that. She's my little girl and blood is thicker than any law all the lawyers in the world can make. He laid the tablet and pencil carefully by the concrete porch support. You think it over awhile. You might come around to my way of thinking.

Clay arose, dusted himself off.

If I ever come to your way of thinking I'll have myself committed to an insane asylum, she told him.

Two nights later something woke her, deep in the night. There was a strong smell of kerosene in the room and a memory of some sound she had heard, perhaps just a dream of a sound. She was instantly awake as if she had been immersed in ice water. She felt as if she had fallen through a deadfall into some other world, a world whose existence she had not even suspected. A square of pale winter light fell flat and white on the patterned linoleum, vanished when she flicked on the light.

In the middle of the floor was a pile of rags, soaked with kerosene. Beside them a box of matches, one out and laid carefully on top of the box. Something more than cold chilled her, moved through her veins sluggishly as ice water. She put on a robe and got Mr. Tippitt's shotgun down from the rack he had made from cedar long ago. As she did so and turned, there was a fleeting glimmer of Mr. Tippett himself regarding her from the chifforobe, the kind thoughtful eyes, the wire-rimmed glasses that lent his face its scholarly, schoolteacher look. Perhaps Mr. Tippitt would have been surprised to see her breech down the gun, check to see that it was loaded.

The yard was empty, an expanse of sloping white that seemed lit by a dim sourceless fluorescence. Dead vines from summer flowers made a shadow of lacy filigrees on the porch trellis. A chill wind blew through them. Wisps of snow fell dreamily. She noticed with some surprise that snow had drifted onto the porch. There looked to be two or three inches on the yard. She peered with head thrust forward but could see no one. There were only shades of black and white, shadows inky and depthless.

She went back in. As she crossed the bedroom sill, Clay appeared beside her and grasped the shotgun. With the same motion that jerked the gun he shoved her so that she fell sideways, doing a grotesque mincing dance step in a vain attempt to recover her equilibrium. She fell heavily against the side of the bed, with the breath knocked out of her, slid into a half-sitting position with her robe rolled under her, the footboard against her shoulders and neck. When she looked up dizzily, Clay was holding the shotgun dangling unbreeched in his left hand and was jiggling the two shells in his right. He was watching her with a pleased expression, as if she had somehow managed to live up to some esoteric standard he had set for her.

Clay had hunkered against the door jamb and had begun to roll a cigarette. He did not speak until he had lit the cigarette and when he did, his voice was thick with smoke. You would of shot me, he said with satisfaction, over them shittin horses. Now how much better than me does that leave you? I was just foolin around with you but you would of killed me, blowed me in two and told about it and prayed about it in church Sunday. I bet you know things about yourself right now you never knowed before.

You get away from here and leave me alone, she said. I never done anything to you.

I'll go, all right. But I'll go when the notion strikes me and not when you order me offa your land. As for not doin anything to me, ever one of you son of bitches is done something to me ever day of my life. The way I got it figured you owe me. For all the years you lived good and all the years I ain't. Then when a way comes along to even things up you won't even write a shittin letter.

You're crazy, she told him. You really are.

No, I ain't crazy. I guess I just got a different way of keepin score. We even right now. You down here with the rest of us now. Jesus is just a hair out of your reach, ain't he now?

There's nothin you can do to me, she said. I can have you put away for the rest of your life for what you've done already.

There's nothin I can't do to you, he corrected her dreamily. I can do all the things anybody ever thought of doing to anybody else and I expect they's a sight of em I might of dreamed up myself. Later on when you get into the spirit of things, you might think of a few on your own and they won't be nobody to stop us, nobody to even know.

You need help, she said. You need a doctor's care.

What I need I can get on my own, Clay said. If I can't it won't be worth havin nohow.

She had begun to cry softly, he swam blurrily in her vision.

Let me tell you something else, Clay said. Your precious husband died screwin that old whore, Susie Hodge, in that very car you beat me out of. He was screwin her and had a heart attack right on top of her and she left him there in the woods where they was.

She began to cry harder. That's a blackguardin lie, she said.

You can ask anybody. It's common knowledge. It was a joke all over town. He laughed, I just figured you ort to know.

It's not the truth. It's a vicious madcap lie.

We won't argue what's the truth and what ain't. It's the truth for us, and that's all that makes any difference. He arose, pocketed the shells and picked up the gun. I got to get on. I'll be checkin back with ye.

She sat until the screen door fell to and then she got up, limped about the room without direction or purpose. The bland face of Mr. Tippitt still watched her, the eyes followed her like those of Jesus in a picture they had once had. But the eyes no longer seemed so kind, seemed now to harbor lies and secrets. They mocked her as she at last left the room, letting the door fall to behind her.

The fire in the living room heater was almost out. She raked down the coals and went onto the porch for more wood. She felt empty, lost, disoriented. She did not know what to do, hardly even cared. Faces that she remembered as having been respectful and friendly now in retrospect seemed to have been sly and knowing, and if there had been some of her friends within screaming distance to ask for help she did not know if she would have taken the trouble. Even if what he had said were lies, they were lies he could have told all over town.

When she turned with the wood a bright funnel of flame arose from the bottom near the creek and she stood as if entranced, the wood in her arms forgotten. It was some time before she realized what it was. He was burning the Buick. Through the flare of flickering orange, snowflakes still drifted pastorally into the sails of fire and beyond them the flame was some vitriolic acid eating away the layer of night, exposing behind it the canes and rushes in the bottom eerily red, and Clay moving through this light lacquered briefly orange then to black like some necromancer of old pagan rites, and then she turned away to the east where there was no dawn or hint of one or even a promise that one would ever be. At last she turned with the wood and opened the screen door and went in out of the cold, there didn't seem to her anything else to do, or anywhere else in all the world for her to go.

On a fine balmy morning in early May, Clay arose as was his habit before daybreak and left the house. He planned to look for work today. Itchy Mama would probably pay him to junk out some of the wrecked cars stacked in her yard. At the very least he might wind up with a pint of whiskey and a dollar or two and it might even save him from having to walk all the way to the Knob. Travelers to and from Goblin's Knob might see Clay abroad on these nights, covert and sullen as some nighttime animal in their headlights, face gone sharp and mean as the bit of an axe turned sidewise. And then sometimes they would not see him as he lurked in the pines behind the Knob forced by pressing monetary needs to lurk in these fabled and haunted pines by night, crouching here or moving among the shadowed trees like a shade, and when someone came out the back way of the Knob and entered into the sepulchral pines to relieve himself, then Clay would relieve him as well, his homemade blackjack falling silent as a guillotine, taut arms easing the slack weight to the ground, fingers swift and sure to the wallet. Clay did not take all their money nor did he strew pictures and papers around. He had replaced the wallets carefully where he found them in some instinctual hope that the victim might decide that he had just passed out. Clay left his victim and then faded quick-footed into the dark.

Cloistered thus in the pines, laughter would sometimes come to him from the honkytonk, shards of feminine gaiety, laughter sharp and splintered like broken glass, and he would sit numb and uncomprehending. This laughter as if it were in another language, some tongue foreign to his ear. About him a past so ancient as to be nearly timeless stirred in the dark, spun tendrils to hold him like gossamer webs. Behind him a scented dark seemed to stretch on forever.

On this morning a comfortable predawn breeze stirred softly, scented with spring as if it blew off fields of wildflowers. A scent of grass in the air. Birds began then in tremulous call. Trilling from the edge of the woods where the remaining darkness hovered as if it gathered there by some force beyond his ken. No windows lit, the world enthralled in sleep. Rocking on the lee of gentler shores. He progressed down the unpaved street. Past the ramshackle house where Elmer and his mother lived. Elmer's wheelchair parked in the pale shadow on the low concrete porch. A litter of amber beer bottles strewn like fool's gold among the grass.

Spring weeds and grass already encroaching onto vacant lots. Past a house long burned, charred rubble rainwashed and sanctified. Broken brick and sundry debris scattered about, a still erect chimney rising bleakly in the May air like an ancient monolith left by some race dead and lost, its meaning forgotten eons ago. Old rusted tin like crumpled and cast off aluminum foil. Past rusted autos stoned sightless by nocturnal miscreants, consigned to this burial above ground on concrete blocks, monuments to better times. Past all those sleeping souls.

Clay left the road and followed a footpath through last winter's weeds, cutting off the corner and approaching out onto the blacktop highway through the corner of Mabel Peter's yard. Just as he made to descend the bank something glimpsed from the corner of his eye gave him pause. A wraithlike paleness of ectoplasm, a shapeless whiteness from beyond the pale. He had been half expecting Son's wraith to appear to him in remonstrance and he whirled now against his will to face this apparition. Wearing a white gown Mabel's daughter Fanny squatted in the sere weed stalks, her skirt gathered about her waist. Her face pale and vacant, her thigh and hip so white Clay felt his breath in his chest. He stood transfixed while Fanny rose ghost-like from amongst the dead weeds and looked about her, the gown still raised aloft so that in the pale and misty light Clay could see the dark tangle of hair between her legs and the still darker and more secret area beneath it. He stood still, bent forward, his mouth slightly agape as one might stand who is peering into his own future. The moment seemed frozen until she dropped the gown and dabbed herself daintily with its hem and then her eyes arose to meet this dark and electric presence gazing upon her. Immediately she fled. Soundless through the weeds and barefoot she made the safety of the caved and canted backporch while Clay still stood gazing after her. At last he sat meditatively on the short bank above the road and smoked a cigarette and gazed down the long road obscured and smoky with mist, fancying he felt eyes on his back from behind mildewed and gauzy curtains. At last he slid down the bank and onto the blacktop and his stride lengthened like one well accustomed to walking. About him birds still sang, behind him the eastern sky streaked with pink and gray and the sun appeared suddenly atop the treeline and hung there, turned blood red by the mist and fog charting his progress malignantly like a malevolent and vengeful eye.

Long a whore in every connotation of the word save that it involved financial transactions, Mabel Peters, in her declining years, saw her erstwhile customers and lovers slip away as irretrievable as the years themselves and fall prey to younger and more comely women. Never attractive or never, as a matter of fact, passable, with the advent of middle age her already squat body thickened as though the upper portion melted and sloped downward and her face became more sallow and reptilian and favored only by an occasional traveling man or someone driven by desperation beyond comprehension, she would sit on her porch days when the weather was suitable, rocking and blinking her lashless eyes in the sun and watch life go by. Old now and righteous with the years and her own past losing clarity, she would watch the young gum-chewing girls walk by switching their butts always laughing as if gaiety itself pursued them, as if wherever they were bound for people would always be glad to see them, thronged always by boys and men who called at them or whistled and Mabel would watch this all with condemnation. Like bitches in heat, she would think righteously, watching them out of sight into the piney dusk. And Fanny alongside her rocking and peering out vacuously at the world as if it were a movie screen on which images of no concern to her flickered in inconsequential arrival and departure.

And on these hot sultry nights while Fanny slept the dreamless sleep of the innocent or the mentally bereft, the sleep of the redeemed was elusive in Mabel's grip. She would lie sweating, awake, and hear all the myriad cries of the night. Drunken laughter came to her somehow, cleansed and nightwashed. Pleas and imprecations, cries of the wronged and the wrongdoers alike borne by the same breezeless air seemed sounds of the past now irrevocably gone. All the cries of people in the throes of life rang like death bells in her ears until at last a vague superiority born of her enforced respectability would mantle her and she would sleep.

On this May evening she was gathering up the supper dishes when she saw Clay approaching the porch. She thought at first he must be headed somewhere else for she had not seen Clay to talk to since he and Roxanne were married. But when she peered out through the opened door Clay was sidling through the weeds toward the porch with a look on his face as near purposeful as Clay's face ever got.

Hidy, Clay said. The girl sat rocking as ever, her hands busy in some cloth, moving like disquieted birds. She did not reply but perhaps Clay did not expect such for he perched comfortably upon the porch's edge like a roosting bird and leaned against a two-by-four stanchion, gauging its strength with his back and then fell into a study of the road below them, gazing outward in abstracted silence.

Git ye a cheer, Mabel told him.

I ain't got but a minute, Clay said. I'll just set here. Clay pulled a flat bottle out of his pocket and stood it on the porch beside him. He picked it up and shook it, canting it against the reddened and roiled western horizon. He studied it carefully, as if its glassine crystal surface was portent with secrets. Then he reached it to Mabel.

Git ye a drink, he said.

I don't drink much anymore, Mabel said. But I might have me just a sip. Let me just get us a glass here.

She entered the house and returned with two jelly glasses and reached one to Clay. Clay handed her the bottle.

They drank silently, Clay ignoring the glass and tipping the bottle. He drank deeply, eyes closed. At last he sat the bottle beside him, stared with unfocused eyes into the yard.

What about her, he said in a strange voice.

She don't drink, Mabel said. Whiskey never touched her lips. She's a good girl.

Clay coughed and spat into the yard. It won't hurt her, he said in his normal voice. Here, he said, proffering the bottle. Git ye a drank.

The girl spoke for the first time. I don't want none of that whiskey. Her voice was curiously high, a tiny singsong voice almost birdlike.

That girl got a voice purty as a mournin dove, Clay said.

She got plenty of sense, Mabel said. She ain't out here runnin up and down the road with God knows who all hours of the night. She sets right here with me on this porch and sees all that goes on. She knows a lot she don't say.

I reckon, Clay said.

He peered into her face which was as blank and receptive as still waters, as though to the depths beneath the surface, to some aberrant chamber where dark forms moved in cloaked silence, in eternal and ambiguous turmoil.

Now dusk had slowly fallen. A stately and timeless quietude creeping from the indigo pines. A hushed and tentative call of insects from the woods. A measured darkening of the bloody and mottled sky. A tangible thickening of the wry air, gone subtly portent with night's promise.

Mabel and Clay finished this bottle and with a look of slyness Clay, like some conjuror or alchemist of old, produced yet another flat bottle and presented it to Mabel. All the while they sat and drank as dark settled over them like coverlets against the cold and the girl sat entranced in the old wooden rocker and rocked effortlessly as if the chair had been set into perpetual motion at its creation and would rock so forevermore. No emotions stirred her face, flickered in her myopic and depthless eyes. No approval or disapproval registered, only a bland sort of acceptance of these early night drinkers here before her and of others in the slipshod shanties about them canted like tugs in uncertain waters with lights beginning to flick on beyond dirty windows, illuminating what chaos this day had wrought. In places voices rose, voices of imprecation, voices of rage. Until the night became electric with their timbre. Voices promised, voices threatened. Faceless voices to which Clay's mind attached countenances or figures, flickers of recognition from beyond this wall of dark. Seeking entry, seeking egress. Seeking anything to make the time rock easier by.

I ever catch you with another son of a bitch like I done then I'll cut your fuckin throat with this very razor, a voice promised. A voice near manic with grief, I won't do it no more, the reply came, faint from the outskirts of death.

From the darkening road disjointed laughter of young girls, eternally renewed. Laughter with an edge of promise, with some curious hint of satisfaction. Mantled with youth like a shield.

Mabel died in the fall and left him to suffer his bereavement in a vacuum, a strange disorientation of his life. Clay had felt cut off and isolated, a dark estrangement from what had come before and what was to be. Big Mabel, he thought (though this was more feeling than conscious thought, some subliminal instinct), had picked him up when he was drifting toward some dire fate and stayed his flight, steered him through perilous shoals toward calmer water; then deserted him when the water quickened, left him at the mercies of chance and happenstance, subject to the whims of unfeeling elements.

Big Mabel had been ten or twelve years older than Clay and she had been a good provider. She had worked in the garment factory in Ackerman's Field since she was seventeen and when she had her stroke, she fell across the sewing machine and expired there, and it was somehow fitting.

Big Mabel had been a woman of awesome proportion who outweighed Clay at least a hundred pounds and whose copious bosom always carried a flat half pint of whiskey. Big Mabel's sister was a bootlegger named Itchy Mama and was therefore the source of a never-ending supply of those flat and potent bottles which Mabel's breasts heated to a steady body temperature and which rode in her brassiere like benign tumors and were always there to minister to Clay's moods. Mabel was a woman of robust, if somewhat random, passion and had kept Clay warm on nights when the winter wind was at the door entreating entry.

After Big Mabel was buried Clay went once or twice and stood dumbly before the steel marker staring at the raw clay as if in query, but it seemed more question than answer and then had walked among the mud-spattered and faded artificial flowers the factory had sent and heard only the wind rushing among the mystic cedars.

A feared and vilified figure thus nurtured on bootleg whiskey at a body acclimating temperature of 98.6 turned even more solitary and silent, turning up unexpectedly on dark roads on darker nights spotlighted shambling in late traveler's headlights like some malignant troll or elemental, staring angrily into the lights as if to turn them aside. Forced now into finding work and survival again a question.

Sitting on Itchy Mama's front porch bereft among the honey-suckles and whiskey now seventy-five cents a half, all family ties sundered. Sitting crosslegged on this porch, an outsider now among the miscreants and outcasts of paler tint, he would look ill at ease as if he were always on his way somewhere, some dark and malign land momentarily taking respite from the air. Until at last he would unfold himself from the edge of the porch speaking no goodbyes, and wind his way among the rusted derelict cars parked shoulder to shoulder like some drive-in movie lot long dead and now only the pitted cars remaining, umber relics of disaster awaiting some show, and coming out into the road and standing as if undecided which way to go, home or walk the ten miles to Goblin's Knob or just walk. At last he would invariably choose the shorter of the distances and go home to Piney.

Now at this time on the southeastern border of Ackerman's Field lay a community called Piney, a collection of shacks and shanties falling away to ruin, appearing as though they had sprouted there like weeds only waiting to be chopped away, for they appeared as temporary as their residents who sat about their canted porches even in midday, workless and luckless and hopeless, children playing naked in the yard and on the faces of the porch sitters, an expression curiously stunned, somehow resembling an old photograph of the survivors of some great holocaust.

Streets and alleys running without plan or pattern and fading at some point into padded, needled paths into the pine woods that gave the community its name. At night police cruisers crawled along these streets like sentries, as if in anticipation of the next fight or wife-beating or cutting, easing among the closed faces in the yards like a threat.

And at night these houses garish with light or perhaps dark and meterless, fallen prey to the idiosyncrasies of the electric company or perhaps a ghostly flickering lamp light, wavering behind gauzy curtains, a smell of coal oil in the air. All manner of expired cars raised on stacked cinder blocks rearing bleakly like curious monuments erected to honor Detroit. Or parked in the uncharted drives, tires flat, blindeyed, and impotent, while their owners walked strung out on the highways like escapees fleeing some region in flames.

In the dusk Clay would cross the grass grown yard and sometimes give the condemned sign the city had put up on the front of the house a sidelong glance of contempt. He had torn three or four of them down but they had always brought another and he felt they must possess an inexhaustible supply of these signs and perhaps employed someone solely to replace the ones he destroyed.

Some nights he would be sleepless and all the sound of his life would reach his ears. Lying in the somber dark and all around him the sound of laughter, sharp-edged and raucous, and sometimes glass would break, a bottle thrown. Clay had come off Coffee Creek before he dwelt here with Mabel and sometimes the night sounds of his childhood would be retrieved over the breaking glass and tires squalling and he would fall asleep to the mesmeric sounds of the crickets.

————

Other bad luck had befallen Clay, so that he had come to feel he lived under a malign sign, had stumbled unknowing on to a pathway sown with salt and brambles, above him gnarled branches obscuring either sun or star, set down here directionless and lost with no way to go but forward into the friendless dark.

Friendless save one and now even that one mouldering in the ground, laid to rest in some country cemetery or another in what Clay began to see as some grand procession marching dirge-like into the earth of every person who had ever bespoke him kind words or passed the time of day with him. Son Pope's wife, Pearl, worked at the garment factory with Mabel and sometimes on Saturday nights Clay and Mabel would visit them and carry a sack of beer and they would sit and talk and drink the beer, Clay quiet even then, their laughter breaking on the reefs of his silence like waves, but a feeling almost of warmth, a momentary thawing of subterranean ice. Sometimes they would ride in Son's old car down to where the Buffalo River's backwaters formed sloughs with flat bottomland lying between them like peninsulas and fish off the bank with the campfire flaring yellowy like council fires, and sit then in their communal dark, no sound save the viscous lap of the turgid yellow water around the twisted tree roots, the flat slap of a fish briefly airborne.

Lying on his back in the grass, the sky stretched to infinity, fall constellations just now rising as if pinned to some gaudy wheel in slow but infinite spin, moving in a silence beyond word, beyond thought, beyond comprehension. And he felt momentarily at one with the dusty bands of galaxies in space, with all the stars burning out in brief and incandescent arcs with all the nebula and nova locked forever in complex and infinite motion, dusty motes locked in the keep of the heavens.

Lying so he would feel outside himself and gone, no part of this slough-locked peninsula, or the square boxy car, highbacked and hearse-like, parked among the weeds, or the strangers moving in occult rites through flickering firelight.

When Mabel died, Son got Clay a job at the rubber factory in Ackerman's Field where he worked. Clay's job was not very complicated and although he was not there long enough to learn all that it entailed, the part he was most familiar with involved rolling a mop bucket around to various areas and mopping the restroom and lunchroom area. As Clay worked the night shift there was no management or office personnel around to give him a hard time and Clay could usually be found on his way to some job, or just returning, rather than actively engaged in some task. A lot of the time he spent standing around in the area where Son worked listening to Son's lies and plans for what he was going to spend his paycheck on. Son's job was a little more complicated than Clay's. Son worked in front of the lead press guiding garden hose coated with lead onto a huge reel which revolved and wound the hose on as a bobbin holds thread. Clay would stand engrossed at the complexity of this huge monolith of a machine extruding forth these silvery strands guided so casually by Son's gloved hand onto the reel and he almost envied Son the disdain with which he performed this task, staring past these hypnotic weaving strands like some demented and glassy-eyed weaver at the shuttle of some monstrous loom fed from the warp of the press while perhaps his mind wandered, attended fields or hills of his youth.

One day in his second week on the job, Clay came up behind him while he stood so entranced and thought how funny it would be to goose Son in the ribs and jolt him back to the present. Clay was never one for practical joking or even joking of any sort and jocularity among men was strange to him. But it was well known how ticklish Son was and seldom did a day pass that someone did not goose him just to watch him jump.

Easing between the presses light-footed and conspiratorial as though his footfalls could be heard above the insane din of clamoring machinery, Clay ascertained that the press operator had left briefly to take a leak or sneak a drag off a cigarette. Cat-footed he eased behind Son. A goose to be long remembered, the fabric of legend.

Clay dug both stiff forefingers into Son's ribs simultaneously. Son rose involuntarily into the air as if the earth itself had catapulted him, soundless, rising as if intent on flight, the reel forgotten, the mindless profusion of leaded hose a thing of no import. He leapt simultaneously forward and upward, a trajectory in direct interception with the reel turning steadily on and felt only the weight of hose close across the palm of his hand like a firm handshake, borne upward then further by this imprisoned hand and carried aloft as if in the grasp of some monstrous bird.

Clay sensed a suspension in the way of things, some strange aberration of events. He felt that this could not be happening. Son was athwart the reel now bound inextricably in these shuttling silver strands struggling as if coupling with some curious gleaming beast and held fast in a dripping web complex far beyond the devising of a spider's wildest dreams.

Clay stood transfixed in horror. Shitfire, he said. He looked wildly about him to see if anyone had seen him goose Son. In the clang and clamor of metal on metal no one had noticed anything amiss. Clay began to run wildly in small insane circles. He had no idea what to do.

Help, help, he screamed. Help, help. He ran to the control panel of the press but it was a maze of buttons and switches and lights with no instructions, no stop, no reverse. If he could but run it backward. By this time the reel had turned in its cycle until the obstruction Pope's body formed was slammed into the steel floor thus locking the reel from movement and it shrieked shrilly as somewhere in the basement the machinery still turned, spinning mindlessly beneath the locked reel. In front of the press shining curves of lead-sheathed hose curled and writhed like a blind headless serpent in knotted and intertwined affliction of coils.

The returning operator saw this rising and coiling lead at the same time the foreman did and he dropped his cup of coffee and began to run. The foreman beat him to the control panel and slammed the stop button. The machine fell instantly silent. Other machines shut down. Men began to run toward the press. On rubber legs Clay moved around the reel.

Great God Almighty, the foreman said in awe. He could not believe that such a thing had happened on his shift.

Clay peered wordlessly, mouth agape. Son had rode the reel overhead foremost, arms akimbo and his skull had been smashed on the steel plate. Son stared sightlessly at the maze of strands as if in mild remonstrance.

Clay left that night without even clocking out or waiting until quitting time and walked among the cars in the parking lot to Son's old sedan and got his coat out of the back seat. It was very cold. His breath plumed palely as he breathed, and his feet rang hollowly as though on stone and the tops and windows of the cars were crinkled with frost. Delicate lace filigrees laid like snowflakes. The air felt dry and cold to his lungs and made him cough when he breathed deeply. Above him the stars seemed remote and colder still, worlds locked in eternal ice.

Clay stood for some time staring back at the grim factory, prison-like and noisy still with hammering machinery. Billowing yellow sulfuric smoke or steam rose from it like brimstone from some fissure in the earth. At last he began to walk as if entranced toward his house in Piney.

Clay did not attend the funeral but he was at the cemetery before the hearse came and he watched the interment of Son from a stand of pines at the edge of the woods above them. Few people came. Clay, thin and diabolical, beholding the widow and orphans in their grief. Figures with bowed heads, fractured shards of sound, a wind-brought cry as old as time itself. A rough final scraping sound of a shovel striking on stone. Nameless feelings assailed him, lurking in the pines, bereft by his own hand. After the family left they filled in the grave and took down the awning and drove the metal nameplate into the ground and Clay stayed through all this with the air of someone who has paid his admittance and will not leave until the show is over. Then he walked down to where the workmen were throwing shovels onto a flatbed truck. A gray December day. Bleak and cold. Two Negroes folded the green striped awning. A mist of rain was in the air. Clay's eyes were drawn to the raw earth, the mawkish and tacky poinsettias. When the truck left he hitched a ride back to Ackerman's Field, the three Black workmen up front and Clay hunkered cursing behind the cab holding his cap on with both hands with the wind whistling about his ears and staring through a hole in the floor at the macadam reeling away beneath him.

Sometimes on these nights he would walk over to the corner of Pine and Walnut to where the old gray stucco house stood and walk slowly past it, possessed by some nameless guilt. Watching the scenes played out behind its yellow windows, Pearl moving past a window, children playing. A paternal eye on the wood pile. Watching for strange men lurking about. He apparently the only one. Some nights he would stand thus beneath the streetlight until Pearl's lights snapped out and once he saw her raise the curtain and peer out at him, her face moonlit and quizzical. The next night he brought a six-pack of beer and got into the old hearse-like sedan by the curb. Sat beneath the steering wheel and drank the beer. One careless hand on the wheel driving away now. Mystic names and places rising before him. Images flickered in his mind. Statelines falling away like windstripped leaves.

A strawtopped face appeared at the window. Colorless eyes in a pale face. Mama says you can come in if you want to.

Henceforth, Clay would sit on their ratty couch with the paper bag between his feet drinking the beer and listening to the big floor model radio. Sometimes he would bring a carton of cold drinks or a sack of candy or Cracker Jacks, and divide them among the children and they would sit about the floor eating and watching with big curious eyes while he and Pearl sat on the sofa drinking the beer. Or some nights they shared a pint jar of popskull moonshine whiskey which they would pass back and forth chasing it with whatever came handy and, behind his turned-in eyes, visions kindled by this liquor flickered like firelight.

Leaving in the clear cold nights, pausing by the big sedan to lay a proprietary arm across the hood. Rust-spotted chrome gleaming dully in the pale starlight. Beneath the hood a suggestion of harnessed power, a tireless devourer of miles. Of many horses held in check.

The day he drew his final paycheck from the rubber plant he read the notice on the bulletin board where Pope's job had been posted for bids. Vacancy, it read. One lead press reel turner. Moving his lips with the sounds. Unshaven face sharp and foxlike below the greasy duck-billed cap. Yellow eyes appalled. He read it like an epitaph, felt there must be more. Surely more. A man gone, living matter bludgeoned into the abstract. A pebble dropped, the last ripple faded, water gone still and receptive above it. All about Clay the hammer and roar of machinery, of life going on.

They fired the son of a bitch that done it, he told Pearl that night. That operator.

They ort to locked him up, Pearl said. They ort to let me cut his throat with a dull rusty Case knife.

Clay nodded his agreement. I may ort to burn 'im out, he said.

They sat in communal silence. Their thirst for vengeance common ground. A glow of alcohol suffused Clay. A man of means now, mailbox portent with Social Security checks. Home fires cherrying the potbellied heater on the side and a bitter wind keening about the windows and a hint of snow in the air. Ample wood on the porch. He felt protective toward Pearl. He felt Son would have wanted it this way.

Then late one night, feeling that the signs were right and fired by white whiskey or a glimpse of Pearl's milky thigh, Clay carried this solicitous protection too far and tried to rape Pearl. Pearl was a big rawboned woman almost a head taller than Clay and with arms as big as Clay's legs and she did not rape easy. As a matter of fact, she did not rape at all. Clay however was persistent and within an hour or so had torn most of Pearl's clothes away and was himself bloody and disheveled. His hair was all in his eyes and his nose was bleeding and all the buttons ripped off his khaki shirt. Clay looked like something the cat had been worrying.

Impatient at last with sweet talk and entreaties, Clay hit her alongside the head as hard as he could with his fist and knocked her back onto the sofa. The sofa tipped against the wall with her weight and fell. Children began to cry. Imploring voices to rise. Clay advanced upon her unbuttoning the fly of his pants. Pearl kicked him in the stomach, and he sat back down hard in the middle of the floor with his breath exploding out of him. Pearl leapt up and threw a stick of kindling at him. It caught him on the neck and bitter yellow bile rose in his throat.

You lowlife son of a bitch, Pearl said. Her florid face was flushed almost to the point of apoplexy and her hair had exploded outward as if it sang with electric current. Her eyes were glassy and malevolent.

Clay shook his head slowly from side to side as if to ensure that his neck still worked. A drop of blood dripped off his nose on to the cracked linoleum floor. He cast one eye painfully to the door, as if measuring. Computing some Einsteinian formula of speed and mass and distance.

You sorry old whore, he told her. I wouldn't screw you atoll anyway.

He got up and walked, bent over, gnomic with pain to the door. Bitter cold air righted his spinning head. He paused by the sedan. Rested there a moment, his forehead on the frosty metal. Eyeing then its graceful lines, bathed in cold moonlight. He began to walk gingerly away, short spider-like steps past the streetlamp.

Within thirty minutes he was back carrying a brown paper bag of sugar. The house now dark, the entire block gone dark and silent with sleep. A twisted shadow on this street of dreams, thwarted and misunderstood. Removing the gas cap softly and surreptitiously. Soundless in the charged air, no rustle even from the sack. A hushed snowfall of sugar down the tank, a miniature avalanche. A dark shadow then moving alleyward and lost among other shadows and only a lean gray cat to chart his passage.

Then on some nights Leck Hixon's old rattletrap of a pickup would be parked next to the car. Clay saw him one night with the hood raised, his arms resting on the fender, staring into the organs of the car as if in deep study.

Clay moving surreptitious now, laying low. Wondering who he had become, whose hand was on the wheel. Aghast at himself crawling on hands and knees deep in the night through frozen and sere weedstalks, rising like some gaunt spectre and pressing his face against the cold glass. By flickering coal oil lamp Hixon dropped his overall galluses and let them fall about his feet. Stepped out of them and moved toward the bed, his arms clutching his chest in some mock pantomime of cold. Pearl slipped her bathrobe off and stood for a moment, facing the window as if posing. Clay's eye drawn as if by magnet to the dark glassy thatch of hair between her legs. The swing of her pendulous breasts as she bent over the coal oil lamp. His breath had fogged the window glass and it was like some erotic scene viewed through smoked glass. Then the light went out. No sounds came to his straining ears, no sighs of Eros, no cries of retribution. A desolate feeling descended upon Clay. He retreated the way he had come, keeping in the shadows more from habit than necessity, for he did not expect them to see him.

Sometime during the night Hixon awoke with the smell of coal oil in his nostrils and the cankered taste of fear in the back of his mouth. He was awake instantly, as if he had been immersed in ice water. The linoleum was cold to his feet. A shapeless mass in the bedroom floor. Someone had bequeathed to them a pile of rags soaked in kerosene. The oily smell hung heavy in the air. Beside them a box of kitchen matches, one lying out and unstruck beside the rags.

Hixon found Pope's old shotgun and came out the door onto the porch breeching it up. But there was no one, only the moonlight etching ebonite shadows on frost so heavy it looked like a snowfall. Hixon stared about him into the yard. Wary eyes searching the shadows where who knew what lurked. No voices came to him. No derisive laughter reached his ears. Only the old winter silence. As he walked back inside his legs felt rubbery. In the front room, he stood for a time by the heater, still holding the shotgun as if he had forgotten it. At last he laid the gun aside and filled the stove with wood. He dragged the bloated armchair to the side of the stove and sat there by the fire, but it would not warm him.

Clay topped out on the ridge just as dawn broke spurious and gray and stood looking down into the bottom where the sawmill was with an expression of anger on his face. Cold winter fog drifted eerily around the creek bank and swirled around the monolith the sawdust made. It rose like pale smoke into the spectral air. Clay could not see the mill with any great clarity but he could see well enough to tell that the truck was gone.

He put down his lunch sack and brought out a sack of Country

Gentleman and began to roll a cigarette. He licked the cigarette and stared bleakly at it. Humped and misshapen. A camel. Even small skills unmastered. His eyes were as blank and cold as steel, expressionless and indecipherable. A thin mean face, eyes yellow and set close together over a nose hooked and thin as a scythe.

He stood smoking in this cold dawn air, leant somehow askew as if by strong winds blowing off his starboard side or else caught in some curious anomaly of gravity. Somewhere cocks crowed in heraldic cries beyond the muting hills and he began to descend the ridge road. When he was parallel with the mill he cut across into a field of sere beggarlice and pigweed white with ice. The frozen and brittle weeds snapped and popped before his advance. Some giant striding across a forest, timber disassembly in his wake.

McNabb was working on the forklift and he did not look at all pleased to look up and see Clay coming through the waist-high weeds, arms aloft like a swimmer heading water. He wore a yellow hard hat and he pushed this back over his thinning hair and stood hipslung against the lift with a ratchet depending from his hand watching this small and angry apparition approaching him through the weeds and then into the frozen mud rutted with log truck tracks and swinging a lunch sack.

I didn't expect to see you today. You're late. The truck's already gone, McNabb said, You laid out two days and today come in late. They's already somebody else doin ye work for ye and drawin the pay for it.

I was sick.

I know how you was sick. You was sick all right.

You firin me?

Hellfire. You been fired.

Clay stood holding the greasy paper sack and regarding McNabb with malevolence, illshaven and graceless in his worn jumper which was faded and tattered and ratty and looking like nothing so much as a lair for small and fur-bearing animals. Standing thin and scarecrow-like in this frozen mire, flinty-eyed and hunched in perpetual cold.

That trial business is the main thing. You know they subpoenaed ever damn hand I got for that trial of yourn and God knows how long that'll drag on. That makes them love you too. They can go set on their butts in the courthouse and listen to em tell all about you beatin the shit out of some school kid that couldn't find his glasses. They can see how that spends at the grocery store.

Clay was staring around the frozen millyard as if he had forgotten where he was or if the mill was already gone from his sight and he were remembering it. A cold wind sucked among the stacked and icy crossties and in the pale light of a wintry and skimpy sun the frosted slab pile gleamed as if snowed on. The ground beneath their feet was frozen hard as rock and rang hollowly when they walked on it. Clay stood rubbing his hands together as if to warm them.

They's people scared of you, McNabb told him. But they ain't none of em goes by the name McNabb.

Clay turned back the way he had come. Eyes small and malevolent below the duck-billed cap. Turbulent with anger. Halfway across the black and frozen mud he turned and with his flinty eyes followed McNabb until he disappeared into the dark ramshackle office. When he turned back around, he felt that he was being watched and a mangy yellow dog came out of the weeds eight or ten feet from him and stood staring at him. When he resumed walking, it again began to pace him. This time when he turned, he looked at the forgotten brown paper bag and then tossed it into the dead weed stalks in the ditch. The yellow hound, who appeared to be starvation personified, walked cautiously down the red clay bank and began to nuzzle the bag about with his nose. After a time, he began to eat wolfishly, his eyes cast upward toward the man on the rim watching him.

What awakened McNabb deep in the night was no nocturnal footsteps or raising and closing of windows, but a curious and subliminal feeling that something was amiss. The first thing he smelled was the coal oil and that brought him awake as suddenly as if his blood had turned to ice. He felt that some malediction had been cast upon him, some curse visited upon him and upon all his descendants, so that never again could he sleep unfettered. He thought of Clay crouched somewhere in this cold, smiling to himself or, by now, long gone into the woods and all he could hope for was that Clay had now forgotten him, upon whom he had bestowed this plague of fire.

After Clay was fired from the sawmill he did not do very much of anything. He knew that he would have to find other work, but he postponed it, although he still rose before good daylight and made his breakfast.

One morning as he was drinking his second cup of bitter coffee, a car stopped outside parallel with the porch and a short little man with a business-like air about him got out and stepped onto the porch. The man was squatly built with short little fat legs like sausages encased in tight blue dress pants and a red agitated face with a big broad nose.

He knocked on the door and the screen slapped loosely.

It ain't locked, Clay said.

The man opened the screen and stuck his head in like a jack-in-the-box.

Your name Herschel Clay?

Clay acknowledged that it was. The little man, who seemed to Clay as though made to appear by some materialized spell or sleight of hand, eased the door further open and came in, remaining near the door in case rapid egress became necessary, as though Clay's reputation was not lost to him.

My name's Rose, the man said. I work for the welfare department.

I ain't on no welfare, Clay told him. Ain't never been.

This house has been condemned, the man told him. You livin here against the law. The city asked me to come by here and talk some sense to you.

If you can, Clay told him, you'll beat anybody that's been here so far.

The man took a package of cigarettes from somewhere inside his suit coat. Clay began to roll a Country Gentleman.

They've sold this house, Rose began. He had a sing-song voice and sounded as though he were reciting the multiplication tables. It belonged to the city and they've sold it to the telephone company.

I don't see how that affects me, Clay said. I'll just pay my rent to the telephone company.

You hadn't paid any rent to anybody in some time, Rose said.

I been laid off, Clay told him.

All of this is beside the point anyway, Rose said. You can't pay rent to the telephone company because they're going to tear this down and clean the whole lot up. They're going to build a telephone exchange here.

A what?

A telephone office. All this is condemned.

Well it ain't no telephone office now, Clay said, it's my house. And I want your fat ass out of it right now.

It ain't your house, Rose resumed. It belongs to the telephone company.

Well are you the goddamned phone company?

No, I ain't. I told you I work for the county.

Well, is it your house?

Hell no, it ain't my house. Rose was getting flustered. You couldn't give me the goddamned house.

Then get your hind end out of it. Clay began to look around as if for something to throw at Rose.

By God you are crazy, Rose told him. They said you was and you damn sure are.

They ain't nobody says I'm crazy, Clay said, picking up a coffee cup.

Everybody says you're crazy, Rose said. If you run me off, they'll just send me back again and they'll send the sheriff.

He turned and went out the door.

They won't send you many more times, Clay told his plaid retreating back. You little bench-legged son of a bitch.

After a moment the car cranked and pulled away. Clay poured himself a cup of coffee and went out onto the porch. Spectral winter sunlight fell on the east end of the porch. Clay sat with his coffee cup in his hand and leant against the clapboard wall, staring with vacant and unfocused eyes into a wild tangle of brittle gray weeds in the yard, as if looking for something he had lost. Among these weeds birds hopped, foraging among the dead stalks. A metallic sky of steely blue above him, winter's days numbered now. Smoke rose from the shacks around him and the scent of it hung in the still air. Beyond their shabby roofs the pines a mist of sea green blurred by distance. Dark lurked beneath their branches like an invitation. Clay drank coffee. Two girls passed arm in arm, giggling, their hips swinging beneath tight skirts, conical breasts of improbable sharpness thrusting forward against their sweaters and he watched them long after their laughter was lost to his ears, the rhythmic and erotic movement playing on in his mind after they were out of sight nearing the junction. He wondered vaguely what they had to laugh at.

Around midmorning, Elmer Pulley came rolling by in his wheelchair and pulled off the shoulder of the road into the edge of the yard. He had an empty tow sack clasped loosely in his lap.

You ain't seen any bottles around this morning, have you, Herschel?

Naw. That where you headed?

Yeah, Pulley said. I got to get going to work.

You ever find very many?

I find several. People just thows em away. Com'ere a minute.

Clay got up and walked toward him, kicking himself a path through the weeds.

You got ary smoke?

Clay wordlessly handed him the tobacco. Pulley began to build himself a cigarette. His hands shook as if with palsy. He had been drunk the night before and a reek of urine and soured vomit and whiskey hung about him blackly like some malignant cloud. Involuntarily Clay stepped back away from him. At last Pulley wordlessly reached the tobacco back to him. He had shredded three papers and sat smokeless and forlorn. Clay rolled him a cigarette and lit it and placed it between Pulley's lips. You want me to hit you in the back to git ye lungs goin? he said.

Pulley laughed, a hacking smoky blue laugh turning into a wracking cough. I'll tell you something if you can keep it to yeself, he said when he could talk.

I don't know what soul in the world I'd tell it to, Clay said.

Well. They goin up to two cents deposit on them Coke bottles, Pulley said, almost in a whisper although no one was visible anywhere.

For a moment Clay stared at him and seemed at a loss for anything to say. At last he said, I reckon you're proud to hear that. You'll be makin twice as much money for the same amount of bottles.

Why hell no, Pulley said. They go up to two cents apiece and everybody'll be jumpin into it. They'll be quittin their jobs to pick up cold drink bottles. A crippled man like me won't stand a chance.

Shit, Clay said.

On a gray and sodden Sunday morning in February the county came and moved Clay out of the condemned house he lived in. The yellow bulldozer came before good daylight and parked by the side of the house, the driver in a rain slicker with a hood like a cowl. He stood on Clay's porch drinking coffee from a thermos bottle and waiting for the truck to come after Clay's things. When it did they loaded everything Clay possessed into a flatbed truck with high sideboards while Clay stood to one side with his hands jammed deeply into his pockets and smoked and shivered in the cold. They threw whatever their hands fell upon into the back of the truck and when the house was bare the truck was not yet full. They threw mattresses and blankets across the top and while they were cutting the clothesline down to lash all this securely, the operator threw his cigarette out into the rain and adjusted the cowl and went out and cranked the bulldozer. It sat idling in the rain.

One of the Negroes yelled at Clay. The truck was ready to go. Before it was out of the yard, the dozer was at the house. Looking back before it was all lost to his sight, Clay thought it resembled some great beast feeding.

Dropping off a long steep hill in the rain, Clay aloft and trying to stay dry under the sodden mattress, cursing and shaking his fist at the elements who, mindful of this, still let the drizzle fall. Past Goblin's Knob, shuttered on this day of rest and cloistered in its stand of pines, mystic and secretive, watching him with lidded eyes. And past further still, descending into a region foreign to him, strange hills and valleys and leaning derelict shacks long abandoned for greener fields and even the names and faces of county politicians nailed to telephone poles were strange to him, people he did not know and never hoped to. Past old lost Churches of God with faith painted on them like scrawled obscenities. At last he became mindful only of the rain.

They stopped finally at an abandoned one-room schoolhouse set atop a hill like a country squire's house, but half hidden by a stand of rank pigweeds. Across a rickety bridge, and then backing up to the high porch, they began to unload and carry Clay's possessions inside. Home sweet home, one of the Blacks said to the other and laughed. Again, Clay did not help. He seemed oblivious to where he was, conscious only of the cold rain.

Within an hour the truck was emptied and gone, and Clay sat in the scholarly gloom of the schoolhouse with the fire he had tried to build smothering and smoking on the hearth of the old fireplace. Old broken school desks and glass from smashed windows lay strewn about him and all around as well his miserable plunder, wet and scattered as if dropped from some great height by strong winds. He sat with no look at all in his eyes, the air of someone who has run out of options, like a yellowed photograph of the stunned survivor of some great natural disaster, all he could wrest from the fates lying in the wreckage about him. After a time, night fell and the dark settled over him like a coverlet against the cold.

On the first morning in March quarterly court met in Ackerman's Field. A gray soulless sodden day. Clay's case had been postponed once and tried once resulting in a hung jury and now they were going to try again. Quite a goodly number of curiosity seekers and people seeking material of conversation had gathered here and Clay passed among them unspeaking and unspoken to, a bitter wraithlike threat of a man still in his ratty jumper and overalls and not making even so small a concession as a show to these curious men in suits and ties carrying briefcases and folders of typewriter papers perhaps containing his name, men who whispered in each other's ears while eyes cold as arctic waters wandered about the room, like performers counting the house.

Clay's case was called first, but he sat for an interminable time while these suited men conferred with one another and whispered to the black-robed judge and rattled papers and moved among them all with purpose and solemnity.

Clay sat at a long table facing the judge and across from him, at an identical table, a boy wearing thick spectacles and his wet hair combed smoothly down sat listening to a fat man wearing an electric blue suit. Clay stared at him malignantly across the blue expanse of the fat man's lowered shoulders but the boy either did not see or chose to ignore Clay for he sat serenely with his huge, magnified eyes fixed on the fat man's face.

The selection of a jury began. Sheriff Bellwether drew numbers from a hat and prospective jurors filed past Clay's table into a double tier of church-like seats and sat regarding Clay with curious and somewhat uneasy eyes.

The man in the blue suit began to query the jury. Did they know Clay? Did they know anything about this case? Had they formed an opinion of Clay's guilt or innocence? Many of them had. They were excused. Could they reach a decision of Clay's guilt or innocence based entirely upon the evidence and sworn testimony presented? An unseemly number could not. All these were excused.

More numbers called. Clay morose, drowsy, perhaps asleep. All about him myriad courthouse smells and noises. A curious timeless smell of polished wood and disinfectant and floor wax and time itself and something still, something indefinable, justice perhaps. Footsteps loud in the sepulchral judicial quiet. Hushed voices from the seats behind him.

More prospective jurors seated, squirming in the hard and uncomfortable chairs. The blue suited fat man again questioning the jury. Did they bear Mr. Clay animosity? No. Or Mr. Long? Here the prosecutor pointed to the bespectacled youth who sat regarding this as from beneath water. No. No animosity anywhere. Had they read about this incident? Heard it from a neighbor? Perhaps from Clay or Long themselves? Well, yes. Some of them had. You are excused.

A sheen of perspiration formed on the prosecutor's face. A glint of disbelief in his eyes. Jurors came and went. He glanced often toward his wristwatch. Above them perched like God in cloaked solemnity the judge sat in apparent kinship with Clay for his eyes were half closed and vacant as if his mind were involved in some insoluble problem in mathematics, perhaps he dozed as well.

At noon only seven jurors were selected, and the judge roused himself to call a recess. Spectators began to straggle into the hall. Almost in resentment, as though the film had broken in some show. Clay went into the hall and rolled a cigarette. A thick blue fog of smoke made shifting patterns in the air. Clay slouched against the polished balustrade, staring about him. All this milling flotsam and jetsam. Women with bruised and broken faces, looking resentfully out of puffed and swollen eyes. Perhaps by their husbands. Women suing for child support, divorces, cars. Men in beatings, dog killings, fence cuttings, timber cuttings, property disputes. Far above them in the jail cells, the real criminals. Burglars and thieves and sellers of whiskey by the drink or by the jar. Stealers of guns or cows. All of them chained like Clay to the wheel of justice, turned by these shiny-cheeked men in suits and ties.

Pushing through the throng of sweating people as if buoyed by the sheer effervescence of noise Clay began to work his way to the basement. Passing two women talking Clay heard one of them say, I'll make that son of a bitch think again before he goes laying out at Goblin's Knob. Clay whirled and glared at the woman bent and frozen like a comic strip character expressing belligerence, but the woman was not talking about him at all yet he continued to glare at her. The woman turned to face him.

Well take a picture, it'll last longer, she said.

Stick it up your wore-out butt, Clay told her, still glaring. I expect they's plenty of room for it.

The bent-over woman turned an ancient croneish face full of shock up to him but could not meet his glassy angry eyes.

In the basement in front of the sheriff's office was a Coke machine. Here Clay drank a Coke sitting on the basement steps. Staring enthralled at his shoelaces as if in deep study of something profound waiting there to be revealed. People wound around him to get to the drink machine. He sat unmindful of them clutching the bottle. Raising his eyes then from the black low quarters up fat khaki legs to the grinning face of the deputy sheriff. Garrison stood leaning against the drink box regarding Clay with amusement.

What do you say, short-timer?

Clay said nothing and began to roll a cigarette. Garrison had a smooth bland face with eyes small as raisins that almost disappeared in fat when he smiled. A young face on its way to cruelty.

How does it feel to be Brushy Mountain-bound?

I don't know, Clay said. How does it feel to kiss Bellwether's ass every morning before breakfast?

I may get to drive you up myself, Garrison said conversationally. We might get to stop two or three times. You know. On them little side roads where we could be by ourselves.

One time would be all it would take, Clay told him. Without you had that pistol on me.

Two or three men laughed and then looked away when Garrison scowled at them. They put their bottles in the wooden cases and went up the stairs grinning. Watch him Clay, he'll set on ye, one of them called. Smothered laughter came, then from the top of the stairs, laughing. Hey, Garrison, ye britches legs is afire. He's done put the torch to ye.

Sure he has, Garrison said, watching Clay. You know goddamn well he has.

Long on the stand. Calm and serious. Eyes huge and myopic behind the glasses, legs crossed casually, polished shoe bouncing awkwardly. Clay stared at the orange clock design on his sock swinging like a berserk metronome. The fat man in the blue suit paced the floor, his face solemn and thoughtful as if searching his mind for a place to begin. Clay wondered at the solemnity of this occasion. His eyes searched the closed faces of the jurors.

Mr. Long, have you ever had occasion to know the defendant, Mr. Herschel Clay?

Yes, I have, Long said, looking toward Clay.

Is the gentleman seated at the table facing you at this moment Mr. Clay? He asked pointing.

Yes.

Tell the jury how you became acquainted with Mr. Clay.

He traded some with my daddy at our store. I used to wait on him sometimes. He bought his groceries there.

Did Mr. Clay pay cash or did he occasionally charge his groceries?

Well, he started out paying cash. After he traded there awhile he got a ticket and then he'd buy em on credit.

Clay's court appointed attorney stood up and objected.

I don't see what Mr. Clay's grocery buying habits have to do with any of this, he said. The prosecutor protested and began to gesture erratically to the judge and Clay did not listen. He had heard it all before and he did not really understand it anyway. Instead he stared past his seedy lawyer and past and above the jurors' heads to where somber windows rose bleakly and even past them to the rain falling grayly like a winter rain and imagined that he was somewhere else and he could hear it falling dully on a tin roof and that he was alone there with only the rain and the floor beneath him. He closed his eyes. The objection was overruled.

He paid at first. Then he quit.

Quit what? Quit trading or paying?

Both, Long said. He'd come in every now and then and buy a little dib of snuff. Then when he got pretty far behind he just quit and he'd cross the street instead of walking past the front of the store.

Would you tell us what transpired on the seventh of August in this past year?

Daddy sent me out to the sawmill where Mr. Clay there worked. It was on a Friday and that's payday. Daddy'd been over to his house and never could catch him at home. So I went out there to dun him about his ticket.

What happened?

Why, he beat me up, Long said. Here the jury looked at Clay with disapproval. A boy with glasses on.

Tell us everything you remember about it.

Well. It was raining. It sat in just as I was gettin out of the car and the hands was goin into the shack, this little house they got out there. It was about dinner and some of em had their dinner buckets out. Clay started in last. I tapped his arm. I told him I needed to talk to him. He never did say anything. He went in the shack and when I stepped up inside he hit me and knocked me back out into the rain. I fell in the mud and the first thing happened was my glasses got knocked off. I never could find em. I crawled around huntin em and Clay kept kickin me.

Did you make any effort to defend yourself?

I might of if I could have found my glasses. I couldn't even see him.

Did Mr. Clay stop this abuse of his own accord?

Objection, Clay's lawyer said. The witness has already testified twice that he could not see.

I assume he could still hear, the prosecutor said. I assume he could tell when the kicking stopped.

Overruled.

They pulled him off of me. I could hear them hollerin and cussin he was goin to kill me if he didn't quit. When I finally did find my glasses he had stomped em and I couldn't even see to get back to town.

Did Mr. Clay at any time threaten you?

Well he said he was goin to kill me.

I guess we could consider that a threat, the prosecutor told the jury. What exactly did he say, Mr. Long?

It was cussin, Long said. He looked at the jury. Leaned forward as one in anticipation.

If you please, the prosecutor said. Just his exact words.

He said: Just another son of a bitch after my paycheck. I'll kill the little four-eyed bastard.

That's all the questions I have for this witness, the prosecutor said. You may cross examine.

Tinney approached the witness chair and stood regarding Long for some moments. Long sat and stared at some point about Tinney's knees. At last Tinney said, We've all listened to your description of what transpired. But isn't the truth a little different? Did you not in fact assault Mr. Clay? Did you not grasp his arm and pull him out into the rain and attempt to jerk his paycheck from his shirt pocket, ripping his shirt in the process? Did you not in fact say Give me that money, you deadbeat son of a bitch?

Why Lord no, Long said.

Tinney stood regarding him as though shocked that such a blatant untruth could issue forth from the human tongue.

That's all, he said.

———

Clay now incongruous in the chair. Illshaven and shapeless, a dark thin slash of a man, a slap in the face of all decency, telling his story grudgingly to his solicitous lawyer.

He'd been following me around two or three weeks. Comin out to the house and beatin and bangin on the door. Hollerin about some money. I didn't have no money. Then he came down to the yard wantin my check. I told him I had to pay my rent and then he tried to take it away from me. Started cussin me and tearin my shirt. Hit at me a time or two and I shoved him. He fell over the doorsill and his glasses flew off and busted. That's all I know about it till they come and served me with the papers.

Did you ever strike Mr. Long with your fist?

No.

Did you break his glasses or kick him at any time?

No.

All right. You may cross examine.

The prosecutor picked up several sheets of paper and stood for some time studying these sheets of type oblivious to Clay or to the jury. Clay sat in some nervousness, occasionally shifting his weight in the chair and staring at his scuffed and broken shoes. His hands intertwined moving as if in grief.

The prosecutor looked up as though he had just noticed Clay sitting there. As though since Clay were here anyway he might as well ask him a question or two.

Mr. Clay, I guess you're pretty well known in this county?

Clay said nothing. He glanced once at the prosecutor's sallow face and then at the jury, in a curious jerking abrupt motion as if he had performed some sleight or magic and it did appear so for the face went momentarily thin and slatlike as a knife wound and the yellow eyes looked arrogant and smug.

I'm waiting for your reply, Mr. Clay.

Why, I don't know how to answer nothin like that. What you guess? What you guess it ain't none of my business?

All right. We won't quibble over a word. Are you well known in this county?

I don't know. No more than anybody else who was born and raised around here. I reckon most everyone knows who I am.

I reckon they do, the prosecutor said, and I think you are a little too modest. I submit that you are very well known indeed. How would you characterize this esteem, Mr. Clay?

What?

How would you characterize it? Is it like, dislike, envy, respect? What sort of response do you feel you evoke in your neighbors?

Clay looked as if in desperation toward Tinney, but his lawyer seemed not to be listening. I don't even know what you're talkin about, he said.

I'm talking about fear, the man said. I submit that most everyone around here is afraid of you. Do you have any idea why such a thing could be?

They ain't nobody afraid of me, Clay said. I tend to my own business.

They're afraid you'll burn them out, the prosecutor said. They're afraid they'll wake up in the middle of the night with everything they own in flames around them. Or worse yet they're afraid they won't wake up at all. You instill a very primitive fear in people, Mr. Clay. They know your propensity for matches, for threats, for innuendo. Short of killing you there's not much they can do except to try to stay out of your way, and your disfavor for the average person is a very serious thing to contemplate.

That's a lie, Clay said. Who told you any such lies as that?

I'm not afraid of you. What would you do to me? Come all the way to Nashville and burn me out? I intend to put you where you won't have any matches or anything to use them on.

I believe this has gone on about long enough, Tinney said. As far as I've been able to understand Mr. Clay is not on trial here for arson. I doubt if any purpose is being served by baiting the defendant and making these wild accusations. There hasn't been an iota of testimony about threats or house burnings.

I'll withdraw it, your honor, the fat man said. I think we've proved what we sat out to prove, that Mr. Clay viciously assaulted Mr. Long, with full intent to murder him.

You may step down, Mr. Clay.

Familiar faces then parading past Clay, all the mill hands who were at work that day of the fight. Caps in hands, cleanshaven angular Anglo-Saxon faces, dressed today in Sunday's raiment, washed and ironed, telling one and all the selfsame story. They did not see much of what happened. It sort of looked like Clay got shoved by Long going into the shack. Nobody saw Long get kicked. Clay might have shoved him a little.

The district attorney took exception to all this. When the defense rested its case he told the jury that he did not see how you could shove somebody a little and crack two of his ribs. Especially if you were as little as Clay was and Long was as big as he was. The jury listened to the district attorney attentively with somber inscrutable looks on their faces and then trooped solemnly into the jury room. They were locked up thirteen minutes and when they came back into the courtroom, they had found Clay not guilty.

The throng of people parted before him like waters and he walked through them like a pariah looking neither to the right or to the left. They could not have existed. In fact, they did not exist, any of them. They were all gone. Even Long and the district attorney were losing reality like a photograph fading before his eyes. He descended the concrete staircase, footfalls loud and disrespectful in these halls of justice. The big iron door creaked behind him, folding slowly in on itself. He stood on the courthouse steps. It was almost dark. The somber winter drizzle still fell. A gust of wind arose, spraying and slanting the rain. He breathed deeply, held the wet air in his distended lungs. Freedom sang in his blood like alcohol. He began to walk. Air leaden and dripping all about him. He paused once when he was some distance from the courthouse and looked back over his shoulder. The red brick courthouse sat ruminating on its square of winter grass. Watching him with lidded and satiated eyes. He went on warily as though the courthouse were somehow following him, stalking him from behind a curtain of brush until it blurred out of his sight in the slanting rain.

Early in April as Clay mounted the high porch steps to the Knob he saw Hixon's pickup in the parking lot, a doghouse on the back with deer hounds watching him solemnly. He stood for a moment as if undecided about entering and then sidled through the door, scanning the room as he came. All the tables were empty. Only Hines behind the bar. Hines had his glasses on far down his nose and he was looking through a cigar box of ginseng. Clay sat on one of the spinning stools and began to rock gently to and fro.

What can I do for ye?

Sack me up about twelve of them cold ones.

Hines, who had dealt with Clay before, was not to be had so easily.

You got any money?

Well. I wanted em before payday.

When's payday? I didn't know they'd got to where they paid off for settin on your butt or traipsing up and down the road.

I'm workin for a outfit putting in sewer line, Clay protested. I run a big machine what they call a jumpin jack. Got a motor on it like a chainsaw. Jumps up and down and sort of tromps the dirt down.

Shitfire, Hines said.

I could take my business elsewhere, Clay said.

Hines went back to inspecting his ginseng.

Clay sat for a time in silence looking about him at the dry poplar beams, the pine floor worn smooth and oily by the years.

It's lucky you ain't never had a fire here, he said at last. This place'd go up like a pasteboard box. A person ever get it in for you likely that's what'll happen.

I wish to hell it would hurry up, Hines said. I got fifteen thousand dollars' worth of insurance on this place I've never needed. Do you know where I'd be if I had fifteen thousand dollars? I'd be in Florida. I'd be laying on my belly in that white sand with a big-titted woman rubbing oil on my back. Instead of settin here listening to some fool jaw about settin fires. Do you know where I might get a hold of such a person?

Clay let silence stretch toward infinity. At last he said sack em up anyway. He pulled a greasy five-dollar bill from his watch pocket and began to unfold it.

Clay came out of Goblin's Knob with the sack of beer under his arm just as Pearl and Hixon walked out of the stand of pines. He began to walk toward the blacktop, his stride lengthening as he accustomed to the walk.

Hey there, Clay, a voice called, halting him.

You want a ride?

No. I'll just walk. Clay heard the truck door open and shut.

We'll be goin in a minute. You just wait. I got something I want to ask you.

Clay turned at the same time he heard the shotgun breech up and stopped as if frozen.

Come on, Hixon said. He was pointing the gun toward the ground in the vicinity of Clay's feet.

I found something might be yourn, Hixon said. A pair of overalls and a woman's blue dress. Belonged to a stout lady, looked like it'd fit your old lady.

Pearl was standing silent and staring off toward the treeline, as if by concentrating very hard all this would go away.

I ain't lost none I know of, Clay said, and I ain't got enough clothes so that I'd not miss anything.

They wouldn't of been much benefit, Hixon said. Soaked down like they was with coal oil.

Hixon looked like he had been on a two-week drunk. His eyes were red and pained and his florid face was covered with a red gray stubble of beard. His hands were unsteady on the shotgun.

You was at the window.

I was not. Clay's mouth was dry.

You think a lot of old Pearl, don't you?

Clay did not answer.

I bet you do. I bet you'd eat them drawers, wouldn't you.

He turned toward Pearl. Pull them drawers off, he said.

What?

Pull em off.

No.

I said pull em off. Hand em to me. I'll lay this whole goddamn bunch out.

Pearl lifted her skirt and slid the panties down and stepped unsteadily out of them. She was a little drunk. She dropped the skirt and leaned against the hood of the truck.

Hixon tossed the panties to Clay.

Eat them, he said. You been wantin to.

Clay was as stiff jointed as a wooden man. Carefully he set the sack of beer between his feet. The bottles clanked musically. He held the panties in both hands. A look on his face like pleading, a mute supplication. Hixon had raised the shotgun and sighted along the double barrels, one eye closed in a grotesque wink.

Eat them son of a bitches.

Clay put the panties in his mouth and began to chew. Tears stood in his eyes, welled and ran across the working cheeks.

He likes them, Hixon said. He'll get em down here in a minute.

Please, Pearl said, to Hixon or Clay or to no one at all. Please.

They stood so a long time, Clay mouthing the white panties.

At last Hixon lowered the gun. He held his hand wordlessly for the panties. Clay tossed them to him. Hixon half turned toward Pearl. He slobbered all over em, he said. She was shaking her head from side to side and crying soundlessly.

Git em on. He stood watching her pull the underwear up bemusedly, the fatal glimpse of dark sliding hair.

Clay was upon him in an instant. The hawkbilled knife hooked under the point of Hixon's jaw, and his throat erupted in a jaunty smile, so that for an instant Hixon seemed to have two mouths, one smiling, one screaming in soundless rage and pain.

Clay whirled and ran, grabbing for the beer as he went like a broken-field runner picking up a fumble.

The shotgun blast blew out his old jumper like a sudden gust of wind, picking him up and spinning him weightlessly about like a straw man, a fine mist of splintered glass and beer and blood flying all about him as he fell.

Hines came running down the steps.

Jesus Christ, he was saying, still carrying the cigar box of ginseng.

Clay was dead before Hines got there, the eyes filming and going blank like a slate slowly being erased. Clay's face had the look of a man who has run for a long time toward some point with no real hope of attaining it then suddenly feeling it within his grasp.

RIDING OFF INTO THE SUNSET:
STARRING GARY COOPER

In the west the sun had gone as the last vestiges flared in chromatic red and orange and windrows of lavender clouds dulled to smoke gray. Somewhere westward night was already facing him, and he went on toward it as if he and the darkness had some appointment to keep. For some time he'd been aware of sounds, the equable cries of birds, a truck somewhere laboring through the gears.

The next morning Bascom woke with light the color of haze heavy on his eyelids, heat bearing down on the flesh of his face and throat. His throat felt as if it had been cut with a rusty pocketknife and he had a thought to feel and see, but some old caution stayed his hand. Some things are better not known. He judged it better to enter into the day with caution, who knows what lay ahead?

Or behind. He lay very still and tried to locate himself. Where he was, where he'd been. Jagged images of the night before came unsequenced and painful, little dayglow snippets of chaos. Like snapshots brought back from a demented backroads vacation. He'd been in a car, six or seven men sitting crammed tightly shoulder to shoulder. Had there been a woman? He seemed to remember perfume, soft drunken laughter. A siren, the systole and diastole of a cruiser's lights. Riding through the actual woods down to a hollow, brush whipping the car, the breathless impact of a tree trunk. The protest of warped metal and a final shard of glass falling like an afterthought.

Running through the woods. One picture of him frozen in air, limbs all outflung and his mouth an O of surprise and an outstretched vine or bramble or perhaps clothesline hooking him beneath the chin and his terrific momentum slinging him into the air. Later on, the cry of some beast he suspected was yet unrecognized by science, some horrible hybrid of loon and mountain cat. Oh Lord, he said aloud, then immediately wondered if there'd been anyone about to hear it and opened his eyes to see.

The first thing he saw was the sun and he wrenched his face away in agony and saw a field of grass, a horizon of stems and clover blossoms like trees in miniature. A sky of a malefic bluegreen that seemed to be alive, pulsing and throbbing. He looked back into the ball of white pain that stood at midmorning.

An enormous blue monolith seemed to rise above him, and it took him a few moments to realize that it was his left leg distended into the air, rising at a precipitous angle and tending out of sight into the malicious sky he wanted no part of. As if some celestial beast or outlaw aberrant angel had snatched him up by the left leg to hove him off, found him ungainly or not worth having and departed or simply paused to rest.

Well now, Bascom said tentatively.

After a time, he realized that the cuff of his jeans was caught on the top of the chain link fence and hung him here in dismissal. Well son of a bitch, he thought. Reckon I was chasin something or runnin from it. He remembered voices and gunfire and riders and their steeds that seemed to have been lithographed on the stormtossed heavens themselves. By inching forward, he was able to jiggle his leg. He looked as if he was climbing the fence with his buttocks, using them as a snake uses its ribs. In this manner he was able to accumulate enough slack in the denim to wrench his leg free. He rolled backward and sat up in the grass with his legs folded under him and his face in his hands.

Oh Lord, he said. A person ought not have to live like this.

He looked about cautiously, like a player sweating over the last down card in a poker game. Who knew what he'd find? A dead body, a canvas bag of money stenciled First National Bank, a knife with blood crusted on its blade, a dead sheriff with a bloody and unserved warrant clutched in his fist. But there was just the fierce arsenical green of the field he was in, a distant treeline, birds moving above it like random or malignant spores on a glass slide. When he rose he noticed the white flaps of his pockets turned wrong side out and when he patted himself down he found he had no more than the nothing whatsoever he'd come into the world with. Just these ragged vestments of jeans and tee shirt. A right shoe. But he was of a philosophical turn of mind and this served him in good stead here. If you don't know what you had you can't miss it when it's gone.

He judged the road southward for he'd seen the sun glare off the tops of occasional cars and, as this was the only sign of civilization he'd seen, he followed the chainlink fence toward it through the stunned hot silence of the day. He was enormously thirsty and all he could think of was water. When the fence ended by the roadbed momentary indecision halted him. He looked left, he looked right. Right was touched by some vague familiarity, ephemeral as social memory and, never one for covering the same ground twice, he turned left and plodded along the shoulder of the road head down as if he were looking for something he'd lost among the brackery of dewberry vines and honeysuckle.

Each footfall brought a shock of electricity to his brain. As if his feet completed some bygone telluric circuit when they touched the earth. He thought of white rats and other small laboratory animals whose job it was to close the electrical circuit painfully until they learned better. He began to feel watched by some celestial scientists that studied him from on high, watched one step after another. This is an exceedingly slow subject, why doesn't he learn? But Bascom was of an optimistic nature and after he began to sweat he felt better, and he thought if he could find some water he might actually live.

He saw the sign long before he could read the letters and beyond it the screen of a drive-in theater and the green of earth shaped in curved tiers where the rowed speaker posts stood like some esoteric crops. Centered in the back of the convoluted earth a white stucco building warped itself up out of the sundazed landscape. Past that a white frame house sat in the blue shade of the hills.

A figure he judged female was moving purposefully along a row of speakers at some obscene chore, bending and straightening, stooping and rising up the rows going on like someone picking cotton. After a time she turned past the white building toward the house in the woods and vanished in the trees.

He could read the sign now. FREE CAR THURSDAY, it said. He stopped and studied it bemusedly perhaps looking for amendments, fine print. There was none. He wondered what day it was. He spat a cottony mass onto the roadbed. Probably a catch to it, he said aloud. He went on.

He was soon upon the car itself. It was sitting aloft parked on a platform framed atop creosoted poles. A ramp of sawmill lumber led from the earth up to the platform. Bascom crossed and peered through the fence. A faded green Studebaker that looked as if it had been ridden hard and illy used. But free was free and a gift mouth not to be examined. It had presumably been driven up the steep ramp.

He left the roadbed. He turned in where a narrow cherted drive branched off past a sign that said Star Vue Drive-In and crossed between the screen where it rose enormous on tall posts and an untenanted ticket booth and followed the curving drive to the stucco building.

He walked all around the building. He was looking for a spigot, but he didn't find one. He felt dry as gunpowder, weightless as dry leaves. He pushed open a door hinged to open either way like the batwing doors of a saloon. Hey in there, he called. No answer. Just the hum of machinery, the whir of an unseen fan blowing. Looking about he saw that he was in the concession stand, a cornucopia of boxed candy bars and gum, bagged potato chips, and the soda fountain with its gleaming chrome appurtenances. Its cunning pump levers like knobbed gearshifts. Compartmented paper cups you pulled free one by one, a sliding door under the counter that revealed miniature ice cubes in a stainless-steel bin.

He'd learned how to work the dispenser and he'd finished a Coca-Cola and half an Orange Crush when the door opened and a redhaired woman stepped through it. She was looking back over her shoulder and didn't see Bascom until she'd slammed into him. Shit, she said, and leapt away wildeyed, orange soda all down her front.

What are you doing in here? Who are you?

Bascom was picking up ice cubes and replacing them in the paper cup. He looked about for something to mop up the soda.

I just come in off the road. I was needin a drink of water.

I guess if you was broke you'd just walk in a bank and help yourself, she said. Just fill up your pockets and be gone.

I been broke all my life and ain't robbed no bank yet.

Well, you're young, she said. Give yourself time. No need in rushing into things.

Bascom set the ice on the counter and studied her. She had bright green eyes and pale skin faintly freckled. A medusa-like head of red curls sprayed so heavily in place they seemed to have been glazed and fired in a kiln. He judged her somewhere in her forties, maybe forty-five. She was dressed heavily for the weather in warm men's clothing and he could tell nothing about her body.

Well? Do you want to see my teeth?

What?

You're looking me over like a horse at an auction barn.

He looked away and said nothing.

You just pushed the door open and walked in like you owned the place. We're closed here. You can't show movies in the daytime.

I was just lookin for a faucet and couldn't find one. I'll get a drink and be on my way.

On your way to where?

I don't know. Whatever's down that road.

Where'd you come from?

He gave a one-armed gesture so meaningless it seemed to encompass the horizon, the world itself, nowhere at all.

Haven't you got folks?

He finished off the orange drink and crunched the ice cubes in his teeth. He'd never seen ice cubes that cunning and small. As if they'd been served only half-grown. He'd always been perplexed by the origin of things and he wondered how they were formed.

Everybody's got folks or he wouldn't be here, he said. But mine are all dead. I'm an orphan. I fell in with a bad bunch and got robbed. It is a rough bunch on the road these days. What about that car?

What about it?

Is it free like the sign says?

We hold a drawing on Thursday night. A raffle. All week long the tickets are put into a box and one is drawn out. If the person who bought that ticket is here, he wins the car.

It still seems fixed to me. You got to already have a car to win this car.

No. We get a lot of walkers. It's hard times. Lots of folks don't have a car.

Oh. Then it ain't really free.

What?

If you have to buy a ticket and come to the show.

The car is free. You buy the ticket to see the movie and speaking of free, the drinks are not. They're fifteen cents apiece.

Like I told you I was robbed. They turned my pockets wrong side out. I reckon I owe you fifteen cents. He wadded the cup, wondering if there was some kind of chemical test she could do to detect residue of Coca-Cola amidst the Orange, a lie detector test. You got something I could do to work it off?

I'd not charge a thirsty man for a cold drink. Even one who helped himself without asking. But there's work here if you want to make a few dollars.

He had given up on the Studebaker. No free car today.

He went out dragging an enormous aluminum garbage can into the rowed speakers and stopped to survey the grounds. They were strewn with popcorn bags and Coke cups and cigarette packs and napkins. Windtossed paper that looked like debris from some huge storm. Every son of a bitch that passed in the night must of just raked out his car and drove off, he said.

But it was light easy work and he went at it with a good heart, down the tiers picking up scrap bothhanded like a man picking cotton. Sweat soaked his shirt as he worked, but it was good to be in a day that seemed guided by purpose. He began to whistle some old lost song from his childhood. He'd police an area around the can then he'd move the garbage can and commence again. When the can was full, he dumped it into a steel mesh incinerator behind the concession stand and set it afire and went back to the field. Once when he was dumping the can into the mesh cylinder she came out to check on him. Well, she told him, you will work. I'll say that for you.

On the last tier next to the woods the findings were of a different nature. Beer cans, a few half-pint bottles. A thin tube of latex like a sea fluke left by the recession of a briny tide. Eros's calling card, a semenstained container love had come in. I ain't touchin that, he said aloud. He hunkered on the earth to think about it. He didn't know what the protocol was here. He wondered what she did in this situation. Should he go ask her? How to phrase it? He couldn't think of a delicate way to put it, and perhaps it had never happened before. As so often it was of no moment. At length he rose and caught it up on a length of a stick and carried it out to the garbage can, holding his arm stiffly extended and slightly to the side as if germs were blowing off it.

When the last papers were burned, he sat for a time behind the concession stand in the shaded silence and just listened to the day. Every sound seemed separate and distinct, a thing to itself, and each seemed to possess significance beyond themselves, as if each sound stood for something. A truck passed on some distant unseen road. Doves called from the woods beyond the house, soft and sad as if they had some loss to mourn to him about. He looked up. The sky was cloudless and blue and bottomless and within it birds shifted and spun in the wind's keep like small dark kites that had come untethered. He rose to go inside and tell her he was finished. For the first time in weeks he felt at peace with himself.

That night he was inside the dark booth watching as the projectionist showed a Gary Cooper western of one man backed to the wall and ultimately making his stand. To Bascom the projectionist tending his whirring machines was an alchemist laboring over his potions. As if he'd concocted this parable, decoded it from some collective unconscious. Never had Bascom seen rugged individualism so rewarded, yet so neatly thwarted. He watched as the projectionist switched between the reels, learned to watch for the white circle in the upper right hand corner of the frame that signaled the end of the reel: ever after he would imagine this appearing to him like a sign of a celestial guidance and he would know that whatever particular reel he was in was ending, and he would think, got to go, time to fold these cards, time to walk off down the road. Start another show.

Long after the lights had come on and the last car gone, he was still transfixed by the play he'd seen. As if in some manner he'd acquired a friend in Gary Cooper, some stoic black and white familiar who'd stand beside him when the going got tough.

How'd you like that part where his wife finally shoots that last outlaw? he asked.

I've seen it too many times, the woman said. I always know what's coming. I don't even like movies anymore. The bad guy always gets shot, the good guy always gets the girl. It never shows what happens after that.

Her name was Willodene Roth and he'd learned she was from Michigan.

How'd you wind up way down here, he asked.

My husband was looking for the ideal spot to drink himself to death, she said. He figured this was the perfect place. As it turned out, he was right.

She was cleaning the grill. Bascom was sweeping up cigarette butts and trampled Coke cups.

I don't see how you've managed to run this place, he said. Sellin tickets and all. Cookin all night, these hamburgers and all. It's run us both to death.

I had a helper until a few nights ago, she said. She was at emptying the cash register, stowing the money in a white canvas bag.

Why'd he quit?

He didn't quit. I fired him.

How come? Looks like you'd need the help.

I didn't need that kind of help, she said. He knew I was a widow and he thought that gave him a license to take advantage.

Mmmm, Bascom said. At the back of his mind he'd been idly wondering where he was going to sleep tonight and guessed this told him where he wasn't.

He wound up sleeping on a sort of chaise longue in the concession stand. From the house she brought blankets, a pillow. There's a shower back there in the bathroom, she told him. I don't want to get personal, but I believe you could stand one. I guess hygiene is different on the road.

When she'd gone he examined the place at his leisure. There was a back room with a freezer. He opened it, cold air smoked out. Bags of frozen hamburgers, neat bundles of wieners corded in their plastic sarcophagus. He'd never seen such largesse. In the other room tiers of cartoned candy bars, each identical in the cellophane wrapper. So accessible all you had to do was tear off the paper. The Coke machine was inexhaustible as the lemonade spring told of in some old song.

He ate three leftover hot dogs and a bag of potato chips and then he ate a candy bar and drank a cherry cola. He looked about. Well now, he said. He was enormously content, master of his domain, lord of all he surveyed. He'd been idly thinking about lovestarved widows and lonely mile-scarred drifters, but this no longer seemed applicable here. At length he made his bed, crawled into it and pulled up the covers. He lay for a time, marveling at the switchbacks and reversals life can take, the odd trips it can take you on. This very morning he'd awakened lost and penniless, even the next meal a dim prospect. Now he was sated and content, semiproprietor of a prosperous business. For a while he lay as he tried to concoct a plan to jerry-rig the drawing for the car. An accomplice perhaps, raising aloft the ticket Bascom had slipped him. That's me, the accomplice cried, that's my number.

But the day had been too full and he was enormously weary. The icemaker made a comforting drone. His eyes closed. When he opened them halfdozing he imagined his head was resting on the bone of a saddle, the ceiling sprent with stars, and that from the dying campfire Coop watched him with bemused and tolerant eyes. Regret haunted him already for all that was lost to him as he went on, Coop shrugged sadly and rode off.

THE DREAM

Sometime between midnight and daybreak, the old man began to dream and the dream was so vivid that every smell and sound and detail was so real that his life became a blurred, half-forgotten dream. It was late June or early July and he was in Alabama. It was early morning, the dew was still on and he was on his way to the new ground to grub bushes. The dream was so real he could feel the sun through his work shirt and the weight of the mattock on his shoulder and, although he was walking ground he had not trod in sixty-odd years, he knew exactly where he was and he knew that if he turned in the red dust of the road he would be facing the house he had been born in. He turned and there beyond the fencerow was the log house, weathered gray, two sides with a dogtrot between. A thin wraith of smoke from the cook stove rose and dissipated in the surreal blue sky. As he watched it he heard the back screen door creak and slam shut and saw his mother carry out a basket of wet clothes and begin to hang them on the line. She threw a sheet across the wire and spread it and it hung slack and straight in the breezeless air. He could hear her singing some old church song and he turned back the way that he was headed.

The winding clay road was bound on either side by a fence of split rails and thick with vines and briars. He began to follow it. He crested an undulating rise and in the distance he could see the field where his father plowed and disked behind the mules. The distance was a soft tapestry in muted greens and browns. He curved past the barn, angled steeply down toward the bottoms flanking Deerlick Creek, and then through trees that made a shady bower for his passage. He was aware of the calling of birds he had not heard since his childhood and of a distant tranquil murmuring from the creek that sounded as no creek had murmured to him since.

He came onto the new ground where the sassafras bushes were and as he passed the last elm he saw his brother Isaac sitting on the bank in the shade of a gnarled apple tree and watching his passage as if it afforded him some secret amusement. Isaac was bare to his waist and his skinny shoulders brown from the sun. He sat calmly, his elbows resting across his knees, as if he had sat so forever and would continue into infinity.

He stopped in the road. There was a roaring in his ears that diminished the birds, the creek, all the myriad sounds of the summer day. He swung the mattock from his shoulder and leaned on it, the head of it settled in the dust beside his bare feet. Then he dropped the mattock and began to climb the bank.

Isaac watched his approach without interest as if there was nothing extraordinary in the fact that he had come back to the field where they had grubbed together so many days.

He dreamed that he put his arms around Isaac's neck, felt the heat of him, smelled the clean scent of his hair, then Isaac shoved him roughly away.

What's the matter with you?

You're supposed to be dead.

What's the matter with you? he asked again. Are you sunstruck? Has the old man worked what little sense you had out of you?

Them lines, he said. You was tangled in the lines and the horses drug you to death. You was twelve years old.

Isaac laughed and looked away toward the creek. Beyond it, limestone bluffs climbed steep and sheer and above its dizzy precipice hawks or buzzards circled against the immeasurable blue.

I seen you laid out, he said in wonder, and felt how inadequate that was in the face of what he beheld: Isaac in the flesh, the pale eyes so long forgotten, the freckles dusting his thin arms, the calm irrefutable corporeality of the flesh. Love so strong it ached like pain rose in his chest, his throat constricted with emotion so that he felt he might asphyxiate. They lied, he thought. They had all lied, then.

Then the dream altered subtly, took on another dimension as if a curious muted light had come on somewhere. He saw that he was in the early part of the summer Isaac died in, that all the horror was yet to come, that Isaac sat before him doomed as surely as there was a God Almighty. That he was powerless to alter what lay ahead, and that he was double cursed by its foreknowledge. He saw that he had curiously gone two directions in time, backward to the time preceding Isaac's death and yet possessing knowledge of what was to come. He felt weary and impatient with helpless anger.

Then Isaac arose and started down the bank toward the creek. Come on, Isaac said. He followed down the bank, picked up the mattock from the road. Isaac had started into the deep cool shade near the creek's edge, then turned impatiently back toward him. Come on. What are you waiting on?

Some inexplicable fear had touched him, chilled the sweat running down his ribs. I don't want to, he said.

What's the matter? Isaac asked. Are you afraid? He gestured toward the viney undergrowth and its cool humming stillness, motioning for him to come on. It's cooler in here, and quieter.

No, he said. Wait. Let me just sit here and rest a minute.

He came awake. It was near day and the moon on the snow created an illusion of a spurious dawn outside his window. He lay for a time, half wanting to recapture the dream and half dreading what lay ahead. But it was lost to him. A feeling of sorrow touched him, for Isaac or perhaps for himself. There was an unpleasant taste in his mouth, a metallic taste of canker.

UP TO BAT WITH THE BASES LOADED

He got married all in a rush that summer. Things were getting out of hand, his life winding down roads he didn't want to be on. I've got to get a hold on myself, he had thought, turn myself around, make something out of myself. At twenty-one, life already seemed to be picking up speed and outdistancing him. The people he had graduated with two years before were in college, in business, their futures as secure as if some celestial hand had outlined the routes for them to take with a ballpoint pen. They were programming computers, going away to school, being shoved without ceremony into plastic bags in Vietnam. He had gone from being a high school baseball hero to pumping gas and occasionally working on other folks' cars, chasing pussy, parked nights in moonlit country sideroads, the yellowlit radio playing, reading by starlight the timeless wisdom encoded on beercans.

Then he got involved with Carmie and met her sister Cathy Liskus. Carmie's real name was Carmelita, but everybody knew her as Carmie. Raymer had yet to meet anyone in Ackerman's Field who didn't call her Carmie. Carmie pulled into the station in a little bright yellow Pinto with an overheated engine. She got out and slammed the door. Raymer just stood there with a greaserag dangling from his hand looking at her, not breathing. There was something about Carmie that literally took his breath. She was tanned very dark and had on a white bikini as brief as sinners' prayers and he could see the white untanned edges of her breasts where the halter had slipped a little. The bottom seemed pulled up into her crotch and the sight of all that tanned healthy young skin made him feel as dull and numb as if his head had been shot full of Novocain.

It got hot coming from the lake, she said. Can you fix it?

We'll soon see, Raymer said above the roaring in his ears. Raymer raised the hood and unscrewed the radiator cap. The explosion of steam rolled the cap off the sealing and jerked the greaserag from his hand and scalded the inside of his forearm. Oh my Lord, the girl cried. Raymer was leant clutching his wrist. He rubbed it and skin slipped away. Hellfire, he cried.

Raymer turned and Adcox was watching him. Adcox owned the station and it was he who wrote Raymer's paychecks on Friday afternoons. He was watching Raymer with a look both bemused and tolerant. He just shook his head and went on into the office. Raymer felt like a coin with the face on both sides, it came up fool no matter which way you flipped it.

Pretty hot all right, he said, calmly listening to the hiss of steam. She might of just been low of water. He was pretending his arm wasn't burning, that it didn't ache and that he had encased it in a shirtsleeve of ice that froze away the pain.

I'm sorry, she said. I thought, you know, you working in a service station, I figured you knew what you were doing.

I do know what I'm doing.

I don't know, are you sure? she asked wryly. If this happens every time you take off a radiator cap I got to wonder how long you'll be in the garage business.

She had a bottle of Jergens lotion in the glove box and she made him let her bathe his arm with it. He sat on a stack of old automobile tires and she knelt before him, rubbing the lotion over the quilted angry flesh. He felt big and clumsy and slowmoving, more the fool than ever as she was concentrating on his burn, her face serious and intent. She was overpowering him, drowning him, sucking up all the oxygen he needed to exist; she knelt before him seemingly unaware that her halter top had slipped another notch and that he could see half a breast. Her knees were touching him, parted a little, he could see the flesh pressed against the crotch of her bikini bottom.

He was angling desperately for something clever to say. You live around here? he asked her.

Nobody lives around here, she said.

He watched the Pinto drive away. Adcox came out and watched it too.

I'm glad she didn't have a flat tire, he said. I never yet seen a man commit suicide with a tire changer and I am glad you didn't put me through it.

Raymer looked at the angry flesh of his arm. I never did anything like that before, Raymer said. I don't know what I was thinking.

The hell you say, Adcox told him.

Next day she was back and she had Cathy with her. They were a wonder to Raymer. They were identical twins and he had never seen two people alike. Though after he had been around them awhile, he could tell them apart with ease, not by their looks but by something in their characters he divined, though he could not articulate it. Carmie was hardedged and brittle where Cathy was quiet and soft, her edges blurred and undefined.

Cathy looked five years younger than Carmie. She was fair where Carmie was dark. She wasn't such a knockout as her sister either. Raymer thought she was pretty, but she did not cut off his breath and set his flesh on edge the way Carmie did and, in a way, that was a relief.

I come to see about you, I didn't sleep a wink last night, she told him. She turned to Cathy. Look at that blonde hair. Didn't I tell you he was cute?

Cathy was watching him levelly through the lens of amber sunglasses. Yes, she said, composedly. You told me he was cute.

Carmie didn't have on the white bikini today. She had on a yellow sundress Raymer was trying not to look down the front of, or, rather, he was trying not to be obvious about it. He decided that Carmie wasn't as lovely as he remembered. Her face was too sharp for that, though her eyes and body made up for it. She just seemed so intensely alive, and alive in a threatening way, if you didn't get out of her way she'd roll right over you, if you couldn't stand the heat you had no business in the kitchen.

Want to ride around with me and my twin sis? We'll let you sit in the middle.

At that moment Raymer made a decision. He didn't plan it out or even think about it. He just didn't figure he had any business in that particular kitchen. Anyway, he could always go out with Peggy Lindsay down at Shipp's Bend. She didn't look like this but then again, she didn't eat him alive either. I have to work, he said.

Come on, Carmie said. We won't bite you. Where it'd show, anyway?

Raymer just smiled. I can't get off tonight.

Raymer could tell she wasn't used to people not being able to get off. She was used to getting next to people the way she had done him and she enjoyed it. He could tell.

He went over to Shipp's Bend that night but this time something was missing. Peggy Lindsay seemed lethargic and dull, her every motion made as if she were sleepwalking, her every word like something she had repeated a hundred times before. So, he wound up checking around to find out where the Liskus sisters lived and Saturday night he drove out to Beech Creek.

The Liskuses lived in a ramshackle frame house at the mouth of a hollow. A tilted mailbox had shown him the way. There seemed no soul about. The yard was treeless and grassless and the gray house had the stark austerity of a landscape by Wyeth.

As Raymer sat in his car the door opened and a man stood in it holding a beercan. He was naked to the waist and the pale expanse of his belly looped over the waist of his jeans. He gave Raymer a fierce malevolent look as if he bore him some old unsettled grudge and then he vanished back inside the house.

The yellow Pinto was gone but Cathy was sitting on the porch swing watching him drive up. She came out to the car.

If you come out for your treatment you'll have to come back, she said. Carmie's not at home.

I didn't come over here to see Carmie, he told her. I came to see you.

They started going out together. She was everything Carmie wasn't. There was a calmness about her, composure, order, Raymer thought. Order she ought to be able to bring to his life, a pattern of conformity she could force him into. Raymer guessed he was in love. Things went the way they go sometimes and that August they were married at the courthouse and some of his so-called buddies had let the air out of all four tires and written all over the car with soap. GRAND OPENING TONIGHT, the windshield advertised. Son of a bitch, Raymer said to himself. He was already feeling qualmy about being an old married man. He was going to have to learn how to handle things.

He had to walk clear across town to Adcox's and borrow a pickup truck and a tank of air. At Adcox's he took two beers out of the cooler and knocked them back one after the other in the men's room. He watched his face in the mirror. He thought he looked thinner, more mature, older somehow and he looked like he belonged. He was part of the enormous pulsating mainstream of life; he had finally made it into the river of humanity rushing toward the oceans. I got an old lady, he told himself. Behind him in the wonky glass he thought he glimpsed the hazy reflection of the dark demon that had always been pursuing him, that in the last year was gaining on him. It was falling back. Raymer's face was sharp and saturnine. He thought of an old song by Chuck Berry. *You can't catch me,* he told the demon.

Adcox owned a white frame house out in the country and he rented it to Raymer and Cathy for eighty-five dollars a month. The house was small but neatly kept and Raymer liked the way it looked set against the rolling green slope of grass. There were two oak shadetrees in the front yard. The chimney was built of red brick and it had ivy climbing on it. There were even roses in the front yard. It was everything you could have asked for in a house.

He liked the way the house looked coming home in the evenings. Knowing Cathy was inside waiting for him made it look that way. A kind of nervous anticipation would build up inside him and it felt to Raymer as if he could see her through the walls.

This was all a new world for him. He would come home for lunch and start fooling around with her on the couch. He just couldn't seem to keep his hands off her. They'd wind up in bed and he'd be late getting back to work. He had a phone installed so Cathy could talk to her mother, and they'd take the phone off the hook so Adcox wouldn't call.

Back in July an old friend of his named Keith had found a raccoon somewhere and thought how funny it would be to lock it in Raymer's car while Raymer and Cathy were in the movie theater.

The raccoon had wanted to be somewhere else very badly. It had ripped out the Naugahyde seat covers Raymer had mailordered from JC Whitney and the places it had shat showed desperation or a great deal of imagination. Keith had been watching from the sidewalk as Raymer opened the car door and the look on Raymer's face as the coon shot over him like an animate furred projectile had Keith down on the sidewalk rolling and pounding the concrete with his fists.

Not for long. Raymer hadn't been amused and he and Keith had a fistfight in front of the theater with folks yelling and Cathy trying to pull them apart. He had beat the hell out of Keith. Ultimately a cop pried him off with a flashlight. Any raccoons Keith came upon in the future years were allowed to go on their way unmolested.

All the same Raymer had to learn to handle things. There had been a time when he and Keith were close as brothers.

Carmie had man trouble that year, was in love with a married man, with men who didn't love her back, with too many men loving her at once. She was twenty-two that year and things weren't going the way they were supposed to go.

Then a terrible thing happened to Raymer: Carmie moved in with them. He came in from work and the yellow Pinto was in his parking space. Cathy had a look of tenseness on her usually calm face.

Raymer was washing the grease off his hands at the bathroom sink. Where is she?

She's in her room. Cryin I guess. They had a fight.

She doesn't have a room.

The extra room then.

We don't have an extra room, Cathy. We have two bedrooms. Neither one is Carmie's.

Well, she's my sister, R. C. I don't exactly like it either, but I didn't have any choice. She didn't ask me, she just sort of told me.

This is nothing but trouble.

Raymer was sometimes wrong, but he wasn't this time. His idyllic life was shot to hell in a handcart. The honeymoon was over.

That night a car stopped before the house. Raymer went out to see. A man was hastily unloading cardboard boxes of clothing out of the backseat onto the lawn. When he saw Raymer, he kicked the last box toward him scattering the clothing, gave Raymer the finger and got back in the car. Hey, Raymer yelled. The car spun gravel leaving, slewing sideways when it hit the blacktop. Raymer stood looking about him. Pale ghosts of Carmie's unmentionables were strewn about the lawn, random as undrifted leaves.

She was coming and going at all hours of the day and night. No hour seemed too early, none too late. Men would drive up and blow their horns and she would grab her purse and go. Strange men homing on Raymer's driveway these humid nights. He saw only their glassed-in profiles, their faces lit orange by pulsing cigarettes, their beercans tossed carelessly onto his meticulously-crafted lawn. He began to hate her. To hate himself for enduring it.

She was becoming more casual in her ways. Raymer was watching a baseball game on television. He didn't look at her until he heard Cathy's voice. There was something different in it.

Carmie, go put some clothes on.

Raymer looked. Carmie had on a short black nightgown. He could see the shape of her bare breasts, her underpants.

I've got on clothes.

No, you haven't. Not enough to suit me.

I never knew I dressed to suit you. Besides what does it matter? R. C.'s family.

Yeah, my family. Not yours. This is my house too, Carmie.

Well, she said, airily rolling the hairbrush through her short black hair, pulling the neartransparent black silk tight against her breasts. Raymer could see her nipples, the smudge of stubble in her armpits. I may not be here much longer anyway.

That suits me right down to the ground, Cathy said.

Carmie fell in love with a married diesel mechanic from Town Creek, Alabama. She met him at a square dance. His name was Jack. It was Jack this and Jack that. Raymer didn't know if he had a last name or not. He gladly forsook wife and children for her, and she went to live with him in a house trailer in Tuscumbia, Alabama. Raymer was very happy for them, he wished them all the happiness in the world.

They didn't hear from her for a month. Then the phone rang in the middle of the night.

Put Cathy on, she said.

Sorry you got a wrong number, Raymer thought. But he reached her the phone. Raymer lay back on the pillow listening to them or rather listening to Cathy's part of it, which was brief. All he could hear of Carmie was a frantic electronic buzzing.

He heard Cathy ask, Where could we meet you?

He said, Oh, hellfire, and pulled the covers up over his head.

Cathy hung up the phone. She pulled on her bra and panties and stood before the open closet a moment in sleepy indecision.

Where are you going?

Alabama, she said. We got to go and get Carmie.

We, hell, Raymer said. He was watching her over the covers. Have you got a mouse in your pocket?

They've had a fight and he beat her up. She's somewhere on the road hitchhiking.

Jesus. Walking? From Alabama. Nobody walks from Alabama.

Carmie does. When she wants to go she just sets out afoot.

Yeah, to the nearest telephone. What happened to her car?

She didn't say, maybe Jack took it.

Then let Jack worry about her. I got to work tomorrow.

Look, I don't want to go any more than you do. But when you come right down to it, she's my sister and I love her. If I won't go, who will? If you don't want to go, I'll do it myself.

It had begun to rain. They drove toward the stateline in silence, save the steady swish of the windshield wipers, the radio turned to a country music station, sad tales of infidelity and poisoned love. Cathy dozing, head pillowed against the dark glass. As they neared the Tennessee–Alabama line, they passed a long string of beerjoints shuttered and barred one after another against the night. They were dark and silent, gravel strewn parking lots barren of cars. He slowed, trying to differentiate between them: they all looked alike, featureless cubicles of concrete blocks or stucco. He saw Big John's, inscribed in dead neon. Big John's had a wrought-iron table and chairs on the lawn beneath a magnolia tree and it was here that Carmie awaited them, for all the world like the lady of the manor awaiting the serving of afternoon tea. She sat penned by the merciless stare of the headlights for a moment, defenseless, recognized the car and came and got in.

She had neither purse nor shoes. I never even stopped to grab a toothbrush, she said. I couldn't even get my car, the transmission's tore up. I left everything. He was drunk and beating me and finally he said he'd kill me and be done with it. He grabbed his big old pistol and shot a hole as big as my head in the end of his trailer.

Good God, Cathy said.

Look at my eye, she said, turning her face toward a fleeting light.

Her eye was almost closed, the flesh beneath it pouched and bluish yellow.

You got a shiner all right, Raymer said with satisfaction.

Cathy was sympathetic. She had an arm about Carmie's shoulders, Carmie's face pressed into her throat. She was crying, perhaps her bruises hurt or her pride was hurt or maybe she missed Jack already,

Raymer didn't know or care. Cathy was patting her shoulder. There, there, she said. We'll have R. C. go get your car this weekend and he'll teach that Jack a lesson.

The hell you say, Raymer said.

Raymer didn't know why she had quit Jack's bed and board but he would have bet money he caught her stepping out on him and beat the hell out of her. Raymer figured somebody was always going to be catching Carmie with another man. That was the scorn of her life. If there were only two men left in the world one of them was going to be catching Carmie with the other. Carmie was always going to be stepping out on somebody and somebody else was always going to be catching her and beating the hell out of her and she was always going to be doing it again. He saw an unbroken future of betrayal and reprisal, history recycling itself and teaching her nothing. He saw her as an old grayhaired toothless harridan, illy used and limping toward a telephone. He saw the perimeter widening, his trips into the rainy night lengthened.

There was one bright spot. She didn't come live with them. She had money, he didn't know or care where from. Perhaps she had been working, stealing from Jack, selling herself. She rented an aluminum house trailer on Beech Creek. She cut her losses with the Pinto and bought on time a '77 orange Firebird with an enormous eagle emblazoned on the hood. It was a very sporty car. Her fortune seemed to be changing for the better.

That year the Yankees were playing the Dodgers in the World Series and Raymer was always for the Yankees. He had been since he was a child. Adcox was for the Dodgers. The Yankees took the first two games but Adcox was unperturbed.

We done got twenty on it. You want twenty-one?

Hell yeah, Raymer said. I'll take your money. Keep on and I'll win enough to take a week off.

I don't know why you'd be for them damn Yankees.

I like to watch Reggie Jackson bat, he said, but it was more than that, more than he could articulate. He liked the self-possessed way Jackson came to the plate, big and confident and placid, the calm air of composure that hovered about him. Control. The air of authority that said, It's all right. We may be one or two down, but I'll take care of that here in a minute. Big hands clasping the bat, leant a little in anticipation. Then the clean crack of the bat and the ball long gone, the hot core of excitement in Raymer's belly. All he had ever wanted was to be able to do one thing as good as Reggie Jackson could hit a baseball.

Looks like you got a customer comin, Adcox said.

The way Adcox said, *You* got a customer, made Raymer look to see the orange Firebird easing past the gaspumps. Raymer got up. He could hear the Firebird knocking before he opened the door.

What on earth's the matter with it, R. C.?

A professional interest in the car's malady momentarily overcame Raymer's resentment. Let's see, he said. Raymer raised the hood and peered into the complexities of cables and wires. Rev her up a little.

When she did the knocking intensified. All right, ease off, he yelled. He leaned over the motor listening intently.

It sounds like a broke flywheel to me, he finally said.

Well, shit.

You'd have to drop the transmission to find out for sure.

Can you do that?

Well. It takes a while.

When can you come out and do it?

Come out where?

Home. It'll make it home won't it?

Sure, I guess so. Raymer closed the hood and came around the window on the driver's side. I was you I'd take it easy though. Drive forty or fifty and don't do no squealin the tires and she'll be all right.

He could smell her perfume. Her dress had ridden up on her thighs and she made no move to pull it down. He was leant abstractly studying the dark expanse of her legs, flesh so smooth and perfect it appeared boneless, the iridescent sheen of nylon serpentine in the play of light. He looked away, back to the station. Adcox's dark bulk leant against the cigarette machine. She traced the line of lipstick with a sharp pointed tongue, frosted pink, her lips gleamed.

When can you come out?

I don't know for sure, Carmie.

Well you come as soon as you can.

All right.

Okay. Thanks a lot, R. C.

She eased the car into gear, drove cautiously back into the pattern of traffic.

What'd she want?

She wanted her car fixed.

The shit she did. What else did she want?

Nothin, I don't reckon.

Nothin. Boy, I don't know how an ugly horse's ass like you does it. Two of them that looks that good.

I ain't steppin out on Cathy, Raymer said.

Well, I never meant you was. I meant you could. If you won't get mad at me I'll tell what I heard on her.

If I did you'd just tell me anyway.

I heard she was one these here nymphermaniacs, couldn't get enough of it, what I hear.

You can hear any goddamn thing. All she wants is her Firebird fixed for nothin.

Charity work. What's she got?

A broke flywheel.

Charity work. Adcox whistled. Then that flywheel's like the man said about the cat pissin in the cash register.

Raymer bit. What? He asked.

It soon runs into money, Adcox said.

Cathy came and sat on his lap. Her hands in his hair. Quit a minute, he said. Past her shoulder Graig Nettles made an impossible catch and the side was retired, but the Yankees were down three runs anyway.

When will you fix Carmie's car?

Damn it, Cathy. I fix cars all day. Right now I'm tryin to watch a baseball game.

You didn't fix Carmie's.

I diagnosed it and didn't charge her a shittin penny, either. She's got to stop that, too. Come in there askin about every little thing that goes wrong. Adcox is beginning to wonder who's payin me, him or Carmie. She's done been in there three times this week.

I can't help it.

You can hush about it.

Well, I feel sorry for her. She don't know how to fix it. She wouldn't know how to start. She can't afford it, and you're so good at things like that. Grimes won't do it.

She bought it from Grimes. Let him do it.

She don't trust him to do it right.

Oh Cathy, let me watch the damn game for Christ's sake.

She called this evening. She thinks you hate her.

Eighty-five bucks for a new one. He'd been lucky to find one at a junkyard for forty, but still that was forty dollars and it was going to have to come from somewhere. Raymer and Cathy were saving up for the down payment on a place of their own and every penny counted.

You at it already? A voice asked.

He twisted, the gravel beneath his back cutting into his flesh through the shirt and jacket. All he could see were her bare feet, the calves of her legs.

I been at it, he said.

I always sleep late Saturdays. She squatted beside the car. You need anything?

I need about three more hands.

Anything I can do to help?

I guess not. I've about got it off now.

How about some coffee? I got a fresh pot.

All right. It's still cold here in the shade. When he had the broken flywheel off, he got beside the car in the sun and drank the coffee. Above the pines the sun looked wintry, remote. He shivered. Carmie wore a faded flowered housecoat, without makeup her face looked younger and somehow defenseless, vulnerable.

Why didn't Cathy come? Carmie asked.

I don't know. I asked her and she said no. I guess she didn't figure it'd take this long.

How long will it take?

I don't know. A little after dinner maybe.

The sun was already sinking when he finished, the world being swallowed alive by blue shadows. That was the trouble with being a shadetree mechanic: you never had anything to work with. In the garage he wouldn't have had any trouble but out here it was different. In the end Carmie had to help him, lying beside him and helping him push on the transmission with their combined weight, holding it in place until he got a bolt through to keep it from falling. He looked at her when he had it secured, her hair was awry and her arms trembling and her face red from exertion and he felt kindly toward her for the first time.

Adcox ever needs another mechanic I'll put in a good word for you.

Thanks, she said wryly.

He washed up in the bathroom. Looking up from scrubbing the grease off his hands, he saw her reflection float up in the watermarked mirror. She stood watching his hands.

What'd you do to your knuckle?

He glanced at it. It had started to bleed again. Skint it I reckon.

I'm always making you hurt yourself.

He looked at the inside of his arm. The new skin there was still soft and red and tender.

You have to go now?

Yeah.

I don't want you to. I wish you wouldn't.

Well. I have to go anyway.

I had a postcard from Jack at Daddy's yesterday. He's comin up here tonight. I'm scared of him, R. C. He tried to kill me, and he told me then he'd come up here and finish the job. I'm afraid to be by myself.

Carmie, I can't help it. He may just want to make up with you. That's your life, you have to run it yourself. Cathy's there by herself, she'll be afraid if I don't come in. He paused a moment, remembering her face when they had been lifting the transmission, then said grudgingly: If you're afraid, come to the house with me and Cathy.

I'd rather you stay here. She suddenly reached out and lightly touched his shoulder, and he turned, as if he had been waiting for it, and before he knew what he was doing he was kissing her, her hands pulling him to her, the length of her slim body laid against him like hot steel. He pulled away. It ought to have been me and you all the time, Carmie said raggedly. It ought to be me you're come to, not me you're leaving.

They were standing very close. Her black eyes were wet and luminous. He could feel the heat of her mouth still on his face.

Come on, she said, her voice sounded strange, not like Carmie. She backed out the bathroom door and turned and went down the hall to where Raymer guessed the bedroom was. Inside the door she turned facing him and began unbuttoning her blouse. I got to go, Raymer started to say, but he felt like a child standing before a darkened room, wanting something that was inside it very much but at the same time knowing there is something dread hidden in the room, waiting in the shadows. But in the end he was compelled to go into the room.

She sat crosslegged naked on the bed, watching him. Her breasts were small and pointed, her legs slim. Her hair was mussed but she smoothed it back with her fingers, her face was dark and gypsy-looking. He couldn't get over how much she looked like Cathy.

What are you thinking about?

Why did you do it, Carmie?

Why did I do it? she smiled. I seem to remember having a little help.

You know what I mean.

Why did you do it then?

I'll be damned if I know, he said. He felt sick at heart, thinking about Cathy. I couldn't help myself. A goddamned flywheel, he said bitterly.

She stretched out a leg, massaged the thigh gently. She seemed to enjoy Raymer watching her. He felt a mixture of longing and self-disgust rise in him.

If it hadn't been the flywheel it would have been something else. It was bound to happen sooner or later.

I don't want Cathy to ever know.

Why not? Cathy wouldn't care. She'll get a kick out of it.

Are you crazy, Carmie?

I know her better than you ever will. We always used to share things. We used to play tricks on our boyfriends. How do you know I'm not Cathy? How do you know Carmie's not back at your house waiting on you?

I know all right. Just shut up, will you.

Yeah, I guess that'd be different. I guess you could tell by that. Who's the best, R. C.? Me or Cathy?

Just shut up goddamn it.

What'll you do if I don't? Hit me?

I'm not your Jack. I ain't never hit a woman.

Hit me if you want to. I wouldn't mind it from you.

You're crazy. I believe you want men to hit you. You're crazy or sick or something.

Cathy'd catch us sooner or later even if I didn't tell her. Carmie got up and stood beside the bed, silhouetted for a moment against the window: outside dusk was falling, the world washed with twilight. The soft blur of her pubic hair black against the smooth mound of her belly. She leant and took cigarettes from the nightstand drawer, lit one.

Sooner or later? The hell you say. There won't be no later. It will never happen again. I'd never do her that way again.

Carmie was watching him with a cold amusement. You'd do it in a minute. I could make you anytime I wanted to. You been wanting it so bad from the first time you saw me. I bet you dreamed about it at night.

Shut up.

I bet you screw Cathy and pretend it's me.

Shut up, I said.

You're cute, but you're kind of dumb. You look at things and just see them one way. You never think about all the different ways a thing can be. She drew on the cigarette, exhaled, and when she spoke her voice was blurred from the smoke. Think about all the possibilities. Did it ever occur to you that Cathy might know about this all the time? That me and her set it up? That she wanted to know how loyal to her you were, whether you'd do it to me or not, and she's just sitting there watchin TV now and waiting for me to report back. Or look at it like this. Maybe she's got a fella on the side, somebody she met or used to know, and had me get you in bed out here so she could be with him. You got to...

Raymer hit her. He was up and had hit her the same way he had kissed her, without knowing he was going to and harder than he meant to. He caught her on the point of the jaw with his right fist and she toppled sideways, her neck slamming against the edge of the nightstand with a sickening crack and she hit the floor hard, slack and rubberlegged, the back of her head popping against the tile floor. He had her up immediately. Oh shit, he said. He caught her up by the shoulders, but her head lolled loosely back. Her eyes were open. Her mouth was open too and he could see the clean white line of her teeth and the sharp tip of her tongue. He held her shoulder onehanded and clasped the back of her head in the palm of his left hand, positioning her head where it ought to go: as if he might fix her, secure her with a bolt, slide a cotter pin and hold her the way she had been before. I've played hell now, Raymer said. For no reason he thought of the raccoon hightailing out of his car in front of the Strand Theater, his own hot unfocused anger, its scared intent eyes.

He sat looking at her. Her eyes were dulling, or the room was growing dark. He touched her breast, feeling for a heartbeat. Her breast was warm, but the warmth was fugitive and fleeting. He thought he could detect heat fleeing like summer's vestigial heat leaking from the dry leaves of autumn. There was a smear of his semen drying on her inner thigh. He touched it, thinking of life, of how alive she had been, they had both been, and he began to cry brokenly.

He came out the trailer door and down the stacked concrete blocks carrying her cradled in his arms and he went around the end of the trailer. The trailer was set on the site where years ago, a house had burned and the basement was still there, half-filled with rubble and halfburned embers and brick covered with a thick growth of honeysuckle. He could still smell the honeysuckle. You'd think it'd all be gone by October. He stood at the edge and looked westward. The sky was a metallic pink, the dark pines against it harsh and artificial-looking, a mockup horizon stamped raggedly from tin.

He knelt with her. He sat holding her slackly across his knees. He couldn't roll her off the edge. If she had tormented him in life, in death it was immeasurably worse. In the end, he climbed laboriously down the side with her, laid her gently on the honeysuckle, pillowed her head with a stone. He could see the pale length of her naked body against the blacklooking honeysuckle.

He had meant to cover her body with rubble, but he couldn't do that either: the thought of a stone striking her white body was not to be borne, the charred timbers held rusted nails that would pierce her soft flesh like scalpel knives.

Ultimately, he struggled back up the side, his breath coming hard and ragged and he carried her back into the trailer.

He laid her in the bedroom floor beside the bed. He overturned the nightstand and scattered clothing about. In the kitchen he swept the dishes from the countertop with a broom, went out gingerly through the broken glass. Come on in, Jack, he thought. Glad you could drop in.

He went out. The moon was cradling up over the dark pines and by the cold light the Firebird looked sleek and wetlooking. He sat in his own car for a time, his fingertips drumming numbly on the steering wheel. He fled outside himself, foreign, as if he were the protagonist of someone else's nightmare. After a time, he seemed to have another thought and he went back in.

He had seen a bottle of rubbing alcohol in the bathroom. He emptied it in the floor and on the scattered bedclothes. When he lit it, thin blue flames scampered across the slick tile, lapped at the edges of clothing, climbed like vines of flame, biting in, the surface beneath the transparent blue fire beginning to char. He got up and left before the flames touched Carmie's body.

He lay in the darkness trying to keep his mind focused on the ballgame, but it kept scampering nimbly away, out of control, alien; it wanted to think about money, Carmie, Cathy. The series was tied up two to two and the Yanks seemed to be falling apart, the players making errors, the managers and Steinbrenner making stupid decisions. Even with Reggie Jackson at the center, the center was not holding. Forty dollars bet on the series, forty dollars for a used flywheel...

Sleeping Cathy stirred against him and he looked at her. Moonlight fell oblique and illusory on her face and, for a moment, he thought she was Carmie, and then he didn't know who she was.

Or who he was.

He thought of Reggie Jackson. Reggie still had the power to make things right. Stoic, confident, in command. Holding the bat between his knees, adjusting his glasses. Eyes focused on the right field stands. Watching. Then a concentrated explosion of energy focused until it was occult almost, magic: the clean crack of the bat, the ball, though he could not see it, not spherical anymore, crushed by the force of the bat into an ellipsoid, soaring upward and arching toward a surreal void of openmouthed faces.

He couldn't sleep. He lay taut and fearful, waiting for the crack of the bat, for the phone to ring, headlights to wash the dark windows, for his world to end.

TIDEWATER'S EDEN

When he pulled up in the yard Tidewater recapped the bottle with a jerk, sloshing whiskey on his best pants. He saw the screen door open and the old woman herself come out on the porch. Tidewater had cherished a vague hope that she would be off somewhere saving souls and was reluctant to abandon this even when he had seen her ratty old station wagon parked under the walnut tree.

Underminin old bitch'll live forever, he said to himself and began to get out. The old woman had meanwhile crossed to the edge of the porch and was peering myopically at the car with eyes shaded and her head thrust forward like some ancient mud turtle with its teeth locked onto a stick. She had her Bible depending from her hand as she eternally did as if it were some strange growth she was loath to have removed, or as if it had been welded to her in some blinding flash of divine retribution. The door opened again, and the old woman's widowed daughter-in-law came out as well and, as if by some signal beyond his sight, the children began to spill out on the porch and cluster around the old woman. Under all their watching eyes he felt giddily that they were watching the progress of some stranger, someone who had not traversed their yard a hundred times before.

When he had seated himself on the edge of the porch and had a stanchion against his back their eyes still regarded him as though he were burdened with some great secret that was about to be revealed. He looked away from them toward the blue hazy treeline and above this to the sky, already a hot and brassy blue.

He could hear someone stirring in the house, soft furtive movements he knew belonged to Jasmine. Even these sounds were imbued with mysticism. Everything about her seemed touched with magic. His mouth felt dry.

You stirrin early, the old woman said, and dressed fit to kill. They ain't nobody dead is they?

Not as I know of, Tidewater said through clenched teeth. I expect they is somewhere. Tidewater hated the old woman and she hated him just as thoroughly. She had put a permanent edge on his teeth long ago and to sit here and carry on what pretended to be a normal conversation with her was almost more than he could bear. He lit a cigarette and noticed that his hands shook. He laid his right on his thigh, steading it surreptitiously with his left and blew smoke palely out.

I got somethin I got to talk to Mrs. Morton about, he said.

Well, you talking to me. But you don't have to make yourself uncomfortable to do it.

I meant the other Mrs. Morton. Jasmine's mama. This don't concern you.

The old woman regarded him with deepening suspicion. Anything goes on in this house is my concern, she said.

Tidewater looked past her to the younger woman standing slightly to the rear of the squat old woman, but her face looked vague and he found no help there. Since her husband's death she had seemed to lose identity and now she looked like nothing so much as an extension of the old woman, some misshapen and elongated shadow she had thrown.

Me and Jasmine aim to get married, Tidewater told the younger woman, but her eyes fell, and he had to turn to where the old woman was regarding him with a self-satisfied expression as if her worst suspicions had been confirmed. Then the old eyes went hard and cold, became chunks of dirty ice flickering with the cold fire that flared behind them.

Maybe when I'm gone to my maker, she said. Not while I've got breath in my body and the strength to stop you.

You can tighten your jaws all you want to, Tidewater said. But you can't stop me. Jasmine'll be old enough in less than a month and we already made up our minds. You can postmark me to hell if you want to. We aim to marry. The only reason I'm even here now is because we wanted your blessin.

My blessin? She looked as if all reason had fled the world leaving her alone to preach logic to gibbering madmen. Bless a sinner and a drunkard like you? Oh, you're proving everthing I ever thought about you. You're a bigger fool than I ever dreamed you was.

I quit drinking, Tidewater said. I aim to make a lot of changes from the way I was when me and Wesley run around together.

Any snake can change, she said. It can shed its whole skin. But when it does it's a snake all over again. Why you won't even work. Where you claimin to be workin now?

Tidewater knew that she knew full well where he worked, but he answered her anyway.

I'm still out at the shoe factory like I have been two years.

The old woman squinted into his face. Why, you been drinkin right today, she said. Your eyes look plumb out of focus.

Tidewater felt what little control he had over the situation beginning to slip away from him, began to feel that it was sliding irrevocably out of his hands. He knew that the Morton family had always considered Jasmine an asset because of her looks and expected that she would eventually marry a rich man. Tidewater was not a rich man, but he was becoming a desperate one and he began to press his case with what few assets he could muster. He had a job, he reminded them. A steady year-round inside job and he would quit drinking. Since Wesley had died the place was running down and beginning to show the lack of a man around the house. The old woman's lip curled at this last, as if to express her opinion of his ability towards remedying this situation.

Tidewater wished that Jasmine's father Wesley was still alive. He and Tidewater had passed many pleasant evenings drinking beer or whiskey or whatever fell to hand while Tidewater covertly watched Jasmine grow up and made plans he dare not even put a name to. Until one night he went into the kitchen for a drink of water while she was washing dishes and without conscious planning, he had turned her toward him and kissed her and she had momentarily stiffened and then went slack. Her hands, warm and slick from the water, came up around his neck and rested there, just where the hair line began. He could feel them there yet as if he had been singed by electric current. When he opened his eyes, Jasmine's eyes were open below his, dark and secret pools, swift moving, depthless waters where, even then, he knew that perils were strung like rocky shoals for such a foolhardy mariner as himself. When he had been drinking with Wesley at Goblin's Knob or in his old pickup truck parked in some uncharted log road, the sweet face was always in the back of his mind, as if etched there by acid or love or what passed for it, a face and name by some alchemy transformed to mystery and magic. A name to conjure with, surely walls would fall and waters recede before its hypnotic chant and it was at one such moment that one small miracle did occur: for one brief moment all of Tidewater's past and present and future merged, like layers of images superimposed with the hot burning rush of whiskey singing in his blood, and Wesley beside him already drunk and droning mindlessly on while in the hot darkness Tidewater dreamed of his daughter. Beyond the truck, dark lurked and deepened where the trees began and, from this dark, whippoorwills called forlornly and without hope. Evoking a place where the girl was by some slight already his wife, hand in hand forever, through life together, who cared what adversity raised its hooded head? Growing old and gray as one, her eyes soft with memories, her hands gentle and careworn with honest toil. From the whiskey or this vision his eyes grew moist. Tidewater was in love.

When Wesley died of cirrhosis of the liver Tidewater felt he had lost a friend. He had also lost any excuse for hanging around Jasmine for the old woman was deeply involved with Jesus and saw her son's death as divine punishment for his years of heavy drinking and hanging around with such as him.

Jasmine's pale face was valentine shaped and framed by smooth black hair. Beneath her checked dress were all the secrets of the universe that one day he might unlock. At last Jasmine began to cry with a childlike desperation, a broken-hearted sobbing as if breath was denied her, life itself being wrested from her grasp. She told the old woman that, if she were not allowed to marry, she would leave, and if they brought her back, she would leave again. She would go to Memphis and work in a honkytonk. The old woman fell into an uneasy silence. Then they stood by the side of Tidewater's old car, him in a heady daze of triumph, not believing that it could be true. She was going to marry him. All the world lay within his grasp. He left her at last and drove the four miles to the community of Flatrock, where he lived. He drove through the magic summer greenery at the rate of fifteen or twenty miles an hour and, although he negotiated the curves and stayed on the blacktop, he could not have told you where he was or where he was going. Only when a car with out of state tags pulled up behind him and savagely blew its horn did reality infringe on his mindless dreams.

He pulled off onto the sodded shoulder of the road to let the car go by. He cut the switch off. He lit a cigarette. From the woods jays called as if maddened or drunk from the sun. The highway shimmered whitely. Tidewater's face wore a confident complacent look that was almost a sort of stunned smirk. It was the sort of calm expression that intimated that everything was going to be all right and that everything in the world was under control. A steady hand was at the helm. It was an expression you would only find on the face of a saint or a madman.

They were married on Saturday the twenty-fifth of June and came back elated from the wedding. They were to eat supper with Jasmine's mother and at the supper table the old woman had her stroke. She fell to the kitchen floor with histrionic anguish and began to thrash about and moan. Tidewater could not believe it. He laid his fork down and stared at her. In her stricken face, her calm little eyes studied their reaction, like a performer peering beyond the footlights. They got her to her bed. A measure of calm on her face against her white pillow slip. Iron gray hair smoothed from her brow by Jasmine's trembling hand. Jasmine's eyes wide and amazed at this display of mortality.

I better get a doctor, Tidewater said.

The old woman could not speak. Apparently her hearing was not impaired. She shook her head vigorously from side to side.

She don't believe in doctors, Jasmine said.

I'll just bet she don't, Tidewater told her.

In the living room Jasmine's mother wrung her hands and wondered aloud how she was going to pay for another funeral.

I wouldn't have thought she'd need one, Tidewater said bitterly. I figured she'd just rise right into heaven without havin to fool with any of the paperwork like everybody else.

Long after midnight they sat up and ministered to the old woman. Tidewater had given up entreating Jasmine to leave and sat on the bloated front room sofa and drank cup after cup of coffee and smoked one cigarette after another. He wore an expression alternately martyred and malevolent, and the temptation to go to the Knob and buy a half pint off Hines was running high. As he felt that this was what the old woman was trying to drive him to, he resisted and even managed to venture into the sick room from time to time and inquire solicitously after the old woman's health.

Tidewater walking about the yard. A pale quarter moon hung above the jagged velvet of the trees, canted in a paler blue, shot dimly through with stars. Night birds called, whippoorwills and distant owls dropping lonely cries into a pool of stillness, faint ripples outward bound and lost. He walked about the yard, his ankles clammy in the dewy grass. He peered into the old woman's station wagon. He walked to his own car. From beneath the seat he brought forth a length of coat hanger and walked back to the old station wagon. He inserted this wire over the top of window glass through the inch of clearance and hooked the wire over the door handle. It opened with ease. This was an old game with him. Years past he had discovered that the old woman kept treats hidden here, locked in midnight stealth from the children. Twinkies, Goo Goo Clusters, cold drinks, tins of Vienna sausages. He imagined her in there, eating covertly in midnight greed, hurriedly dispensing of the evidence and returning to bed. He seated himself in the driver's seat and began to rummage under the seat. After he had eaten two candy bars and drank a treacly and tepid grape drink he began to search further.

In the back he found the old metal toolbox. It was locked. He could not remember precisely when he had last looked at the toolbox, but he did know that it had not had a lock on it. Locks bothered Tidewater. They intimated secrets kept from him. Things not safe for common eyes like his own. He climbed out and went to find a screwdriver. The house was quiet. He peered through the bedroom window. They were grouped about the old woman's bed in an attitude of waiting.

The screwdriver would not work at opening the lock, so he chiseled the rivets holding the latch on. Among the rusty wrenches and pliers, he came upon something wrapped in a cloth. A scrap of some slick material, satin or velvet wrapped around a pint fruit jar. Something of ceremony here, some religious artifact hidden from heathen eyes. The Shroud of Turin or perhaps an ancient chalice.

He stared at it, squinting in faltering light, a pickled weenie, he breathed, and held it aloft to pale intangible moonlight, lowered it and struck a match. He dropped the jar. It hit without breaking, rolled across the floor of the bed, ceased against the wall.

God almighty damn, Tidewater said.

What lay revealed was a human penis afloat in some nameless and colorless fluid like some strange, eviscerated animal swimming in uncharted depths. The match went out. He retrieved the jar with a kind of delicate distaste, wrapped it daintily in its shroud. He sat for a time entranced as if his mind had caved in under the weight of this strange discovery. He could not comprehend this new, dark side of the old woman that stood revealed, as if he had turned over a rotten log in the woods to reveal a motley of centipedes, wood roaches, and sexton beetles scurrying and burrowing away from his gaze. He saw the old woman in stoic grief laying out Papa John. Saw her quick little surgeon hands with knife, perhaps John's old straight edge razor. Sharp steel against cooling and flaccid flesh. A midnight necromaniac moving in dreadful stealth. What morbid sentiments harbor such a souvenir? What infidelity could have brought this terrible retribution, could send an old man to his maker in such a fashion?

When Tidewater did get out, he was swinging the jar along in his hand and his step was quick and light. He hid the jar beneath the seat in his own car. He looked calm and self-satisfied, as if his meditation had in some manner eased and cleansed him. He had the look of someone who had some great power fall into his hands by happenstance, as if he had discovered the secret of eternal life or perhaps the formula for Coca-Cola.

Fast in the siege of guilt, Jasmine sobbed in Tidewater's arms. She had driven the old woman to such a pass, had moved her to her death. The old woman lay framed by a dark rectangle of raw yawning earth. Tidewater patted Jasmine's back. There, there, he would say. There, there. He was unmoved. He seemed determined to let her play out her charade. With such a weapon in his hands he felt no need for haste.

In the morning she found her voice, made a rusty and unused sound such as might be expected to erupt from a misty river on a moonless night. A light came into her eyes. They grouped about the bed to watch this miracle. The jaws began to work spasmodically, words to form. They felt mantled by gentle celestial light that seemed to emanate from the sickbed.

By midmorning the crisis had passed and she was sitting propped up in bed and she was speaking with ease. Jasmine and her mother were asleep and Tidewater was sitting by her bedside. He felt lightheaded and hungover from lack of sleep and reality seemed to ebb and flow.

The old woman watched Tidewater with satisfaction.

The ways of the Lord are beyond the understanding of such as you, she said. God works in mysterious ways.

God is not the only one, Tidewater told her. People put curious things in fruit jars of alcohol and lock them up in old toolboxes.

He thought she was having another stroke. Her skin went a sickish white as if all the blood had been sucked from her body in a rush and then went purple when it flowed back in. Her mouth was open and her jaws worked but no sound came, only wheezing expulsion of air as from a bellows possessed by some satanic force.

You got everybody thinking you and God laid out this whole

mess, Tidewater said. But I seen the other side of your face. I know what your hold card is. He left the room. He went into Jasmine's room and shook her awake. Git your plunder, he said. We goin home.

When they came outside the sun was near its zenith and the day was sultry and hot. As he opened the door on the passenger side, pious voices raised in hymn drifted from the Primitive Baptist Church next door, like some celestial blessing indiscriminately bestowed.

A new world opened for Tidewater, a lush world of senses whose existence he had never known. He had been on his own since he was fifteen. His parents had moved to Detroit where his father had a job in an automobile assembly plant, and they moved into an apartment there. After six months Tidewater himself had felt he could stand it no longer and hitchhiked from Detroit. It took him a week to arrive back at the peeling clapboard house he had been born in and he had come close to starving to death. His parents were never able to get him out of Tennessee again. He felt he did not know them, had felt once that he did but that they had deceived him, that they had sold themselves too cheaply. Their voices had taken on a northern brogue almost at the instant they crossed the Tennessee line and now, when he did see them, they were strangers to him, curious tourists in checked shirts and shorts with their minds always on going away.

Now with his marriage he gained a new dignity. Tidewater would not fit back into place. Days away from her became drab and commonplace. He had been transformed.

Sleeping, she would be dappled by morning light, the sheets tousled and cast off. The alabaster mounds of her breasts, incredibly soft, cherry-teated, were shrines to some esoteric ancient religion. Light teased in the faint down at the nipples, the hair at the base of her stomach, the faint blue veins that metronomed in her throat, as if light were some alchemy transforming her before his eyes. He would touch her gently, as if unsure of her corporeality, feel the heat of her nearness, the sweetness of her sleeping breath beneath his cheek. In a system of checks and balances she was a reward for some good deed long forgotten. Searching his mind, he could find nothing he had done to deserve her.

Deep in sweaty darkness he might come wide awake with her arms around him, a leg across his body in errant abandon, a night-time fantasy beyond his wildest dream come to life, her face then beneath his own, the eyes vacant and abstracted as though her body did some other's bidding than her own.

A horn blew shrieking, fell silent, repeated itself. Birds called in vexed alarm, rose into a lightning-blasted oak, and watched the car with tiny black eyes as expressionless as glass. The horn blew again. Tidewater walked out of the house into nine o'clock sunshine, buckling his belt, blinking his eyes and scowling at the man in the car. A cat ran through his feet, fluid black grace gone beneath the underpinning of the porch. Tidewater kicked at the cat and came on. Well, goddamn, he said. He was looking at the car as if he could not quite believe it was real and parked in his front yard on this hot July morning. Tidewater looked angry. The closer he got to the automobile the angrier he looked.

The man in the car rolled down the glass and just watched Tidewater come. He did not appear to be perturbed.

The foreman sent me out after you, he said.

Tidewater had a cigarette in his mouth and he kept going through all his pockets, one by one looking for matches.

I never seen a goddamned place would come after you, he said. He done this ever day I'd save a lot on gas.

He just sent me is all, the man said. It ain't nothing to me whether you go or not.

Sent for, by God, Tidewater kept saying.

He said you been layin out a lot lately. Sayin you was sick. He said if you wanted to keep your job you better get on in there.

Well piss on him. I never seen a goddamn pissy-ass factory would send somebody out and roll a man out his own goddamned bed. You tell him I said kiss my ass.

He said he needs you in that cuttin room, the man said.

You tell him I said kiss my ass and call it workin in the cuttin room.

It don't matter to me, the man said, one way or another. He cranked the car and began to back it around the yard. Tidewater crossed the yard and mounted the porch. He turned once toward the room where she still slept. It was very still. No sound or motion or sign of life came up from the hollow. Dust settled slowly through motionless air. He sat uncertainly on the front porch with the unlit cigarette still in his mouth. Well goddamn it anyway, he said at last.

He told her he got in a fight and quit. They were starting a night shift and wanted to put him on it.

What Tidewater did do was to use up what grocery credits he could find and lay up in bed mornings with Jasmine. In the afternoons he would dig ginseng, combing the hollows and walking the ridges back deep into the woods where no houses were built and even hunters and barbed wire did not trespass. In the shady quiet of the woods, peace flowed over him like soothing balm. No creditors assailed him here and the old woman did not have the breath for the hills. In hollows grown chest high with briars he sometimes came upon the remains of houses, like falling ruins of some forgotten race. He wandered through them, kicking aside ancient rubbish, passing through shades of lives lived out long hence.

That was the way summer was that year. The July heat hung shimmering over the land seared and blighted. A dark malaise crept softly into Tidewater's Eden, so surreptitiously that later it was impossible for him to pinpoint the moment it arrived, perhaps it started when he quit his job. Or when the grandmother was on her appointed rounds and he would come upon the old woman's station wagon parked in his yard, and he would go back into the woods until she left. He imagined her trying to talk Jasmine home, anger lay in the pit of his stomach like scalded stones. Or it could have been when the radio broke.

She met him at the door, lights already lit behind her, dusk following him home and across the sill.

The radio's tore up, she said. I want it fixed.

What's the matter with it? He laid the ginseng down, crossed the room to the radio.

I don't know. It quit, it won't play. I need it for company.

Tidewater had taken out his pocketknife and was taking the screws out of the back of the radio. Now, let's just see here. Peering into the dark interior of the radio in the false hope of some obvious defect, a broken tube, a luckless mouse electrocuted. Nothing save neatly wound wires and a curious smell of ozone, an air of burnt out electrical storms.

He wriggled a tube here, adjusted a wire there.

Now that ought to do it, Tidewater said, a note of triumph in his voice, placing the back in position and beginning to adjust screws.

Did you fix it? Faint hope in her voice, Tidewater noticed for the first time that she had been crying.

Well, we'll just see. Tidewater plugged the cord into the wall. They waited expectedly. Nothing happened. It has to warm up, Tidewater explained to her. She sat waiting patiently as if Tidewater was a conjuror about to reveal some fiat of legerdemain. The dead radio mocked them with its silence.

I'll carry it into town in the morning and get it fixed, Tidewater said at last.

In bed she would have none of him. For the first time she lay cold and unresponsive as stone. As if from afar, her voice accused him, paraded his failures with tearful threats to leave, to start over somewhere anew.

Tidewater suffered all this in silence. He pondered the duplicity of flesh, that now she could not suffer his touch. He felt he should be defending himself, shoring up the levees, slow the recession of these waters. He knew that his life was going to change drastically in the next few minutes and that he could control the outcome by what he said, if he could just think of the right words to say. No words offered themselves, no chants came to mind. He lay sweating in the humming electric darkness as if he was perpetually waiting for something. At last he sidled up to her.

You wasn't no virgin, he said. You tried to act like you was but you wasn't, no more than the Bible-totin old grandmaw of yours is. I reckon you thought I was born in the last five or ten minutes.

He had played his last card and waited for his opponent to tell which it was, high or low. He raised up on one elbow and peered down into her face, as if from some great height. In the pale fluorescence of the pooling moonlight he saw that her eyes were luminous with tears unshed. Then she turned her face to the wall and her angry silence rang in his ears like accusations left unvoiced.

In the morning they drove into Flatrock to have the radio repaired. She held it against her breast all the way as if it were some peculiar shield she was cradling, some misbegotten electronic offspring of their strange union. They sat half a day and waited and then drove back in silence through stifling motionless July air, through a benumbed, wilted countryside, sumac branches talcumed with road dust. A fiery orb of sun paced them like a malignant and vengeful eye, sinking slowly as a stone in water through a throbbing and brassy sky.

When they got home the fan would not work. Tidewater began to curse. He felt himself set upon by all manner of mechanical conundrum, saw himself beginning a long procession in and out of repair shops. Nothing would work. The lights would not come on. The old refrigerator sat in a sullen silence.

He ransacked drawers for fuses, changed them one by one. At last, fearful of what he must find, he walked out the back door and peered cautiously at the wall. A feeling of panic seized him, of things being out of his control.

He sat on the edge of the porch, swinging his feet in uncut crass. The lowlife son of a bitches, he said. His worst fears were realized. The meter was gone. He could see where the light truck had turned in the grass. He sighed and went back into the house. She was taking clothes out of the closet, laying them across the bed.

What's the matter?

They took the goddamned meter, he said. Son of a bitches can't give a man till Saturday.

Well, she said, as if that decided something. She went back to sorting clothes.

You can just take me home, she said. I'm not waitin any longer for you to get another job and try to make something out of yourself. We're never goin to have nothin.

I don't give a goddamn one way or another, Tidewater told Hines's bland face, hands laid flat on the bar, thumbs touching the mug of pale beer.

She can tell what she wants to. I never laid a hand on that girl. No matter what her crazy old grandma says.

She never said you hit her. She said you mistreated her. Hines tried to placate him.

Well, hell. I done all I could. I didn't buy her no mink coat, but

I done all else I could. Hines did not reply, did not seem interested, chin deep in stories of marital mishaps and victim of countless ones himself, one more-or-less did not seem much to him. He knew what the boy could never comprehend: that it was the way of things. That some things were foreordained to end in such a manner, that others were born with fault lines where they might or might not splinter. That it went on all the time, was read in unconscious glances and the set of the mouth. That he could have seen it coming. That in the long view of things it did not matter very much at all. It was just the nature of things.

Tidewater's throat worked spasmodically pumping the beer down while behind him the plaintive jukebox sang as if to underline what he had been saying and thinking:

> *Ashes of love,*
> *cold as ice*
> *I paid the price.*

And such a price it was. Coming irrevocably awake in winter night, lying alone in the unmade bed, or on the couch, or floor. Wherever random chance decreed him be. The house seemed vast and empty, some lost abandoned spacious mansion inhabited only by nightbirds and winter winds. Pale-eyed and sleep long gone, he would stare at the ceiling, so dark it was unperceived, yet so familiar darkness itself served no purpose, was thwarted. The flyspecked roses cracked and fading, a shard of begrimed paper falling away with painful slowness hanging suspended, a victim of its own weight.

The ceiling, all the house falling away from neglect assailed him with guilt. Let go, let go, it sang with December wind as he had let all things go. As if things once yours needed no maintenance, no care, no small kindnesses to keep them yours, and are yours forevermore till death do you part.

Cut off before his time, Tidewater became righteous, would flounder in the seize of grandiose plans only to have them melt like frost when the sun warms the ground. Moist sadness would come for all his unborn sons, an aching throb somewhere in the vicinity of where his heart was for who would have been cast in his mold, his alone, and like no other man on earth. Visions of what would never be flickered before his unblinking eyes like scenes viewed through a crack into hell. Leading the child, perhaps four or five, walking into the sparse beginning of the woods, the gun shouldered, steps slowed to accommodate the child at his side. The scent of the woods in fall, everything, everything so right. Squatting before the boy, letting him touch and perhaps briefly hold the rifle, the eyes growing big, face so like his own. You got to learn what a gun can do, son. You got to respect a gun. When they were coming out of the woods at dusk, the woman met them at its darkening edge, lifted the child to her breast, grasped Tidewater's hand with her own. Before them, the house was lighted, warm, a vague scent of cooking and woodsmoke drew them into the home and hearth and sealed the door.

She laid her old bewenned hand against the door jamb, the flesh shifting on her arm as if corporeal reality were fleeing her as all things were. The pale winter light caught briefly in her wedding band and it flickered, flitting across Tidewater's face and was gone. Old, old. Will you not ever die? Why will you just not die?

She don't want to see you.

Why don't you let her talk for herself? Tidewater said. You been doing her thinking and talking all her days. Let's see what she has to say about things.

I don't want to see you, the girl said from the back room, enunciating each word clearly.

I need to talk to you, Tidewater called, raising his voice and yelling directly into the old woman's face. Under his liquored breath her eyes flitted wildly about like insects being sprayed and she took an involuntary half step back though she did not relinquish the makeshift doorblock her arm made.

You got nothing to say to me, she told him. No more than I got to say to you. She made as if to close the door, but he caught it. You lettin the heat out.

Then I reckon I need to talk to you, he told the old woman, watching her face form the sneer effortlessly, years of practice not for naught.

With that filth on your breath, she said contemptuously. You ain't got anything to say that Christian ears wouldn't be better off not knowin.

About your cannin, he told her gently, and turned then and walked into the frozen grassless yard toward his car. He halted without looking back. He had left the motor running against the cold and the exhaust paled in the cold air and rose like smoke. He took a cigarette packet from his coat pocket, looked at it, creased it flat and threw it from him. He shoved his hands into his pockets and hunched his shoulders against the wind.

She came out wearing a ratty black coat and a man's old felt hat pulled down on her head and approached him cautiously, feeling her way across the icy ground. Then they were face to face. From a distance they appeared a strange pair of conspirators, two dark figures in bleak and bare December ice, every tree seized in winter's crystal grip, two plotters caught unaware and forever locked timeless in some old Currier and Ives woodcut.

Where is my property? the old woman asked.

If you mean that fruitjar with a man's dick floatin belly up like a drowned fish in it, it's in a safe place.

Her face flinched as if he had just slapped her, the bleary eyes batting rapidly as a frog, as if some unmarked boundary had been crossed, or if they had met on some dreadful common ground. Then she swallowed and steadied herself. I want it back.

Well. I've got almost attached to it, Tidewater said. It keeps me company on these long winter nights. Where if it wadn't for you and your meddlin, I'd be a little less lonesome and a whole lot warmer.

What's been done you've done yourself. I never liked you, but I never brought her back here. She come on her own and you know it and should have known it long before she did.

You sorry, turtlefaced old bitch, Tidewater said into her unflinching flinty face. You stabbed me in the back every time somebody laid a knife in your hand since I was ten year old and you doin it right today and you think after I git finally somethin to give me a little leverage I'm goin to tie a ribbon on it and lie it right in your little hands? Sure I am. You think I was born in the last fifteen minutes? Like shit I was.

She blew her breath out, pale smoke the wind got, behind her glasses her eyes were rheumy and wet, tearing in this selfsame wind. Her hands rose in faint protest, fluttered like pale birds and fell. Behind her, faces occasionally peered out the foggy windows. Tidewater began to laugh. It struck him funny that he and this old woman who looked like a caricature of all the grandmothers who ever lived were arguing over a Mason fruit jar laden in such a manner as to be beyond even the wildest of its manufacturer's expectations.

If this got out, she began. If people knew—all my good works lost—they would misunderstand.

Tidewater's mirth fled. His face, sharp as an axe bit turned sidewise, was bitter, leant almost onto her own like a threat. All of your good works could be folded five ways and shoved up a gnat's ass without causing him any great discomfort. And how you could misunderstand a cut-off dick in a jar of alcohol is a mystery over my head.

What do you want?

I want her back. You got her here, you send her to me.

I can't. You know I can't. I told her not to marry you and she did anyway. If both of you had listened to me at the start there'd been a lot less grief.

How you do it don't bother me. I want her out here. If you can't get her to come back to me today just get her where I can talk to her. I'm going out, I got a promise of a job Monday and I mean to talk her into coming back. I'll get her anything she thinks she wants even if it has to be still warm from somebody else's hands.

The old woman had no reply. There was nothing she could say that would affect him, nothing that could alter the pinched near-bloodless face, that could bank the fires that flickered behind his eyes like campfires in dementia. She shivered in the cold.

I'll do what I can. But I've got to have that back.

I know you have, Tidewater said. So, you'd better do what you can, then back off awhile and do some more.

Tidewater sat in the car with the engine running and found cigarettes in the glove compartment and smoked and drank orange vodka and watched the heat gauge rise up and hover near the redline. He knew the car was running on fumes and getting hot to boot and did not care. Blow up you SOB, he told it. He felt weak somewhere in his stomach, a dizzy mixture of dread and anticipation. As he tipped the bottle again, the door opened, Jasmine came out on the stoop, tossed her hair casually back over her shoulder, a gesture almost of defiance. Dearer to him than she could know.

When she got in, she sat without speaking, a calm attitude of waiting, as if great secrets were about to be imparted to her.

I missed you, he said, voice thick from the vodka.

I didn't mean you to miss me. I'm sorry you did. What I wanted you to do was to forget me. The only reason I'm here is because Grandma talked me into it. She said you had something to tell me that was important. What did you do to her, anyway?

Tidewater laughed. I know where the dead body is at, he said. Well I ain't and I won't. I'm going to work Monday on a construction job. Makin good money. Reckon you'd come back if I do?

As if she had heard only half of what he said, she said, I'm going to work too. In the Dari-Dip out of town.

I don't believe in no wife of mine working, Tidewater told her. She stared at him in disbelief.

A wife of yours would work or starve to death, she said. There are things I want you can't give me. She halted momentarily, as if there were no words for what she had to say. Things you can't give if you tried all your life. Because you don't even know what they are.

What kind of things?

Oh, nice clothes, smart clothes. Pretty new furniture and a new car to ride around in.

I might get you all them things someday, Tidewater said.

She sighed as if this was beyond Tidewater's comprehension, as if it was something that should have been ingrained in him from birth. As if he should never have had to ask.

It wouldn't matter, she said. It would just be us havin em.

Oh, Tidewater said.

I want, she began and could go no further, as if her wants were of no concern to him. I thought you were my ticket out of here, she said. But you was just another dead-end.

He put his arm around her, drew her nearer him, a weight without protest or acquiescence. He caught the scent of her hair, the clean smell of soap, the way she had smelled when she had been a little girl.

What are you drinking? It looks funny, not like whiskey.

Orange vodka. You want a drink? It's sweet.

I don't reckon. I believe I can put up with you better drunk, she said. I guess I never seen you sober till we married.

Tidewater felt congested, overladen with emotions, as if

pressures were building in him from the inside out, from some hot core deep in his abdomen. He felt that he would explode or burst into flames. The fingers of his right hand stroked her ear, delicately as a bird alighting, dropped to the graceful throat. He sat the bottle clumsily in the floorboard, dropped his left hand on her thigh, half turned toward her. As if it had an existence separate from him, the hand crept toward the crotch of her jeans, rubbed her gently. Her thighs were clenched. Then they parted slightly, allowed the flat of his hand between them, permitted it without acknowledgement to do its will, parted more.

So, you can't always do what your head tells you to, Tidewater told her. Did you miss me too?

She didn't say if she did or she didn't.

Suddenly the car engine sputtered, coughed and died. He reached up and turned the switch off. They sat in uneasy silence. Tidewater began to feel a dull and aching anger at whatever remorseless gods controlled his fate. He had had brief visions of a tearful reunion and now even this sorry semblance of victory had been wrested from him. He glared beyond the windshield to where heat radiated upward from the cooling hood. Beyond this further the dark horizon was aswim in coming dusk and seemed to be in motion, roiled and twisted by some distant cataclysm that had not reached them as yet. Above it birds moved in ever expanding circles in their flight.

I just don't believe this, Jasmine said. We can't even separate right.

Hell, it's been running on fumes a week, Tidewater said. It had to quit sometime.

She opened the door as if to get out.

Well. Let it go. I'm goin on. I'll have Grandma come and pick up my clothes.

Like hell you will, Tidewater said. Grandma don't pick up nothin at my house. Grandma don't bring her God-fearin butt through my front yard gate.

Go ahead and run my people down. It's too late now. You can't hurt me that way anymore.

Tidewater fell silent. He was thinking of Jasmine's grandmother. She had seemed always to dislike Tidewater. Once when he was fourteen or fifteen, the government had stocked a lake near Flatrock with a rare species of geese and the old woman had told him that there was a ten-dollar bounty on them. After some days and no small amount of effort Tidewater strode purposefully into the courthouse laden with five of them and tossed them casually onto the counter of the Fish and Game Commission office and thus found himself in the wrathful grasp of the game warden. They did not send him to the penitentiary as he had feared they would but when he finally was allowed to leave the courthouse his face was bright with humiliation and he did not walk like a man who had a fifty-dollar windfall drop into his lap.

An orange coal of rage smoldered somewhere inside him and plans for vengeance smoked in his mind. If Tidewater was nothing else, he was a good grudge-bearer. The anger was as real to him now as it had been then.

The girl sat poised with the door half open. He tried to find some resemblance to the grandmother. If he could have willed the old woman's face to appear, perhaps he could easily let her go.

It was a fearfully cold winter, a winter out of old men's tales, a winter dredged out of their very youth. He stared at the winter harshness, at the bleakness unrelieved by bird, or evergreen, or even a deerhunter's cap: as if another ice age had descended in the long winter nights, seizing every twig in ice, skimming the highway with glass, chilling the bones with surreal cold settling first in the vitals of all humankind, hearts transpired to chunks of bloody ice and, through Tidewater's eyes, hearth or heating stove was never enough.

Treadless tires spinning and sliding, Tidewater kept his rounds, kept between the ditches by some seemingly inexhaustible supply of luck or perhaps only by God's predilection for drunkards and fools, the old car easing in the night past the house where she lay dreaming, imbued with magic, touched with grace, a sleeping tousled figure more myth than flesh and blood, the estranged half of his soul.

Propelled by bootleg fumes and what gas he could buy on credit or steal under cover of dark he kept his rounds like a sentry charged with some watch, alert for strange cars in her driveway, once even getting out and looking at tiretracks in their drive. Past the cemetery where Papa John had slept peckerless these long years and then on to the Knob, where Hines's old potbellied coal stove and cool halfpint bottles of sloe liquor kept the cold momentarily at bay.

A cheerless gray drizzle fell, cold as ice. It had already begun to freeze on trees and on the dozers and graders parked seemingly random about the gaping ditch. In the east the sky paled minutely, dawn coming without apology or promise.

Tidewater and another man stood beneath a group of dripping trees which afforded them no shelter.

You reckon they'll work today?

I don't know, Tidewater said.

I hope they do, the man said. I hope they hirin. I've got to git a job somewhere. They ain't no work. The man was shorter than Tidewater but broad and deep as an over-rolled barrel, a wide red neckless face rose out of the jumper collar and his deepset eyes were black and curiously piglike. He wiped his nose on the jumper sleeve. The goddamn woods is froze up and a man can't get in and out to log. I reckon they mean for us all to starve to death.

Tidewater did not reply. He was watching the approach of a pickup truck with chains on its rear wheels. It stopped in front of an aluminum trailer and a man dressed in a yellow slicker and raincoat climbed out. He walked cautiously across the ice toward the trailer door, fumbling keys out of his pocket as he went.

I heard if they's only one job they hire the one with kids, the man said. Tidewater made no reply, and after a time the man asked: you got any kids?

Four or five, Tidewater told him. He was watching the trailer. Two more pickups had arrived and several men had gotten out, glancing covertly at them, stamping their feet in the cold, their breath white in the frosty air.

Four or five, the man repeated, scrutinizing him from head to toe.

You aim to work in them shoes? he asked in disbelief. Tidewater looked down. He was wearing his only shoes, a pair of black penny loafers. The man was wearing heavy lace-up leather boots.

I didn't plan on barefoot, Tidewater said.

A man carrying a clipboard came out of the trailer and looked around at the gathering of men and then approached Tidewater and the other man. You men wantin to work?

Yes sir, the other man said. You damn right.

All right. We several short this morning and I can use you both and a halfdozen more if I had em. We running way behind schedule here and got to get through. You ever run a tamper? A jumpin jack?

Hell yes, the man said.

You?

Yes, Tidewater told him.

Sure you have, the man said and nodded. But no matter. We got thirty or forty foot of pipe laid up there needs tampin. Git that one out of the truck over there and start tampin. Give me ye names and you can sign ye W-2s later this morning.

The ditch was six or eight feet deep with earth banked on both sides and they had to lower the tamper with a rope. When they had the tamper down in the ditch Tidewater sat down breathing hard and looked at it closely. It had a set of handles on either side similar to lawn mower grips, a steel shaft on its bottom ending in a flat steel footlike plate about eighteen inches or so square. To Tidewater it had a squat, froglike look about it.

You crank it like a chainsaw, the man said. You hold one side and I hold the othern and you pull that crankrope. It jumps up and down and packs the dirt down. You just stick with me and let me do the thinkin and you'll be all right.

You ain't no more seen one of them son of a bitches than I have, Tidewater said. He arose and took his place opposite the man, gripping the handlebars.

Hold it tighter, the man said. Here we go. He flipped the toggle switch to on and jerked the crankrope. It didn't start. Cold, the man said. He looked about him, grinned up and down the yawning ditch. All aboard that's coming aboard, he yelled. He jerked the rope. The engine caught, sputtered, caught again. The man flipped another switch and the tamper began to leap into the air and descend and slap against the frozen ground. The man grinned and winked, Hold'er steady, she's a rarin, he yelled. Tidewater could barely hear him above the motor.

Almost immediately the steel foot caught Tidewater on the shin and peeled the skin from knee to ankle and then caught one penny loafer between the steel foot and the frozen dirt.

You son of a bitch, Tidewater shrieked. He released the handles and began to hop about on one foot and then finally he ceased and kicked the tamper as hard as he could.

Help me hold it, goddammit, the man yelled. He was manhandling the tamper, trying to restrain it with one hand and find the switch with his other. Control was slipping away from him and panic swept into his face like rising waters. He began to curse at the top of his lungs, the tamper or Tidewater or both. The tamper descended on his foot and he scrambled to maintain his balance, feet backpedaling madly on the uncertain shale until at last he fell, only to scramble wildly to his knees, hands clawing the smooth ditch sides for purchase.

Whoa, goddammit, whoa, he screamed, but the tamper was past all such earthly admonitions. Like some gross and demented frog it leapt wildly into the air, descending and random with dull thumps on the ground only to rise aloft again, as if it had been freed from restraint by some divine intervention and was bent on wreaking havoc and exacting revenge for its years of past subservience.

Help me grab it, the man screamed at Tidewater. Help me bulldog it and hold it till we can turn it off. He was making half-hearted grabs at the tamper whenever it chanced near him.

Tidewater had meanwhile begun to scramble up the side of the ditch. When he reached the top he paused and rubbed his leg, peering at the raw flesh beneath the shredded skin. He rolled the trouser leg down delicately. Below him the man had fallen again and was trying to arise, cursing all the while and flailing at the attacking tamper. He turned tormented eyes up to Tidewater.

Tidewater passed the trailer and the group of dispersing men who looked at him curiously and then headed for the ditch. Tidewater did not pause until he reached the top of the rise where he had parked his car. He looked back once and below him in the distance the men were gathered all about the length of ditch like mourners at some grotesque grave.

Tidewater had been leaning against the plate glass window of the Belly Stretcher Café for a half hour and in that time he had neither altered his stance or had to move aside to allow any prospective diners to enter. Behind his shoulders a canted sign inside beckoned, FISH DINNERS ALL YOU CAN EAT $1.00. But the sign was flyspecked and faded and the clumsy drawing of an unlikely fish stared at Tidewater with round hopeless eyes.

The door opened and Hinson came out and peered up and down the frozen streets.

What say, Tidewater? What you know?

Very damn little, Tidewater said. Hinson nodded as if this was in line with his expectations.

How's business?

It would be all right if they was any. But they ain't.

Tidewater made a ritual of feeling through all his pockets. Coming up empty, he said, Give me a cigarette, will ye?

Hinson pecked a Camel half out of the pack and proffered it to Tidewater. He took it and lit it, pulling the smoke deep into his lungs.

You broke?

Tidewater acknowledged that he was. I got laid off, he told Hinson. They fell silent and then after a time Hinson laid a brotherly arm across Tidewater's shoulders and said, Come on in where it's warm. I got a proposition I need to put to you.

When Tidewater came out twenty minutes later he was a changed man. There was a deliberation to his stride and four packs of Camels bulged from his pockets, two in his front jeans and one each shirt pocket. There was a look of purpose about him; he had the look of one who had been lost and then shown the way.

Tidewater eased the crowbar between the door and jamb, soundlessly applied his weight. There was a dull click as metal gave somewhere. The door pushed inward, Tidewater easing into the greasy-smelling dark. Feeling his way in the kitchen, peering through it to where tables set in staggered rows and light fell whitely from the ghostly streetlights beyond. Tidewater stood behind the counter. What'll it be, he said softly, then, Yes sir. He gathered rags from the counter, carried them into the deeper dark of the kitchen. Accident, accident, he murmured to himself busily. He lit a match and located a garbage can. Then he lit one of the rags, a fine thread of red eating the rag, a thread of black where it had fed. Into the can now, its greasy brothers piled atop. Tidewater eased into the alley with quick little panicky steps, slowed his pace, shoulders squaring, lighting a casual cigarette.

He sat in his car behind the dark old hotel and waited. Time went by with painful slowness. His ears strained against the silence, but no sounds reached him. No running feet, no screaming fire trucks, no shouts, no breaking glass.

At last he went back. The door stood ajar; a faint smell of greasy smoke hung in the stale air but there were no flames. He paused at the garbage can. The fire had gone out. Tidewater relit it, waited until it blazed merrily, then fleet-footed it back to the car.

He repeated the waiting. Again, there was silence. He got out and looked once about him, staring eastward toward the horizon. Pale day hung there like a threat. Cursing, he retraced his steps. He kicked the charred garbage about with disbelief. Well kiss my ass, he said.

He sat on a stool and smoked. After a time he arose. Accident's ass, he said, and went out.

When he came through the door this time he was carrying a five-gallon can of gas that canted him sideways with its weight and he was wearing the look of a man who has burned all his bridges and will brook no further nonsense. He unscrewed the cap and began immediately to pour the gasoline about the kitchen. Fumes rose about him ropily like vapors rising from a swamp. Now burn, you son of a bitch, Tidewater told it.

When the gasoline hit a smoldering rag there was a muffled thud like a fifty-gallon oil drum exploding and Tidewater was lifted bodily and slammed backward with its force. A wall of flames blossomed about him. The explosion had blown Tidewater up and across the counter and set him, with clothes afire, down amidst turned over tables. He leapt up and peered wildly about him. The kitchen was a solid sheet of crackling orange and it gave off a steady roar like an approaching locomotive. Trying for the back door did not even cross his mind. He threw a chair through the plate glass window and leapt through into the cold air, sliding down on the icy sidewalk. He arose and batted at his flaming clothes. His brows and lashes were singed away and even the hair that had stuck out from under the bill of his cap and it gave his face a featureless unformed look.

Tidewater knew his luck was running true to form when the first car to come around the corner was the city police.

Tidewater was in jail for four days and he thought it not bad at all. The food was nothing extra but it was better than anything he would have cooked on his own and there was a routine to cell life that shaped the formlessness of his life. He had even found a stub of pencil and written his name on the cell wall and upon rising each morning he would affix a number after it.

On the fourth day the old woman came and signed his bond, but it did not surprise him. He had lain on his bunk and put himself in her mind and he knew that that was all she had left to do. She would not find the jar; he was confident of that. She would have spent the days searching the house and car, but she would have come up empty-handed. He imagined that old woman was half-crazy, must feel that she had slipped over and was living someone else's life by mistake, had taken some dread side road that should have been let alone.

When he followed the turnkey down the Lysol-smelling stairs he was not surprised to be meeting her, jaws tight and more reptilian than ever, clutching the old pocketbook as if it were something that was going to save her from drowning.

You look like a six-winged chicken, she told him with satisfaction when they got into the old station wagon. Tidewater slammed the door and had no words to say.

She inched cautiously into the street, humped over the wheel and occasionally glancing at him.

A sinner, she said, and laughed. How much money did you get out of him?

I didn't get none, Tidewater said tiredly. I was to of got it out of the insurance money.

A sinner and a fool besides, she said as if he had done something that pleased her greatly. Nobody would get mixed up in such a deal as that.

You did, Tidewater told her. What did you ever do such a crazy thing for? What'd make a woman cut a man so and then keep it like a souvenir ashtray or pillowcase? After some silence Tidewater said, I guess there's things better not asked. Silence. Then, and better not answered.

The old woman maneuvered the car out of the street, parked near the curb. Shoppers passed the car. A child's laughter, brittle as glass, came to Tidewater. Go on and get out. Go to the pool room or wherever it is you go.

I'll just ride on out with you, Tidewater said. I need to see Jasmine.

Well you won't see her there, the old woman said. She's been gone three days. She's workin at that old Dari-Dip and got her a room.

A what?

A room. You do know what a room is, don't you? She's left.

The old woman's hands clenched the wheel. The knuckles were white, almost yellow. The eyes looked through Tidewater, past him, to visions he would never behold. The old jaws worked as she shook her gray head from side to side. When the words finally came, she had somehow steadied herself and her voice was calm and clear. I've wrote her off, washed my hands of her. She's where I can't reach her now.

Well you better reach her.

The old woman shrugged. She's gone, she said, and Tidewater

knew she was talking about more than a room, or a job at the Dari-Dip. He opened the door, began to climb out.

You seem to forget what I got, he said, his voice rising. A matter of a little Mason fruit jar.

But the car had begun already to roll, the door on the passenger side, flapping like a broken wing.

You remember the bounty on them ducks, Tidewater screamed after her. You payin it right now. He began to walk. He passed the burned-out café, halted and stared in for a time. As if this gutted building were the only work he had accomplished, the only mark he had made on life.

He made a fist and with it cleared a small round place on the plate glass window at the front of the Dari-Dip, and peered in. A warm domestic scene within, Jasmine at the grill, frying something, steam rising, her face intent on her work. She glanced at the window once without seeing him. Into the moist circle a man came, wearing a white cap set at a jaunty angle, over blonde short hair, a slim cigar clamped in his jaws. He came up and stood behind her.

It was like looking up from under water. Tidewater remembered making love to her once, peering downward into her roiled eyes as if from some lofty height, the dark hair plumed on the pillow as if stirred by restless waters. The eyes did not see him, never saw him, felt only the thrusts he made. There was a moment then, when the eyes looked blank and opaque as a corpse's, as if no one lived there anymore. With the hair like that she looked like a drowned woman, thrashing only at the will of the current that bore her on. He thought of her so now.

The man had approached her, touching her with his body, reached out his arms and encircled her, cupping both her breasts with his hands. Tidewater's knees went to water. He waited for her to turn, to slap him, to flail at him with the spatula she held, he reached automatically for his pocketknife. He saw her body go slowly limp, her hips settle comfortable against the front of his body, the slight thrust of his hips toward her, her dark head lean gently back. There was something in their manner that told Tidewater they had stood so many times before. His breath fogged the spot, as if the waters had engulfed them all.

The old woman stood staring at him, as if waiting for him to speak. None of the things he had planned to say seemed suitable now. He could have gloated, could have said, She is lost to you, too. Or that she was gone as irrevocably as if she had drowned. But he saw that he could not tell her anything she had not known long before him.

Then as if in answer to some unasked question he spoke. I buried it, he said. In that cemetery. It's deep down in old Papa John's grave.

She studied his face a long time as if looking for signs of guile, then nodded once. I thank ye, she said.

He turned and began to walk toward the car. She called to him once, but it put no falter in his pace. She fell silent then. He looked at her once across the top of his car and across the moon-silvered yard and his head bobbed below the level of the car and was gone.

She felt suddenly powerless and old. There was nothing she could have said. She had meant to ask him about the bail, to caution him. But there was something in his white browless face that told her that nothing she said could keep him here, nothing could make him go.

HOMECOMING

Winer in unaccustomed and more opulent surroundings. A house of near palatial proportions rising above him, yellow light from its windows spilling out onto slashed red earth tilled and seeded and strewn with wheatstraw. She peered down at him through the glass of the storm door, her blue eyes limpid and myopic, a solemn and inquisitive owl's face. Then he saw recognition form there as if she were reconstructing his child's face in the lines of his older face and he heard the latch click.

Sure it's me, he said. Who did you reckon it was?

Come in, come in. Well, I didn't think it was anybody in particular. It's just been so long since I saw you, you look like you're standing on a box or something. Lord, I haven't seen you in years.

He entered into a high foyer where to his left carpeted stairs curved upward out of sight. Above his head a glittering chandelier hung from a gilded chain. She guided him into a large room with subdued lighting. The room was more cluttered than opulent, high-ceilinged, the walls papered with what appeared to be black and red velvet. Well, well, he said awkwardly, looking about the room. He seemed unaccustomed to such splendor. Expensive pieces of furniture set at random about the room showed a predilection for the same rich wines and purples, the plusher fabrics. The room seemed happenstantial, undirected, as if too much money had been spent to no good purpose.

He brushed magazines aside and seated himself on the edge of the sofa, weight on his calves and ankles, as if he must soon be off again. The room held a vast profusion of *True Story* magazines. They littered the tables and chairs, their covers and titles as lurid as the furniture they adorned, perhaps she'd won a lifetime supply of them in some obscure contest.

Is anything wrong?

Not that I know of. Why?

Well, I didn't know, she said. I never see any of the family unless somebody's dead or in the hospital, my own first cousin and I can't remember when I saw you last. How's your mama?

All right. I was just in town and I thought I'd come by and see you a few minutes.

When she sat beside him on the sofa he could smell a strong scent of gin on her breath and he recalled talk that his mother's niece had been wild when she was growing up, before she had married well, but if she had there was no vestige of it left in her face. She looked placid and almost matronly, though she could not have been over thirty. She took up a pair of glasses from the table and put them on, her face altering with the addition, becoming somehow more confident. She was a bigboned statuesque woman, yellowhaired, and there was something intimidating about her. Winer sat with his hands in his lap, seemingly lost in a deep study of his fingers. When he looked up she was smiling at him.

What's so funny?

You are. You talk as if you came all the way cross country instead of three or four miles out of town.

I just don't get out much.

She was studying him appraisingly. My guess is that's going to change before long. I'll bet you've got a lot of little freshman girls with their caps set for you.

If that's so it's been kept mighty quiet.

And modest on top of it.

He was already wishing he had not come but could think of no reason for leaving so quickly. He could not remember what he had once liked about her or what kind of thing she had said to him, what her face would be like with ten years gone from it and he could see little resemblance between the photograph of a smiling schoolgirl and this woman sitting beside him. There was some vague memory of his father's leaving, the slight weight of her forearm across the back of his neck.

You want a Coke or something? I think I'll have a nice glass of ice water.

I'll drink a glass of water if you don't mind.

She arose and passed through a curtained doorway into an adjoining room. The curtain was gold plush, tassels of satin depending from the doorway, a gold fringe that swayed against the passage of her yellow hair. For no good reason he thought of history books, of the decadence they said was Rome. He picked up two or three of the magazines and thumbed through them. Raped and strangled, they said. Beaten, assaulted by their fathers, unwed and pregnant. Bereft, orphaned, dragged screaming to their stepfather's beds. Mad confessionals here of the reviled, the undone, hard times on the land.

He laid them aside when she came in with two iced glasses. He drank water from the glass she handed him, mildly surprised to discover it was indeed water; he could smell the juniper scent of the gin in her glass and he felt a cynical sort of disillusionment about her, it seemed a needless and shoddy attempt at deception. It was her house, she was three times nine, it was none of his business if she chose to drink kerosene.

She had pictures she would show him.

Here, she said. Have you ever seen this picture of you and your daddy?

He studied it. He laid it face up on the coffee table, sat staring at the image of himself, four or five years old. The picture seemed curiously and profoundly prophetic. His eyes were held by the image of his childhood eyes, calm, unquestioning. They seemed already at some cold remove from the scenery that locked them. From the big man holding his hand. The man towering above him dwarfed him, the face stern and flinty. He wore a black slouch hat and, as he stared into the sun, the shadow of its brim fell across his eyes like a bandit's mask so that he appeared already a fugitive of the order of this life, or of life itself.

Wasn't you the cutest thing? she asked. I always thought you were anyway. Still do, for that matter. Look, here's one of me, wasn't I the ugliest girl there ever was?

There were others. Old folks he barely remembered or never knew. Snippets of time like souvenirs saved from some vague wars, moments preserved in perpetuity that seemed better let alone and forgotten. Ultimately the pictures seemed to depress them both and she laid them aside.

She picked up one of the magazines, let it fall. They keep me company, she said. I'm by myself a lot with George running the restaurant and movie house both, it's generally late when he gets in.

Is that where he is tonight?

She sipped the gin. It's where he's supposed to be. I couldn't say for sure where he is.

I guess he has a big night Fridays. The football game and all.

George has a big night every night, she said obscurely.

This didn't seem to call for a reply and Winer made none. She seemed different, as if she had passed some unnamed border down whatever road the gin was taking her. Winer realized it had been foolish of him to come here, the past was here no more than it was anywhere else. It was dead. He could not imagine anything they ever had in common save some idiosyncrasy of the blood. They sat in a deepening silence, for Winer realized he had nothing to say to her, nor she to him. He wished bitterly he had not come, had let the random debris of the years lie undisturbed. All this was, was a soft sofa beneath him and a cold glass in his hand. The silence did not seem to bother her, she seemed in some manner used to it, nourished by it, and there was an undercurrent of tension beneath her placid flesh; she seemed to be waiting for something to happen.

Has the cat got your tongue? Surely you didn't come all this way for a glass of water.

I wasn't even sure you'd be here. I knew you used to cook at The General. I figured George would have you frying hamburgers.

George says it's unseemly for me to fry hamburgers, she said. George finds many things unseemly.

Winer could smell her. He could smell her makeup and perfume and the gin and, beneath all these separate fragrances, the almost indefinable female smell of her.

How is George? Winer noticed she had almost finished the gin.

I don't know. He has to go to the doctor now and again and get a little something out of him. His stomach, I guess. She was silent for a time, then as if in reply to something Winer should have been perceptive enough to ask but was not, she said, So I sit. And, every once in a while, I get up and look in the mirror and watch myself get older.

He's built you a fine house here, Winer said nervously. He shifted his weight to the edge of the sofa. He seemed to be making ready to go.

I suppose, she said, dismissing it with the words. George's folks all had money you know, and I reckon it's George's ambition to spend it all before he dies. He lost money on that theatre he put in. He's losing more on that damned café. He doesn't care, it makes him feel important. George likes businesses where he gets to hire little high school girls with short skirts he can look up.

I got to get on, Winer said. He set his glass atop the table. He did not need or want any of this. He was finding he liked certain doors better left closed.

Why you haven't been here but a few minutes, Nathan. Lean back and rest a while, you look tired out. I'll hush about George. You leave now and you won't be back for another four or five years.

When he saw the face at the window he jumped involuntarily and knocked the tumbler of water over. Hellfire, he said. The face was pressing itself against the fogged glass, a cheek and one eye, then as he watched it turn full face to the room, two blue eyes and hands coming up to shade them, the nose twisted onesided, two rubbery lips misshapen with the weight of the glass. He leapt up. Somebody's trying to break in, he told her. I'll see if I can catch him.

She had a hand on his arm. Oh, it's just George. Sit back down and act like you don't see him. He does this sometimes.

What's the matter with him? Why would a man sneak around looking in his own window?

I guess he's drunk, she said. He thinks folks come here to see me, you know, menfolks. He thinks I entertain men when he's not here and he's always sneaking back and peeping in trying to see something. She laid an arm around Winer's neck. You want to give him a thrill? Her head rested against Winer's cheek.

Not so's you'd notice it, Winer said.

Their eyes opened wider then blinked closed in a solemn dual wink.

They opened again and Winer pulled away from her and began to pick the ice cubes from the carpet and put them back in the glass and when he looked back toward the window he was gone. George must have run all the way around the house for almost immediately there were two loud taps at the front door and then Winer heard it open and close. Crazy, crazy, crazy, the woman said to herself. She was agitatedly smoothing back her curly hair. The curtains parted and George came into the room. He flipped a wall switch, and the room sprang into bright relief. He stood there watching them and batting his eyes rapidly.

He was smaller than Winer remembered, wasted, dried up. He had on a plaid sportcoat and gray flannel slacks too large for him. He appeared to be very drunk. He swayed from the knees up and his left eye showed a tendency to wander, as if it must see all the world at once and refused to be confined. His left cheek bore a mauve birthmark the size of a woman's hand, the area where the fingers would be cleft the hairline and his smooth hair was brushed to cover it. From across the room the birthmark stood out in livid relief. It looked purple velvet or yet some fungoid growth spreading from his face. He stood slowly twirling his hat in his hand, watching Winer.

Figured I better knock, he said. Liked to caught you anyway, didn't I? He laughed dryly through his nose, wandered toward them across the room, sidestepping such furniture as he chanced to notice. Ain't I seen you around town, boy? And what are you doing on my couch, you little cockhound.

Oh shut up, the woman said. For God's sakes, George, this is my cousin Nathan. You remember Nathan.

Yet another cousin, George said. Then as if he hadn't heard he said, Oh yes, I liked to caught you. Don't think I didn't see you with your hand up her dress there. Ahh yes, the voice went on slurred and somehow mechanical, like a voice issuing from a tape played too slow. The voice had the singsong quality of litany, a child repeating an oft-told story to hurry sleep. Yeah, I seen you with your hand between her legs, rubbing the straddle of her drawers.

Winer started toward him. The coffee table banged his shins and he kicked it viciously out of the way without looking down.

George threw his hands up before his face. No, young man, you hold up a minute. You're in my house. You lay a hand on me and you'll wake up in that jailhouse. How do I know you ain't broke and entered? How do I know you ain't raped my wife or vice versa? As if he had suddenly remembered Adell he whirled to face her.

What have you been up to?

I'll tell you what I haven't been up to, she said. I haven't been bumped up in a hot little broom closet peeping through a hole I bored in the ladies' room wall.

You whoring slut.

You pathetic drunken sot.

Winer was looking aghast from one to the other. George seemed momentarily to sober himself. He squared his narrow shoulders and adjusted his tie and smoothed a hand across the bird's wing of his gray hair.

All right, he told Winer. I apologize. I'll go back out and you go right ahead and do it to her. All I ask is for you to let me watch through the window.

All I ask is to be out of this crazyhouse, Winer said. Just move the hell out of my way. He turned to his cousin. Her face was convulsed, and he thought at first she was crying but she was not. She was laughing. By God you're as crazy as he is, Winer told her shaking shoulders. She was laughing uncontrollably. Her glass tilted, gin pooled like oil on the satin pillows of the sofa. An ice cube slid, fell soundlessly to the carpet.

George had his wallet out, he was peering shortsightedly at its contents. His weight shifted drunkenly; the floor was adrift on uncertain waters.

All right, you cockhound, he said, I've got your number. How about your rockbottom dollar?

I don't know what the hell you're even talking about.

Adell had brought herself under a semblance of control. Don't pay him any attention, she said. He's sick.

He sure as hell is, Winer said. And I think it's contagious.

Why sure you do, son. You know you been settin' here wantin' to screw her like all the rest of the little cockhounds around town. All right then, go ahead. Here's…twenty dollars for you. Go on and get started and I'll ease on out. All I want to do is watch through the window.

All you'll get is a basketweaving course up at Bolivar, Adell said. And me living high on the hog spending your money. You better get a grip on yourself or you're going to be in a place where the rooms got rubber walls.

Winer stepped past George and George grasped his arm. Thirty's my absolute top dollar, he said. Winer turned and slapped the wallet out of his hand. George fell, fumbling for the money on the carpet. His glasses fell off. He felt for them, pale hands weaving like drunken spiders above the nap of the carpet. Winer kicked the glasses out of his way and started for the door.

You ought to go on and take the money, Adell told him. You've got to humor him.

You humor him, Winer told her. You married him. He went out the door without looking back. Come back sometime, Nathan, she called after him, but he heard the voice through the wooden door he'd already closed behind him. He went on down the steps.

It was late. He paused in the yard, filling his lungs with fresh cold air, holding it, his chest swelling, expelling it slowly. It had grown chill and he could see the vapor of his breath. He looked up. The sky was full of stars, broken jewelry slung in anger against a velvet backdrop. The moon rode high above the rooftops of town and the distant woods were a constant presence he divined rather than saw. In the distance a few scattered tin roofs winked back the light but here the dark-shingled roofs sucked the darkness to them, they were mere negations of the moonlight.

He walked on. Here slept the rich, what would their dreams be like? Their untroubled scions reposed as well; their lives assured, they slept clutching roadmaps to the future. The daughters of the well-to-do lay in tousled musky darkness. He went past porch and façade, stone lions that watched him go with silent contempt. The town was sleeping, curtains drawn, the houses of the monied fell away and here were tacky porches steeped in dark silence, pockets of deeper night, watchdogs that watched the shadow of hedges with wary, surly eyes.

He rested once where Mill and Holy intersected, sitting on the curb, his feet in the street. Above him the traffic light blinked red to green, unnoticed save by the moths flailing blindly at it. He wondered what time it was. He was tired, exhaustion was a weight he carried that grew heavier and heavier. He got up and walked on listening to the hollow sound of his footfalls.

After a while he smiled to himself and shook his head. Crazy son of a bitches, he said. As he walked toward town his weariness seemed to leave him little by little and a sense of elation seized him. The world he was moving toward seemed infinite in its possibilities, the lives he could lead, the people he could be, limitless and complex. The world was full of places he could go to, people he could meet, emotions he could make his own.

MEMOIRS

THE WRECK ON THE HIGHWAY

Opportunity only knocks once; ruin will kick the door down and barge on in. Some enormous concussion had gone off in the world, a horrendous cataclysm of rending metal and breaking glass he'd heard or dreamed, the waves of destruction rolling outward, dark waters lapping about his ankles. Then he saw that the heavy book had fallen from his chest when he sat up from the couch he'd fallen asleep on. Everything was happening at once. The phone was ringing and strobic light raked the windows like cold blue claws and something was pounding at the door, a truncheon, a mailed fist.

He sat for a moment disoriented and then he looked at his watch. It was two o'clock in the morning. The pounding went on. Distant thunder rumbled. He picked up the book and laid it on the table and arose and crossed to the door and opened it. A cop stood there, nightstick poised to strike the door.

Is your name Vestal?

A stormtrooper blown out of imminent storm. Khaki and leather and holstered blue steel. Behind him looking anomolaic and sinister in Vestal's front yard a police cruiser idling, crouched like some beast on its forepaws poised to spring. Revolving blue light washed the porch. Vestal could smell mimosa, rain, he could already hear it in the treetops and singing on the tin roof.

I'm Vestal. What's the matter?

You have a minor son named—he tilted an opened notepad toward the porchlight—Butler?

Yes, Vestal said. But he's not here. You want to tell me what's the matter?

Mr. Vestal, I'm Deputy Sheriff Rossen. There's been an accident, and your son is involved in it. I need you to come with me.

What sort of accident? Is my son all right?

We think he's just shook up. But he's a minor and he's asking for you. Everything's still under investigation, I don't have any answers for you yet. Come on and we'll find out. You might want to get a shirt on, he's being transported to the emergency room at Centre.

Vestal looked down at himself. He went back inside, and the deputy followed into the living room. While Vestal pulled on a tee shirt Rossen stood studying the four walls as if evidence of a crime might be framed there, as if he'd catalogue the room's contents should he be called upon to testify before an oaken bench.

Let's roll, Vestal said.

You got everything you need? You'll probably have to accompany him to Centre. You might want to turn everything off.

I'm packed, Vestal said, impatient to see his son, but the deputy's eyes swept the room one last time to see was there anything forgotten. He had careful cop's eyes. Vestal guessed he always made sure the lights were out before he left a room, the campfire pissed on, his prayers said before his head touched the pillow.

They went down the stone steps into a world coming alive with storm. The wind was up and running the pale leaves like quicksilver and he could hear it making a harp of the winds and lightning was pacing frantically beyond the restive trees and the heavens were a dome of absolute blackness.

We better move before the bottom falls out, Rossen said. Goin to be like a cow pissing on a flat rock here in a minute. No, don't bother with your vehicle, you'll ride with me.

In his youthful longhaired days as a protestor of wars Vestal had ridden in the backseat of cruisers, caged left and right by handleless doors and forward by a steel mesh screen, but here he was ushered like a guest of honor to the shotgun front seat and the car was backing up as soon as he'd closed the door.

Buckle up there, Rossen said.

Easing down the hill Vestal could hear the lick the cam was hitting and the supercharged engine sounded impatient with such constraint. Rossen opened it up on the main road jerking Vestal back against the leather. The headlights cut away the night. The countryside came at him in windblown tatters like a jigsaw landscape the wind had dissembled. Garbled dispatches from the front lines of chaos crackled over the scanner, cut away Vestal's enforced calm like broken glass.

The country was flat here and to the right and in the distance Vestal could see a battery of flashing lights, blue and red, bleeding into the sky like a caustic violet stain.

He didn't know why the deputy wouldn't tell him anything. He didn't know what he'd find here, what had found him. Inside he felt cold and enormous, he contained worlds beyond number barren and icelocked the wind whistled across.

Rossen turned right at the crossroad. The first thing Vestal saw was an ambulance, its rear doors cocked open, light pulsing in waves across the field. Two EMTs were sliding a hardboard gurney into the rear. He tried to take all this in. There were two other police cruisers. His son's red Nissan was on its right side in the ditch, its lights still on. In its headlights a woven wire fence strung away into the darkness.

The night had taken on a sort of hyper reality. Vestal was drawn into a world where everything was deeply symbolic and every motion and word had a secret meaning. Everything was outlined in bold strokes, the brightness down, the contrast cranked all the way clockwise. Vestal knew that his life had changed in some irrevocable way and for now all he could do was just lean into the changes and go where they took him.

He was out of the car without being told and running toward the medics but the high sheriff stepped around the ambulance and held up a restraining hand, stop.

This is just a precaution, Mr. Vestal. We're having him transported to the emergency room at Centre to be checked out. He appears to be just shaken up, this is just standard procedure.

He'd had a quick glimpse of Butler's face as the gurney was tipped into the ambulance and slid forward. He heard the gurney lock into place. He was looking for blood and he hadn't seen any. He hadn't seen much, but he'd seen Butler's eyes seeking him out and they hadn't looked like Butler's eyes. They'd looked like the startled eyes you've seen trapped in your headlights.

Your son was in an accident, the high sheriff said. There was no emotion in his voice; here these curious malfunctions of time and space seemed his daily fare.

Not here. Well, here and somewhere else. Two accidents then. He was involved in a collision with another vehicle, he hit it or it hit him, we're still sorting it out. Anyway, he fled the scene.

Apparently he was trying to get to you.

Vestal shook his head. He looked at the Nissan. Part of the roof was peeled back and the driver's side looked as if it had been raked with enormous claws by the bucket of a steam shovel. The car was on its side in tall grass and the random orbs of fireflies moved through the rainswept weeds like St. Elmo's fire on the roiled surface of some winedark sea.

These boys need to roll, the high sheriff said. There's a hell of a storm east of here and they need to beat it to Centre. If it touches down, they'll be all over the place the rest of the night.

Vestal climbed into the rear of the ambulance. An attendant closed the door behind him and it latched with the decisive finality of a casket lid slamming shut. They were rolling almost immediately, rain streaking the windshield and the siren wailing down the night like a banshee, lights painting the fleeing roadside trees with a fierce electric lacquer.

What happened? Vestal was crouching on a metal bench by the gurney. He was trying to smell alcohol, but he hadn't yet.

Butler's eyes were moving jerkily beneath their neartranslucent lids. The longlashed lids raised and the dark eyes skittered jerkily searching for something and then they fixed on Vestal's face. The eyes looked frightened, tormented. The face beseeched him. Fix this. Make it go away. Make it not be.

But the voice was Butler's confident own. I had a wreck, he said. I couldn't see shit. Wind and rain. I pulled out from a crossroads and this motorcycle just came out of nowhere and slammed me in the side.

His eyes looked focused on some point Vestal's own eyes couldn't get to. He passed a hand before his eyes as if he'd erase these visions. He shook his head. Out of nowhere, he said again.

Why didn't you stay there? Call the law.

Butler's face looked confused. Uncertain. Soft dark shadow of attempted mustache. The face said everything was a mystery, even its own motivations.

I don't think anybody was bad hurt. This guy was up walking around yelling at me. I had Tina and a friend of hers, this other girl, and they were all screaming at me. Take me home, take me home. God. They were all yelling at me, all at once. I freaked out. The guy in the grass was screaming at me. I let them out at Tina's and then I was trying to get to you. I figured you'd call the law.

Anyway, we've got plenty of that, Vestal said.

What'll they do to me?

Vestal was staring out the glass. The night was coming at them with dizzying speed as if the entire landscape, house and tree and stony field, had been flattened into a two-dimensional strip of fabric that fed beneath their wheels at an ever-increasing clip and he imagined it being wound onto an enormous reel turning somewhere in the night behind them. He pretended he hadn't heard.

They went through Ackerman's Field, night lights on, doors locked, guard dogs dozing at their watch. Vestal envied these folks in their tousled beds, covers drawn to their chins, limbs unscathed and their dreams untroubled. At the railroad tracks by the tie yard the ambulance rocked on its heavyduty springs and leapt into the darkness at town's edge, speedometer in a dizzy climb, windshield wipers ratcheting away the rain.

The night was throwing everything it had at them. Storm to the east, the high sheriff had said. Rain was coming horizontally, and the driver had to fight the steering wheel against the buffeting winds that came broadside and tried to jerk the ambulance off the road. The wind carried tree branches, plastic garbage cans; the air was full of leaves the wind had stripped.

Vestal kept expecting to see windblown old ladies in rocking chairs, restraining hands raised to their hair, folk clutching the handles of umbrellas, families aligned to the last dog and cat on the ridgepoles of uprooted houses. Beyond the glass the wind was howling down the hillsides and trees were leaned westward into the calm the nightwind was blowing away.

Nearing Centre they met another ambulance, its siren wailing and red lights bleeding into the rain and Vestal wondered if the storm had touched down and in his disassociate frame of mind it seemed to him that they'd met themselves in some dark fairytale mirror, or yet descended to a world of dimensional displacement, ambulance and antiambulance passing each other in the night and going their separate ways.

_____

He'd seen his son two nights ago. He'd just set down at the bar of a place called The Highlander and drank half a beer and when he'd looked up he could see reflected in the bar mirror the green baize of the pool table and beyond it Butler watching him. His still eyes, his closecropped black hair. The other player was leaned to shoot and on the far side of the table Butler stood with his cuestick held bothhanded before his chest like a weapon at parade rest.

Vestal drained the beer and set the bottle down and shoved his change across the bar for a tip and arose. He went past a makeshift plywood stage with a karaoke machine and a fat man in a porkpie hat singing Sam Cooke with his eyes closed. *Bring it to me, bring your sweet loving, bring it on home to me.* He went through batwing doors and out into the failing heat and crossed the street to the parking lot.

It was at just the end of twilight and beyond the parking lot the western sky was a burnished red that cooled to smoke gray even as he watched it. Feeding nighthawks came to dart and check above the streetlamps, random as spores moving on a glass slide.

Hey.

He turned. His son had come out of the bar and was crossing the pavement toward him.

No need to run off.

I wasn't running off.

I could have sworn you were running off. Saw me there in the mirror and split.

Vestal slid his hands in his jean pockets and didn't say anything.

Hell, I know you started drinking again. We could have had a beer or two. Shot a game. Talked about olden times. I guess they're all olden now.

I had a hard day, Butler. I worked my butt off. I left because every time we talk it works around into a situation where you're chewing my ass and I just can't handle it today.

What are you doing?

Roofing a house. Putting on shingles. It was hot up there today, too.

Yeah. I heard they fired your ass up at the college. I expect it's harder toting shingles up a thirty-foot ladder than it was looking up co-eds' dresses there in that air conditioning. Though I guess that got to be hot work too.

The look on Butler's face was a complicated one but Vestal knew this calm confident face so well he could have deciphered it, but he didn't want to go there. He went anyway. The face looked confused and disappointed in him and it showed pain and the shame he felt saying these things or even being in this conversation and beneath it all anger burned like a banked fire.

The face looked like old photographs of Vestal's father. They were both constructed on the same paradigm. Compact bodies and high cheekbones and go-to-hell grins and sleepy moviestar eyes. The three of them, grandfather and father and son, looked as alike as if they'd all been stamped with the same faulted die and Vestal wondered how many of them had been shipped into an unsuspecting world. Butler always looked like a coiled spring, like a volatile liquid kept under pressure.

Any truth in that about you getting fired?

We came to a mutual understanding.

Yeah. We mutually understand they fired your ass. I heard about that student. How old was she? Mama heard twenty-two at the factory. How about fixing me up sometime?

Vestal ran a hand through his hair and turned toward his truck.

Hey.

What?

You got any money.

Vestal felt in his front pocket. A bill there, who knew what denomination. He withdrew it, glanced at it by the streetlamp. It was a fifty-dollar bill. He reached it to Butler.

You got a date?

Yeah. I'm taking Tina out to eat.

Don't drink, okay?

That's funny advice, coming from you.

Take it anyway. Why don't you drop by the house? Bring Tina by.

Well. Maybe later. When all this dies down. This goddamned divorce.

A year ago, Butler wouldn't have said goddamned divorce but a year ago was back in what Butler himself had called the olden times. The olden times were lost and gone and they weren't coming back. The olden times were beyond the pale.

Now here is the emergency room in Centre, Tennessee, at three o'clock of a Saturday morning. Bedlam reduced to its purest essence, a bus stop on the way to dementia praecox. No-nonsense attendants sped the gurney down a tiled hall, automatic doors opened with their arrival, closed at their passage. Butler's eyes darted about, taking in all these wonders. They paused in the receiving room. The receiving room was the foyer to hell, a Felliniesque motley of overdosed teenagers and miscarried mothers and the remnants of children set upon by pit bulls or their mother's boyfriends and a cleanshaven middle-aged man who kept asking, Did they ever get the bleeding to stop?

Forms were filled out; insurance questions must be answered. Vestal, a voice called. They rolled the gurney through stainless steel doors into the bowels of the hospital. Where harpies wait with their poised knives.

When he'd finished the forms, Vestal went and found a seat in this disparate madness. He could hear wind and rain at the glass, and he could hear the constant coming and going of ambulances and police cars and, after a time, the tattered orphans of the storm began to be carried in or to arrive under their own power. Halfclad or wrapped in blankets and all wearing the selfsame look that Butler had worn. As if they'd been suckerpunched by life. They looked like the sorriest of refugees, the wet and bedraggled remainders of some distant shipwreck who'd stumbled ashore and found themselves in this waiting room. One man with a hightop boot on one foot and a bedroom slipper on the other and some unshod altogether. Beyond these walls a rising tide of human voices taking on. Calling on God and determined that He pick up the phone.

Elizabeth? Elizabeth? Come on baby say something. Oh Lord. Oh Lord.

He tried not to see, he tried not to hear. He laid the back of his head against the vinyl and closed his eyes.

He thought about his father. Or rather an eight-by-ten photograph of his father that had set for long years on his mother's bureau. Dust gathered there like the dust on the family Bible his father sang about. His father and three other men. His father who wanted to be Hank Williams and three other men who wanted to be his Drifting Cowboys. A fiddler with his instrument tucked beneath his chin, a player riding a standup bass for comic relief, a seated man with a lap steel guitar. His father with his Gibson hung like a trophy about his neck. Those high Cherokee cheekbones, that shiteating country grin. Howdy friends and neighbors. So glad you all could set a spell and listen to us pick. Cool a while, ain't it been hot in the field? They all wore white Stetsons; they all wore white Palm Beach suits like Hank. Sharptoed city slicker shoes. He'd wanted to be famous, he'd dreamed about it at night, could taste it at the back of his tongue or at the bottom of a whiskey bottle, cashed checks on a future that had been delayed indefinitely. Killed time waiting for opportunity's knock at a tiny dirt road radio station; Vestal could hear the voice coming out of the fabric of the radio speaker. Hello out there in radioland. Now let's get serious for a few minutes, folks. Here's a gospel number I know will be a blessing to all you shut-ins,

The Wreck on the Highway.

His mother's voice. I can smell that whore on you from across the room, that cheap perfume is stronger than the whiskey on your breath. Goddamn you. You've got lipstick all over the side of your mouth.

Coming back from a gig in a honkytonk two counties over, the Cadillac he was driving (again in emulation of his hero) had occupied for a microsecond of time the same space as a bridge abutment God had thrown at him and this drifting cowboy had drifted across the lone prairie to the last roundup. His Gibson Dove guitar looked like something a stick of dynamite had dismantled, like shredded wood you'd use to kindle a fire on a cold winter's night.

Mr. Vestal?

He opened his eyes. A harried-looking nurse was standing before him.

Your son asked me to tell you he wants you with him. Just through those doors and the third door down the hall on the right.

So directed he went through the doors. The noise diminished and here there seemed a semblance, the cooling hand of competence laid on fevered chaos. He went into the third room. His son was alone. He was still on the board but unstrapped now. He was covered to the shoulders with a sheet and his arms and shoulders were bare and Vestal guessed they'd disrobed him for examination.

They tell you anything?

No. I'm all right though. Starting to stiffen up and get sore. I ache all over and my knees feel banged up.

The room was divided by a heavy curtain suspended from the ceiling to give the illusion of privacy. There was someone on the other side of the curtain: Vestal could hear stertorous breathing, an occasional moan.

A doctor came into the room. His white tunic was spotted with blood as a butcher's might be. Your son'll be fine, he said. He has no broken bones, no spinal injuries, nothing like that. He's been X-rayed and we ran a CAT scan. From what I understand about his accident he's a very lucky young man. He's a little bruised and shaken up, but he'll be fine.

Then we can go?

He won't be released for a few minutes. I believe they want a specimen for a blood alcohol test.

When the doctor had gone Butler started to speak but Vestal leaned and placed a palm over his son's mouth. Butler's eyes cut around to Vestal's face. Vestal shook his head. Some sort of defensive mode seemed to have kicked in. He hadn't known he had it; it had just lain dormant until needed. He needed it now. He could feel paranoia staining the edges of his mind like ink on litmus paper. He looked about the room. He suspected recording devices, video cameras, depositions taken unbeknownst. He raised his hand and Butler said, I'm about ready to get the hell out of Dodge.

Rubbersoled footsteps next door. Someone spoke in a druggy spacedout voice. Where's my father? the voice asked. Dad?

Mr. Mayberry?

Yeah.

I know you're in a lot of pain, Mr. Mayberry. We're going to do all we can to ease you and then we're going to have to transport you.

Transport me? Transport me where?

I'm sending you to Vanderbilt, they can do more for you there than I can. You're going to need surgery at once and they're very good there, the best. There's a chopper, there's a helicopter on its way here now.

A helicopter, the voice said.

Were you in an automobile accident?

A car, a car at a crossroads. It pulled out in front of us. We were on a motorcycle. The voice changed, as if had just remembered something. Where's my father? I want my father in here.

I have to give you something for pain now, the voice said. Where's my father, the drugged voice kept asking, and the placating voice kept responding. It's all right, it's all right, while whatever ministrations were going on kept going on and Mayberry's voice grew drowsy and drowsier still and little by little slurred into silence and Vestal realized he'd been brought to this selfsame room from the selfsame accident. Small world, he thought dementedly, we've got to stop meeting like this. Someone will talk. It grew quiet. He could hear oiled rollers moving away across the tile floor. A door closed.

A highway patrolman and a nurse came into the room. The officer wore the flatbrimmed Smokey Bear hat of the Tennessee Highway Patrol, he carried a clipboard. He didn't speak, he didn't even glance at Vestal. The nurse leaned and swabbed the inside of Butler's left elbow and inserted a hypodermic needle. Butler looked away. She pulled back on the syringe and blood with pink froth boiled into the tube. Vestal watching, what have we here, does alcohol discolor the blood, what color is doom?

He stared at the wall. There was a framed print of van Gogh's cypresses reared against a hot electric sky. Vestal imagined himself lost in them, the warm citrus smell of cypress, thick-needled earth beneath his feet. He'd slip into them like stepping through a curtain and this world would be no more.

She withdrew the needle and swabbed the spot with alcohol again. She turned to Vestal. We're through here, she said. You can go wait on him out front. His clothes are here and he can dress and meet you in the waiting room.

I'll be outside, Vestal told him.

The din outside had subsided now, disaster's rush hour over, a time for taking stock. Vestal stood before the admittance desk until a nurse acknowledged him.

Sir?

Hard night for you?

She looked exhausted, out on her feet, as if she'd been out in the storm, leaning too long into a high keening wind. That tornado touched down, she said.

I wanted some information about Mr. Mayberry.

All I can tell you is that Mr. Mayberry is being transported to Vanderbilt for surgery. That's all I know.

No, the other Mr. Mayberry. The father.

Her eyes changed. Are you a relative?

First cousin, Vestal said.

Then I'm sorry to tell you this. Mr. Mayberry wasn't brought here, she said. He didn't survive. He was pronounced dead at the scene.

He turned away. The distance across the geometric tile to the door was enormous. He wondered could he make it. Left foot, right foot. Sometimes you can just see too far down the road. To know all things is to suffer all consequence. He wished for ignorance. His head felt full of light and winds, his body a drifting string. The door opened without his touching it and he went through it into the pale dawn.

The rain had stopped and the storm had passed. Above the streetlamps the sky was a deep purple and high winds that never touched the earth shuttled lavender clouds across as if they had appointments to keep elsewhere. They passed and a capsized crescent moon stood above the trees like an omen.

He was smoking a cigarette when Butler came out. Butler was fumbling in his pockets, he'd lost his own cigarettes somewhere along the troubled path this night had taken. He reached for one of Vestal's. I'm ready to get the hell out of here.

We'll have to call somebody. Or call a cab.

Call who?

Your mother I guess. I don't know. We'll call a cab.

Then let's call it. I've about had it.

You saw that man up walking around?

Yeah. He seemed okay. He was okay enough to chew my ass and yell at me.

Vestal wondered if your mind would tell you lies. If there was some part of your brain that spoonfed you the news it thought you couldn't handle. That held the poison in abeyance and fed it drop by drop like fluid in an IV.

He wondered if Butler had stopped the car. He figured he had. That he'd leapt out into a growing storm to the carnage in the weeds with behind him the rising voices of horror and exhortation, take me home, let this not be, sprung door ajar and light spilling out like something toxic from a broken container.

Here his vision failed him. There was no way to know what Butler had seen but there were scorched images in his seared-looking eyes. Vestal wished he could shoulder this burden and just walk off with it. Spare Butler. All he could do was hang onto it a few minutes longer. His life felt like a flung stone.

Vestal believed you had to take responsibility for everything you did, all the commissions and omissions, the deeds and undeeds. Everything was accounting, everything went into columns marked profit or loss, there was no column marked good intentions, none for holding your own.

The wrong moves you made were noted and it might be years down the line when they handed you the check, but they always hand it to you. Too much stuff in the air and you drop the plate and it shatters and your son leans to the bloodspattered weeds and closes a dead man's eyes with a gentle thumb, one, the other.

He felt slow and swollen, a slow-moving copperhead laden with summer poison, pregnant with the direst of news.

Yet blood was blood and it was the strongest thing there was. It had always been so. It reeled backward into time when the first families huddled about their guttering fire and it reeled forward into a wavering and provisional future. It transcended the dread familiars that will come in nightmare and the ministrations of lawyers and the exhortations of judges leaned from oaken benches which will surely come too and it transcended the dead long in the cold, cold ground bowered beneath rotted silk, sewn mouths gone slack and features crept with indigo mold.

Day was coming now and the world forming itself anew. A band of the palest pink lay above the eastern buildings and one by one the stars had gone.

He touched Butler's shoulder, a touch so brief and light it might have been a bird alighting momentarily then taking to the air again. I'm about ready to get the hell out of Dodge myself, he said. I'll go look for a phone.

He was counting the moments now before he had to say what he was going to have to say but there was peace in this interim before the firestorm hit and he figured he might as well give him that.

FUMBLING FOR THE KEYS TO THE DOORS OF PERCEPTION

A MEMOIR,
MOSTLY TRUE BUT WITH SOME STRETCHES,
AS MARK TWAIN ONCE SAID

We'll starve to death, she said.

I was married then and my wife was appalled because I had quit my job.

Something will turn up, I said.

I'll get another job.

I sounded confident but I wasn't so sure. New jobs weren't so easy to come by and I was young and possessed no marketable skills. The only thing I had to offer the job market was a warm body. I had been working construction but when that job wound down, I had taken a position in a shoe factory for minimum wage operating a sort of press that cut shoe uppers from sheets of leather. Nobody had made production on this job since about 1947 and things did not appear to be picking up any speed. I could hardly keep up with the hands reaching out for my cut uppers to carry them to the folks who were gluing them to the soles.

This factory was a place of clamorous noise and the smell of hot glue and leather, and I had come to see it as a sweat factory run by petty tyrants and their footlings and toadies who lorded it over the folks like me who were just trying to work out a grocery bill or car payment. Its only advantage was it ran all day every day.

Which was another thing.

You all work every day? Sheets asked me once.

Sheets was a new hand hired fresh out of the log woods and was not yet acclimated to the doings of factories.

All day every day, I said.

No matter what the weather is?

There is a roof, I pointed out.

The hell with this, Sheets said. I ain't working nowhere you can't get rained out just every now and then.

Now that job was gone in a moment of outrage and I could not call it back. Could I have rewound events and altered them perhaps I would have. But probably not, for I had been sent for.

I was married then only a few weeks and used to drive home for lunch. Occasionally one thing would lead to another and I did not always make it back to clock in on time. On this particular lunch hour, the time I was sent for, I had decided to take the rest of the day off and get a fresh start in the morning.

About one o'clock a car drove up the gravel drive to the house and into the yard and immediately the horn began to blow.

Who in the world could that be? she asked.

I went to look. I couldn't believe it. It was my foreman from the cutting room.

Car broke down? He asked.

No. Why are you here?

The floor boss sent me. Thought you might need a ride back to the plant. We sure do need you out in that cutting room.

I was outraged. Sent for. Sent for like some incompetent who had forgotten the way to town, or could not find something the size of a shoe factory.

That cutting room can kiss my ass. I quit.

Why Lord, you can't quit. There ain't no work. You'll starve to death.

I can maybe get you on at the boat paddle plant, my brother-in-law Curtis said a few days later. Curtis was new at the job himself but was the sort of confident fellow who fell easily into the way of things and saw no reason why he could not hire and fire after a couple of weeks on the job.

Curtis had himself been recently fired. He had been a city policeman who had used a little too much force blackjacking miscreants and had been summarily dismissed. Or penalized for unnecessary roughness as he called it. He had been outraged too. Hellfire, he said to me. That's what the law is supposed to do. I just made em too good a hand. What's the point of being a police if you can't beat nobody up?

What makes you think you can get me on?

There is a lot of turnover, he said. Folks comin and goin. There is generally some kind of opening.

Let's try it, I said. I've got to do something till construction picks back up.

The boat paddle plant was a couple of towns over, almost fifty miles away. We drove there in Curtis's lovingly restored '59 Chevrolet. Anyone else would have had a '57 but Curtis fancied himself a bit of an eccentric and much preferred the fine aesthetics of the '59. He was the opposing viewpoint to every proposition. The perennial devil's advocate, his head always cocked slightly sidewise, as if listening for the first faint beat of a different drummer.

The plant was a huge sheet metal building full of machines and the folks who ran them. Saws, sanders, blades. The place was full of noise like the shrieking from a slaughterhouse. But it smelled like freshly sawn wood, which was already an improvement over the cutting room.

I could put you on the dipper, the foreman said. Son of a bitch walks off the job last night. Never said a word. But you have to work nights and you'd have to be here every night.

I'll be here, I said.

It's warmer back by the dipper too. That's a little benefit we don't charge for.

It is a little cold in here, I said. Why is it so cold?

It's December, the foreman said. December has been a cold month all my life.

When do I start?

How about right now, the foreman said.

It was indeed a little warmer back by the dipper. The dipper consisted of a circular concrete vat perhaps sixteen feet in diameter and filled to some unknowable depth with lacquer or varnish, some kind of waterproofing sealant. There was a crane-like device you operated to lift bailed bundles of forty-eight boat paddles and lower them into the hot lacquer. You left them there a time and then raised them out with the crane and stacked them to the side to dry. You always had bails soaking up lacquer, bails waiting for their turn in the vat, bails drying, new bails being fork-lifted over from the sanders. Enough oars for the entire population of the world to be sitting in flat-bottomed boats rowing upstream. An imponderable amount of boat paddles.

Hell, this is a job with all the work picked out, Curtis said. The machine does all the lifting. You're in the tall cotton on the dipper.

It did not take many nights on the job to discover there was another aspect of the dipper no one had bothered to mention. You got drunk. You got high on the miasmic fumes rolling from the heated vat. Drunker as the night progressed. Not just gently high but drunk as a lord, drunk as a bicycle, drunk as a fiddler's bitch, sleeping it off in the gutter drunk. By shift's end your head would be filled with helium, your boot soles touched the concrete floor only occasionally and a strong wind would have blown you into the next county. It took enormous snake-eyed concentration to raise the bundled oars and set them down gently on the concrete without breaking the bails. You ran into things. Things did not look right. Perceived distances were fey and compasses unreliable.

The ride home seemed endless or it passed in a flash. Time was a fabric gone slack on the loom or stretched tautly past the breaking point. Every morning you woke with a headache you had been aware of while you slept. It was there before you opened your eyes. There was a taste in your mouth like you had been drinking formaldehyde. Every morning was like sobering up from a two-week drunk.

I need a mask, I told the foreman, after a couple of weeks.

A mask? Who the hell are you, the Lone Ranger?

Some kind of safety thing to breathe through, I said, a filter like. Something to filter out the fumes. I get drunk every night.

And perfectly legally too, the foreman said. You ain't been hassled by the law, have you? You'll notice on your pay stub you are not being charged for these drugs. As a matter of fact, you are even being paid for getting high. Drug addicts would tramp each other to death trying to get to this job. We ain't got no masks. The budget don't allow for no safety equipment. Take it up with OSHA.

Perhaps there was an upside to this, I told myself, ever the optimist. This was the twilight waning of psychedelia, of Timothy Leary and LSD, but rumors of mind expansion had drifted down to my hometown through the people at *Rolling Stone*. Perhaps even now my mind was being expanded. Dylan had used LSD, the Beatles had tried it. Writing about mescaline Aldous Huxley had quoted Blake's line about opening the doors of perception. I had always written and was trying to be a writer. Perhaps these doors of perception would swing wide and I would be ceded a wider vision of things. The gift of the world bestowed upon me. The world writ large, infinite distance made comprehensible; the imponderable mysteries of this world printed out in simple block letters like a ransom note. My mind opened to the windy reaches of the universe.

None of this happened. My mind did not expand. My mind went into a darkened house and closed all the doors and windows. It went down to the basement and sat down in the tiniest closet in the house and pulled the door shut.

I had been there a little over a month and the shift was close to over when I dropped a bundle of oars. Lacquer in the vat seethed and frothed like some malignant potion. The foreman came back. Boat paddles had scattered all over hell and some of them would have to be refinished. What the hell happened? the foreman asked.

I don't know, I said. I got dizzy and let them down too fast or something. I think I need some fresh air.

Maybe you need some fresh air, he said, as if he hadn't heard. Go outside and take a break. Curtis's machine is down, and I'll put him on the dipper.

It was very cold outside. A starless expanse of sky, purple in the floodlights it seemed very close to the earth, the air was freezing, going opaque. A few flakes of snow listed and fell. I sat against the side of the building and smoked a cigarette and thought about things. The cold was beginning to clear my mind. Blow out the smoky fumes that smelled like nightside chemicals.

Perhaps I was damaging myself. Perhaps what brain I had was shriveling instead of expanding, drawing down to the size of a walnut. Perhaps things were turning black inside me, organs charring, becoming brittle at the edges, and flaking off. My blood slowing, clotting in my veins until all motion ceased. I might be getting cancer, sterility, impotence. Perhaps generations unborn, generations unconceived, would be tainted by the blight of the dipper.

It was snowing harder when the shifts changed and Curtis came out bobbing and weaving like a punchdrunk fighter, just a few feet this side of the blind staggers.

Goddamn I'm drunk, Curtis said. I feel like I fell in a whiskey barrel and had to drink my way out. Let's get the hell out of here.

Curtis cranked the Chevrolet and waited a few moments for the engine to smooth out. Then he revved the engine and dropped it down into first and stamped the accelerator. He came out of the parking lot into the street too fast. There was one tree there, an enormous elm, and he drove directly into it. He seemed to have aimed the Chevrolet at it and hit it dead center. The hood buckled and I grabbed the dash to keep from being thrown into the windshield.

Where'd that come from? Curtis asked. He had bumped the steering wheel with his mouth and his lip was bleeding a little. He wiped it with a sleeve.

It's been there all the time, I said.

I could have sworn that son of a bitch was over yonder, he said.

I opened the door and got out into the cold. It was snowing harder and beginning to whiten the leaves in the edge of yards, the cold metal roof of the Chevrolet. Curtis got out to inspect the damage. He shook his head as if to clear it, as if when he looked back all would be restored. Headlights unshattered, pristine paint made right. I've ruined my car, he said.

A good body man can hammer most of that right out, I said.

I believe I busted my radiator.

Is it drivable?

Are we on the same page here? Drivable with a busted radiator?

I started up the street toward the highway.

Hey. Where you goin?

To the house, I said.

To the house? Hellfire, the house is fifty miles away.

We'll catch a ride, I said. Come a car. Somebody will stop for us, let's go.

I can't leave my car.

It'll be here, I said. It's not drivable.

Somebody will steal all my tapes. Take my tape player out. Hang around and we will catch somebody when the shifts change.

I'm gone, I said. I started up the street.

How'll you get here tomorrow?

I won't be here tomorrow, I said. I won't be back.

You mean you quit? What'll you do?

Go to the house, I said. If I see a wrecker, I'll send it your way.

By the time I got to the highway it was snowing harder. What will you do? Curtis had asked, and I wondered that myself. I would find some way to make a living and I would write at night. I had no words for the way the snow looked drifting down in the streetlights and I wanted those words. If they were anywhere, I would find them.

I thought of things I could do; I was working on a novel that might come to something but more likely would not. I did not yet know how to write a story anyone would publish. I did not yet know how to frame houses or hang and finish drywall. Perhaps I could devise a territory no one else was working. I might become a sweat expert, I thought. Go out to Hollywood and advise people making movies. You ever notice in scenes where people are working, a chain gang in the hot sun for example, the sweat is never in the right place? They need someone for that, to show the makeup people where it goes, someone who has actually sweated, a perspiration technician. They could create an award for that. And for best art direction, perspiration department, the Oscar goes to…

I went on. I had no way of knowing what might happen. The doors of perception had not opened, and I could see down the road no further than the darkness permitted but I was on that road anyway. It was long but it was straight and wide and clean, and my house lay at the end of it.

I went on into the night. I would just take what might come. And hope nobody starved to death.

READING THE SOUTH

(PAPERBACK EDITION)

In those days the B&O Pharmacy stood on the corner of West Main and Park Avenue North, and since childhood it had seemed to me a place of magic and wonder. I always felt a moment of anticipation when I pushed open the pneumatic door: you never knew what you'd find. As you went in the door, the magazine rack was on your left. On the right, before the plate-glass window that looked out onto Park Avenue, stood the paperback book carousel and the comic books.

By the time I am writing about, I had largely outgrown the furry animals (except for Walt Kelly's Pogo and Carl Bark's Uncle Scrooge McDuck) and the movie cowboys in their gaudy shirts and postmodern gun belts. I devoted most of my time to the paperback rack, though every month or so there would be new issues of *Tales from the Crypt* and *The Haunt of Fear*, horror comics which featured the work of Graham Ingels, an artist I had been keeping up with. He illustrated the old witch's stories with panels so morbid and grotesque they seemed to be decomposing as you read, and rubber gloves were needed to handle them. However, there hadn't been any new issues for some time. I was to learn later that a psychologist had written a book named *The Seduction of the Innocent* that had so inflamed parents and righteous citizens that the ten-cent comics were being blamed for everything from sex crimes to juvenile delinquency. Soon these artists would be looking for other jobs, and the publisher would be out of business.

But on a typical visit in the mid-fifties, I was looking for two paperbacks I had read about: James Jones's *From Here to Eternity*, and *I, the Jury* by a man named Mickey Spillane. The Jones book, I had learned, was the last book edited by Maxwell Perkins, who had been Thomas Wolfe's editor during the years when he was publishing *Look Homeward Angel* and *Of Time and the River*, two books I held in the highest regard. The Spillane book I was curious about because I had seen my cousin reading it.

This was an older cousin who had a job and a girlfriend and an automobile, all the trappings of adulthood.

Let me read that when you're done with it, I said.

You're too little, he said, you'll have to wait a few years.

I read about Mickey Spillane in *True Magazine*, I said. Let me read it.

It's a grown people book. It's full of naked people doing it, he said.

There are no pictures, I pointed out. And Mike Hammer shoots his girlfriend in the gut with a forty-five automatic.

But today neither book was on the rack, though I knew which day the magazine distributor came, and my lunch money was in my pocket. I checked every title, having struck gold here before: the best thirty-five cents I have ever spent was in the B&O for the Signet paperback edition of *A Good Man is Hard to Find* by Flannery O'Connor, but you don't come across a book like that on every trip to the drugstore.

I was so often in the store that I had become acquainted with Buzzy, the clerk who was always behind the counter. Buzzy was a recent high school graduate who still wore the jacket with its school colors and his basketball letter. Buzzy so looked like a typical teenager that he himself could have been an illustration from a comic book.

He looked like Archie Andrews, except for his impeccable flattop haircut, and he even had the right name, Buzzy Bailey. When he opened his mouth to speak, you expected him to say something about a sock hop or pep rally, but he never did.

Got some more magazines for you, he said today.

From beneath the counter he brought up an armload-sized stack of magazines.

There's a new *True* in there, Buzzy said. Got a piece by that Keyhoe fella about UFOs. The magazines all had covers torn off. I had learned that unsold copies of magazines would be discarded after the covers had been removed to be returned to the distributor for credit. Buzzy and I had come to an arrangement: he'd get first choice and pass the rest on to me.

The magazines could be anything, and it was always an adventure riffling through them. *True, Saga, Confidential, Modern Screen, Male*, some pulp crime and Western stories. The junk titles like *True Confessions* and the hunting magazines I could jettison in a garbage can somewhere to lighten the load.

On this day I went up Park Avenue to an older friend who had an office there. Typically, Doc would be in the back with a patient, and I would look around the waiting room. It was like a museum. Doc collected Native American artifacts he had found or bought or despoiled graves for—framed panels of arrowheads so delicate they looked like works of art rather than tools or weapons, tiny, perfectly executed sculptures. A white spear point chipped from some stone veined with red threads. Behind glass a human skull was stained brown with the varnish of time.

Can I leave this stuff here and pick it up after school? I asked when Doc came out of the back.

Stack it anywhere, he said. How'll you get it in time to catch the school bus?

I'll walk home after school.

That's a hell of a walk. It's a long way to Grinder's Creek.

I'll probably get a ride.

Doc sometimes gave back magazines from the waiting room, magazines with good fiction like *The Saturday Evening Post* and *The American Magazine*. I particularly liked these because they often had novellas by Rex Stout chronicling the adventures of his corpulent, genius private detective, Nero Wolfe.

He also had some boxes of paperbacks in a back room. I was going to be late because the school lunch hour was already over, so I didn't have time to look through them again. Doc knew I liked reading and had difficulty finding books, and he had been kind enough in times past to help me out. Doc liked reading himself. I had once asked him who his favorite writer was.

He didn't hesitate. James M. Cain, he said. He's the best writer to ever draw a breath. Everybody talks about Shakespeare. William Shakespeare is not worthy to kiss James M. Cain's ass.

I had liked the first book I read by Cain, but he seemed to fall into a pattern of *femme fatales* seducing folks into committing murders for them. Also, he had a curious obsession with opera singers. I found this a little effete and much preferred Raymond Chandler's wisecracking private eye Phillip Marlow in *The Long Goodbye* or Hemingway's ambulance drivers who fell in love with World War I nurses.

Going home carrying the magazines, I would wish for a ride. Even from Arthur Quillen, who was known to drive with abandon and a reckless disregard for his own life and whoever was riding shotgun. This was a time when, as Robert Penn Warren had written, the internal combustion engine had come into its own. Every young man who was lucky enough to own an automobile was perpetually overhauling the engine or rebuilding the carburetor, boring and stroking, putting in lowering blocks or jacking up the rear end. Social status was measured in horsepower.

Arthur had picked up my father and me once when we were walking from town with bags of groceries. Arthur liked the slow drift of the wheels on graveled curves you almost couldn't negotiate, the throaty roar of the engine when he shot past slower traffic, or the mule-drawn wagons he held in contempt. My father was never quite comfortable with automobiles, perhaps because they did not obey verbal commands. Perhaps he had never understood my passion for reading because books didn't obey either, although he would have bought me all the books I wanted if he was able. This day he slammed the dash with his fist and demanded to be let out of Arthur's car. As we watched the yellow Mercury disappear around a curve, he said, Well, I've rode with that crazy son of a bitch twice now. My first time and my last.

Getting books and magazines had not always been so easy. When I was in the third grade, I asked my maternal grandmother if there were any books in the house.

I don't know why there would be, she said.

This was an allusion to the fact neither she nor my grandfather could read. This was no news to me, as I was charged with walking up to their house every Thursday and reading to them two weekly newspapers that came in the mail. They had left Alabama in the 1930s and settled in Tennessee but still subscribed to two papers, *The Limestone Democrat* and *The Alabama Courier*, to keep up with the doings of folks they had known. Most of them seemed to be dying off.

Read the deaths first, my grandmother would say.

I had come to dread the obituaries. Survived by so-and-so, interred in the Rosebrier Cemetery. My grandparents were old, and I knew death was in the rearview mirror. But it seemed morbid and wasteful to care about nothing except folks who died.

Is there anything about that girl? she asked. For a while we had been following the story of a steel casket dug up by heavy equipment at a building site. This casket had a glass panel inset, beyond which lay pillowed the face of a young girl, undecomposed and as pristine as the day the earth had been shoveled over her. I always thought how terrible it would be if your eyes came open. For all of eternity, you'd be staring through the glass at nothing but impacted earth.

No, I would say, for the story had played itself out without resolution, none of us finding out who the girl was or who had interred her there.

But even if they couldn't read, I reasoned, my grandparents had raised a houseful of sons and daughters who'd grown up and gone into worlds of their own, and surely one of them must have read a book. So I found two books in a closet, at the bottom of a box of photographs of ancient relatives. A thin hardcover titled *1000 Jokes to Make You the Life of the Party*, and a battered, coverless copy of Zane Grey's *Wildfire*. The joke book was useless, and the idea of one of my uncles memorizing jokes out of it and attempting to become the life of some long-gone party was somehow a little sad. The jokes were antiquated and hoary even then and must have predated vaudeville and perhaps even minstrelsy. I still remember one of them: a bandit says, I'm going to rob all the men and kiss all the ladies. A man leaps to his feet and says, You can't treat these ladies with such disrespect. His wife grasps his arm to restrain him. Sit down and shut up, she says. Who's robbing this train, you or Jesse James?

But the other book was something else. *Wildfire* was the first novel I ever owned, and for a while I was scouting around for other Zane Grey novels. As a kid I thought they had everything—gunplay and fisticuffs, romance and honor, great descriptions of Western landscapes.

About this time the high school librarian, who had learned somehow that I was always looking for books, sent me a beat-up and worn copy of Mark Twain's *Huckleberry Finn* the library was discarding. It was the first book for which I rationed myself pages when I was nearing the end, allowing myself ten pages a day. The book amazed me. The wild humor of Pap's drunken monologues, the doings of the Duke and the King's *Royal Nonesuch*, the moment of revelation when Huck says, Alright, I'll go to hell then. It falls off toward the end once Tom Sawyer shows up, but it's still a great book. Hemingway said that all American writing came from *Huckleberry Finn*. I saw no reason to dispute that then, and I see none now.

Growing up I read a lot of books by folks who had been impressed with Hemingway's less-is-more use of understatement and stoicism. A lot of these writers no one remembers anymore, but the last few paragraphs of *A Farewell to Arms* probably inspired more paperback noir than any other book. The scene at the end, when the protagonist walks into the room to look at the lover who has died in childbirth and then leaves, sent a lot of noir antiheroes walking off into the lonely rain, turning up their collars against the cold. Someday someone will write an essay giving Signet books the credit they deserve for educating a certain segment of the young South. For twenty-five cents (thirty-five for *Signet Giants*) you could own a novel you would read time and time again. And Signet had everyone: Faulkner and O'Connor and Truman Capote. Their big gun was Erskine Caldwell, who at the time sold more paperback books than anyone in America (except maybe for Mickey Spillane's Mike Hammer novels—Signet again, naturally).

I was not a huge fan of Caldwell. I was gravitating more and more toward Southern fiction, primarily because of Flannery O'Connor. If Southern writing can be divided into two camps, as some critics have postulated, with the Walker Percys and Eudora Weltys on the uptown side of the tracks and the Cormac McCarthys and Larry Browns on the other, then O'Connor seems to bridge the gap between the two. She wrote a lot, especially in the short stories, about middle-class women from comfortable circumstances, but whose worlds were usually undone by characters like the Misfit from

"A Good Man is Hard to Find" or Mr. Shiftlet (great name, by the way) from "The Life You Save May Be Your Own."

But Caldwell wrote about a type of Southerner I was not acquainted with, and he seemed to deny his characters any dignity or even humanity. He seemed to view them as objects of ridicule, his priapic men all libido, his women all tempting seductresses. Everyone seemed in a perpetual state of arousal even as they starved to death, a combination of circumstances that seemed unlikely to me even as a teenager.

I worked during a few summers for a man named Weiss for whom no one else would work. This was at a time when there was almost no work to be had, and folks were headed north to work in auto plants and steel mills. Weiss was from New England or somewhere up East and had a clipped Yankee way of talking. None of the men wanted to work for him because he had a tendency toward verbal abuse and a sort of unspoken arrogant contempt for the redneck culture he had moved into. He only paid me half of what was the normal wage for farm workers, what was then, believe it or not, about four dollars a day. But I was glad to get it.

He had two enormous poultry houses, each of which housed six thousand chickens from chick stage to maturity, when they would be caught and crated and loaded onto a trailer truck and hauled away. My job was to feed and water them early in the morning and again before nightfall. Eventually, after the chickens had been hauled away, we would clean out the houses and bring fresh sawdust and shavings to re-floor it.

Everyone called him Old Man Weiss, though he was scarcely into middle age, his hair still black and crinkly beneath the pith helmet he wore summer and winter. He was never verbally abusive to me, perhaps because I was all the help he could get. When we were working together, he talked incessantly. His stories were so grandiose that to simply call them lies does not do them justice. He had invented Coca-Cola, he said, only to have the formula stolen by his blackguard of a partner. Though only a private, he had become a confidante of Eisenhower and Patton during the war, and his military expertise had saved them from any grievous errors. He had in earlier days worked in Hollywood as a stand-in for Errol Flynn. That's my swordplay you see in *The Adventures of Robin Hood*, he said. I had to do all his stunts. He wouldn't do them. We used to go out on the town a lot. I used to fix him up with women.

I didn't believe any of this even then, but it was entertaining and harmless and passed the time.

Everyone called Weiss and his wife rich, and I suppose by the standards of the folks they lived among they were. They lived in a new brick house and drove a late-model car. I thought they were rich because I had never known people who subscribed to magazines: each week they got *Life, Look*, and *The Saturday Evening Post* in their mailbox, and his wife, who was sickly and always down with something, would give them to me after they had looked through them. She told me that if I would clean out their garage, she would give me a box of books stored there. They turned out to be paperbacks, a cornucopia of books, a treasure chest of books, mostly Signets.

I discovered *The Grass Harp* and *A Tree of Night* and *Other Voices, Other Rooms* by Capote, *Sanctuary* by Faulkner. I fell in love with the strange, slightly surreal stories in *A Tree of Night*, stories roughed with gothic fantasy: "Miriam," "The Headless Hawk," "The Ballad of the Sad Café" by Carson McCullers, which obviously had been read by Capote. The genius of these paperbacks was that the reader didn't know what he was getting. The covers were usually lurid. Beautiful, young women in peril. Their clothing in disarray, breasts half exposed, their expressions a curious hybrid of anticipation and terror, huddled on a bed of straw-strewn barn floor. A man with his back to the reader's eyes, his intentions clear. Folks read them for the hot sex, the blurbs promised, but intentionally got a sort of education in literature. Also, in the box was a book by the man who invented Southern noir called *They Don't Dance Much*. And naturally it was a Signet paperback. The author was James Ross, a newspaperman from North Carolina who only wrote the one book—maybe one was enough. This book was as noir as novels get. It made the pseudo-tough style of Cain read like *Dick and Jane Go to the Seashore* and reminded me of one of the early short stories of Ernest Hemingway. It was told in the first-person voice of Jack MacDonald in a tough, take-no-prisoners style that was surprisingly frank and ahead of its time. At the novel's beginning Jack is looking for a drink of whiskey. The bank is foreclosing on his one-horse farm. He is broke and being dunned by the undertaker that buried his mother. He hires out to Smut Milligan, a bootlegger and gambler who runs a roadhouse, and the tale spirals downward into adultery and prostitution, torture and robbery, and eventually into murder. The style is simplicity itself, unadorned and beautiful in its understatement. At the end, Jack, like one of Hemingway's lonely protagonists, is headed out into the rain—the stolen money gone, several folks, including Smut Milligan, dead, and the future: a moving question mark.

The book finally became lost and out of print. Here's what the internet is good for: a friend of mine a few years ago had heard me talk about the book so often she searched the web until she found a copy, a pristine hardcover copy, and gave it to me as a Christmas present. It was one of the best presents I ever received. It had been reprinted in the seventies by Southern Illinois University as part of a series of lost American fiction. As far as I'm concerned, this book is where dark Southern fiction began, and any writer who works in the field owes Ross a debt of gratitude, whether he or she has read *They Don't Dance Much* or not.

But there are so many books I haven't mentioned. I haven't mentioned a certified Southern classic, Davis Grubb's *The Night of the Hunter*, which still influences me all these years later. Or the way

I felt the first time I read Cormac McCarthy's *The Orchard Keeper*. Or Nelson Algren's Depression-era New Orleans novel, *A Walk on the Wildside*. I have heard people say that a book has changed their lives. If it is possible that a book can change a person's life, then the book that changed mine, that sharpened everything and brought it into focus and pointed it toward a purpose, was Thomas Wolfe's *Look Homeward Angel*. A schoolteacher saw that I was reading a lot of Earle Stanley Gardner and gave me Wolfe's masterpiece, in the *Modern Library* edition.

This is a young man's book, he said. If you'll promise to read it, it's yours. It's worth a boxcar load of that junk you've been reading.

I began that night, and I could scarcely believe this book. I was stunned by that power of the language. I had not known you could make language do the things Wolfe made it do.

The book was intensely alive. The characters walked and talked and lived their lives and they would not abide the page. The sense of utter October aloneness, the rhapsodic poetry to the stone, to the leaf, to the unfound door. The death of Ben Gant was the most powerful thing I had ever read. Wolfe took the ordinary lives of ordinary people and made them transcendent.

I thought this was a very fine thing to do, and I wanted to learn how to do it myself. That was what I thought then, and all these years later that's one thing that hasn't changed.

But forget about writing the Great American Novel—Thomas Wolfe got there first.

READING THE SOUTH PART II

(FAULKNER'S *AS I LAY DYING*)

As a young boy growing up in rural Tennessee, and already knowing I was going to try to be a writer, I was especially interested in authors who were chronicling the American South. Signet seemed to publish everybody. Thomas Wolfe, Flannery O'Connor, Truman Capote. Their heavy hitter was Erskine Caldwell, who probably sold more copies of *Tobacco Road* and *God's Little Acre* than all these authors combined. I had read all of Caldwell because I read everything I could get my hands on, and because Caldwell's books, being hot numbers in the used paperback line, were widely available.

I was a little put off by him. I was growing up in the selfsame South that he was describing and in similar sharecropper circumstances, yet I did not know anyone like the people he wrote about. I did not personally know anyone who abused people of African-American descent. I had never attended a lynching or lusted after a relative. These people seemed gross mock-ups of the rural poor, with appetites and libidos so enormous their skin scarcely contained them. They seemed shoddy caricatures devised solely to titillate and sell books and convince folks in other regions of the country that everyone down South was like them.

Faulkner never stoops to this. One of the first things that struck me about his books was that his characters were actually people.

I had known people like them, heard their voices. Though Faulkner has written at times about depraved people doing depraved things, he never denies his characters their basic humanity. He does not condescend to them and he always allows them whatever modicum of dignity they are entitled to; his humor and compassion are always in evidence.

William Faulkner took up his pen and wrote *As I Lay Dying* on a sheet of blank paper. He took his title from Agamemnon's speech in the *Odyssey*. "As I lay dying, the woman with the dog's eyes would not close my eyelids for me as I descended into Hades." As he underlined it twice and wrote the date in the top right corner, he must have felt that he was at some sort of crossroads, that something had to be done. Faulkner never doubted that he was an artist, but the commercial aspects of his career seemed at an impasse and he must have felt apprehension about responsibilities he had taken on.

It was October 25, 1929. He had published four novels and yet was working nights at the University of Mississippi power plant, charged with keeping the furnaces stoked for the manufacture of electricity. 1929 was an eventful year. In June he had married his childhood sweetheart, the former Estelle Oldham. It was her second marriage and there were two children from her first marriage for whom Faulkner was now responsible. His masterpiece *The Sound and the Fury* had been published to generally good critical reception, and a few reviews were insightful enough to recognize the book's importance. Joyce was mentioned, Dostoevsky. Yet the first printing was less than two thousand copies. This would be a sufficient number to meet demand for some time to come.

Faulkner never seemed to doubt his ability or the worth of what he was doing, but he must have felt that it was taking the rest of the world a long time to catch up. He was at the peak of his powers when he began this novel. He was in the middle of a creative cycle that would produce *The Sound and the Fury, As I Lay Dying, Sanctuary* and *Light in August* all in close succession, yet he was constantly beset with financial troubles. He had not yet begun his periodic excursions to Hollywood as a screenwriter, and when he set out to write a base potboiler that would sell— "the most horrible tale I could imagine," as he said later—he wound up with *Sanctuary*. At this stage in his career it was apparently impossible for him to even deliberately write a bad book. Advances on his novels had generally been in the neighborhood of two or three hundred dollars: not a particularly lucrative neighborhood. He was better known in France than he was in his own country, and none of his published work had sold in adequate quantities for supporting a growing family. He would not see any real financial security until he was awarded the Nobel Prize in Literature in 1949.

And yet he knew exactly what he was doing. "I set out deliberately to write a tour de force" he said later. "Before I ever put pen to paper and set down the first word I knew what the last word would be. Before I began I said, I am going to write a book by which, at a pinch, I can stand or fall if I never touch ink again."

He certainly did that. From the opening scene, with the Bundren family returning from the field to the house where Addie, the wife and mother, lies dying, listening to the sound of the adze as her carpenter son Cash is already constructing her coffin, with the family awaiting her death to set their fates in motion, there is never a misstep or false note. I believe *As I Lay Dying* to be Faulkner's most perfectly realized novel. I love other of his books, especially *The Sound and the Fury*, but this is the one I return to every year or so, rereading it for the mythic sweep of the story and the sheer beauty of the language.

As Faulkner chronicles the misbegotten odyssey of Anse Bundren and his family to get Addie's body to Jefferson for the burial, there are moments when his rhetoric evokes Shakespeare, Homer, the Old Testament itself. And yet he manages to do this without his narrators ever stepping out of character as they speak or think in letter-perfect dialogue that is always true to who they are; and though their story is told through the shifting *Rashomon*-like viewpoints of fifteen different narrators, it never loses focus. The narrators never bleed one into the other. Each voice is distinct and true to itself and wonderfully accurate, from the first word to the last.

The voice of the son, Darl most closely resembles Faulkner's own, and it possesses a quality Faulkner was drawn to and fascinated with: madness touched by poetry. Here, as the Bundrens work desperately to get Addie's coffin finished and the wagon and team underway before the rivers flood, the natural world itself seems to be conspiring against them:

Cash works on, half turned into the feeble light, one thigh and one pole-thin arm braced, his face sloped into the light with a rapt, dynamic immobility above his tireless elbow. Below the sky sheet-lightning slumbers lightly; against it the trees, motionless, are ruffled out to the last twig, swollen, increased as though quick with young.

It began to rain. The first harsh, sparse, swift drips rush through the leaves and across the ground in a long sigh, as though of relief from intolerable suspense. They are big as buckshot, warm as though fired from a gun; they sweep across the lantern in a vicious hissing.

I came upon Faulkner in my early teens, in used Signet paperback novels. Knowing that I loved to read and had difficulty acquiring books, someone had given me a bag of paperbacks, most of which had lurid covers that enticed you inside. I remember the cover of *Sanctuary* depicting a young woman, presumably Temple Drake, sprawled backward on what appears to be hay. Her clothes are partially ripped open and a man (Popeye, apparently) looms in the foreground, his back to the reader's eyes. His intentions seem clear, though there is no corncob in evidence. The genius of these books was that, while you read them for the sex scenes promised by the covers, you were actually getting an education in literature.

Though some of Faulkner's preoccupations (genteel Southern

aristocracy crushed by the Civil War, race and miscegenation) are not in evidence in *As I Lay Dying*, he does return to a theme he had used before and would use again: the abnormally close relationship between a brother and sister. Darl and Dewey Dell (a great name, by the way—one of Faulkner's best for his sultry seductive maidens) share a closeness that, while not incestuous, approaches the supernatural: Dewey Dell knows, through Darl, that their mother is dying and Darl knows, without being told, that Dewey Dell is pregnant by her lover.

With Addie in her coffin and loaded into the mule-drawn wagon, the Bundrens—Anse and Dewey Dell and the four sons: Jewel, Cash, Darl and the child Vardaman—begin their laborious and circuitous trek. The ostensible reason is to haul Addie's body to Jefferson for burial, but everyone here has their own agenda. Anse, for one thing, wants a set of dentures—his other purpose will become clear in the closing pages of the novel. Dewey Dell has been given ten dollars by her lover and hopes to buy medicine that will induce an abortion. A neighbor has sent cakes to be sold. Vardaman, the youngest, has seen a toy train in a shop window that he wants to see again—he has no hope of ever owning it, he just wants to see it.

"If ever was a misfortunate man," Anse remarks several times in the course of the novel. He blames the road constructed near his home for making it easier for bad luck and trouble to find him. Anything meant to travel is made longways like a snake or horse or a road, he believes. Anything meant to stay where it grows is upright like a tree or a man. It seems, however, that most of his misfortunes arise through stubbornness and wrongheaded decisions. On a greater, almost cosmic scale it is easy to believe that by keeping Addie out of the ground and hauling her decomposing body all over the countryside, with buzzards circling and following, and, in macabre touches of the Gothic, perching on her coffin, by turning her death into an opportunity to fulfill his own purposes, he has outraged not only his neighbors (especially the women, who recognize that a woman's lot in the rural South, especially one married to Anse Bundren, is hard enough already), but the fates that control them and, beyond that, the hostile world itself.

There are set pieces here of stunning power. The first comes when the Bundrens are forced to take a roundabout route and must cross a flooded river, in the process losing Cash's carpentry tools and breaking his leg (an injury that will leave him a permanent cripple), drowning the team of mules, and almost losing Addie's body. Here they have approached the river: it seems implacable, more foe than natural phenomenon. They know how dangerous it is but seem locked into the inevitability they have set in motion. Caught in dread and caught in the caesura before actually driving the team into the water, Darl studies the swollen river and recognizes its sinister undercurrent:

Before us the thick dark current runs. It talks up to us in a murmur become ceaseless and myriad, the yellow surface dimpled monstrously into fading swirls travelling along the surface for an instant, silent, impermanent and profoundly significant, as though just beneath the surface something huge and alive waked for a moment of lazy alertness out of and into light slumber again.

This novel influenced a lot of Southern writers who came later. Ghosts of Anse Bundren, like echoes, show up in the work of several, including my own. The wry comments and ironic humor of storekeepers and country doctors that Faulkner seems to have invented and patented affected the way dialogue was written in later novels, and essentially changed the way characters in Southern novels talked. Doc Peabody (a character Faulkner had used before and would return to again), who has been summoned to attend to the dying Addie, muses that simply the fact that Anse Bundren has sent for a doctor is evidence enough to know that she is already past saving; faced with the prospect of treating Cash's leg, which Anse has cobbled up in a concrete cast, he says, "I be damned if the man that'd let Anse Bundren treat him with raw cement aint got more spare legs than I have." Peabody serves as the voice of practicality and common sense, a counterpoint to the more bizarre monologues of the Bundrens.

In a larger sense the novel was influential to Faulkner as well. The panoramic vision of his "little postage stamp of earth" as he had called it, was becoming clearer. He had begun to paint on a larger canvas. He had named his county Yoknapatawpha and its county seat Jefferson, his stand-in for Oxford, Mississippi. Its geography and its myriad denizens, from the Chickasaws in the primeval forest to the Varners and Compsons and the avaricious Snopeses who would ultimately despoil it, were gaining clarity in his mind and on the page. Stories told by the residents of Yoknapatawpha take on the quality of myth, like real events turned to legend by the alchemy of their constant retelling. Every incident seems interconnected to another. The horse that Jewel rides is a descendant of the spotted horses Flem Snopes brought into the county twenty-five years before, but this story would not be fully told until Faulkner published *The Hamlet* in 1940.

The book approaches its conclusion with a steadily-accumulating quiet power. Stronger occasionally for being understated. Scenes like Dewey Dell's darkly comic misadventures with the drugstore clerk, Jewel's confrontation with a knife-wielding townsman, and especially the rescue of the animals and Addie's coffin from the burning barn, once read, are not easily forgotten.

If Doc Peabody is the practical voice of reason, then Cash is probably the book's most unreliable narrator. But Cash seems to be able to take the world as it is, accept it on its own terms, take things as they come with a sort of stoic bemusement. Misfortune and ill luck are recounted with an almost bland equanimity. Even Darl's fate is treated with a kind of rueful acceptance; this world is not his world.

But if Cash has learned to shape himself to accommodate the world, Darl is unable to shape the world to accommodate him. Darl is the one who realizes that when the tab is added up for this outrage and folly, the sum will be enormous.

It is indeed hard to pay. They have succeeded in burying Addie, but the team of mules has been drowned, Jewel's spotted horse traded to replace them, and Cash has been rendered a cripple. Dewey Dell has not been able to see to her own needs. Only Anse has been able to accomplish what he set out to do. And Darl has paid the highest cost of all.

Darl is sick of the world, sick of life. Outraged by the atrocities being committed upon his mother's body and unmoored by powerlessness, he begins to hear his mother's voice speak to him from her coffin, asking to be hidden in the ground, away from the eyes of men. He is deliberately disconnecting the cables that link him to the material world, his poet's imagination is being ungrounded: "If you could just ravel out into time," he thinks. "That would be nice. It would be nice if you could just ravel out into time."

How do our lives ravel out into the no-wind, no-sound, the weary gestures wearily recapitulant: echoes of old compulsions with no-hand on no-strings: in sunset we fall into furious attitudes, dead gestures of dolls. Cash broke his leg and now sawdust is running out. He is bleeding to death is Cash.

There is nothing contrived about this novel, and when the end comes it is inevitable and irrevocable. It is the finest ending Faulkner ever wrote, and Faulkner was no slouch at endings. The last sentence is devastating, and it seems at once the result and summation of everything that has gone before.

FRAGMENTS

STONEBURNER IN LOVE

Before he fell in love that summer Stoneburner felt that he had attained a measure of contentment that was almost, but not quite, happiness and that it would sustain him all his days. He sensed an almost infinitesimal movement in the hours and minutes and seconds of his life that hot dry summer, as if he were being drawn toward something he had never seen but had known about on some deep level since he had opened his eyes for the first time and now that world loomed about him. He felt on the cusp of something new and foreign, drawn by a force as strong as gravity but that acted under a different set of laws, as if a new and unexplained kind of physics was asserting itself. Something unseen was tugging at his sleeve the way black holes are told to affect the movement of any other body that strays within the pull of their gravity.

It would not rain that year. Crops died in the field. Beads of corn dried hard and sharp as a knife's edge and they would slice the flesh like a blade when they crumbled on themselves and shrank and recoiled like a spider's limbs dancing in a hot globed light. Faultlines appeared in the pale baked earth and the crust dried to a fine powder like dust from a kiln. Had there been a breeze it would have blown listlessly away but there was not. Drinkers at Goblin's Knob shook their heads and tried to remember if they had ever seen a summer so dry. None could. The world had the hot winy smell of scorching greenery. At the Knob, the proprietor, Sharp, said that that crazy Waters witch had hexed the countryside for three or four counties around. An itinerant rainmaker came and burned his chemicals and fired cannons into the implacable sky and ultimately became so embittered that he returned such money as he had collected, and it was told he left for a state so beset with rain folks were willing to pay to have it stop.

Stoneburner was working with a mason that year, building a series of rock fireplaces and foundations and retaining walls for a contractor. He made mortar in a concrete mixer and carried it in five-gallon buckets and wrestled the stones onto the scaffolding then climbed up. Hinson, the mason, was teaching him how to lay rock. He thought Stoneburner, now apt for once, set on learning this craft and he called him Stonebuilder.

Stoneburner liked setting the stones in place, bedding the layer with mortar and casting about for the perfect stone, the one that would make a perfect contribution toward order and symmetry turning the stone just so until it was like setting one piece of a puzzle into the whole. Slicing the drying mortar away with the trowel then brushing the joints with a whiskbroom. The finished stone had a look of ancient permanence about it, as if time itself could not prevail against it. For the first time that summer, Stoneburner could look about and see changes that he himself had wrought upon the face of the world.

He grew lean and hard and bronzed by the sun. When the workday was over the sun still hung flaring in the sky like some imminent conflagration and he would drive his truck down to Sinking Creek where he lived alone in a huge old farmhouse he had rented cheap. It was said the farmhouse was haunted by the ghosts of the family who had been murdered there.

Sinking Creek flowed beneath a wooden bridge in front of the house and every day that summer Stoneburner swam in it. The water was so cold it seemed to have seeped up from a core of ice at the center of the world. Below the bridge there was a sinkhole of a depth Stoneburner never ascertained and he used that year to dive into it, hitting the water as hard as he could and arcing downward, stroking toward a bottom he never touched past jagged stone, his body twisting in the cold still water until his lungs burned like constrained fire and he turned in the darkening water and rose toward the light, rising in a cold black silence, until his face broke the surface like a projectile, being born into the world alive with birdsong and the hot reek of honeysuckle, upturned toward a sky that seemed to ascend into forever and that was a violet cerulean blue so breathtaking and perfect it ought not to exist in this world at all.

On some afternoons Stoneburner would arrive at the Knob before the factory workers and farmers off Beech Creek got there and the place would seem seized in an aberration of time, the cool still interior of the Knob seemed caught in a caesura, waiting for the world to jolt awake and time to lurch grudgingly forward. Sharp might be playing his fiddle so softly it was for his ears alone, some old song that seemed to have seeped through the walls of the past.

Stoneburner would cross to the cooler and get a longnecked bottle of beer and pop the lid and sit on a stool at the bar. Sharp kept the cooler cranked so high there would be crystals of ice trapped in the beer and in the hot air sweat crept down the brown glass of the bottle. He drank deeply, the taste of hops on the back of his tongue. He held the cold glass against his forehead and thought about the girl.

He had gone into Waters's store and, instead of the old woman, there was someone new behind the counter. A slim young girl with long dark hair that seemed to flow down her back. He went down the aisle to the cooler and got a pint of chocolate milk. At the cash register he handed the girl a dollar bill.

God, you're brown, she said. I believe they should have took you out when you were done.

What's your name? he asked her.

Sarah, she said, and laid his change in his palm, their flesh touching for perhaps a moment longer than necessary. Something palpable passed between them and his flesh tingled as if a current of electricity had coursed through it. He withdrew his hand and pocketed his change without looking at it.

He went with the milk outside and drank it sitting on a Coke crate in the shade of the porch. She came out behind him, the screen door slapping to, and stood in the sun looking into a horizon that shimmered like glass. She glanced back at him.

He couldn't seem to move his eyes from her face. There was a curious look on it, and he divined that the look was as old as time itself, and that he was lost. The look seemed the summation of unreckonable moments of all the looks, the essence of knowledge, fraught at once with promise and sinister with implication, and it went back to the moment when the world hung in the balance between innocence and awareness. The moment passed and she laid the apple aside, the excised bite showing the marks of her perfect teeth, the blue eyes widening with curiosity then narrowing in bemused speculation. Her hair looked blueblack in the flat sunlight and her eyes were as deep as the sinkhole and the exact hue of the sky he would see when his upturned face thrust through the surface.

Hey, Stoneburner called.

Hey what? Sharp said.

Who's that blackhaired girl working over at the store at the crossroads?

Leave her be, Sharp said. If I was you I might consider taking my business somewhere else.

Do you know her?

She's some kin to old lady Waters. Granddaughter maybe. Likely as crazy as the old woman, that secondsight voodoo shit runs in the family. So does bad news. I'd let her be.

Stoneburner didn't say anything. He made a series of interlocking circles on the green Formica with the wet beer bottle.

College never learned you a shittin thing, did it? Sharp said.

THE TRACE

The road from Natchez to Nashboro was a rough place. There was no law there and there was no God. God had thrown up his hands in disgust and disowned responsibility for any of it. Denied even the making of it, the granting of permission for it to be made. Another made that road, God said, and peopled it with his minions. There is evil in the world I have not gotten around to straightening out yet. We'll let it run awhile and they will drown in their own blood.

He was sleeping in the front room that year. The house was divided by a dogtrot and on the side there were three rooms, the small parlor where the cot was and the room where his father lay abed and the room where his sister-in-law slept. Sleep would not come that year. The summer held on into what should have been fall. It did not rain and a malign heat clung on resistant as the plague. Crops died in the field. Stars went streaking down the black well of the night in such numbers that the heavens seemed to be depleting themselves, as if they were moving night by night toward ultimate blackness. They'd plunge in blackness halfway across the sky leaving just the streak they'd made burning on his retinas and he wondered where they went when they did that. There was no obstruction, no horizon, just the limitless enigma of the night and they moved like fire focused to a fine line of unreckonable intensity and abruptly guttered like a candle in the rain.

Heat lightning flared and died, flared and died. The window opened inward on hinges cut from leather. He'd tie it back and stand naked before it hoping for a wind to dry the sweat. That year there did not seem to be any wind. The window faced to the south and somewhere to the south was the twin brother he'd betrayed three times already this summer and who, given the slightest of chances, would betray again.

He could hear her, restless, trying to sleep. He wondered was she trying to work up the nerve to ease into the room. He never knew what she was thinking. If she was thinking. Perhaps she just did things on the cusp of the instant, waited until the turn of the card had begun to place her bet. If she comes it will be on her, he thought. I will not go this time, if I don't go, even if she does come it will not count. It will not count.

After a while he went back and lay atop his covers with his fingers laced behind his skull and thought about his brother. How of all the instants there were two that might align themselves. Out of all the times that the door might push inward under the weight of his brother's hand or might not, and all the instants that she might be lying under him or might not, if these two instants miraculously coincided, in all the vast dizzy spread of time it might force things to some kind of conclusion. Any kind of an end at all seemed better than this.

He was up again and standing by the window when she did come. It must have been far past midnight, halfway past midnight, the stars seemed strange, foreign constellations rolled up like configurations he might see from the antipode of his sleepless bed.

Her skin was white as milk; it was lightly dusted with freckles though you could not see them now. Palely, leant with a knee on the bed, she looked like a wraith, translucent as a spectre that had come to warn him of the evil of his ways, of the life he was aspiring to. Her green eyes burned out of a milky mask of a face luminous as a cat's.

He drew her into the bed anyway and, dissolving against his, her flesh seemed to bring with it all of the world, or at the least all of the world worth having. She had unbraided her long hair and where the braids had been the hair held crimps and they turned the light like hammerworks in soft copper.

Andrew Blount was barely fifty yet and he was an old man. Whatever was killing him from the inside out had wasted him to a handful of skin and bones, weightless and dry as cornshucks, something you might kick across in the woods after the witching hour. Something that had not survived the bitter winter past. Leaning to study the caved face as if he might read there already intimations of the darker world imprinting themselves in perverse stigmata, palimpsest, young Blount saw little of the religious zealot who'd handled rattlesnakes and cottonmouth moccasins as you might pet a housecat and drank strychnine that did not even set his teeth on edge and young Blount wondered if such mad faith was already being rewarded, if celestial cobblers were already at work on golden slippers, seamstresses measuring the wasted shoulderblades for the stitching on of wings.

You was always looking for it, Blount silently told the sleeping face. Is it all shaping up the way you thought it would?

He had commenced the serious business of dying sometime during the night. Of course, he had been dying for some time but now he was dying in earnest. Young Saul Blount went into the room. The raspy breathing filled the room. Some machine of destruction seemed to have kicked on inside him; everything speeded up as if to regain a schedule that had been lagging. Some old long ago grandmother had woven from split willow switches an armchair and Blount found it by feel in the darkness and seated himself beside the bed like a member of an audience aligned for the performance of some show that will be performed once then never again, never again.

The night drew on. He dozed and woke with head aching and his joints stiff and the ragged breathing like that of an animal somewhere out of sight in the darkness. He began to think he could discern incremental gradations in the degree of darkness. From black to the darkest hues of charcoal to lusterless and opaque gray, light through the glass of palest pearl. Somewhere a cock cried. Blount's face came forming itself out of sheer nothingness like something in a bad dream. The grain of pine slab walls ran with dizzying complexity. The spirals in the bull ends of logs began to spin in a counterclockwise motion. Sparse furnishings of the room, a drysink, a black walnut armoire, appeared like things that had not been there in the night but were magically forming themselves as if the day might bring forth a use for them.

He could hear her arising in the next room, stirring about, putting on her clothing. The door to the room was open and she didn't bother much about closing it anymore. She came through the doorway and paused and stood for a moment looking at him where the dying and the one left with the contention of the world seemed timeless as its representation caught in dark oils on old canvas might be or some solemn moment graven in stone. She didn't say anything. There seemed to be nothing to be said.

She shook down the ashes in the woodstove and took kindling from the woodbox and laid a fire. She went out with the waterbucket and he could hear the skirting of the well chain and then she came back in and put water on for coffee. He knew she would begin to ready things for the road having seen the old man not long for this world and almost immediately she began to do so, sorting among the cutlery and her cooking utensils, judging what would be essential and what just a burdensome weight to bother with. When he turned, she was raking dried peaches from a stone crock onto an unfolded cloth.

Leave that off for a while, he said.

Everything not done now will have to be done later, she said. It will just be more delay.

Let it rest anyway. We don't need all that anyway. It's like he's holding us up. Like he's not dying fast enough to suit us.

She put the things away and stood by the table watching him for a moment and then she crossed the room and laid a hand on his shoulder, the palm turned inward, the fingers cool and smooth against the side of his neck. The fingers were cool, but he felt if she moved they'd leave scars, the imprint of her palm cauterized, smoking into his flesh.

We've waited too long anyway, she said.

He didn't know what that meant but he didn't ask. He turned the covers up from the foot of the bed and felt the old man's flesh just above the ankle. It had the clammy quality of a dead man's flesh and already there was a degree of rigidity. He felt the arms and they felt the same. As if his father was dying from the extremities inward and whatever life or fire or whatever had moved him jerkily through the events of his life was retreating toward a cooling core at Blount's center. Where it might gather strength and regroup it in faster or it might flicker once then go abruptly as the light goes when you clasp the wick of a candle between your fingers.

I'll fix your breakfast, Rachel said. He didn't reply. He went outside. The heat of the day had already commenced but there was a different quality to the light and the sky looked different as well with a look of immeasurable distances like leaning and peering into the depths of a bottomless well where all the light that remains of the world had pooled. Even the horizons were altered, detail vanishing in the remoteness, the eye charged not only with seeing them but reconstructing them from memory so that it was hard to say what was seen and what remembered. They seemed to have somehow been moved outward during the night. A bank of dark clouds lay in the southwest and they blended into the blue void seamless as the shadow of something enormous cast against the heavens and he thought it might be rain. He didn't see what it mattered. Everything burned in the fields and all the work he'd done was represented by twisted tortured stalks the birds would not even husband and the fields looked the result of some perverse misplanting as if the corn seed had been saved not from a better year but like seeds thriftily saved from plague or pestilence to keep these things from dying out in the world and that was what the fields yielded. He remembered the old man praying wretchedly for rain some time back but perhaps the prayer had been misrouted or backlogged under the weight of more pressing prayers and he thought it a shame Blount would not live to see his order filled.

By his trade Andrew Blount had been a maker and seller of furniture. Young Blount went into the room off the barn that had served as workshop and it was the room where his father's casket was stored. The casket was setting on two sawhorses. It was made of cherrywood smoothed and buffed and stained and it would not have looked much out of place in a fine parlor with a silver service atop it. Blount had lined it carefully with thin copperleaf so that he could await the rapture comfortable in the dry. The corners were mitered and strengthened by copperplate and all the joinings were mortised and doweled, but Blount was not thinking about any of this. He was wondering how he was going to get it off the sawhorses and out of the shop and up the slope to where the others were buried.

He did not even consider pallbearers. There were neighbors of Blounts in Nashboro who'd have an interest in his passing, but Saul had no intention of telling anyone. He was now living in the house with his brother's wife and already the subject of conjecture and a certain amount of gossip about the tavern and he felt knowledge of her could be read on his face.

Once when asked about Paul's prolonged absence he had pretended confusion. They were in a tavern. He had drank off the ale and wiped the foam from his lip and smiled. Saul's is the one down the river to New Orleans, he said. Saul is a single man with no wife to see for and father sent him to sell the furniture.

The man looked as if he didn't know whether he believed it or not. He sort of didn't but then he sort of did, too. He was studying Saul as if there might be some fault to his face that would set him apart from his brother. There was not.

Does he look like you? The man asked.

As much as mirror image except nothing is reversed. Everything is the same.

Well, none would dispute you, the man said. I reckon you can be either one if you want to be.

Once, thrusting deeply into his brother's wife, orgasm about to wash over him like something that would drown him, he had felt his identity shift as if his fundamental being was so fragile it had not permanence or foundation to it and for an eerie moment he had slipped away, annihilated so that Rachel's taut nipples were rubbing against Paul's flesh, Paul's hand was knotted in Rachel's sweatsoaked hair as if it was some handhold that would save him from flood.

He could barely lift one end of the casket. They goddamn, he said. He worked the sawhorse toward the foot of the casket then balanced the casket precariously on the edge of the sawhorse. He took up a length of heavy doweling and slammed the sawhorse hard and it capsized coffin and all. The casket sliding off the remaining sawhorse and slamming the floor hard in an explosion of shavings and sawdust that rattled the floorboards.

He threw a shovel into the coffin and with some effort set the lid atop it. He couldn't even drag it. You heavy son of a bitch, he told it. He saw the ornate casket as an expression of some vanity the old man had hidden successfully in life but could not deny in death. The fanciest thing you ever shoveled dirt over and that worms ever tried to bore through, he thought. He pried the coffin up and set blocking beneath it and found a rope coiled on the wall and tied the rope athwart it in a slipknot and went out of the shop.

The black horse came backing skittishly through the door. Blount had geared the horse for pulling and he looped the rope to the singletree and drew the line tight and leading the horse by the halter pulled the casket through the doorway into the barnlot.

They went on up the grade toward the cemetery. The coffin plowed out a furrow as it went until they reached the pasture where it rode easily on the grass. It looked an impossibly ornate groundslide. Horse and man drew the coffin to a rough alignment with the other graves. His mother's grave and five small others in a line beside hers and he'd often thought how many bitter tears had been shed here over the five diminutive plots, so many tears the ground should have been sown with salt and it was a wonder to him that grass grew. Hopes raised and hopes dashed. How did you go on? He imagined her in black broadcloth sitting beside her children in the twilight. Fading light rosecolored and goldcolored and oblique. He saw her only in his imagination for she had died bearing him or bearing his twin. No one knew which had killed her, but it seemed to him that she had been snatched roughly into the darkness as the culmination of some bargain she'd struck to give him life.

When he went back in from digging the grave Blount had died. Rachel had stripped the bed and stripped Blount and washed the body and dressed him in the black suit he always wore when the call to preach was heavy on him but he lay last in the clothing like a man cobbled up from sticks and twigs. A gross mockup, a viciously parodic image of Blount. Saul stood for a moment staring down at Blount wondering where he had gone. I should have been the one in New Orleans, he thought. I should not even be here. You are a good boy, but you are weakwilled, Andrew Blount had said. I want you where I can keep my eyes on you. You would fall in with the drunkards and gamblers. I've noticed that the jug fits the crook of your arm too readily. You have a weakness for loose women, whores bring out all that is worst in you. They don't even have to expend much effort to do it. You would squander the money in whorehouses and fall in with bad companions and you would be ashamed to come home and I would never see you again. I want you where I can keep my eyes on you.

I could have laid him out myself, Blount said.

It had to be done, whoever did it.

I mean I'm not sure it was proper.

Proper?

I don't know for sure what I mean.

Well, the Lord knows, I don't.

I mean, he would have been ashamed, you washing him and all. Dressing him.

He wasn't ashamed, she said. He wasn't anything at all. He's a dead man. What difference does it make?

None, I guess. He noticed for the first time that she had been crying and he was a little surprised.

He was so thin, she said. So thin there was hardly anything to him at all, you could handle him as easy as a doll. Like a bird that looks big, but you pick it up and it's all feathers and bones. What will you read over him?

I don't know.

You've got to read something.

I expect I have.

In the end he read from Ecclesiastes. He had managed to get the coffin into the ground first because he could not imagine tumbling it about with the old man inside it and he had to lay Blount beside the grave and climb down himself inside the open casket and stand in it and take up Blount in his arms and position him. He read Ecclesiastes about death and the mourners going about the streets and about the failure of desire but the word desire made him think of Rachel and he glanced at her where she stood beside the grave and at the word *desire* she looked up at him. He read on but he wasn't sure his heart was pure or that the reading would take, and he suspected that Blount would have been disappointed in his performance. He had seen the old man from time to time studying him, a look of speculation and he wondered what the old man knew or did not know about Rachel. He had seen or imagined he had seen satisfaction in his eyes as if Saul was living down to Blount's expectations of him. It tumbled with a reality as provisional as a dream someone is beginning to wake from.

Descending the slope after he'd filled in the grave, she ran up alongside him like a child given an unexpected freedom and took his hand. There was no one to see them. No one in all the world whose eyes remarked her grasping his hand. They moved in a grail of light and shade. The shadows of clouds moved over the pasture so that the earth looked ephemeral, an illusion of light and shadow. A darker shadow circled, the shadow of a great hawk spiraling earthward on the updrafts. He looked up. There was nothing. Translucent clouds sliding beneath the sun. No hawk, yet the black shadow darted and checked, darted and checked. It vanished beneath their feet where they stood hand in hand and Blount felt the solid earth itself had betrayed him, opened for an instant to absorb the hawk but beneath his fingers the earth was firm and solid and between the tufted grass, as if expecting to find shards of shattered dark glass, splintered shadows, there was nothing.

Wasn't that the oddest thing, she said.

Late in the day he went up the slope again to the raw grave where Blount lay and past that to the edge of the woods. He sat on a stump and smoked and thought of Blount lying in his opulent quarters beneath the mounded earth with his hands clasped atop his abdomen waiting patiently for whatever would happen next. You're in for a wait, Saul thought. We've just started this mess; you're in for a hellacious wait.

He sat and thought about things. He couldn't take her and he couldn't leave her. He couldn't go and yet he had to. She would be a burden to take and a worry if he left her and there was no one at all to leave her with.

In his heart he believed his brother was dead. He believed he would know that. A thin silver cord that connected half the brother to the other had severed and half had drifted away into the twilight. He did not know when it had happened. There was no moment when he felt the onset of loss. It was just there one morning when he woke, and he suspected that whatever had happened to Paul had happened to him at night.

There were bandits who plied their craft on the Trace road. Men floated down the Cumberland to the Ohio to the Gulf of Mexico and sold what they'd transported to market. They dismantled the rafts and sold them for lumber. Walking back up the Trace was the only road there was. People traveled in groups for the safety that lay in numbers. Larger groups of land pirates came boiling out of the woods and slaughtered them to the last child. There were inns and doss houses where the proprietor drugged your ale and cut your throat while you slept and dragged your body into the woods for the animals to feast on. The animals developed a taste for human flesh. When Andrew Jackson went back up to Nashboro in 1802 he traveled in a party of fifty men. It was a great excursion and he and his bride Rachel slept in tents apart from the slaves and guards. Guards were posted who did not need to be told to shoot to kill and the lovers' sleep was disturbed only by the nightbirds. Travelers to the Cumberland Gap, which was considered a jumping off place into the unknown, traveled in numbers sufficing for their protection. Most of these bandits were white. The white men had been able to negotiate terms with the Chickasaws and Choctaws and Natchez but he was not able to negotiate with himself.

Paul had been gone seven weeks and she was eager to get underway. She had kin down the Trace somewhere on the Tennessee River where Paul had met her. She wanted to know if Paul was alive or dead and he wondered that. If Paul were dead, she would simply shift him into her life in Paul's stead and continue on as before. Perhaps she would begin to address him as Paul. It was even possible he was Paul, as children they'd shifted identities countless times to play games on their father or on neighbors. In the end what did it matter? What difference did it make? He didn't know but the answer troubled him, and he thought there ought to be one and he sat for a time trying to puzzle it out.

After a while he heard the door of the house slap to and she came out into the backyard. She stood looking about for him. She didn't see him, but she turned toward the slope anyway and came on, a thin girl in a long black dress winding toward him graceless as an injured bird, and he felt she must have had some instinct where he would be.

He thought what they ought to do was nothing at all. Stay off the Trace, stay out of Natchez, Mississippi, the longest and bloodiest mudhole in the world, they called it in the taverns. Live here as man and wife. Paul was dead, his bones were scarred by the teeth of predators. They would work the fields and at night she would sleep in his arms and in time she would bear him children. Perhaps twins, they run in families. He had his father's skill with a drawing knife and adze, he could work in wood and carry on the business of Blount Fine Furniture. After a certain length of time people would forget which twin he was. They would remember only that he was not the dead one.

She came up and knelt in the grass. What are you thinking about? Were you thinking about him? She was looking toward the raw red earth.

No.

He had a good life.

He had a terrible life, Blount said. The things he wanted to do were the things he found fault with. He could only be happy doing things and if he'd done them he would have been miserable. That is a terrible life.

I was thinking how foolish this all is.

It has to be done. There's no one else to do it. We could wait until winter. The road would be froze solid then.

Likely we would as well, she said, smiling up at him.

I know it has to be done, Blount said. I'm just talking to myself.

If he's dead, I have to find him and bury him here.

He's not dead.

He's dead, Blount said.

When we find him we'll all laugh about what we thought.

Blount felt there'd be precious little laughing done but he didn't say so. He sat in silence and picked the charred ash out of the bowl of his pipe and scraped it with his knife.

Did you load the wagon?

Yes, he said.

Did you think of everything we might need?

More than we'll need.

Some of that parafined canvas for waterproofing things. It's going to rain.

I thought of everything, he said. We don't have to go if it's raining. We can wait.

We've already waited too long, she said. A little rain won't hurt us.

She was watching in the tense way she had when she wanted to say something she wasn't sure how to say. Finally she just said, Saul.

What?

When we see Paul you're going to want to tell him. To get it off yourself. Don't. The telling could hurt more than the silence and it wouldn't help you.

About us you mean?

Yes. About us.

I won't have to tell him.

He won't hear it from me. Nor read it in my face.

Nobody could read your face. But he'll read it in mine. He'll know the minute he sees me. Before that. If he's alive. He knows it now.

She stood up and brushed the dried stems of grass from her dress.

I think you made far too much of this, she said.

And I think you made far too little.

I've never lied to you about this, Rachel said. You knew I was married. You knew it could never be anything other than what it was because in the beginning you said it could never even be that. Because you don't know yourself. You don't know what you'll do until you've done it.

I know that's what you said.

Then why can't you believe me? I have to cook supper. You know this'll be our last meal here for a while.

It's the last meal here forever, he said.

He sat for a time after she'd left. The day was falling. Just a wirethin rim of sun that seemed to be sinking into a conflagration that flared behind the spiked horizon. Salmoncolored clouds were reefed with fierce metallic light. When the sun vanished, they faded to a dull gray, like forged iron cooling. The very air turned golden, seemed alive, everything was transitory, and everything was in motion. A mauve light swept down, and the gold vanished and deepened, turned somber. As if awaiting just such a moment, a whippoorwill called out of the deep blue timber.

———————

Sometime in the night the rain began and when it did he awoke. He lay listening to the steady drumming on the shakes and to distant thunder rumbling away to the west. She was sleeping against him and she stirred in her sleep but did not awaken. He lay listening to the rain and for something else and then he realized he was listening for the sound of Blount's tortured breathing. He began to imagine he could hear the tortured rasp filling the room and to drown it, he held his ear closer to his face so that he could feel her heart beating and hers was the only breathing he could hear. Her breath was warm against his face and there was a cleanmilk smell to her like a baby's breath.

They were four days out before they approached Duck River and for four days rain fell in a cold unremitting downpour. The very air seemed composed of water and a wet mist rolled out of the hollows like smoke. The Trace in places had turned into sucking quagmire that ran with red mud and at times he was forced to maneuver the wagon onto the shoulder of the road, team and wagon at a precipitous attitude aslant on the slick clay banks and it was a good thing he'd kept a chopping axe handy for he was called upon often to clamber down and clear the shoulder of halfgrown saplings and cedars drooping wetly into the rain and, from these cedars, with the first blow of the axe dozens of sodden birds who'd sheltered in the thick branches would plummet, startled out of their makeshift quarters, on fiercely whirring wings. Toiling on they met other travelers on this refugee road different from themselves only in the direction they were headed. And like themselves they seemed much subdued by the rain and sitting on the wagonseats or trudging through the mud driving cattle or oxen they seemed less individuals, less remnants of humanity but symbols or archetypes of human misery set adrift in the world to serve as warnings.

She sat on the wagon seat beside him and didn't complain. He kept wanting her to complain but she never did. In her black clothing and bonnet and the beeswaxed cloth wound about her shoulders she perched the wagon seat like a sodden and enormously disconsolate bird.

He grinned at her from beneath the dripping rain of his hat. He wiped water out of his eyes. A little rain won't hurt us, he said.

They could smell the river before they could hear it and hear it before they could see it and when they topped out on the last ridge and the river lay below them he drew on the lines and halted the horses and just stared down into a world going to water.

Good God, he said. He glanced at her and her eyes had widened. Her face ran with rain as if she was weeping. Yellow water shoaled almost up to the ferryman's house, and he couldn't even see where a ferry might have been. He wondered if the ferryman had been able to drag it to higher ground or if it had been lost to the waters. The far bank vanished in a mud-red sea that seemed to rotate in a slow clockwise direction and in the center the paler current churned and occasionally he could see the black trunks of entire trees dislodged and spinning lazily downriver. Travelers waiting recession of these waters thronged the banks and some stood tiny as block stickmen close as if to make out just what manner of beast the river had become. He could see other teams ungeared and tied to wagons and wagons thrown with oilcloth to form makeshift shelter and the blue woodsmoke from cookfires guttered in the thick damp air and slank along the ground like dirty grease. The ferryman's house was a two-story brick, opulent for this country which looked taller than it was because of its small width and depth. The house had four chimneys, all of them smoking, and there was smoke from the kitchen situated behind the main body of the house. He thought of fire that engendered this smoke and he thought of Rachel's thin body inside the rooked empire of homespun broadcloth and wondered if the ferryman might rent them a bed and sell them a hot meal and allow them to stand before the fire while their clothing steamed and dried.

He snapped the lines and started down the slope. The wagon began to turn slightly in the mud as if it might overrun the team and he began to ride the brake, applying it, easing off, a dissonant skirling of metal on metal. Going down he met a teamster and his family who'd apparently given up hope of the rain's cessation or any decline in the river's level. Perhaps he sought a way around the river or perhaps he'd given up on the journey entirely. Wagonwheels steered slickly in the mud and the slipping horses nearly floundered on the steep grade and their hooves made huge streaks in the slick mud. The man just shook his head as they met in a gesture that needed no words to augment it and Blount nodded and drove the team to a clearing well back from the shoals and away from the other wagons.

There's probably not a stick in this world dry enough to burn, Rachel said.

We're going to do better than that, he said. He climbed down and ungeared the horses save their halters and stood holding the lines. Let's go to the barn and see if we can get a meal for the horses, he said. And find out about one for ourselves. Hold these lines just a minute.

While she held the lines, the horses stood with lowered heads slack and mute in the downpour. Blount fumbled in the covered wagonbed until he found the pistol in its watertight wrapping and unbundled it and, holding it in the dry, checked the charge. He shoved it into the waistband of his trousers and rebuttoned the sodden coat over it. When he glanced up, she was watching him.

You won't need a pistol, she said. It'll be rougher and bloodier still with you toting a gun.

Yes, it will, he said. But maybe for somebody besides us. Let's find a cup of hot coffee big enough to just swim around in.

The ferryman had died but the ferryman's wife had continued the lease and most of the work seemed done by a halfbreed Choctaw. Some of the men called him Colbert and some Nine Eyes as if he had dual names, one for each side of his parentage, or perhaps his name was Nine Eyes Colbert.

A man named Scrimshaw sold them baskets of oats. These are hard places and hard folks that cross them, Scrimshaw said. I've seen some times so hard I thought the world had turned cold forever. Froze itself up in ice and the thaw a long time coming. I lived in a hollow tree all one winter.

A tree? Blount asked in disbelief.

A tree. There was a salt lick at the roots of it and I lived on deer that came to lick the salt.

It must have been mighty crowded.

Not so. No room much for company but it was roomy enough for me. I never been hard to please. The world will take care of you if you'll let it, if you go in the same direction nature wants to go but cross it and it will destroy you. Fight it and it'll break you like a prisoner on the wheel and rack.

Rachel and Blount stood in the rain feeding the horses for there was no barn or shed to quarter them. Every time Blount glanced at Rachel, she was watching the river with a look almost of speculation on her face. The road that wound from the ferryman's house around the hillside to the ferry just vanished and followed some unguessed course into the swift yellow maw of the river.

They climbed the steps to the porch, but a small wind had arisen, and spray of rain strung off the cornice so that it was little better than being out in the weathers.

The ferryman's wife had come out and stood leaned against the door staring past the men thronging the porch to the valley where the river boiled away into the low. She was a squat woman, sturdy as if she'd been broadaxed of tough dark hardwood and Blount guessed she was thinking about the gold she was losing while the ferry didn't run.

We ought to just swim them across, she said. He just looked at her as if she'd taken leave of her senses.

You haven't even a guess as to when the ferry can cross? Blount asked.

She just gestured toward the yard where the rain still fell and ran in rivulets toward the river and didn't say anything.

We'd like a bed and a meal if they are available, Blount said.

They come dear at times like these, the woman said. My beds are at a premium with the world underwater. Are you man and wife?

Yes, Blount said.

Or passing for it, the ferryman's wife said. She was looking closely at Rachel. I've met you before, she said.

I don't know you, Rachel said.

Oh, but I know you. I saw you in a place they call The Cove In Rock. In company I don't want to mention.

Rachel was silent for a time. Then what was your business there? she asked.

Blount stood looking at the floorboards. Gray water ran out of the hem of his long coat and pooled around his feet. He felt the weight of eyes and looked up. The Indian was watching him. Nine Eyes was hunkered against the wall with his long knees drawn up and he was cleaning his nails with a broadknife. His hands were small and smooth as a woman's and the nails were clean and meticulously kept.

I don't deny I've been around rough folks, but their ways are not my ways, Rachel said.

Or rougher ways than your own maybe, the ferryman's wife said. You're not man and wife. I make you to be brother and sister. You're finefeatured alike and your hair the same color. An ungodly and incestuous lot. Goings-on that are permitted in that cave of perdition will not take place under my roof. Or even on my property. She gave a two-armed gesture so expansive it seemed to encompass the world itself.

To hell with that kind of talk, Blount said. You don't owe her anything.

Some kind of confrontation seemed to be shaping up here and Blount didn't know why. He looked away toward the trees. Through the windy rain they looked nightconjured and intangible as trees the imagination might conjure.

Blount looked at the ferryman's wife. I don't suppose you'd charge for a man swimming a team across, he said.

She gave him a flinty smile that never reached her eyes. I might even pay to see such a thing, she said.

I'd not sleep in this pesthole anyhow, Rachel said.

Blount leaned and spat off the porch. He looked at Nine Eyes. Whose bed does he sleep in? he asked the ferryman's wife.

Her face went for a moment flat and absolutely expressionless, as slack as a dead face in repose.

A man who came scarcely to Blount's shoulder nudged him. Blount turned. A wizened little man wearing a greasy coonskin cap, dirty water was coursing out of it, with one brown eye and one of clear fluorescent blue that was almost luminous. He closed the blue one in a slow wink.

Somebody's goin to die on this porch, he said. And it would be a shame if it was me. He backed down the steps into the rain.

The ferryman's wife looked at Nine Eyes. Get these vermin off my porch, she said.

The Indian unfolded himself. He was a head taller than Blount. He was still holding the knife and a crazylooking smile flickered around his mouth.

Blount unbuttoned the bottom two buttons on the overcoat and held the butt of the pistol against his cupped palm.

The Indian stopped. He was still smiling. You only have one shot, he pointed out.

You only have one brain, Blount said. And if you want a lead ball laid in it take one stride toward me.

The Indian waited. Blount watched the flicker of thoughts. He had the pistol drawn now. Nine Eyes's face said it would and then it thought maybe not. He turned. He jolted the ferryman's wife aside and went into the house. There was an explosive curse, glass broke as if he'd flung something against the wall.

Blount glanced at Rachel. One corner of his mouth was turned up in a curious smile. I guess we know whose bed he won't be in tonight, Blount said.

They went down the steps, Blount descending backward as if he'd see if Nine Eyes came out with a gun. They paused in the yard and Blount stood looking at the river.

I'll see about something for supper, Rachel said. Since I guess we're not eating with the ferryman tonight.

We need to think about this. We've either got to go on or go back. We can't sleep here. He'll cut our throats while we sleep or have a few friends do it for him.

I say we go on.

If we do that then we're going to have to do it quick. Overcast as it is, it'll be dark early and it would be madness to try it in the dark. It's madness anyway.

He walked down and stood with a group of other men looking at the water. He glanced back once and Rachel was going on toward the wagon, picking her way through puddles to higher ground. The man in the coonskin cap came up beside him. The man had put on little wirerimmed bifocals as if he'd study the river more carefully than other men. The roar of water was almost deafening and when the man spoke to Blount he had to shout and Blount had to lean toward him.

You're not thinking about it are ye?

I'm thinking about it, Blount shouted back.

The man grinned and shook his head. He turned to the man next and shouted something into the tumult and the man looked at Blount studying him closely as you might study the very embodiment of insanity.

I believe the swiftness has slackened, Blount shouted.

That's like saying hell's cooled off a few degrees, the man said.

There's them would say hell was just a handy place to warm their hands, he said.

When they'd made a meal from jerky and dried fruit and tea from jars, he put the handgun and Paul's patent rifle back in oilcloth. He put in as well matches and some jerky and dried peaches and what powder and shot he had. He rolled the bundle and laced it as tight as he could draw it with rawhide thongs and just stood looking dubiously at it. He looped at each end a leather strap so that he could sling it across his shoulders and have both hands free for the lines. Then working in the shelter of the oilcloth he melted paraffin with a candle and worked it into the seams.

Are you ready to drown? he asked Rachel.

As wagon and team wound down the road past the ferryman's house men straggled along to watch. The little man in the bifocals halted him with an upraised arm. He was pointing riverward with his left arm where the road vanished into the water. He thought the swirling yellow river looked crazy as if it aspired to some state of madness not attainable by insensate matter.

There's a stream fore you get to the river, the man said. Or was, I guess it's all one now. A stream and a bridge, if you miss the bridge you're lost. It ortn't be under a foot or two of water and there it ain't too swift. Go slow and trust ye horses, let them feel the way. They can tell what's road and what ain't. Angle with the current and don't fight it. Try to aim where yon beech trees are.

———

Blount studied the farther shore and thanked him and tipped the brim of his hat and snapped the lines and the wagon followed the curving descent of the road toward the river. At the point where the road vanished in a seamless yellow turmoil the horses hesitated, and he snapped the lines harder and they stepped into the water. Almost immediately it was about their knees, then up to their chests. He could tell they were on the road though there was little to mark it save scrub brush and the way the wagon felt, the iron rimmed wheels turning steady against the hardpacked earth.

He pulled on the lines and stalled the horses. The roar of the water was overpowering. Everything seemed lost. Road, bridge, any moorings the world might have posted out of all that yellow waste. Trees leaned halfsubmerged and straining against the current. A shattered skiff went by spinning dizzily. Blount didn't even suspect where anything was: he knew back from front, left from right, and that was all he knew: the world was at his back and the flood in front, left was upstream, right down. Ahead of them was an area about twenty feet wide where the current quickened and churned thick gouts of yellow foam like dirty cream. Chunks of wood spun, sank, rose again in endless repetition.

I don't care for the look of this, Blount said.

We have to go on. I doubt we could even turn around.

There was some truth in that. He sat watching the river with mounting apprehension. It didn't look like a river, like water. He thought it looked crazy. It looked like the very focus point of insanity, as if the river had aspired to and attained a degree of madness not normally granted insensate matter.

He listened to its myriad of voices weaving in and out like aberrant threads in a tapestry, murmurous and placating then baleful and malign, gleeful mad laughter and soft ribald banter, then a ceaseless senseless muttering, endless and cyclic repetition as if all the moods of the world were becoming encountered at random.

I'll hold on to you, she shouted into his ear.

A lot of good that'll do, he said. I don't know where I'm going myself. But he didn't even bother to shout. It didn't seem to matter.

When he snapped the lines the horses tossed their heads and looked back as if they'd see what manner of madman had taken control but when he popped them again they leaned into the traces and the wagon rolled smoothly on, the creaking and grating submerged now and moving in an eerie silence with the wheels turning silent as wheels spinning in oil and she slid across the seat toward him and wrapped his waist tight in both arms. Water rose in the floorboards and straw and chaff rode its surface. She moved her feet out of the water, but it came on a swift remorseless tide and she just hung on to him.

At the point where the swiftness began, he realized too late that that was where the bridge had been and when the horses stepped into it, they vanished momentarily and came up wildeyed and blowing, crazed with fear. There one instant and gone the next, the wagon upended and the horses jerked hard to the right and gone into the yellow foam, the wagon turning on itself until he felt the tongue break underwater, Blount himself spinning in mad rotation so that the landscape strung itself out in incredible elongation, an endless repetition of unreeling canvas of burntlooking trees rushing past the shores of the motionless water, the ferryman's house adrift and lost in the flood, black depthless figures of men along the water's edge with arms raised in parodic remonstration, depthless as a string of paperdolls scissored from black paper.

When he went under he felt her grip loosen and stabbed out blindly for her and felt her fingers clasped on his bicep, she turned toward him and lay silent and invisible against him as if they swayed in silence to some mad ballet, spinning slow in an upright position. Until then the wagon he'd thought longgone heaved out of the depths like some malevolent accomplice of the river itself and slammed them hard and he felt the rawhide thong from the pack saw along his neck like a giant knifeblade. The wagon was rising like some enormous sea creature surfacing and when they surfaced he had only a momentary vision of the sky and her plastered hair and wild eyes and they were under again and spinning with the wagon as if the river turned on some shifting and offcenter axis, a wheel against his back as the wagon passed above them. He felt the pack loosen but he was afraid if he released her, he'd release her forever and he worked the thong around onehanded and took it in his teeth and felt for her other hand. He had his eyes open, but the water was almost opaque with silt and debris and she was just a vague sepia wraith swaying disembodied before him. He turned her back to him and clasped her mouth and nose as they surfaced. They came up gasping for air and spitting water. He still had an arm about her and they were swept along with just their faces out of the water upturned so that the rain fell on them cold and clean and hissed in the river. The current seemed to have spat them into the slower doldrums near the river's farther shore. The countryside was streaking away and he turned and saw they were far downriver with the ferryman's house gone and with it all other evidence of the presence of man.

When Blount woke he was lying on his back and it had quit raining. He could hear the river and when he opened his eyes the first thing he saw were moving clouds rimlit by a hidden sun. Their edges smoldered with banked fire.

God, he said. He struggled up and his vision darkened and the world took motion and swung rightward and he sat down again. He closed his eyes and the world moved in a slow sickening orbit. When he opened them, he peered at a tilting world of minutiae, sticks and sodden black leaves, a crayfish that darted backward and vanished in the muddy water as if it closed a door behind it. A stranded black hellgrammite moved like a centipede in the mud in a slow rhythmic agony. Arcane life moved in a slow ballet and no object held precedence over any other.

Are you all right?

He opened his eyes. The world righted itself. She was sitting on a beached windfall combing her hair with her fingers. What sun there was moving in it and it seemed to glow with an inner copper fire of its own manufacture and he thought for a dizzy moment he could have seen her on the darkest night there was.

Have you got a comb? she asked him.

He just looked at her.

Oh Lord I guess you don't have much of anything.

No, he said. No, I don't.

She had to raise her voice to drown out the river. I drug you out of the shallows, she said. By your legs. I thought you were drowned. Then you puked enough to fix most anything there might have been wrong with you.

He felt for the wallet belted around his waist. It was there and such currency and silver as they had was there too. His knife was in his pocket and he could feel its weight without looking at it. I was trying to save you, he said. He grinned weakly and shook his head. I reckon you turned around on me. I reckon you got me now.

I had you already, she said.

Is there anything to be saved? Have you seen the horses?

I ain't seen em since they went out of sight in the river. I don't care if I ever see them again. I wish we'd turned and gone back and waited on him some more. Can we go back?

He looked at her. Then across the vast expanse of roiling water where the far shore lay like a fading dream.

No, he said.

I think the wagon caught in them trees down yonder.

They had the guns and he unrolled the parcel and shook the water out of it. He cleaned the sodden loads from them and wiped them as best he could on his shirt. He wished for oil of some kind but there was none. With the guns lay the flat pint of medicinal whiskey he'd packed. He'd forgotten that but it seemed less than useless. Sulfur matches in a stoppered jar that were not useless.

He went through a canebreak to where the wagon was on its side in a stand of willows. It was banked with soupy thick clay mud and he thrust his arms to the elbows feeling around for anything that might be there. All seemed gone. Clothes, utensils, food. Finally, he fished up a crockery jar with dried fruit seized in a layer of beeswax dripping with mud and that was all he found. He rinsed it in the river and beneath the thin beeswax the fruit looked like something exotic and precious seized in amber. There were a few feet of rope around the pole brakelever and he set the stone for safety and untied the rope and went on.

A quarter mile below he found one horse. The horse itself standing ankledeep in the eddied backwater ungeared by the river with its head lowered as if it were cropping grass or studying its reflection in the still water. Its mahogany sides moved in a steady rhythmic heave and occasionally it flared its hide in a lightninglike shudder to dislodge flies.

He waded out to the horse and stroked its head. That first step is hell, ain't it? he asked. The horse looked up at him and its soft limpid eye mirrored Blount and the world behind him in a veiled anamorphic sepia image with the river rolling ceaselessly like something he was peering at moving inside the horse's skull.

Naked as the day you come into the world, Blount told the horse. Where's your brother? he asked it. Rolling toward the Mississippi River, he answered himself.

He fashioned a rope bridle and led the horse to where grass was thick enough for grazing and hitched it to an ironwood sapling. It wouldn't graze and he guessed it queasy as he himself felt. He went on down river, sometimes on the bank, taking to the shallows to avoid the tangles of blackberry briars and clots of black locust with murderous thorns like spikes in some deadfall laid to snare him.

He went perhaps a mile and a half but he found neither horse or corpse of horse watching all the while with cautious eye the sun between the timbered hills falling swift as a trapdoor in a gallows down the western quadrant while the air cooled and nameless birds moved endlessly over the vast watergone world as if there was nowhere to alight.

This ruin of a world seemed deserted. No survivors of this latter-day deluge save he and one other who hovered at the periphery of his sight like a view of the familiar. If they're all gone it's all to the good, he thought, and felt his sanity veer like the slick flint shale beneath his feet.

He came upon, to his wonder, an entire house uprooted and swept away and set down in a sumac thicket where no one had intended to live. The house set canted on a slope with its windows shuttered but its door open to the world, porch gone and chimney gone save its shape in a chimneyshaped palimpsest of drying mud.

The house offered next to nothing in the way of protection or even shelter for the cries of the nightbirds through the unchinked walls were scarcely diminished and the walls seemed to be less indicative of security than simply a boundary that walled off the larger world or even so fundamental a thing as nightfall itself.

Anybody home? he asked it. He peered in. Floor awash with mud, a loggerhead watching him redeyed from a stone hearth. A ceiling so low it seemed tailored to gnomes or some other form of littlefolk, to children bereft and left to construct their own dwelling, half playhouse and half shelter, left to fend for themselves in the world.

A brokenlegged truncheon table lay against the wall. A section of split leg with augured holes for the legs. Nothing else. Either they had owned nothing, or the river had winnowed it clean. Perhaps the littlefolk had filed into the maw of the river and taken all their possessions with them, bags packed, and fares prepaid to some yellow downriver world where silence prevailed, and the landscape turned forever in a slow drifting of silt.

He went back. She didn't even ask about the other horse. She was sitting on the windfall log sunning herself like a cat on a windowsill. Clothes steaming on a white expanse of limestone. I looked for your comb, but I guess the mermaids got it, he said.

Mudpuppies more likely. They're welcome to it. Did you not get the wagon?

What on earth for?

Can he not pull it by hisself?

Blount was trying not to look at her. He stared out across the river. He looked away from the water toward a greengold world of trees, bushes with thorns so diabolical you'd think only fairytale or nightmare could conjure them. The forest stretched untouched and primeval toward the lowering hills where the idea of roads was heretical or, as yet unknown.

Pull it where? he finally asked her.

I see what you mean.

I guess we foot it from here.

All right. Where are we footing it to?

I don't know. Southeast. So we angle that way and hold to it, we'll come out to the Trace somewhere. The first stand is not supposed to be too far from the ferry.

If we knew where the ferry was.

Well. We can't miss that. Or where it was anyway. Since it crossed the river. Which is it, back up the riverbank or overland across the woods?

The woods, she said. I'm sick of water.

I found a washedaway house down there, he said. Little shanty setting right there like somebody built it in a sumac grove.

You didn't see nobody?

Nobody alive or dead.

I wouldn't want anybody to happen along and see me naked like this. I had to have dry clothes though. Them wet ones were chappin me.

Then you'll have to get your clothes on wet or dry. We need to move.

You're usually trying to get me to pull them off. Now you say put them on. I guess there's just no satisfying you.

I guess not, he said, for a moment thinking what the odds might be that Paul would step out of the undergrowth like his mirror image, lefthanded where he was right, northward bound as he passed south, heel touching as he set toe, the storming copper woman watching cateyed and poised, her own property, nothing that belonged to either of them. For a moment fearful in its dreadful intensity he could almost hear Paul's footfall in the brush, see his red hair through the translucent greenery, hear the remembered cadence of his voice, and he thought they might flee westward instead of south, become fishers of river or diggers of herbs or miners of whatever minerals the earth held, set up housekeeping in the crooked mudfloored house in the sumac grove.

When they came out of the bordering willows and ironwood with her riding the horse and Blount leading, they were in a lush green valley that lay between two steeply ascending hills and day was already beginning to fail. The light thrown down through the trees was first turquoise, deepened to lavender, with twilight it went the deepest of amber, and the black pines and cedars looked undimensional and unreal.

He had come to believe only the world he was walking into existed, that perhaps it was so ephemeral it shifted its shape moment to moment so that it existed as perceived only in the instant he passed through it and that behind him it was already fading. Events and folds and landscapes so seized in nothingness they were gray and static holding their shape momentarily like brittle leaves burned to ash before the wind dismantles them.

A void, an anti-world. Life had not come or had long fled. The world rolled away in a series of scenes each growing a paler blue until at last they had the transparency of deep water. No wind blew and nothing moved in all that world of void. Nothing existed save trees and rocky bluffs and the sky that covered them. He found himself holding his breath. He hadn't known that he'd come this far, that there was so much distance to cover, that the world was that far.

A thunderhead had risen in the west and lay like a tumor. It ascended, clouds stringing away and obscuring what there was of the sun, fleeing eastward in the keep of some wind Blount could not feel. Shadows of clouds moved across the tall grasses like a broad swath of alien light.

The valley began to accommodate itself to the shape of the hills and rising toward them to the horizon the hills met in a bottleneck of sky and when the thunder came it seemed to be coming from there and lightning flickered side by side in this crucible that seemed to contain it, as if the aperture in the trees channeled it. The storm seemed to be fermenting and growing there and the next time the lightning came it ascended above the bottleneck as if it would no longer be contained and ran horizontally like fractures in blown glass as if the dome of the sky was faulted and so whitehot the glare of the lightning's path burned itself onto his retinas in negative image and remained a moment charred to black like a star the lightning had left on the firmament.

Her turned toward her. We got to move, he said. It's goin to do something. We got to get somewhere.

Where? she asked.

He didn't know. He looked around and decided to strike for the nearest trees, in the hollow where the hills met. When they neared them their tops were clashing in constant motion and he could hear the wind bearing down out of the bottleneck and the thunder sounded the constant fire of armaments that the altered air had changed and elongated roll on rumbling roll like the ghost of armament or yet some satiric comment upon them.

MY BROTHER'S KEEPER

The kid climbed up the ridge to the top where it flattened out and then he stopped for a minute and looked at the valley below. He could see the houses, but it did not look the same; but then he could not tell much about it. Rain fell like a blue mist between him and the house and made it look hazy and gray.

Unmindful of the rain he sat down under an oak tree and stared at the house. He took a sack of tobacco out of his inside pocket and rolled a cigarette and lit it with a match he extracted from a can. He smoked the cigarette slowly, inhaling the smoke deeply because he was almost out of tobacco and this was his first one today, and once his hand shook a little. He did not notice. In his mind when he had seen himself coming back to this place, he had not expected to be nervous. It had seemed as normal as breathing and he had known all the time he would return. He smiled a little with one lifted side of his mouth, perhaps at something he remembered, though there had been little enough to smile at, and that was god's truth, but it could have been something his brother Samuel had done once a long time ago or something Judith had said, before he left. Now thinking of Judith this way made him more uncertain still because he had come back to ask Judith to marry him. But between Judith and his brother, he would have had difficulty choosing which one he was more eager to see.

He watched the house for a long time, but he saw no one. A blue plume of smoke rose from the chimney and the wind blew it away into the rain. But no one came out or went in.

Because of the rain, he said, and the sound of his voice surprised him, so that he laughed. He threw the cigarette butt away when it burned his fingers and watched the rain tear away the paper and wash the grains of tobacco. Water ran down his neck, and he tried to adjust the old black felt hat to prevent it, but the water ran off the brim in greater quantity and he gave it up. He took the hat off and shook the water off it. There was a hole in the crown of it so that his black hair was wet too. Water ran out of it and coursed down his face, and he wiped his sleeve across it and put the hat back on. After a few minutes he got up and walked down the ridge to the hollow where he had tethered his horse. I'll come back tomorrow, he said. I'll go down then and just walk up to him.

And later on, just as the November dusk was falling, he found an abandoned cabin with a roof that did not leak too much, and that is where he spent the night.

He walked the horse across the yard and stopped him halfway to the door and walked almost up to the door. Then it opened and a man came out. He stood on the porch and did not go into the yard, for the drizzle still fell, and it ran heavily off the edge of the roof.

Come out of the rain, he yelled into the yard. The kid made no motion to come on to the porch but looked at the ground and his feet and then briefly off at the dark timbered hills surrounding the valley.

Well, I dunno, he said, I'm looking for a man. You know a feller named Leigh? Samuel Leigh, I believe it is.

I'm him, the man on the porch said. Come on up here out of the rain. Wait a minute. God damn! It is, ain't it? He peered out at him. I thought the way you walked—ain't it Caleb?

Yeah, it sure is me alright, the kid said, grinning foolishly, standing there as if he did not quite know what to do.

Well, hell, don't just stand there. Get up on the porch, same as if you had good sense.

The kid laughed and caught one of the porch supports in one hand and leapt onto the porch. Leigh slapped Caleb hard on the back and laughed again, and his face looked as though he could not keep from grinning, as though he no longer had control of it. He kept looking around him as if he were looking for changes that had been made in his absence, and then looking back at Caleb, as though he could not look at him enough.

I clean forgot, he said. I got to put up my horse. Poor feller had enough of this rain last couple of days.

Wait till I get my slicker, Samuel said. I'll walk out to the barn with you. What happened to your slicker anyway?

The kid paused a moment and then said carefully: It was took from me. Then seeing the look in Samuel's eyes, he added, almost apologetically, took in a card game.

Samuel laughed and said, Still the same kid brother, and then he went into the house and came out with two oil slickers.

The barn was warm and dry. It smelled of animals and dry hay, and somehow, to the kid, it smelled like summer. The kid was rubbing his horse down. When he finished, he hung the burlap sack over a stall and hunkered down on his feet. He took out his tobacco and rolled and lit a cigarette. He spoke as he exhaled the smoke and it made his voice sound furry and deep. Couple of changes, here and there, he said.

Things change, kid. Give it a little time, turn your back on it, it'll change. And three years is room for a lot of changes.

That's so, the kid said, and looked up at Samuel leaning against the stall. You changed a little yourself. Boy, you are looking prosperous. You find a gold mine, or turn outlaw?

Just about a gold mine, boy. I'll tell you about it at supper. I'll let you in on it, you turned up at the right time. I looked for you earlier, lot of places.

I wrote some, the kid said.

Yeah, Samuel said, but you sure didn't linger long after you wrote, did you? The kid laughed at this, as if it were some private joke, and Samuel said: Got a whole box of letters I wrote you. Come back, all of em. All but a couple, anyway. Got snowed in last winter, and nothing to do, I got out that box and read em to myself. Every last one of them. He laughed a little. Some of them made pretty good reading. Well, it ain't like it once was. We almost starved once. You remember that? Me and you?

The kid straightened up and looked away and when he spoke his voice sounded flat. Yeah, he said. I sure do remember that. It ain't a thing you forget.

Well, we ain't going to starve no longer. Not us. I seen to that.

They were silent for a moment and there seemed to be an unanswered, or even unasked, question between them, but the kid did not know what it was.

Well, come on up to the house, he said. It's a hell of a lot warmer than it is here. He looked closely at the kid and said, You changed a little bit too. You know that? Your eyes look different. And what're you doing? Growing a mustache?

Foolin' around with it. I grow one, cut it off, just foolin around, have somethin to do.

The kid's slicker was open and then Samuel saw the gun. He saw the way the belt was fitted and the worn, polished-smooth leather holster and dull gray sheen of the gun, and he looked at the kid's face.

I hope you worked all that wild out of you these three years. I just hope that streak in you is gone.

The kid smiled, a flash of white teeth in his brown face, and he said, Oh, yeah, Sam. You don't have to worry about it. Not that. I worked that out, all right. I'm back here ain't I? Didn't I come back?

You won't need that then.

I reckon not, he said, and touched it momentarily, but he did not take it off.

Then let's go eat.

They walked through the rain to the house. Samuel talking a mile a minute as if he wanted to fill all at the once the gap three years had made, the kid beside him silent, but close silent; he was trying to get back the feeling of home. He was trying to get used to just being here.

I got a surprise for you, kid, Samuel said.

A lot of em, I'll bet, Caleb said. You sure are full of surprises, ain't you? Well, what is it?

You'll see. This here isn't just any surprise. This is a big one.

He laughed very loudly, and punched Caleb in the shoulder and almost shouted, By God, I am happy. This is a big day for me, and it just about gives me everything I could want. You coming home caps everything off for me.

Now they were at the porch and they walked across into the house, Caleb heard someone in the house, and he started. Sam laughed. In the kitchen, he said, and Caleb walked fast to the kitchen door. A woman was taking a pan of bread from the stove. She had her back to him and did not hear him.

My wife, kid, Samuel laughed. I'm married, boy!

She turned then but she did not have to. He had seen only the back of her and the yellow of her hair, but he knew from the moment he saw her that it was Judith.

Judith had fried a chicken and there were hot biscuits with butter and honey. There was plenty of cold milk. The kid ate hungrily, and Samuel watched him with something like pride. He kept grinning. Kept filling the kid's plate and pouring more milk till the kid almost choked laughing.

Sam, he said, you're goin to kill me. Every time I take a bite, you shove another one at me. Fast as I can eat, I do believe you can shove faster.

There was a time, Samuel grinned, you could eat a hell of a lot faster than I could shove.

That's so, the kid said, staring moodily at his plate. That is truly so, Sam.

When he finished, he pushed the plate back and stretched and ran a hand through his long hair. He looked at Judith, but she would not meet his eye and she had not looked at him once during the course of the entire meal.

I just don't know how to tell you how good that was, Judith, Caleb said. She smiled and looked at him then, just for a moment, and then looked away.

Thank you, Cal, she said.

He and Samuel rolled cigarettes in silence. After a moment Samuel said, Well, let us in on it, kid. Don't keep it a secret. We want to know where you been, what you been up to. Man goes off to join up in the civil war, it ends, and he don't come back then. Hell, Cal, it's been over two years. Cal looked down at his plate and then took a deep drag off the cigarette.

Well, I'll tell you, he said. I did go off to fight. But I wasn't born early enough, I reckon. I meant to get in it early. I came in on the tag-tail end of that one. They give up the ghost at Appomattox and left me holding the sack. Didn't have nothing to do.

You could have come back home, Samuel said.

I know that, Cal said, and his eyes looked perplexed, as if they asked for understanding. His words were slow and halting. I don't know exactly. Seemed like I was all set to fight a war, and all at once there wasn't any war. So, I started traveling. Hung around New Orleans for a spell; left there. Bummed around a little of everywhere without getting attached to anywhere. Dealt a little cards, played a little cards. Worked on ranches. Started back here many a time, but something'd always jump out in front of me. Seen a whole lot of the country.

Them's the kind of things interest me, Sam said, but I guess they're more fun for me to listen to than to do. You was always more interested in that than me. I bet you seen a lot of things, too.

Yeah, the kid said slowly. The telling of them always comes out different than the way they was, you know that? Like you said, there's more fun in the telling of them than in the doing.

If that's so I don't see why you didn't come home sooner, then.

I was just looking around, the kid said. He looked about self-consciously for a place to put his ashes, and just as Sam said, Hell put them in your plate like I do, Judith got up and got him an ash tray.

Thanks, the kid said. This here is a lot more than I've been used to. This is all going to take some getting reacquainted with.

I'm going to see that you do, though. I got plans for us, boy. When Sam said this he leaned back comfortably in his chair against the wall. He lifted one foot up and crossed it across his knee and the kid looked at the fine stitching on the tailored boot. Sam took a drag of the Bull Durham roll-your-own and somehow gave the impression it was a dollar cigar, he looked so contented.

The kid looked away from him, not looking at Judith, turning instead his face toward the windows and looking out at the night. It was completely dark now and the weeping rain still fell against the glass panes dismally. There seemed to be nothing to say.

Yeah, you sure changed the looks of this old place.

Sam uncrossed his legs and leaned forward and put his cigarette out in his plate.

Give me five years, he said. Five years, Cal, and you won't know this place.

Well, what do you do, anyway, Sam? What kind of fortune have you hooded up with, anyway?

Sam was silent for a moment. The kid picked up the tobacco and began to build a cigarette.

The war interested me a lot too, Sam said. Only in a different way. I knew the wreckage of it. I seen pictures of Atlanta, Georgia, where they burned it. Where Sherman wrecked all them houses, clear to the sea. I read all that. And I started thinking. I knew them people was going to rebuild. There's money in wars. There's money in the tearing down, and money in the building back.

Judith got up and began to clear the table. Sam smiled at her and said, That sure was a good meal, honey. He looked again at the kid, who seemed to be staring at the design of the tablecloth.

I borrowed money. I borrowed, begged, I hit everybody I ever knew. You remember that old mill Jason had? No. Well, you remember Jason. He died, and I bought that mill from his kin. Cheap. I contracted for every log I could get. Without a dime in my pocket, kid, but I knew I was right. A blind hog has to find an acorn sometime, Paw said. We run that mill around the clock, we sawed every log we could get. And we sold lumber. Right and left, boy, ever stick we could saw. Houses they're building all over the country, we sawed their goddamn lumber. Or a good part of it. Right here, and we're shipping it all over the states now.

You still selling it?

Still selling it? Hell yes, we're still selling it. We got back orders on it. We're behind, and the money just keeps rolling in. Like it was falling from the sky, boy. Like it grows on trees, and it does. For me, for us, it does grow on trees, on them hickory and oak and stunty old blackjack.

It sounds like a mighty good thing, the kid said. He looked closely at Sam. When he talked of the mill and the money Sam's eyes grew bright, his face flushed and excited, and the kid looked at him almost in wonder, for he had never seen Sam get excited before. You sure got lucky.

You're right. I was lucky. But it was more'n luck. I knew. I don't know how but I did. And I want to bring you in. A partner. I need somebody with a head on his shoulders.

You reckon I could do that?

Hell yes, I reckon you could do that. You're my brother, ain't you? Didn't I do it?

It sure is a lot to think about, Cal said. He grinned and ran his fingers through his hair. It sure is a lot to stumble into all at once.

I'll break you in easy, kid. Nothing all at once. We'll take our time.

It sounds all right, Sam. It sure does sound good to me.

Now Judith had finished cleaning the table and Cal could hear her in the kitchen pouring water, the clinking sounds the dishes made as she put them into the pan. He could hear the soft movement of her feet in the kitchen and creaking of a board sometimes when she stepped on it.

They sat in silence for a few moments, and then the kid put his cigarette out in the ash tray and got up.

I believe I'll step out on the porch and see how the weather looks.

He walked outside and listened to the rain drum steadily on the tin roof. The sky was dull and solid cloudy. The hills looked like shadows beneath it. He walked to the end of the porch, in front of the dark windows of the living room, and after a moment the screen door opened and Sam came out. He stood in the square of yellow light from the door and looked around.

Cal?

Over here.

Sam crossed over to the dark end.

It ain't going to let up. It's going to rain a while yet, Cal said.

I wish it'd stop. Gets on your nerves after a while.

I like it.

Too lonesome for me. Maybe that's why you like it. Ever think of that?

I reckon, the kid said.

Seems like you never minded lonesome things. You ain't different in that way now. He slapped Cal lightly on the shoulder and laughed.

You ought to get married, kid, he said.

Suddenly there was an awkward silence and the kid laughed shortly to break it and said, I'm a little too young for that, Sam.

It's a sure cure for lonesomeness, Sam said lamely. If a man's got somebody else to worry about it ain't so bad.

I don't worry much, the kid said lightly. I'm like a gambler. I just stay wild and loose and play the percentages. And they ain't no percentage in marrying.

They sat down in chairs and watched the rain course off the tin roof and make little rivers in the bare front yard. The kid could sense that Sam had something on his mind but that he didn't know how to begin, and he knew that Sam was working it out in his head, turning it around and around and looking at it from all sides. He felt a vague anger and almost a hurt toward Sam as if they were children again, and then he had remembered times when Sam had went hungry so he could eat. The silence grew between them until it felt like a tangible thing, and he could feel discontent growing in him. He felt suddenly like he wanted to just jump off the porch and run out through the rain and get his horse and cut out across the valley.

I'll go to New Orleans, he thought, and grinned into the night. And then he thought, no, by God, this is what you wanted so long, and now you're here, and you can make a go out of it or just do whatever happens.

He stood up.

I'm a little tired, Sam, he said. I reckon I'll bed down early tonight.

Hell kid, set and talk awhile. It ain't as if you just came back from visiting. Tomorrow's Sunday. Sleep late.

Reckon I'm just tired is all, Cal said, his voice very low. The old room back here?

Yeah. I'll get Judith to throw some clean bed clothes on the lot for you.

That's all right. He paused at the door, uncertain. He touched his cheek with his hand, feeling the beginning of soft whiskers there. He looked at Sam a moment.

If that's what's bothering you, he said, forget about it. We was kids. There wasn't never anything between us. You ain't hurt me.

For a moment Sam sat silent, as if he did not believe what he heard. Then he said, Is that the truth, Cal?

Damn sure is, Cal said. I'd forgot all about her till I seen her there in that kitchen.

I don't know whether to believe you or not. Never could tell nothing about you.

Cal laughed. You do worry too much, don't you?

Boy, Sam said, if you ain't lying to me, then it's a load off my mind.

Cal laughed softly and let the screen door fall shut behind him.

When Judith put the blankets on the cot, she didn't say a word to him, although she looked at him long once and her eyes seemed to search his face like fingers, feeling. He turned to the window and said, That old rain just keeps on coming, and she did not answer him. She stopped in the door for a moment as though she were going to say something, then she turned and softly closed it behind her.

He got into bed and lay there feeling the strangeness of it. He was not used to the softness. He saw that he had forgotten to blow out the coal oil lamp and lay there watching it intently.

You can believe it or not, he said, just whichever you want to do, and if you don't want to answer you can just sit there and burn, for all of me.

After a while he laughed and got up and blew the lamp out. The floor felt cold to his feet. Then in the darkness he crawled back into the bed and lay there listening to the rain and thinking and it was a long time before he went to sleep.

When they knew for sure that he was coming back after all that time, they told my grandmother about it, and she sat in silence for some time, and then she said, I will never see him. It's all the same to me if he is in Georgia or here, there's not a speck of difference to me. When he left, he left and it's a door better closed. He might as well be dead.

I guess he's pretty stove up, my Uncle Brady said, lighting a cigarette. In the letter he said he couldn't hardly get around, even if they did say it was a mild stroke. He blew out smoke and looked at the fire and his eyes looked very far away and when he spoke his voice sounded as though he were apologizing to someone who was not there. No, he said, You won't ever have to see him, Ma. He was quiet, then, and he looked around at everyone. It was all we could do. There was nothing else. But I was agin it. But he is my father, even if he was no kind of one. In the end it's the blood. If you're blood kin to anyone you can't let them die a stranger in a place you never been.

This was a long speech for Uncle Brady, and he sat there, and his face worked as if he were going to say something else, and his eyes darted around beseeching, wanting someone else to speak. But nobody did.

We sat there this Sunday afternoon, a bitter cold day late in November, and listened to the wind blowing up the cedar row, glad for the heat from the stove. My grandmother and Uncle Brady and his brother Job and my brother Dug and me. But Dug and me don't count. I was fifteen and Dug was twelve, that year. We were family but we didn't talk. We sat there all ears and listened to them talk about the grandfather we had never seen and who was coming back after twenty years.

He's coming back for you, Ma, Brady said. He's going to take you to Atlanta and show you the sights.

She said nothing but I looked at her and I could see her chew her lower lip. She would not look at Brady or any of us. She looked out the window into the dirt yard.

He'll most likely take you down to the burlesque shows. All them night clubs and bars and dens of whiskey and women he could never get out of him.

My Uncle Brady had a streak of meanness in him. He would probe you and search until he found a weakness. Then it would become a weapon in his hands, and he would twist it in you like a knife. All the time he would be watching you with a funny look to see what you would do.

Hush your mouth, Job said. Job was older than Brady and there was no meanness in him. Job let people take advantage of him. People said, Job will let you walk all over him.

Ain't that what he said? Ain't it?

My grandmother's eyes had a glisten to them like the ghost of unshed tears. They were faded blue with memories. She did not say a word. She got up and fumbled for her crutches and started hobbling toward the kitchen. Then, so that we would know she was not going to cry or be mad at Brady, she said, I have to see about supper. It ain't goin to cook itself.

I'll help you, Ma, Brady said, and I knew that in spite of his meanness he loved his Ma and that he could not help his meanness. It was in him. It was blood.

Then I got up and when I did Dug got up too. He kept looking out the window at the way the wind blew the naked brittle tree limbs and listening to the little whistle, lonesome around the windowsills.

We got to go, I said. I guess we better head down the ridge home.

It's cold, Bud, Dug said. Let's stay a little while.

We can't, I said. They'll be out looking for us.

Let 'em look, Dug said. It's colder'n Alaska out there. He began to pretend to look for his cap. He always did that. He'd hide it somewhere so he couldn't leave.

I can't find my cap, he said.

It's under the bed, I said. Behind that box of old books. I seen you when you hid it there at dinner.

Dug was a good loser. When you had him dead to rights, and he knew it, he'd grin and give up. We got his cap and said goodbye to Grandma and Brady. Job walked out into the yard with us.

Boys, he said, if I had me a car I'd sure run you home. If Wesley and his wife was here they'd take you. I dread that walk for you.

It's all alright, I said. Job was always apologizing for things that he had no power over whatsoever. He thought we wouldn't like him because he did not have an automobile.

We started to walk, me and Dug. We were bundled up, but the wind cut cold like knives with blades of ice.

He dreads it, Dug said.

I'm glad he does, I dread for him too. I dread for him to go sit by that nice hot fire while we walk them three miles home.

You didn't have to come. And it won't be so bad when we get to the woods. Pretend it ain't cold. Pretend like you're in Africa and its hotter'n July.

Pretend, hell, Dug said. My doggamn ears is about to fall off and break. Do your ears fall off in Africa?

I don't know, I said. But I do know you ain't to cuss. You been told.

You won't tell. We walked in silence and then out of nowhere he said, I wonder what does he look like?

You seen his pictures. You know as well as I do. And they say he's big like Pa. Pa takes after him, except Pa ain't got no mustache.

Yeah, Dug said. But he could have one if he wanted to. Let's walk fast.

———

Pa was sitting on the porch waiting and our mother was cooking supper. By now it was dark, an early November winter dusk, and I could barely make Pa out. He was sitting in his leather-bottomed chair, smoking a cigarette. When he puffed it, I could see his hands and his face lit red by the fire.

How was they? he asked. He always asked that.

About the same. I always said that.

He's coming back, Dug said. Grandpa is. They got a letter.

Pa showed no sign that he heard what Dug said. He sat for a long minute and then he looked at me. When he spoke, I could see the gleam of the two gold-capped teeth. A flash of gold, sheathed by his lips.

Is that true?

Yes, I said, that's so.

He had a stroke, Dug said. A mild one. He'll probably take Grandma to Atlanta. All them burlesque and bars and women.

What in the name of God are you talking about? my father asked.

Some of Brady's foolishness, I said.

He's all stove up, Dug said.

That Brady has got a mean tongue, my father said. He always did. But I wonder at him coming home. It puzzles me that he'd do that.

Pa said the same at the supper table, when he was cleaning the last bit of gravy out of his plate with a piece of bread. He was sopping his plate. He was using a fork to do it with but that's what it amounted to all the same. Then he said that it puzzled him.

Me too, Dug said. It puzzles me.

My mother laid her fork down and looked across the length of the table at Pa. It don't puzzle me, she said. Not in the least. He's an old man, and he's crippled up with that stroke or whatever. What else can he do? Where else is there to go but to his family?

Some of them places he went during that twenty years, Pa said.

He ain't got no family. He might think he does, but he don't. And he'll find that soon enough when he does get here.

He fixed his eyes angry on Ma, and she picked up her fork and began eating again with her eyes on her plate.

It seems a shame to me, she said. Him having to come to a place where his own kin don't even claim him.

I wanted her to hush, but at the same time I admired her, because I knew what it cost her to say it.

He's blood kin ain't he? Dug asked.

Mister man, Pa said, if I want anything out of you I'll call you by name. He looked at Ma.

You would take his part, he said. You would. I sat there silent and didn't want them to argue. Sometimes Pa can say things in a way where they cut like a knife. Over and over I said to myself, Please, let them not fight. Let him not say anymore. And he didn't. He sat there a minute and then went back to eating. He looked out as if he wasn't seeing any of us, his eyes unfocused on distance, and put butter on a biscuit and laid it on his plate. He laid his forearms on either side of his place.

A thing like that would break Pa, he said. Pa's finally broke then, as he wouldn't do a thing like that. He was always a prideful man.

What's he look like, Pa? Dug asked. Ma motioned for him to be quiet, but there was no need of that; Pa sat there not hearing. It was as if he was a world away. After a while he finished eating and screeched back his chair and went out on the porch.

All the next week me and Dug worked for Uncle Job grubbing new ground. We were working for Christmas money that he was going to give us in return for our getting the field ready for planting in the spring. We worked with double-bitted axes, chopping the young saplings off below the ground and piling the brush to burn. We spent a lot of time by the burning brush piles; it was that cold. The wind would lift the delicate powdered ashes into the air, and they would fall like snow. We worked from early morning till nearly dark. We ate dinner at our grandmother's. It was a strange week, for no reason I can name. It had something to do with Christmas, and part to do with the cold and with him coming, but partly it was me. I felt like I was changing, and it scared me, for I wanted to be a child always, and I did not want Dug to grow up. I wanted it to always be brittle cold November and both of us working there in that field, with birds flying and calling lonesome far above, and looking forward to how good the fire would feel at the end of the day. But that kind of thing can never be, and that is what hurt me like a knife.

I cut the cards neatly into three even piles and Uncle Brady picked up one of the stacks and began to deal them face up one at a time and tell my fortune.

You are going to be married when you are seventeen years old, he said, and turned up a queen and studied it intently.

Who does it say I'm going to marry, then?

Well it don't name no names. But judging from the cards, I can safely tell you that it will be a woman.

That's some relief, I said.

But you are not going to live with her long. You will have one boy by her and then you will separate. After some time you will marry again, from the looks of things a girl away from here.

Uncle Brady was enjoying himself. He always did when he told fortunes. He would look at you like a doctor who has just discovered that you are going to die in six weeks or so and is deciding whether or not to tell you. I have seen him study the cards and then fix his eyes on the person whose fortune he had been telling and have them squirming all over the chair they were sitting in. He went on telling my fortune. It appeared that I was going to do considerable traveling, and never want for anything. And in three or four weeks I was due to get a package in the mail. I knew I would too. Even if Brady had to mail it himself.

What about me? Dug asked. Do I get a package too?

I couldn't tell you, Brady said. I can't tell but one at a time.

Tell mine next then.

Not today.

Why not, then? It's a mystery to me why you always tell Buddy's fortune and never tell mine.

It wouldn't work on you, Brady said. You got to be at least fifteen years old to have your fortune told. Why, you're too young to even have a fortune.

Brady picked up all the cards and shuffled them and put them back into the worn pasteboard box. Then he put them on the shelf inside the old tall clock that stood in the corner. Walking over to the windows, he stared out at the yard. He said it looked like it was going to snow.

I hear the old man's got a trailer. I can imagine what kind of trailer it is too. A little claptrap affair that'll keep out the cold about as good as mosquito netting. He'll freeze hisself to death this winter the way the wind blows over them crossroads.

Is that the part you're giving him to put it on? By the pond? I asked.

Yes, by the pond. The old frog pond. Come spring them frogs'll drive him crazy.

I imagine he's heard frogs before, I said. I was beginning to be a little mad at Brady. It wasn't nearly as much fun coming over here on Sundays as it had been. All he wanted to talk about was Grandpa and the meanness he had done that even he was too young to remember. He talked of the way he had treated Grandma a long time ago, so long ago that to me who had not even been born then, the time seemed vague and misty, like the poison vapor that hangs over a swamp dark with night.

What's he like? Dug asked.

All right, you asked me, Brady said. I'll tell you. He is like sin. He is evil with a shirt and a pair of pants on walking. That is exactly what he is like.

Brady, I said. I think you hate your own Pa.

I do hate him, Brady said. I know, it's not right but I do. I hate him so bad that, if he wasn't blood kin to me, he would not set foot on this place. Anyplace he was, I would want to be far away, so far that I would never have to see his face.

In the kitchen I could hear my grandmother moving around, the slide of her houseslipper-clad feet moving across the old linoleum, the somehow hurried and almost frantic sound the rubber-pointed crutches made when she stabbed the floor with them. She was moving as hurriedly as she could, between the kitchen stove and the table and back again, and I could imagine the mindless moving of pans and banging of them together to close out the words she could not help but hear, and it built up in me so much that I wanted to hit Brady. I got up and went outside and walked around the house in the cold, feeling the cold dry wind take the anger out of me. I walked around the yard and played with the dogs and listened to the wind rattle the loose metal sheeting on the crib. Brady had been going to fix that for as long as I could remember, and it is not fixed to this day. I went there once long after when the old house was empty and the siding gone and the invisible ghosts of them shifting silently and endlessly and restlessly from room to room, with the sounds of their movements (though it could have been the dark rustling of dead tree branches), I thought I could hear them somehow. I could hear the wind, rattling that loose metal roof, lifting and dropping it, eternally lifting and dropping.

I loved her, though. Maybe more than anyone, because she was never old, and I could talk to her. No, not to her, nor did she talk to me. We talked with, not to, and we could talk about anything, and these are some of the subjects we exhausted: foreign countries, and which one we'd rather go to (for her, England, and Africa for me). Do you think there is life on other planets, and why; and the best one: ghosts. She could tell ghost stories better than anyone. Ghosts and warnings, harbingers of death, watching through winter-frosted glass at the wind restless in the pines. She told of a time her mother saw a mystic figure in white cross a field covered with snow, no sound, no tracks, and it was unreal, like a painting, or a half-remembered dream.

The old man came the first week in December, although Dug and I did not seek him that week. The weather had turned bad and we were not cutting brush for Job. It had us ever sour, waiting for a White Christmas, I guess.

THE WRECK OF THE TENNESSEE
GRAVY TRAIN

Pennyroyal was known for seeing into the future and for telling fortunes, but he hadn't seen this one coming. You'd think he would have just woke up that morning and locked all the doors. But no.

They'd blown in one Sunday morning like gypsies, like a band of gaudy carnival folk wended up from a nightmare. Two trucks. A sideboarded one-ton truck loaded with tarpaulined plunder and a pickup truck sitting low on its springs with what looked like refrigerators and cook stoves and washing machines. Both trucks stopped a ways up the driveway past the barn and doors sprung open and folks began to climb out. An ungodly number of them, still more sliding down like eels from the tarpaulined heights of the sideboards. They walked around stiffly, stretching their legs as if they'd come a long way. He watched in disbelief as the man and one of the biggest boys with him hauled out their peckers and began pissing into the weeds along the roadside ditch. Then they aligned themselves in a ragged phalanx along the barbedwire fence and stood looking out across the pasture toward the woods. One of them pointed out toward a great mulberry tree. They looked for all the world like folks picking out a house site.

Lost, he decided. He figured he'd get them turned around and pointed right.

It was the first warm day in May and he was taking the sun in an old lawn chair in his front yard, reading the Sunday paper but sometimes he'd just close his eyes and feel the warm weight of promised summer and breathe the citrusy wind looping up from the cedar row. He'd planned on spending the day doing nothing but this, yet he didn't figure getting these people pointed the right way would take long and he could get right back at it. He folded the Sunday paper and laid it atop an old sewing machine cabinet that served as a table and sat his coffee cup atop that against the wind. He rose and started up the driveway.

They saw him coming, all their eyes on him. He didn't get much company and wasn't used to this. Not as many as he'd thought; they seemed always in motion and it was hard to get a fix on them. A redheaded man about forty who separated himself from the others came striding toward him, hand outstretched like a preacher or insurance salesman. Built close to the ground with his upper torso leant forward as if he could not wait for some place he was about to get to and his feet had to peddle along smartly to keep up. Others. Two grown or halfgrown boys and a skinny teenaged girl, a toddler and a babe in the arms of a carrothaired woman with the darkringed raccoon eyes of tiredness.

You know me? the man called.

Pennyroyal stopped. This was the moment his life altered, and he knew it, not in retrospect, he knew it then. Everything past this moment would bear no relation to what had gone before. Like being dunked in some dark baptismal waters that perversely washed away the good things and left the sins.

No, Pennyroyal said. Who the hell are you?

Damn, you ain't much on welcomin kinfolks are you? I'm Ernest's boy, Alvin. Don't you remember me?

I couldn't remember you if I never saw you.

You must have heard about us.

Pennyroyal didn't reply. Alvin kept hanging onto his hand as if he were hauling the old man from a quicksand bog. Pennyroyal had heard vague rumors drifted up from Mississippi like bad weather moving northeast. Cuttings and shootings and penitentiaries. Ernest shot dead by a whore in a Memphis motel room. Old faded bad news, newspapers the ill winds blew down alleys, lodged fluttering in hedges.

Alvin clasped his hand. It was like shaking hands with a preacher who was thinking about the choir leader's fine titties or a man who was plotting to steal a gun from his brother and blame it on a burglar. Good to finally see you, Uncle Alton.

Sometimes Pennyroyal got a jolt of knowledge when he shook hands, like a jolt of static electricity. It was almost always knowledge he didn't want, and he generally avoided touching other folks but he couldn't read Alvin. Some low level of red like a banked fire. It was like trying to read a mean bull or a biting dog.

We come to help you.

The old man jerked his hand away. He rubbed it with his left as if he'd been burned. Help me what?

Help you whatever. You ain't got nobody. We come to look after you.

Lord God, Pennyroyal said. I don't want nobody, and I've looked after myself all my born days.

You gettin older now though.

The whole world is getting older ever day, Pennyroyal said. You ain't obligated yourself to look after it have you? There must be somebody somewhere wants lookin after. I'm used to livin by myself.

You're our blood kin. Ain't blood thicker than water?

I don't know, Pennyroyal said.

Alvin took a step backward at this heresy. He studied the old man's face as if it were a puzzle he was charged with deciphering.

We never figured on you being this unfriendly, he finally said.

We expected you'd be glad to see kinfolks. But it's a long way back to Tula. We'll set up our tent out in that field yonder and be out of your way come morning.

This was the moment when Pennyroyal could have said, Alright, that suits me right down to the ground. Rest up and just roll on back to Tula or where the hell you can get on the welfare or a job where you can spot things in the daytime and steal em at night. He could maybe loan them a hammer to stake down the tent that had probably been stolen from nomadic evangelists. He knew all this, and he opened his mouth to say it but instead he closed it without speaking. The day had darkened incrementally so that the air had thickened and taken on an amber tint like a world through smoked glass and above the cedar row to the west ulcerous thunderheads, dark as tumors, had boiled up and two Jersey cows had wandered up to the fence thinking it was feeding time and the woman with the tired eyes had transferred the baby to the girl and raised a toddler so he could get a better look at the cows. He was waving both arms at them.

Pennyroyal was studying the trucks. They'd been loaded haphazardly as if wherever they came from, they'd just knocked out a wall and scooped everything up in a frontend loader and dumped it over the sideboards.

What about them kids? Pennyroyal asked.

What about em?

It's goin to storm after a while. That tent'll sail off like a box kite and leave them chaps trying to hold on to the grass to keep from gettin blown away. Come on down to the house and we'll make do somehow.

Thanks Uncle Alton.

Alvin had a tattoo on his left bicep that said BORN TO RAISE HELL, and Pennyroyal had no cause to doubt its authenticity. He suspected it was as true as anything an old graybeard prophet had carved on a stone tablet off somewhere in the holy land and he felt that Alvin was the summation of every trait he'd fought down in his own life, impulses battered down with a two-by-four, like malignancies sawed out with a rusty pocket knife, as if you'd gathered up every sorry impulse and sudden rage and clinched fist and wrong decision and jammed them hand over fist into an Alvin-shaped plastic bag and then tattooed BORN TO RAISE HELL on the arm of it.

They threatenin about the law, Beryl said. They wantin the money.

People in hell wantin ice water and complainin about the heat, Pennyroyal said. But nobody reachin to turn down the thermostat.

How about money, Uncle Alton, did it show me makin a bunch of money anywhere in them cards? What's the symbol for money?

Work, Pennyroyal said. It didn't show that.

Do you believe all this bullshit? the woman named Beryl asked him. All this telling fortunes business? These widows that come ask you is their love life over. What about that mysterious stranger, that secret admirer? Is all that just a number you run on them? Cause everybody's got their number, everybody's running a game on each other as fast as they can trot. Alvin's running a number, I'm running a number. I guess you runnin your own game, too. Can you really do it?

Pennyroyal sat in silence a time. She'd begun to think he hadn't heard. Then he said, I seen a ghost dog one time. I was twelve years old. His name was Brownie and the summer he died I was choppin cotton for a man named Lineberry. I come in from work one day and he met me on the road by the gate the way he always done and followed me to the house. He was a spoiled yellow and white collie and that day his hair was full of beggar lice. When I got to the house, they was waitin on the porch to tell me Brownie got run over and killed by a peddlin truck. I turned and he was gone, beggar lice and all.

Pennyroyal tipped out a Camel cigarette and raised the thin tube of tobacco to his nose and sniffed delicately then put it in his mouth and fumbled out a worn Zippo lighter and lit it. When he spoke his voice was altered by the smoke.

Was he real? I don't know. Was he a spirit dog caught for a while between this world and the next one? Or was he somethin I drawed up in my mind because I knew he was dead? I don't know. I've never puzzled it out. Later I could witch for a stream of water, dig and it'd be there. Bet on it. Sometimes I knowed what folks were thinkin. Knowed what their reasons was. They'd say one thing, but I could see through their faces and they'd not fool me. Before Annie died, I was comin in from the field and I seen a woman in white through yon bedroom window. A hand to her hair. Why's Annie put on that white dress? I wondered. And why when I come around the porch was Annie halfway from the barn with an apronful of eggs? And why when I looked was there nobody in that bedroom? She was gone. White dress and all. Where'd she go? What's it like there? I don't even want to know that. Was it a warnin? Where's the sense in it? What's the use of being warned somebody's brain's goin to freeze up and die from a stroke? Here's the truth girl. This world is a place of mystery and that's a fact, and there's things in it and not in it that folks'll never figure out.

I still think you just been doin it longer, she told him. You're just better at it than everybody else.

You just the organ grinder monkey, he told her. Alvin turns the crank and you just hold the cup for the pennies.

They'd arrived so weary and laden with road dust and road miles, all these bad-luck reprobates who drew trouble the way iron draws

lightning and so shady and shifty he'd found himself watching the
road they'd come on as if to see the dire ethos of their arrival rise
up out of the settling dust. He'd waited for someone to drive up and
clap them in irons and haul them away, but no one ever came. He
imagined folk dusting their hands good riddance and watching the
state lines with trepidation and posting guards there lest they try to
sneak back in.

He imagined them clustered about the telephone waiting for it
to ring like knelt acolytes at some sacred spot awaiting a promised
miracle, and he could hear it in his head going off sudden as a fire
siren and final as the last clap when the gates of Hell slam to.

All of them seemed to be waiting. Himself included. Like troops
becalmed in the eddies before the onset of some imminent and
decisive battle. Beryl and Alvin and two or three of the kids whose
names he hadn't learned were waiting on him. They'd tried two or
three other things and he guessed it had come down to this.

When Pennyroyal came through the door into the living room,
he'd about figured out what they were up to and he'd decided to just
let it roll. He'd slicked his wild hair down and his cheeks were pink
and slick from the razor and there was a smear of talcum powder on
his throat. He was wearing a longsleeved cowboy shirt with mother
of pearl snaps and a necktie with a leaping bass imaged upon it. He
smelled of aftershave and Sen-Sen. He was so clean you could have
spread him out like a picnic cloth and eaten a meal off him.

Oh, Uncle Alton, you look so nice, Beryl told him. Who'd have
thought you'd clean up so good?

Pennyroyal looked at her. I ain't your uncle, he told her. Point of
fact, I don't even know who the hell you are.

It didn't bother her. She just gave him a tight one-sided smile as
if she'd humor him and looked at her husband and rolled her eyes.

Alvin took Pennyroyal by the arm. Right over here, Uncle Alton, he said. Sit yourself down. He guided him toward an armchair they'd dragged out from the wall. They had a video camera mounted on an aluminum tripod, and a bar of high intensity lights mounted on another. The lights were very bright, and Pennyroyal blinked and shaded the lights away with a hand. Turn them damn lights down, he said.

Pennyroyal found himself against his will in this present world of computers that were always running your number and video cameras that were always tracking you and there were many things the old man did not hold with and high on that list were moneychangers and banking establishments. He'd come up hard in the Depression when money was no more than a vague rumor, like some old myth handed down orally, and folks were eating wild sorrel as their main course and hickory nut pie for dessert and stripping the bark from sweetgum and sourwood trees and judging every found object they came upon in the daylit world by whether you could eat it or not. The annoyed old man wanted no dealings with paperwork or safety deposit boxes. Whatever he'd accumulated in the world he wanted ready at hand so that when the wildflowers in his front yard were awash in the rising tide of apocalypse he could snatch up the box and be out the kitchen door and down the steps and gone into the deep timber and vanished like a photograph you'd laid in a bed of hot coals, gone in the blink of an eye to wrinkled gray ash and then dust, no more in this world, no more anywhere.

When he was seated in the chair, Beryl came and tucked a shawl about his shoulders. For sweet Jesus's sake, Pennyroyal thought. We right homey, he thought, maybe he should have a cat in his lap to stroke but maybe they hadn't thought of that. We goin all the way here.

This seemed so professional a job Pennyroyal wondered had they rehearsed, or had they done it so often it was rote. He kept expecting a director wearing a beret and a turtleneck sweater to pop out of a closet and start giving everybody orders. Alvin handed him two three-by-five index cards. Here's what you say, he said. It don't have to be word for word. Pennyroyal looked at the top card. It was covered with neat spidery-looking printing and he judged Beryl, or that oldest girl had wrote it out. Privately he suspected Alvin of being illiterate and figured he had to sign Xs when he applied for food stamps or cashed stolen social security checks.

He guessed they considered him stupid, but Pennyroyal knew what was what. He hadn't fallen off some haywagon on the town square. He was reading through the card. All this? he asked deadpan. It seems like a whole lot to memorize.

Just do it in your own words if that's easier for you. Or read it off one. That'd work. Which'd you rather do, just say it or read it off?

Let's do it both ways, Pennyroyal said. And then pick the best one. He figured pillow smothering would come right after the will taping and he guessed he'd put that off.

Something flickered in Alvin's eyes. No one but Pennyroyal would have seen it, but Pennyroyal was attuned to subtleties and nuances and he looked at things closely. His whole hardluck cornercutting history seemed written there. Pennyroyal looked closely. Something dark and sinister had moved swiftly left to right, left eye, right eye and gone, some dark animal moving in depths of Alvin's atavistic eyes or some godless sea life, some beast you wouldn't want to see paddling toward you up a dark alley. Gone. Then there was just a bovine amiability. Pennyroyal looked away, to the lone inscrutable eye of the camera.

Alvin knelt before him. Broad meaty face, Brilliantined hair, the smell of sweat and last night's whiskey. His hands were tufted with red hair rampant as fur. You know this is the best thing, don't you Uncle Alton?

Why sure, Pennyroyal said.

And we'll look out for you. Sickness or health. Never leave you.

Take care of you till you pass over.

Pennyroyal was maddening. Of course you will, he said.

Alvin placed a hand on each meaty knee and rose. Run through it once, he said.

The old man cleared his throat. He took a pair of reading glasses out of a breast pocket and put them on.

My name is Alton Pennyroyal and this is my living will, he read. My wife Annie has passed on and we had no children that lived. I am alone in the world. I am in failing health. My nephew Alvin and his family have come up here from Tula, Mississippi, to take care of me.

He read on. This was a dispensation of all his property to Alvin from the three hundred or so acres of land down through money and his vehicles and buildings and cattle. It seemed needlessly detailed and was a listing of personal belongings so extensive it seemed to include the toilet paper on the dispenser and the bag of dog food on the porch. The old man hadn't known he'd accumulated so much. He guessed he'd done all right.

Alvin seemed to have wearied of this sorry charade. He wanted it done with. Beryl start that thing and film it. He turned to Pennyroyal. Start over and read it like you mean it.

He'd thought it lost but he suspected some stubborn remnant evil that had taken root in his own soul and grown rampant, some wild growth with horns as long as his fingers and blossoms a bright arsenic green and sulfur yellow. He should have just given Alvin the money and been done with it, but some old compulsion would settle for nothing less than destruction.

I think I pretty well got it, Pennyroyal said. He turned to Beryl. She was stooped and squinting at him one-eyed through the camera. You ready? he called.

I guess it's filming, she said.

Pennyroyal rose and faced the camera. He leaned forward, peering deeply into its cyclopean eye. An expression of benevolence washed over his face. Friends, he said. He raised both arms aloft like one quieting multitudes. Friends, he said again. In fact, he could see the room tending away to infinite distance with walls vanishing and folks standing in mute unknowable thousands, folks straining to see, folks with hands cupping ears, folks holding babies aloft the better to see him. Friends, tonight we stand at a crossroads, he called. His hands made calming gestures lest they grow restive. But it is time to move one way or another. It's time to give your soul to Jesus. Now I want each and every one of you to pick them souls up by the nape of their scrawny neck and tote em down here. I'll tag em one and all and pass them on to you.

Alvin moved so swiftly he might have been a coiled spring abruptly released from enormous pressure. You crazy old son of a bitch, he said. He shoved Pennyroyal hard back into the chair and then jerked him up and slapped him hard openhanded, then slung him into the panel of lights. Lights flickered; alarms rang in his ears. Pennyroyal scarcely knew where he was or what was happening. Before the lights toppled and his head slammed the wall Alvin had already jerked the camera from its moorings and hurled it into the fireplace. He kicked the lights over onto Pennyroyal and whirled and was out the door and gone. The door slammed behind him.

Pennyroyal opened his eyes and the world had the wavy provisional quality of a reflection seen in the water. A world in flux, waves moved on it. After a time, he'd struggled to a sitting position. He pushed an upper incisor with his tongue to see did it move. It didn't but he could detect the bright sheared copper taste of blood anyway.

In the moonlight over all the silver and black world everything seemed imbued with enhanced significance, every tree, stone, flower. Not like themselves but like symbols set up to represent them.

Goddamned if I ain't crossed over the edge, Pennyroyal said. His senses seemed accentuated, he became aware of the very heart of the night, the hour clockhand would drag and stutter and was reluctant to measure. Asleep all alike, the holy and the unholy and even the reprobates and miscreants sort through their sugarplum dreams. Like an elfin cobbler laboring with a tackhammer and the last hour when dreamfolk have them shift at the helm of the world. The clockwork itself whirs and slows and threatens to come unsprung.

He lay still for a time. He didn't know if he'd dreamed but he didn't think he had. He felt he'd been vouchsafed a glimpse into the very clockwork of the world and the sheer random malice of it appalled him. Had he been standing, his knees would have buckled and he would have fallen. His spine went to jointed ice and moved in his body like a viper snake striking, a serpent with faulty dentures and diluted venom. It seemed to him that anything could happen. Anything. Nothing was preordained, guarantees weren't worth fifteen cents, weren't worth the foolscap they were printed on. There were no guarantees.

Pennyroyal cautioned himself not to sleep. He'd warmed up a pocket of comfort under the covers, but his hands were cold for the gun would not warm. Can't sleep at the watch, he thought. Doze off and jerk around, pull that trigger. Shoot off a foot and then where would you be, footless and fancy free. He held the pistol bothhanded between his knees and he could feel the thin hard bone of his shanks. All covered with the comforter he felt like some storybook beast all tuckered out in some grandfather guise awaiting the footfalls of the innocent.

He must have slept anyway for shards of dreams came in fits and starts the way Pennyroyal imagined a cat might dream. Broken images appeared out of the mist and vanished like likenesses mounted on an enormous wheel rolling past him. Like turning over yellowed photographs in a picture box, this face, that face, remember when.

Old boxes of letters, with stamps so strange and sinister they might have been moiled from the other side of this world or the outskirts of another one. Half-literate scrawlings of disasters impending, could he turn these events aside? Could he tell them for sure? Now sadly long come to pass. Will she come back? I hate to say it, but I can't live without her. I'm afraid I'll do away with myself. My seven-year-old child has vanished off the face of the earth. You are my last hope. Here is one of her shoes. I believe my husband has took up with another woman and is trying to poison me. Sometimes the old man felt like one of those sin-eaters who consume the accumulated sins of someone who's died in order to allow the deceased's ascension into heaven. Pennyroyal stayed earthbound, freighted with sins that stooped his shoulders, that clanked like leper's balls when he walked. He couldn't bear them. All he could do was try to keep from accumulating more. Whippoorwills tagged like carrier pigeons flew to and fro but communications had broken down and there were no messages. The letters, like despair, felt like tears, like bitter nights when sleep will not come.

He won't leave me alone, Carolina Jessamine said. He's at me all the time for what he wants. It's like he can smell it on me.

I don't need to hear any of this, Pennyroyal said. Take it on away from me.

He was assailed by a sudden wave of anger, a raging fury at the world itself. Pennyroyal had once owned a cat that would present for his approval dead field mice punctured with tiny toothmarks, carrying them in its teeth across his front yard, and now the world itself was doing that, giftwrapping its sorry doings and unacceptable ways and setting them on the doorstep and standing back, staring into his eyes to judge what his reaction would be.

I don't want it.

As if whatever mechanism inside him that permitted him and sentenced him to fragmented images of other people's future had broken or seized or stripped a gear so that faces he knew and the faces of strangers came and went indiscriminately in a dizzy unspooling, like frames in a film reeling past in jerky and incoherent disorder. In such randomness that a face rolled up for his inspection might not reappear for a thousand years and then in some whole other shaping of the world.

They wouldn't hold still. They were always starting and stopping and then heading off again like malignant spores darting and checking on a glass stick and they were always cranking their cars and heading off in an explosion of dust and gravel and worse they were always returning. They seemed the very essence of shoddiness. As if you took white trash and boiled it until it condensed on itself, these were the dregs you have at the bottom of the beaker; to reconstitute, just add beer or whiskey. There seemed such an ungodly myriad of them he couldn't have gotten a count had he wanted one, they were always in motion and always laughing or shouting and playing or fighting, a motley stairstep bunch all garbed up in loud dollarstore clothes like an enormous and gaudy neon parade that imploded on itself and tee shirts imaged with the likenesses of guitar gods or naked women, the shirts emblazoned with the wisdom of these latter day philosophers: SHIT HAPPENS; SHOW ME YOUR TITS; YOU'LL TAKE MY GUN WHEN YOU PRY IT FROM MY COLD DEAD FINGERS. They'd slide to the periphery of your vision and vanish, look away and they'd have your cash and valuables stashed in flour sacks and shoeboxes and tucked under an arm and gone, look back and all you'd see was where they'd been, masked cartoon burglars who never took a breather and avoided all the things that were gaining on them. I'm some place I never been. I've been walkin toward crazy all my life and now I believe yonder it is over that hill. And I believe my feet have picked up the pace some.

Then he was being ushered down a dream hall toward a dream door by some beast that appeared for all the world to be an enormous badger save that it walked upright like a man. Its big hands were curving yellow claws like a predator and one paw was clasped loosely around Pennyroyal's bicep. This beast gave off an earthen odor; Pennyroyal could smell it. It smelled like clay or fetid river mud, graveyard dirt. The hallway was an enormous earthen tunnel that tended downward. They went on. Steam was rising off the floor and condensed on the convoluted walls and the air was growing hot against his face. He looked behind him the way they'd come, and blue flames were darting up and down the walls and skittering about the floor like flaming mice. He looked up far above his face and the ropes of dirty yellow smoke twisted against the ceiling, coiling and uncoiling upon themselves like serpents. He wondered who was in charge here, why didn't they call some sort of authorities?

They went into a small room paneled in limed oak. A desk that seemed hewn from a single block of walnut centered the floor. Behind it a man sat studying papers in a cardboard file that lay open before him. The man had clean ruddy cheeks and was immaculately dressed in a silvergray gabardine suit and a broad necktie the deep color of twilight and he had a magnificent head of silver hair that lay in waves and ringlets. It was exactly the head of hair Pennyroyal would have grown himself, had he been in charge of such things.

The man smoothed the top sheet of paper with a palm and then closed the folder and turned to the computer screen on his desk. He punched a key and figures and numbers and images flew upward out of all the void of history like bats flying out of a cave and filled the screen. They scrolled upward and shifted and constantly reordered themselves. The man studied the monitor for a time and then he looked at Pennyroyal.

This just hasn't worked out, he said. I'm dissatisfied with you.

Pennyroyal didn't speak.

You've taken far too much upon yourself. You were sent to witness history, not to control it. You've tried constantly to usurp my own authority and twist things to your own ends. You've interfered with the rules of my game. I've set stones in folks' passageway and you've picked them up and toted them off. I've set brush fires and you've wet down your britches' legs and stomped them out. I've set speeding automobiles on a path to collision and at the last moment you've grabbed the wheel and steered them aside. The time has come for a reassignment, for a realignment of your duties. We may have to terminate your association with us.

The heat in the room was stifling, like something enormous drifting toward earth from an enormous height, like a mother leaning to kiss a sleeping child goodnight. Pennyroyal looked down and he couldn't see his feet. They were obscured by shifting smoke. In a window that looked out upon a landscape you'd not want to see, windowpanes warped and buckled and melted down the sashes. This place is afire, Pennyroyal shouted. Why don't you do something?

POSTSCRIPT

LOST AND FOUND:
A ROUNDTABLE ON WILLIAM GAY'S
LITERARY LEGACY

Introduction by J.M. White

An earlier version of this roundtable discussion, conducted via email, was hosted by Suzanne Kingsbury and published in the *Chattahoochee Review*, Fall 2018/Winter 2019, Volume XXXVIII, Numbers 2 & 3 by Perimeter College at Georgia State University. It dealt primarily with the story of finding and editing the manuscript of William Gay's novel *The Lost Country*. For the purposes of this publication, I have broadened the scope of the conversation to include all the posthumous works that have come to light so far. These include *Little Sister Death*, *Stoneburner*, *The Lost Country*, *Fugitives of the Heart*, and now this collection of short stories. The publication of this collection of short stories marks the fifth book published from the William Gay archive.

Soon after William's death in 2012 I was asked by the family to review his archive and was totally surprised to find such a wealth of material. He had been writing all his life and had managed to save most of what he wrote. He came into his own stylistically when he was in his thirties and was writing at the peak of his performance from then until his death but, ironically, he didn't get anything published until he was fifty-nine years old. Consequently, most of the material he wrote from age thirty to age fifty-nine was in the archive.

Working on *The Lost Country* was our first project since there was a contract on the book, and it was much anticipated by his readers. A small group of people formed organically and, more or less spontaneously, to work together to get this material typed and edited. These included Susan McDonald, Shelia Kennedy, Lamont Ingalls, Paul Nitsche, and me. Michelle Dotter at Dzanc Books entered the picture fairly early and brought the resources of Dzanc Books to bear on the project. This basic team prepared *The Lost Country* and *Little Sister Death* in rapid succession. As more time passed and this material began to be read, people would get in contact and the team began to expand to include Matt Snope, an English professor who specializes in Southern literature, Dawn Major, who wrote a master's thesis on William, and George Dilworth who turned out to be an eagle-eyed proofreader. Joe Tidwell is a Southern writer and playwright who has been transforming William's books into scripts and showing them around Hollywood. Greg Hobson, a professional photographer and graphic designer, supplied original photos and some graphic design. Randy Mackin teaches English literature at MTSU and had William lecture at his classes, and Brodie Lowe and Jon Sokol are Southern writers who also helped with this collection. Suzanne Kingsbury and Sonny Brewer were both close friends of William and both contributed along the way as well.

What follows is the roundtable convened by Suzanne Kingsbury for the *Chattahoochee Review* article re-edited with new material. Suzanne put together some questions, which appear in bold script, and sent them out to the people who had been involved in *The Lost Country* editing process. I have added some new questions (my questions are bold and in italics to distinguish them from Suzanne's original questions) and sent them out to the original team of editors plus Matt Snope, George Dilworth, Joe Tidwell, Randy Mackin, Greg

Hobson, and Dawn Major. This expanded the scope of the original roundtable to include everyone who had a direct hand in the editing process and broadened the scope of the roundtable to include all William's posthumous works.

Introduction by Suzanne Kingsbury

If you knew William Gay, you have a story about William Gay. An iconic, timeless, literary giant, William Gay was also one of the most beloved writers of the deep South and beyond. The author of three internationally acclaimed, award-winning novels and three short story collections, William was a rough-cut genius whose work climbed out of the hollows of Tennessee and took the literary world by storm.

I first met William Gay at a reading in Oxford, Mississippi at Square Books, where the literati and book-obsessed gathered a few times a week to hear some of the best writing of our generation. By that time, I had studied his work. The pages of his novels had become softened from my constant touch, dog-eared, and hacked up with pen marks, until finally he arrived in Oxford.

My publisher had sent a copy of my first book to him for a blurb, and I was given the dictum to find out if that would actually happen. He was outside, smoking a cigarette. In the breathless way of any die-hard fan, I tried to explain the depth of my feelings about his books while he smoked and stared at the sidewalk. Eventually, we came to a long pause. Finally, William looked up at me and said, "You want to get a drink?"

That was the start of our friendship. Perhaps everyone who knew William felt a special kinship with him, as though he'd allowed you into the secret hermitage of his literary mind. But I sometimes wonder if anyone really knew him in the way he knew, profoundly knew, the characters in his books. To be friends with William was to feel inspired and loved by him. He had a fantastic mind, and a wonderful dry sense of humor, and people wanted to be near him. William's friendships were built around the centrifugal force of the art—of which he was a procurer—music, film, and literature.

And that's what we talked about, riding through the South on our way to conferences and readings. We were quiet, too, for long swaths of time. We both loved Dylan, and that's how I remember the auditory soundtrack on those drives with William. We were both on book tour at the same time, and we often found ourselves at swanky hotels, William was always getting shepherded to special dinners with media and breakfasts with film directors. After one such event, we were walking down the balcony to the parking lot. "Well," he said with that wry smile, "back to the trailer and the three-legged dog."

William's death in 2012 was and was not unexpected. He was an unapologetic smoker, and he drank perhaps to alleviate some of the shyness he'd borne throughout his life. He exercised only when walking with his dog in the woods to pick ginseng by Swan Creek.

The news came to me one cold evening up north, and I don't think I'd ever felt grief like that before. I wanted to hear his soft voice again, get a hit of the dry humor, hear him recite poetry one more time, show me one of the paintings he'd just made. Perhaps what struck us all most was the literary force that was William Gay had run itself out with this death.

When in 2015, we began hearing that a few of his lost novels had been found, a collective sigh of relief came from the literary world. Perhaps the publication of his posthumous work satisfied a fantasy that may be common to all of us—to experience again the person we thought we had lost.

Most people have stories about the first time they met William Gay. He was iconoclastic and that was apparent as soon as you laid eyes on him. He was also gentle and curious about human nature and what made great art. Can you talk about the first time you met him?

MICHAEL WHITE: For many years I did technical writing for non-profit organizations, and one of my best clients was in Hohenwald, a small Tennessee town of about three thousand people. I read *Provinces of Night* and *The Long Home* and was astonished that a writer of his power and talent had been born and raised in this obscure little rural town. I started asking around, but no one knew him. A few people knew some of the family members, especially William's Uncle Scott, who was a famous psychic. However, Scott had been dead for several years, so that was no help.

I drove around different parts of the county and asked at local stores and in neighborhoods. One woman was raking leaves in the front yard. I asked if she had ever heard of William Gay; she leaned on her rake and looked at me, "Yes, I've heard of him, but I don't think you should go looking for him. I hear he might pull a gun on you." I went on my way, more intrigued than ever.

Eventually, I found a farmer who knew one of William's daughters, and he told me how to get to her place. When I drove up to her house, the yard was full of old vehicles, four wheelers, motorcycles, go-karts, trucks, the earth mostly bare, un-mowed clumps of weeds here and there. A young woman came out of a house carrying a boy on her hip. It was his youngest daughter and she assured me it would be alright to go see him and gave me directions. I couldn't believe my luck.

I followed her directions to Grinder's Creek Road and pulled up to the first trailer on the right, a dilapidated single-wide on a scruffy lot. An old white pit bull came across the yard, and a man stepped out. He called the dog Knuckles and said he wouldn't bother me. I had a copy of *Provinces of Night* in my hand and introduced myself. He invited me in, and I stepped through the front door into his living room. There was a couch and an overstuffed chair. Both had the legs removed, so they sat on the floor. There was a coffee table covered with magazines, an ashtray overflowing with cigarette butts, and across the room was a state-of-the-art flatscreen, a stereo component system with big speakers and shelves full of CDs and DVDs. He motioned for me to sit down. He agreed to sign my book. But as he did I could tell he was very uncomfortable. Obviously having fans drive up was not one of his favorite things. I thought I should beat a hasty retreat as soon as possible. I decided to ask a couple of questions before I got out of there and left him alone.

"If you don't mind, are you working on anything new?"

"Yes, I just submitted an article to *Oxford American*, about Harry Smith."

"Harry was an old friend of mine."

William looked up quickly and gave me a piercing stare. "Really, you knew Harry Smith?"

"Yep, I loved Harry. We were friends for the last three years of his life. He was an amazing guy."

"Well, shit, I wish you had come around here before I submitted the article, I tried to find someone who knew him but couldn't make contact with anyone."

I could see a change come over William as I told him stories about Harry Smith. He was now totally relaxed and more than happy to sit and talk for a while. I was relieved but still thought the wisest thing was to get out of there and not sit around talking for a long time so I quickly thanked him and got up to go. As I was leaving he invited me to stop back next time I was in town, and I was off.

I was amazed after reading his books to find him living in such circumstances, although that type of lifestyle was certainly reflected in his books. It was one of those great meetings that happen from time to time if you are lucky.

LAMONT INGALLS: I first met William through Michael White. Michael and I met in March 2001 in Lebanon, Tennessee. Michael told me about William Gay, "this novelist living in Lewis County," and suggested that I read his books.

I was born and raised in Nashville and have been reading Southern writers since the mid-1960s, when I found Faulkner's *The Sound and the Fury* at the Nashville Public Library. Flannery O'Connor and Cormac McCarthy were also longstanding favorites. I had not previously heard of William Gay.

After returning to my cottage in Florida, I read William's first two novels, *The Long Home* and *Provinces of Night*, and became a self-confirmed admirer of this talented, insightful, and somewhat enigmatic author. So, when I met William in Hohenwald in the spring of 2005, I was already enamored of his well-phrased dialog and his characterizations of both person and landscape. With Michael—whom William sometimes called "the Professor"—as an intermediary, I spent a fine spring evening listening in on William's comments about literature, at his home, well-furnished with music, movies on tape and DVD, and shelves and stacks of books and magazines, and more magazines and books.

That evening we found a mutual literary territory in McCarthy and O'Connor and a shared admiration for John D. MacDonald's books featuring Travis McGee, a "knight in tarnished armor" who lives aboard a houseboat in "Fort Lauderdamndale." Another MacDonald, Ross, a writer of detective tales, was also favored by William.

That first meeting I also witnessed William's ability to recite long passages from Flannery O'Connor, an admirable and entertaining skill. He was fabled for having a photographic memory, and I could readily attest to this gift. I recall this first gathering at his cabin as just a simple sharing of two-three hours, probably ordinary for William, but auspicious for me. I had met a few authors before, in New

Orleans and Washington, DC, but this quiet evening get-together beside Swan Creek is one I continue to treasure.

A few years later, Michael asked me to work on a book of William's collected prose that Michael's small publishing house, Wild Dog Press, was producing. I readily agreed, honored to support William's literary legacy. Michael compiled the book from William's previously published prose: short stories, essays, and music criticism. As a lagniappe, the book, *Time Done Been Won't Be No More*, included color plates of eight of William's paintings. I worked on this book as designer, proofreader and editorial consultant, and it was published in 2010. In early 2018, Anomolaic published William's Southern detective noir novel, *Stoneburner*, another production of Team Gay.

SHELIA KENNEDY: I first saw William at literary events in Nashville and Clarksville and, as luck would have it, on the set of *That Evening Sun* (the movie based on William's short story "I Hate To See That Evening Sun Go Down"). One of the farms used for that film is the family farm of my brother-in-law, so my mother and I went to East Tennessee for the final night of filming; William and his family were there.

Fast forward to the following summer when William was speaking at Austin Peay State University in Clarksville. A friend and I went to see him. I had photographs that my sister had made during filming of the movie to give William. When I presented them to him, he gave me his phone number and asked that I call him. I had a broken ankle that summer and had plenty of time to read and talk, so I would call William and we would talk about books and music.

In 2010 and 2011, I gladly volunteered to be William's driver to and from Clarksville for the Clarksville Writers Conference—more time to talk. I think the last time that I saw William was at The Southern Festival of Books in October 2011. The chairwoman for

Clarksville Writers Conference wanted him to participate in the 2012 conference and told William that he could do whatever he wanted at the conference and asked what he liked most about coming to Clarksville. He said, "Riding around with Shelia and talking."

SUSAN McDONALD: I knew William through my relationship with Michael. I went to his readings, visited him in his home, and accompanied him to appearances on occasion. He was such a humble and likeable man that people were enthralled to be in his presence. We were told that during a teaching stay at Sewanee, the students loved him and took every opportunity to hang out with him. He was really a character from his own books, somewhat shy and almost embarrassed by adulation, transparent, generous, appreciative, candid, homespun in his manner, and full of dry humor. In early February 2012, Michael and I were very excited because of an impending visit from William. The day before his visit, we learned that he had died the night before. He was not well due to a heart condition but was reluctant to spend much time around doctors, which, in retrospect, might have hastened his death.

GREG HOBSON: The first time I read anything William had written was just a lucky accident. I had ridden my motorcycle to a small Kansas town that was home to a bookstore where I'd gotten good deals in the past. I was looking through shelves of hardcover books whose pages had been marked along their top edges with streaks of black ink designating them as "cut-outs"—books someone had deemed not worthy of buying at full price. I saw *Provinces of Night* and chose it simply because I liked the cover.

At home, I was just a page or two into the story when I realized I had stumbled onto something special. A few pages farther, and I knew I had stepped into something beyond special and was reading a piece of true literature that was taking me well into a place where only the rarest talent lived. I turned back to the beginning and gave the book a fresh start, this time taking it in much more slowly and savoring every sentence.

Before long, I dug out a yellow highlighter and began marking passages I found especially wonderful. A half hour later, I noticed that page after page contained more yellow than white. I got on the internet and sent off for *The Long Home* and *Twilight* and *I Hate to See That Evening Sun Go Down,* and I read whatever I could find about William Gay. This was fall of 2007. I was fifty-eight, and what amazed me more than anything about the man was that he'd gotten nothing published until he was fifty-five years of age (or maybe older, I discovered when I learned that William granted himself a dose of creative license when it came to his date of birth).

Curious and hungry for more than I would ever find this way, I looked up his address and wrote him a letter telling him how his words spoke to me and asking when his next novel would be published. I had included a stamped self-addressed envelope, hoping he would write back. But that's not what happened. After a few weeks of checking my mailbox, I realized how foolish I'd been to think an author of his stature would take the time to write a letter to someone he'd never met or even heard of. That was my mindset when my phone rang one afternoon in early 2008 and a string of long, kindly spoken vowels asked me if this was the right number for the guy who'd written the flattering letter.

I remember being nervous as hell, like a child in the presence of his hero. I kept calling him sir and he kept telling me that there was no need to call him that. We were about the same age he said, and it made him feel weird, not to mention old, for me to use that elevated word to address him. I also remember feeling like I was talking way too fast and no matter how hard I tried to slow down, my voice seemed like an auctioneer's compared to the one on the line.

We spoke for maybe an hour that day and I would call him a

few times until eventually, with his permission, I drove from Wichita to Hohenwald with my four-month-old English Setter. We'd kept it informal and vague as to when I might be in his neighborhood, so when I knocked on his screen door, I wasn't sure how welcome I would be. The uneasiness didn't last long. The voice I had come to look forward to on the phone, spoke from the cool shade inside his modern log cabin. "Come on in." I asked him if I could bring my dog in from the car and he said, "Sure, I love dogs. Bring him on in."

Someone had poisoned his dog a while back and by the attention he gave Curly, I knew he missed him a great deal. I had promised myself not to take up too much of his time, but I'd brought one of my better still cameras with the hope of taking some photographs. In fact, I had called his publisher about that very thing, and he had encouraged me to get some new shots because he wasn't all that fond of the ones he had. I mentioned this to William, and he grumbled that he didn't much like to have his picture taken. I let it go.

In a short while, one of his sons, Christopher, showed up with his guitar and a soft smile and little to say that went beyond sincere politeness. I decided to wrap things up and let the man spend time with his kid, and was saying my goodbyes when William said, "I thought you were gonna take some pictures. You ought to get some of Christopher while you're here." This, I learned over the next couple of years, was typical William Gay. When it came to his kids, the world was a different place. Entirely changed and for the better.

We would talk on the phone every month or so, and when Michael White asked me to help put together a one-man show of William's paintings, I made sure that Christopher was an integral part of the goings-on by hiring him to perform some of his music at the Southside Gallery in Oxford. William did not drive, nor did he enjoy crowds. Christopher solved both issues by doubling as chauffeur for the trip, and then being at his father's side to help him make his way through the press of well-meaning admirers. Oxford is a place where writers occupy a position that many college towns reserve for coaches of nationally ranked football and basketball teams. In this environment, William was beset for hours by fans of his writing and, to a much lesser extent, now his visual artistry. Eventually his close friend Tom Franklin whisked him away from the crush and humidity. Clearly, the evening had taken its toll.

Since his death, I have often seen something I thought he'd find interesting, and I reflexively think of calling him like I used to. Anyone who admires the man and his work is now, along with me, forever in debt to Michael White who has thrown himself at the gargantuan task of taking faint scribbles inside hundreds of spiral notepads and turning them into entire books filled with the near magical prose of William Gay—a writer whose name will one day be spoken in terms not unlike those used to describe another writer who spent a good deal of time in Oxford. If that sounds adulatory, place your bet now. Let's make it the price of a beer. In five or ten years, let's meet up in that little bar there on Oxford's Square that William liked to haunt. You can buy me a drink.

MICHELLE DOTTER: My first job in publishing was as an intern at MacAdam/Cage, which had acquired William's *Twilight* and *The Long Home* from MacMurray & Beck. They were the first books you saw when you came in the door, shelved right next to *The Time Traveler's Wife*. *The Lost Country* was under contract and slated for publication, though it kept getting moved back; many of my first months there were spent answering phone calls from readers who wanted to know when *The Lost Country* was coming out. So, in that way, this book has been unreal and sort of mystical to me for a long time. I never got to work with William directly, which will likely remain one of my big publishing regrets.

RANDY MACKIN: I actually sought William out, so there was nothing serendipitous about our first meeting. The November/December 1999 issue of *The Oxford American* arrived in the mail, and my eyes caught a few lines that I couldn't ignore from William's short story, "My Hand Is Just Fine Where It Is". It said, "The night before they went to the motel for the first time she twisted his mouth down to hers and said against his teeth, I think you are trying to corrupt me. He didn't deny it." Those words pale in comparison to the lyrical, beautiful prose I found in the rest of that story and all the others, in the novels, even in our conversations, but there was something in those couple of lines that made me have to read more. That issue included a brief interview and mentioned that William lived in Hohenwald, less than a half-hour from where I live in Linden. My initial reaction was, who is this guy and why haven't I heard of him. I didn't show up on the doorstep of his Little Swan Creek cabin, but the following October, at the Southern Festival of Books, between sessions, we spoke, made a brief connection about where we lived, that we both grew up in the South, and I asked William to think about coming to MTSU where I teach and speaking to my literature classes. He did so the next Spring, the first of many trips we made to the university over the next eleven years.

We rarely hear about manuscripts being discovered posthumously. Most writers leave behind manuscripts in progress, half-finished stories, but aside from the "bigs"—Harper Lee's Go Set a Watchman, the early stories of Capote, and one Seuss book—it is not usual that we see a full manuscript. Can you talk about how The Lost Country and the other books in his archive were discovered?

MICHAEL WHITE: A few weeks after William died, William's youngest son called to say he and William's other son, Chris, had three tubs full of William's notebooks and would I like to come and help him figure out what was in there. I stayed up most of the night sorting the notebooks into piles based on the characters. William's writing was nearly indecipherable. Many of the notebooks were filled front to back with tightly written script; many of the pages had notes on the sides of the pages and across the top margins, and lots of them had writing on both sides of the page. He did not cross his t's or dot his i's, so many of the words were very difficult to make out.

As I was going down through one of the tubs there were some pages of typescript, yellowed typewriter paper with notes penciled in between the lines and in the margins. They were loose in the tub between a couple of the yellow pads and spiral bound notebooks he was fond of writing in. At first, I thought it was corrections William had wanted to make, but when I looked closer it wasn't William's handwriting; then suddenly I realized, with a shiver, they were annotations by Cormac McCarthy. William had mentioned Cormac McCarthy had read an early draft of *Provinces of Night* and had commented on it line by line. I was relieved to see the McCarthy annotations.

It didn't take long before I saw pages with the names of Edgewater and Roosterfish in some of the notebooks. I knew they were characters from *The Lost Country*. There were over fifty notebooks and I wound up sorting them into piles by categories like "Works in Progress," "Published Short Stories," "Music Writing," and "Notebooks from *Provinces of Night*." There was also a typescript of a rather long story about a character named Pepper Yates. It was one of the funniest pieces of writing I had ever read.

I felt like a dragon sitting on a horde of gold and gems. William Jr. agreed I could copy them. It was an excruciating job. There were notes on the tops of the pages, and the text ran right up to the edge of the pages. I had to hold it on the copier just right to get it all to copy. When he hadn't written on both sides of the pages, William had made notes on the backs for inserts he wanted to put into the text on that page. I had to watch for those and make sure the copies were associated with the proper pages. None of the pages were numbered, and in some of the notebooks there would be multiple stories. Sometimes stories or episodes from the novels would start or stop in mid-sentence, and a different story or episode would start up on that page or the next page.

It was obvious there was a significant amount of unpublished material. In one of the notebooks, I found a synopsis of *The Lost Country* in a draft of a letter to an agent. I ran across a second synopsis, this one for a book called *Fugitives of the Heart*. I re-sorted the material to separate *The Lost Country* from *Fugitives of the Heart* and used the two synopses to help figure out what went where.

In one of the tubs I found a large sheaf of typescripts, and, luckily, this one was in pretty good shape; the pages were numbered and in order. Here was another complete novel, this one with two main characters, one named Stoneburner, who was a private detective, and another named Thibodeaux, who was on the run with a beautiful blonde and a briefcase full of cash. It was an amazing story. There was an old sheriff obviously modeled on Buford Pusser, a local legend in middle Tennessee who was the inspiration for the movie *Walking Tall*. As I started reading it, I remembered William talking to me about the fact that he had written a novel in the style of a hardboiled detective story and had a publisher ready to publish it. He called it film noir on paper. Then, just as he was ready to publish, Cormac McCarthy released *No Country for Old Men*, a story about a drug deal gone wrong, a protagonist with a briefcase full of money, and an old sheriff on his trail. William decided that if he published his novel it would look like he had stolen the storyline from Cormac, and he was already sensitive to comparisons of his style with Cormac's. So, as he told me, he withheld the manuscript from publication.

Once I had gone through all the notebooks, I got back with

William Jr and Chris and we discussed what to do. They encouraged me to work with the papers and mentioned that there could be more in the attic of the house where they were raised. I eventually went to the house, and it was there I found the bulk of *The Lost Country* in the attic of the old house William moved out of around 1992. He had built the house and raised his four children in the house. Bookcases took up one whole wall of the attic and were filled with paperback books, covered with a deep layer of spider webs and dust. I had never seen so many spider webs—they hung from the rafters like Spanish moss, like gossamer. The floor of the attic was covered with magazines, I immediately saw *Rolling Stones* and *Playboys* along with some more literary stuff like *Harper's* and *The Atlantic*. At the end of the bookshelves, I found an old cardboard box and when I looked inside it was full of hundreds of pages of old cheap typing paper in various stages of decay, some pages with numbers, most not.

When I got home, I showed Susan the box. She opened it with a mixture of curiosity and repulsion on her face because the box smelled like stale smoke mixed with mouse droppings and was covered with a deep layer of grime. The paper was cheap and yellow and brittle with age, some of the pages crumpled and creased, a hodgepodge with no order that I could discern. I saw that Edgewater and Roosterfish were in there along with an array of other characters that I didn't recognize.

I remembered William telling me he couldn't find parts of the manuscript and didn't know what to do about it. We talked about rewriting it, but it was obvious from this and other conversations that he had no interest in rewriting. For him, once the pen had moved across the paper, there was no going back.

I knew from the work I had already done on the notebooks that the main characters in *The Lost Country* were Edgewater, Roosterfish, and Bradshaw, and it didn't take long to notice all three of those names. The papers were not in any order. There were many pages with other names that I didn't recognize. I started sorting the pages, and, in the end, I had five stacks of pages. They were stacked based on the names of the characters that showed up on those pages. I could easily see that I had a big portion of *The Lost Country* here and that some of what I had was the same as what was in the notebooks, although it seemed that some was not. Then I had three stacks that had other characters and represented different time frames as well. One seemed to be set in the 1800s with horses and wagons, another in the 1930s, and finally, one big stack that represented events in 1980 with characters named Binder and Corrie. This turned out to be the manuscript of *Little Sister Death*.

In *The Lost Country* papers I was thrilled to find one page that had "The End" written in pencil at the bottom. And there were pages with handwritten page numbers in the bottom right-hand corner and the page with the words "The End" was numbered 231. By the end of the week, I had all the pages in plastic sheet protectors and had two three-ring notebooks, one for *The Lost Country* and one for *Little Sister Death*. It seemed I had most of *The Lost Country* in order. Only about half of the pages were numbered, so that presented another puzzle, although it wasn't too difficult once the storyline became apparent. However, there were some gaps in the typescript and especially at the end of the book.

This is a remarkable story because you were able, in a sense, to walk around in the mind of a genius. I remember William telling me that as a boy he used to skip school to write. He would find a spot under a tree to wile the day away, working on stories. Because he sometimes did not have a pen, he'd use a stick from a tree and scrape out the inside of a walnut hull for homemade "ink." What was astonishing, when he showed me the early writings, was the quality of that young William's work. He was a protege, and the stories came out almost fully formed. He told me his editing consisted of handwriting the book. With that in mind, what did it entail, typing the notes for this manuscript into book form and editing the final version?

MICHAEL WHITE: William never looked back, and once something was written, that was that. When he started getting published in 1998, he had an archive of four unpublished novels and was working on new things all the time. His old work, like *Stoneburner* and *The Lost Country* were just old manuscripts to him, and, apparently, he had lost track of them. He knew he had written it but had no idea where they were located. Perhaps his ex-wife Diane had put them in the attic after he moved out. Who knows? It is still a mystery.

It took about two years to get everything in the archive typed up, to edit the parts altogether, and get it into a final draft. We had some hopes of being able to scan the typescripts and work on them from a scanned copy, but the pages were old and the typewriter print wouldn't read on the scanners in a way that would allow us to manipulate the text. So, we were stuck with typing everything, the handwritten manuscripts and the typescripts, into the computer.

Susan and Shelia were the first on board and did the bulk of the typing. Plus, Lamont has been the editor of my little press (I brought out two of William's books while he was alive), and Lamont worked on those as well as all the other books my press published (eight and counting). Then Paul got in touch and offered to help, and everyone contributed by reading and reading and reading again, making sure the story fit together properly and correcting typos, etc. Luckily, we had all the story. Team Gay has done *Little Sister Death, Stoneburner, Fugitives of the Heart,* and *The Lost Country,* all discovered in the archive along with this collection of short stories.

SHELIA KENNEDY: Michael emailed me in July of 2012 and told me that he had sixteen notebooks from William and wanted to know if I was interested in helping. I jumped at the chance! William's handwriting made the job difficult, but the more I typed, the easier it was to read. His vocabulary kept me referencing Google to see if what I typed was actually a word, and I found that not only was it a word, it was the perfect word for the situation. Google was also a huge asset with brand names and song lyrics or literary references. William did not write scenes in order, and he wrote along the margins, sometimes indicating where to include those lines, although often I had to use my own judgment.

Susan and Michael were also typing, and by October 2012, at the time of the Southern Festival of Books, we had assembled a rough draft of *The Lost Country*. Michael and I met Tom Franklin and George Singleton, both authors and friends of William's, to discuss what we had found. I remember telling Tom that I felt like we had a great piece of work but really didn't have "the end" of the novel. In our rough draft, we had placed the scenes in order—and there was an end— but there was not enough material to get to that end. Little did we know that in the treasure trove of notebooks that Michael would deliver to me from another trip to the attic, we had the missing section. Edgewater is in the cafe when a young man approaches him and is pimping his wife on their honeymoon. She is the girl with Edgewater at the end!

SUSAN McDONALD: The transcription of William's work was at the same time exciting, challenging and daunting—exciting due to participation in the discovery of William's unpublished work; challenging due to the difficulty of deciphering his penmanship and inserting his marginalized notations in the text in order; and daunting due to my self-imposed obligation and responsibility to accurately convey the meaning and intent of his words. Once I got past the condition of the pages which were often yellowed, ragged and stained from coffee or god knows what, it was a delve into a heretofore undiscovered world. Once I felt I had correctly transcribed a thought or an especially profound scene it was often time to stop and savor it. Since Michael was close by, I usually called to him to share and marvel at it. The process for me was akin to a visit from William as his persona was so reflected in his work so it was both a pleasure and yet there was an admonition: "Don't screw it up"!

PAUL NITSCHE: In April 2014, I received the first manuscript of *The Lost Country* from Michael. He told me that other than himself, I was the fourth person to read the book. As a fan long awaiting *The Lost Country*, this was quite a moment. I worked on the manuscript for the next four months, arranging scenes, editing and proofing, right up until it was delivered to Dzanc in the fall of 2014. Once Dzanc created the proof copy, I again contributed more editing and proofing. Working on the manuscript of *The Lost Country* has been one of the highlights of my life.

MICHELLE DOTTER: *The Lost Country* was pretty daunting. Michael White and his small band of William's friends and fans had already worked their fingers to the bone getting the manuscript to a publishable state, but the big question remaining was whether to edit the book heavily, as we might any first-draft book, or whether to let it stand pretty much as it was. This was an issue we debated for a long time here at Dzanc before it finally fell to me to make the decision.

Ultimately, I chose to do a very sparse edit, looking for factual errors, typos, and grammatical issues only. I'm not sure it's the decision everyone would have made. William's style is lush and dense—a good friend of his told me, with a smile, that William would never use one word where three would do. There were lines we could have cut, or scenes we might have trimmed. But given that this book was found in the attic after William's death and pieced together page by page, I was concerned about authenticity. I want everyone who reads this book, who loves William's work, to see him in it, and not to question whether any quirk of dialogue, description, or voice is the work of some other, invisible hand.

William often talked about his belief in the supernatural, his surety that there was, indeed, more than the human condition. He had an understanding of the occult as something to be both curious about and wary of. He knew its dangers perhaps because he had psychics in the family. When I told him once about fooling around with a Ouija board, he said his previous experience with one was so intense, he cracked the board in half and threw it in a dumpster. The singer songwriter Marshall Chapman, who was a good friend of William's, has said that he has visited her in dreams. Did you feel William "with" you at any part of the process?

MICHAEL WHITE: No, not in any way other than the absolute thrill of reading his unpublished manuscripts. I helped with some of the typing, and one night I was typing a section from a notebook and ran across this:

"I drove the dark highways with the radio tuned to a country music station. I felt myself drowning, inured in woes in a phantasmagoric landscape of lost love and betrayal until these folk became real to me, I was one with them. Ultimately the night and the beer and the trusting black road and the music seemed to alter my very consciousness, making me a character in this single unending epic song that came to seem not to be a song at all but some folk stories whispered and told by a vast and infinitely crowded cast of folk who moved irrevocably toward infidelity with masochistic glee and a dread and near mythic inevitability."

It was a West Texas night. The moon tracking high above me rendered the silver landscape cold and surreal. I stopped and cut the lights, the switch. Silence descended and I got out into it. The desert looked timeless. Save the dark highway beseeching it, this could be the desert of ten thousand years ago or of some vague and unchartered future. I turned. The truck looked anomolaic, Fortean. Above me the dark bowl of the night sky was shot with pinholes of light. I urinated and lit a cigarette. The horizon where the highway and sky met tugged me gently as if bound to me by a webbing of invisible wire and I got back into the truck and drove on.

The thrill of reading something like that for the first time was indescribable. I immediately sent it around to the team. We had no idea where it fit or which book it belonged to, since William would write segments of works in progress in whatever notebook was "at hand". However, that passage turned out to be the ending of *Stoneburner* and, like so many other pieces, there was nowhere else it could fit.

SHELIA KENNEDY: I actually did feel William's spirit as I worked on the manuscript. The intensity of his eyes in a framed photograph on my bookshelf kept me working to get it right.

LAMONT INGALLS: Throughout the recovery and editorial processes, William's written voice remained in the present as a guide. So, yes, he was with me in this sense. William's unique and imaginative voice telling the stories of his country, principally the Harrikin and Ackerman's Field, and peopled by his characters continues always. The essence of William Gay's singular artistry remains. So, yes, he was "with" me in this sense.

For those who knew him, it was clear that William's least favorite part of the writing process was publishing and promotion. When the New York Times called to ask him if they could feature him, he refused, saying to me, "I don't want one of them New York reporters coming down and seeing where I live." This was before he moved to the cabin, when he was still living in the trailer. I remember his telling me, after one fairly strenuous book tour, that he was thinking of going back to drywalling. He said there was a meditative peacefulness to it. He would write all day in his mind and come home to put it on paper. I'm curious about the way the manuscripts went into the publication process without him.

LAMONT INGALLS: In early 2013, the manuscript of *The Lost Country* was essentially ready to circulate to potential publishers. There was a long process of ensuring that the rights reverted to the William Gay estate following the bankruptcy and death of the original publisher at MacAdam/Cage. Once this legal matter was settled, *The Lost Country* could be circulated unencumbered.

The rights for *The Lost Country* and *Little Sister Death*, another novel recovered from the attic in Lewis County, were acquired by Dzanc Books. *Little Sister Death* is William's Southern Gothic retelling and updating of Tennessee's Bell Witch legend. The novel, which I also edited and proofed as a member of Team Gay, was published by Dzanc in September 2015. *The Lost Country* was published in July 2018.

MICHELLE DOTTER: I wasn't the one who acquired *The Lost Country*. I actually inherited *The Lost Country* from my predecessor at Dzanc, Guy Intoci, but William Gay had been on my radar a lot longer than that. As I said, my first job in publishing was as an intern at MacAdam/Cage, which had acquired William's *Twilight* and *The Long Home* from MacMurray & Beck.

After MacAdam/Cage dissolved and the Gay family was finally able to get William's rights back, they approached Dzanc in part because Guy Intoci and Pat Walsh were associated with the press.

Guy, Pat, and I all worked at MacAdam/Cage together, and I know they were both very excited to finally be bringing this legendary book out for William's fans, who have been incredibly loyal and patient. That neither of them was working with Dzanc by the time *The Lost Country* was ready for publication is just one of those funny turns of publishing. I feel like I inherited so many people's love and hopes for the book, and I wanted to honor those hopes above all else.

In terms of promotion, all I can say is we were extremely lucky that this book already had an audience, as well as a group of dedicated fans and friends ready to champion it. Michael White and company, as well as Sonny Brewer, the dedicated folks at the Southern indie bookstores, and the whole vast host of William's devoted readers have helped us spread the word, and we've been grateful for good coverage from significant papers and magazines, too. Sales have been looking good so far, and everyone—from readers to booksellers—has supported us and the book from day one. This has truly been a work of love, and certainly not just by me or the press. I've heard that William was a very good man, a kind man, and it seems he left a mark on a lot of people, who were willing to go the distance and help us get this lost novel into the limelight. Not least of all, Suzanne Kingsbury.

William's work was immediately recognizable, and many of the landscapes and some characters repeated themselves. After his second book, Art Winslow, book editor for The Nation, summed up his work in the New York Times, saying "...his mountain folk are still seeking, with lives of unquiet desperation, what is ever tantalizingly close and for a few heartbeats within their embrace." Do you feel his novel, The Lost County, *is a departure in any way from his others?*

PAUL NITSCHE: Within the posthumous releases, *The Lost Country* is more consistent with William's other work. *Little Sister Death* and *Stoneburner* found William playing within the horror and crime genres that he was fond of. When I would come across pictures of William's cabin, I would study the background book shelves for authors and titles. Among the stacks, one could see Stephen King and Daniel Woodrell titles, authors that certainly influenced *Little Sister Death* and *Stoneburner*, respectively. These novels are stylistically a bit of a departure from his other books. The language and vocabulary are simpler, less developed, and are most likely a stab at popular fiction by William. *The Lost Country*, on the other hand, seems to be a full clasp of William's southern gothic writing and style. Like the novels published during his lifetime, *The Lost Country* follows characters on the fringe of society, some making bad decisions, some villainous, others trying to just get by. These folks feel familiar to the William Gay reader, as does the landscape, which swings from the bucolic to the apocalyptic. Using his crafted language and phrasing, William describes the journeys and humorous antics of some of his most memorable characters. *The Lost Country* is one of William's greatest artistic statements.

LAMONT INGALLS: The exacting use of language that is often poetic, the creative description, the idiomatic conversations and humor, the fully developed characters, and the sense of inevitability that mark William Gay's writing are all especially evident in *The Lost Country*. However, there is a sense of "lostness" in Edgewater that I think is different in degree from characters in his other novels. Others are rooted in place and families, in Ackerman's Field or the Harrikin, and have local histories and kinfolk that are part of their stories. Once Edgewater heads away from Memphis and his brief and tenuous connection with Claire, and toward a reunion, vaguely sensed, with his dying father in East Tennessee, he is traveling through a countryside in which he is unknown to all he meets. He has no kin along all his highways or in the towns and hamlets he wanders into as he travels toward the remnants of his family, presumably in Monteagle, Tennessee. Likewise, the land itself does not seem to contain any portion of his previous history, no memories to which he might momentarily connect. There are no towns through which he may have once passed, or persons he may have previously encountered. As in the traditional song, "Wayfaring Stranger," Edgewater is "traveling through a worrisome land," although without the pilgrim's hope for fulfillment at the end of the road.

MICHELLE DOTTER: For me, William Gay is one of those very special writers because he's a favorite of people in the know—people who don't just have a passing acquaintance with Southern Gothic literature, but people who have a passion for it. When you read widely in a subgenre and you still respect and love a writer, you know he's doing something very right. William Gay's writing astonishes me every time I crack open one of his books, and in addition to reaching lifelong fans, I hope we've honored his memory in our treatment of it, and that he'd be pleased by the efforts of so many of his devoted friends.

Obviously, we are all huge fans of his work, please talk about what drew you to his work and how you found your way to help edit his posthumous books?

MATT SNOPE: In 2003 I was in Las Vegas, it was 112 degrees in the morning, and my then-wife gave me *Provinces of Night* for a birthday gift. She'd learned about it because I was really into Tom Franklin, but I'd never heard of William. I was impressed with the gift since there wasn't as much online in those days as now, but she'd found out about it. I started reading it and was blown away by the prose, earthiness, and William's use of metaphor. Passages that he has related as elating for him to write are also ecstatic for the reader, and I was hooked.

Years went by after William died and *The Lost Country* languished in uncertainty. When it finally came out, I thought: *Fuck yeah— William lives!* I was very moved by Michael's afterword in *The Lost Country*. I actually cried and so reached out to Michael offering editing help and a familiarity with William's work and Southern Gothic and grit lit in general.

DAWN MAJOR: At first, I was drawn to his work because I was personally interested in writing horror and I read Stephen King's blurb about *Twilight* being the scariest novel of 2007. From there I was hooked. I was in graduate school at the same time I found my way to William's works and my critical thesis advisor wisely suggested I choose to write about someone who was relatively unknown, not an author who had been written about so many times there would be little new to say. The amount of academic articles tackling William's work was limited and none of them asserted my argument which was that in addition to being a wonderful Southern Gothic writer, William also belonged on the shelves of authors of horror and magical realism and that he was building a Southern legendarium around the town of Ackerman's Field and his haunted forest, the Harrikin. While I was only required to research and write about one of William's novels to support my thesis, I felt William deserved more and I ended up writing about his entire body of work and twice the amount needed. My critical thesis advisor also suggested that any chapters I wrote could be later published in literary journals. Fortunately for me, the editor of *Five Points Review* was at my graduate lecture where I spoke about William's world-building techniques and particularly how that played into his artwork. After my lecture Megan Sexton asked if I would write an essay about his paintings and that essay was published along with an interview conducted by Michael White with William in the 2020 edition along with images of William's paintings and an image of his map of Ackerman's Field and the Harrikin.

GEORGE DILWORTH: Six years ago, I was rummaging through a basket of books for sale at a small local business and came across a title that caught my attention, *Provinces of Night* by William Gay. I had never heard of Gay, but I saw the Cormac McCarthy quote inside that provided him with the title. I paid a dollar for the book (virtually new) and took it home, where it sat on my bookshelf for almost a year until a nephew told me he'd read an extraordinary book recently called *Twilight*. When he told me the author's name, something clicked in my head, but when I didn't come across the book at home, I went to the library and found *The Long Home* and *Twilight*. (My heroes were Wolfe, Fitzgerald, Faulkner, O'Connor, Saroyan, McCarthy . . .) I read *The Long Home* first and had not been enthralled by a writer's words like that since I read *Look Homeward, Angel* at sixteen! *Twilight* was mesmerizing, stunning, and it felt like I was reading the best of all my heroes condensed in this one incredibly gifted writer. Of course, I found my copy of *Provinces of Night* and afterwards began looking for everything I could find that he'd written. I wanted to know everything knowable about the man who wrote these poems of prose. It made me heartsick to think that William Gay had only been eight hours away from me all these years and I had not heard of him. I kept expecting to be disappointed at some point with a story, essay, or book, but it was not to be, I remained enchanted and hungry for more. I recognized what J.M. White, Ingalls, McDonald, Nitsche, and Kennedy were doing out of pure admiration for Gay's body of work and wanted to thank and encourage them to stick with it to the end. So, I wrote to Michael at the address I found in my copy of *Time Done Been Won't*

Be No More. He was kind enough to reply and we found ourselves corresponding. In a considerate act of generosity (to stave off my craving) he sent me three or four pages from *Fugitives of the Heart* to feast on and tell him what I thought. I printed it off and read it several times, operating on what my wife calls my "teacher spirit", correcting punctuation, spelling, adding and removing hyphens, making comments, etc. I mailed it back, hoping to be helpful, and apologetic if it appeared otherwise. To my good fortune and delight, Michael welcomed the additional assistance and has continued to allow me the privilege of playing a tiny part in bringing this hypnotic material to print.

RANDY MACKIN: After discovering William's work in 1999, I read everything I could by him and about him. Lucky for those of us who so admire what William was able to do, that first novel was followed fast upon by another and his first collection of short stories, plus William was being published in all those magazines whose editors had rejected his work earlier in his career. I knew William had considerable unpublished work, he had told me so, and that was no surprise considering he'd been writing for decades, honing his craft. No writer suddenly bursts onto the literary landscape with a novel as fully imagined and realized as *The Long Home* without having spent years developing such a distinct voice. We had talked extensively about *The Lost Country*, William had shared parts of it with me and others in manuscript, and we discussed the problems he had with his publishers and with completing the novel. He told me that he'd gotten all *The Lost Country's* characters back to Ackerman's Field and he just didn't know what to do with them, couldn't find an ending. I was happy to see that book in print after his death because I knew it contained some exceptional writing, as good as anything William had written. And so too, I was thrilled with the publication of *Little Sister Death* and *Stoneburner,* the former I knew existed and the latter a book I'd never heard about. When *Fugitives of the Heart* came out, I emailed Michael to thank him for all the work he'd done on William's behalf because I knew he'd faced what must have seemed an insurmountable challenge and offered my help. Michael, within days, sent the manuscript for this collection and invited my edits.

JOSEPH G. TIDWELL III: I had never heard of William Gay until a director friend of mine in Los Angeles told me my work reminded him a lot of this Southern writer named William Gay. I'm going who the hell is William Gay? "Man, you need to read this guy's stuff. He creates the same kind of characters and landscapes you write about in Mississippi." After several months I had lunch with him again and that's when he handed me a copy of *Provinces*. Well…I couldn't put the book down. I bought every bit of William's writing I could find. Then one day I found this email address for one JM White in one of the books. I can't remember which book it was, but I wrote a note to myself and forgot about it. Several months later, going through my stack of torn papers, stained bar napkins, a couple of notated parking tickets and other notes on this screenplay I was writing at the time, I ran across the memo and thought what the hell, if something comes of it that would be great. I emailed JM White. If you know anything about living in LA and you deal every day with some of the "sweet assholes" in the film business, you realize that most emails are usually unread. I was expecting that. It's amazing how one little email can create such a wonderful tempest in your mind when I did get a return from JM White. I called him and we talked for a while about novels and short stories and other writing, and the subject moved to screenplays and the film business. I mentioned to him that, if the occasion ever arose, I would be very interested in doing the screen adaptation from one of William's novels. Well…to my great surprise he mentioned *Stoneburner*. It took me about eight months to write the script. I tried to stay as close to the novel as I could as

William changed locations a lot without any transitions. Which is hard to do in a film. If I'm correct William said this was his "film noir on paper." Believe me, I wanted to include transitions along the way, but Michael lovingly held my feet close to the fire. He's pretty damn quick and handy redlining your shit so I held even closer to the novel. To make this short, the rest is history. I am honored that Michael gave me a chance to be a part, even though in a roundabout way, of William's life and legacy. As I was writing the script, I could feel William's presence and I would occasionally talk out loud to him as to how he meant a certain scene to play out. I love painting pictures with words, and as you all know, William held a wide paintbrush with many colors. I feel we would have become good friends had we met. It's a shame that the world has lost this great treasure but what he left us in his characters and stories is priceless and I shall never forget that. My life and writing and artwork have been influenced beyond my wildest dreams by William Gay. Thank ya buddy wherever you are, wish I could have a drink (or eight) with you right now. And thank you Michael White for the opportunity. At this time, I along with my new writing partner, Dawn Major, are in the process of adapting William's last novel *Fugitives of the Heart* into a screenplay. I would love to create more film projects from some of his short stories. What a hoot that would be…

PAUL NITSCHE: After McCarthy's *The Road* in 2006, I took to reading almost exclusively Southern literature. While I was exploring the catalogues of McCarthy, Faulkner, O'Connor, and the like, an astute algorithm kept suggesting the name William Gay. A year later at work, I was flipping through the pages of a *People* magazine, the back page of which was Stephen King's favorite books of that year. There was the name William Gay again, with his latest book *Twilight*. In his recommendation, King believed the book was for lovers of language, and that was enough for me to give this writer a try. Starting with *The*

Long Home, I can still remember that first session of reading, blinking at disbelief at the words crafted together, rereading paragraphs. I knew I had found a special author. *Provinces of Night* followed, and at one point I was so taken by the language and story I had to close the covers. Staring at the front of the book, dreaming about the man who had written it. A bit of an infatuation had taken root, and I read everything of William's, from large to small publisher. My wife was subjected to many of my readings aloud and musings about William. I would search the internet and read every article I could find. If the article included a picture of William in his cabin, I would enlarge his bookshelves to see what he was reading. When *The Lost Country* began to be mentioned, my excitement for a new book by William had peaked. There was a book cover and even some excerpts, but the book release never solidified. When William died in early 2012, I was burdened with regret that I had never reached out to him. In November of that year, I wrote the publisher about the status of the book but got no response back. A Wild Dog Press book had an email address in it, which I contacted but thought a long shot. To my surprise, Michael emailed me back. We began writing each other regularly and he soon shared an unpublished short story. For a superfan, getting something like that was extraordinary. However, I noticed it had quite a few proofing errors, and sheepishly offered to fix them. Michael will have to say why he entrusted me, but soon more short stories followed, and I became part of the small group shaping William's posthumous work, including, unbelievably, *The Lost Country.*

If you have a favorite William Gay story please share it with us.

MATT SNOPE: I unfortunately never met William but in the early 2000s I designed a class in Contemporary Southern Literature for a community college, and both Tom Franklin and William were so nice and easygoing about me using their writing for the class. I talked on the phone with Tom, William was a little more reclusive (yet very happy to have his work studied at the college), but both were easy to interact with, no egos or pretentious bullshit. I also always chuckle thinking about how William knew Stephen King was gonna call him, but he let the phone ring. That is punk rock.

SUSAN McDONALD: I was moved by William's shyness and humility even after he was a well-recognized and respected author. He seemed to suffer a little by being in a large public event during which he had to read or speak. As soon as his part was over, he wanted to "get out of there." On one occasion at a radio event in Franklin, Tennessee, which was held in a venue that sold food, the owner asked him to stay and eat and William just wanted to leave and go home. We had picked him up and were driving him back so were happy to do what he wanted. But we knew he had to be hungry because he had not eaten for hours. The owner then asked if he would like some food to take away and William was thrilled with the offer. He asked "Do you have any fried green tomatoes?" and fortunately they did. So, William left with a box full of fried green tomatoes and barbeque and was delighted.

One year at the Book Festival in Nashville, where William was a speaker, tables were set up after events so authors could sign books. I was in line to get a book signed by Charles Frazier and happened to be standing next to Mrs. Frazier. We somehow began talking about William who was at a table nearby. She said that Charles was very anxious to meet William but had not had an opportunity and was afraid he would leave soon, so Michael and I took him over and introduced him to William. They turned out to be admirers of each other.

RANDY MACKIN: No way can I limit my experiences to a favorite story because in every encounter—mostly in my car, or on the phone, or visiting in the book-lined walls of his home—something memorable happened. One story, however, seems particularly important and appropriate to this collection. In March of 2011, when I pulled up to his house for a trip to MTSU, William was coming out the front door onto the porch. He was wearing his usual: jeans, a print shirt, tennis shoes, and he was slipping on what he called his "writer's jacket," a black sportscoat with satiny lapels, something he'd purchased at a Goodwill store. He was carrying a Mason jar of black coffee. As soon as he sat down in the car—no hello, how are you, chit-chat—William said, "I finished a new story last night." On our way back to Highway 412, following the curves of Little Swan Creek and cutting through that morning's fog, William told me about the story, with a working title of "Ashes of Love" from the old Jim & Jesse song—a tune he said was quoted in this tale about a penis in a fruit jar and the man who finds it and tries to blackmail an old woman to fulfill his own designs on her granddaughter. I told William I'd love to read it. He said it was still in longhand but I could take a look if he ever got it typed up. Of course, that didn't happen. William was gone less than a year later. But, that day in two of my classes, William shared the news about his story with my students, told them how the idea had originated from a twenty-year-old newspaper clipping about a woman who'd robbed her husband's corpse of his private part because she didn't want him enjoying it in the afterlife, the unfaithful way he had in this one. My students heard firsthand from a writer what it was like to finish a story but also how that piece of fiction developed from a stranger-than-fiction real event, and how William had shaped it into an exploration of human nature and selfishness and manipulation. I did not see that story until I began editing this manuscript, and there it was, with a different title—"Tidewater's Eden"—and I think it's the best piece in his collection, an example of William at the height of his writing powers.

DAWN MAJOR: I didn't know William personally. He passed away before I was even aware of his writing. My experiences all relate to meeting those who knew him. If I met an author that I knew was a friend of William's, I made a point of getting a story out them. George Singleton was the keynote speaker at my graduation when I got my MFA in creative writing and when I met him, I immediately asked him to share William Gay stories with me. In truth, I was nervous because George is one of my all-time favorite short story writers. I wanted to ask him about his work, but I basically skimmed over him and launched into William. It was kind of rude really, but I've embarrassed myself before in front of writers I admire and I'm sure to do it again. George is as likable as his stories and was gracious about it. Later that night, we were all hanging out in my dorm room and in walks George with a case of PBR and those stories about William. I still have one can of PBR from that night. As for the stories, I'll let George share those when William's biography is published.

MICHAEL WHITE: After William died, I spent as much time as I could afford in Hohenwald and interviewed all his family members. There were no phone calls involved, I just showed up at their houses and everyone seemed happy to see me. At first, I wanted to call and make appointments but quickly learned that the Gay family didn't operate that way, it was perfectly fine to just drop in whenever I was in town. So, I would sit there with a yellow pad on my knee and take notes while I asked them questions about their life with William. Once, talking to his brother Cody, he told me about a time William was living in an old house and when he would visit, they would sit and talk in the living room and there was this big spider who would inevitably come out and roam around the room. Cody eyed the spider and motioned to William to make sure he saw it, but William's only response was, "Yeah, he lives here." That was William, he never owned a gun, and never hunted and never killed a thing, not even a spider.

Please describe the role you have played in helping work on his posthumous books.

MATT SNOPE: I was living in Atlanta and had lots of time on my hands due to poverty and unemployment, so I first worked on helping edit the novel *Fugitives of the Heart*. I have a pretty light touch when it comes to editing William, because I find his work so beautiful, and so much of it has a final draft quality to it, probably because while working his construction day jobs, he was writing in his head.

DAWN MAJOR: I've actively sought literary journal editors to publish William's short stories and books. As I mentioned previously, *Five Points Review* published my essay, "A Window into William Gay, A Southern Writer, A Southern Painter," as well as an interview with Michael White and William in 2020 edition Vol. 19, No. 3. Along with the essay and interview, one of William's paintings was featured on the cover with seven images of William's paintings and the map of Ackerman's Field in the middle. I was recently interviewed about William with *Five Points Review* which should air on their podcast in December 2020 and also included information about upcoming publications for William. The *James Dickey Review* published "The Dream" in Vol. 2019 along with an introduction from me and how the story was acquired.

For me, it's not just about publications, but about reaching professors, teachers, and the public. In 2019, I presented at Georgia State University's New Voice Graduate Conference where I discussed William's methodology and treatment of the supernatural. I also lectured about mapping and William's treatment of the fairy tale during my internship. I know many professors and because of my enthusiasm some of them have added William's stories to their curriculum, which I think is simply wonderful.

I provided editorial assistance on *Fugitives of the Heart* and the latest collection obviously. I'm still seeking other journals to place articles about his work. Prior to the pandemic, I was scheduled to present at Georgia State University's Lost Southern Voices Conference Reader's Festival. That's on hold for now.

GEORGE DILWORTH: Since *Fugitives of the Heart* through *Stories from the Attic*, I've helped with the editing of manuscripts. To have played the least part in this project to publish William's contribution to literature has been an incredible privilege and delight. A highlight in my life for which I am most grateful.

RANDY MACKIN: My work on his posthumous books has been limited to this collection, but I'm so proud to have been invited to participate, and I'm grateful beyond measure for what the William Gay team has done to get as much of his work in print as possible.

PAUL NITSCHE: Through some inconceivable fortuity, I have edited and proofed all the posthumous material: *This Ride Ain't Over Yet* (an early unpublished version of *Stories from the Attic*), *Little Sister Death*, *Stoneburner*, *The Lost Country*, *Fugitives of the Heart*, and *Stories from the Attic*. I did the jacket and book design for the Anomolaic Press release of *Stoneburner*, as well as designing and illustrating the two headed whippoorwill and typography for the Anomolaic Press logo. I am also responsible for constructing and maintaining the modest website at williamgay.net. Reflecting on the last decade, I feel grateful to Michael White, Team Gay, and William's family for giving me the opportunity to contribute to the legacy of one of my favorite authors.

What is your favorite book by William? If you have a favorite quote from any of the books, please share it.

DAWN MAJOR: Because I'm a huge fan of the modern fairy tale, I naturally gravitate towards *Twilight*. It was also the first novel I read of William's so it's sentimental for me. What William did in *Twilight* was similar to what Angela Carter did with her collection of short stories in *The Bloody Chamber*. William basically rewired the fairy tale "Little Red Riding Hood" and gave it a modern twist, but he also recognized that, at the heart of most fairy tales, there's an element of terror.

As to favorites, just one? Really? I must mention *Provinces of Night*, because I love Uncle Brady's character. Uncle Brady was the deciding factor in my conclusion that William's works could be viewed through both a realistic fictional lens and a speculative fiction lens. It's kind of brilliant really. If you choose to negate the paranormal and contend that those supernatural elements in his works can be explained away by dreams, dementia, poor vision or old age then William's endings become vaguer. However, if you practice the willing suspension of disbelief, meaning Uncle Brady had the powers he claimed to possess, then the evil wizard won. I also love the Oedipus Rex connotations surrounding that novel…Uncle Brady killed his father to be with his mother. It amazes me that William was completely self-taught based on the sheer amount of allusions from philosophy, literature, religion, music, poetry, and even physics; one would think you were dealing with an academic who had an extensive education.

I cannot possibly stick to one quote, either.

When you see "Somethin's goin to happen" it means something terrible is about to occur. This phrase occurs in *Little Sister Death*, *Twilight*, and *The Lost Country* and each time the protagonists ignore the warning or omen it's to his (protagonists are male) detriment. I always imagine William chuckling to himself when he wrote that phrase. In *Little Sister Death*, Swaw and Binder both think these words while in the orchard, in *Twilight* Sutter is described as waiting outside for Tyler and waiting for something to happen, and in *The Lost Country* Sudy tells Edgewater she saw an omen and she speaks these words like some portent of death. Readers familiar with what happens after these words occur in a William Gay story should recognize the protagonist is in for a ride, and not a joy ride. I liken it to scrying in a mirror and repeating a spell three time. If words are magical, and I believe William felt they were, then "Somethin's goin to happen" is a curse.

The second example isn't just one quote or phrase. The four pages (98-101) prior to Book Two of *Twilight* are way too long to quote, so I'll just mention what I found appealing. The real-time narration is momentarily suspended as the supernatural world of the Harrikin opens its doors to Tyler and Sutter. It starts with instructions told in second-person point-of-view giving the reader directions to the Harrikin, and William piles on poetic language here—the initial sentence lasts six lines. William ends it by telling the reader the antagonist (Sutter) and protagonist (Tyler) are "fleeing chronologically" backwards. Essentially, they're going into the past.

Finally, I love the language of the scene described below from *Provinces of Night* because it's so beautifully constructed and I can envision it even better because William (maybe) painted it. Michael White pointed this out to me, and I tend to agree.

"The feeling that off somewhere in the bracken man and boy still walked rose in him nor would it abate. With their steps locked in sync with his, they paced him in the silent black wood, passed through the boles of trees like revenants. A moon the color of yellowed ivory cradled up out of the dark and he could see them moving through the trees transparent as water, insubstantial as a handful of smoke." (72-73)

The cover for *Time Done Been Won't Be No More* is a twilight scene of a white cottage set back from the road with smoke piping from the chimney and in between the woods, if you look closely, are these dark forms that don't seem to belong to the painting, but you can easily imagine they're the revenants Fleming walked amongst.

MATT SNOPE: While *Provinces* remains my favorite and I think William's magnum opus, I keep returning to *Little Sister Death*. I'm a skeptic of supernatural things by nature, but there's something generally creepy about that book, and I can read it over and over. I love its blend of almost clinical descriptions of evil, violence, insanity, and incest, yet it's also a semi-autobiographical book about William trying to be both a writer and loving family man.

GEORGE DILWORTH: I suppose it's possible to have a favorite book by William, but when you read them over and over as I do, your favorite is ever-changing. Right now, it's *Fugitives of the Heart*. Before that, it was *The Lost Country*. For short stories, as a main-line addict, there are too many favorites to choose from...however, high on the list would be "The Paperhanger," "Sugarbaby," and "Nighttime Awakenings." "Sugarbaby" is a gem of a tragicomedy. A commentary on a man's (mostly) futile attempts to humble himself and conquer his pride. Gay could have included the quote from Jeremiah 17:9 on the title page: "The heart is more deceitful than anything else and mortally sick. Who can fathom it?" A simple tale, yet, soaked with insight on the nature of man.

As far as a favorite quote, there again, from the works of Gay you're asking the impossible. There are simply too many. However, because they are so easily found in all his books, I shall select one for the pure joy of setting it down.

"Lying there sleeping on the mossy concrete, his face jerking with the troubled passage of his dreams, he is provisionally still brother to all humankind. He has strayed far from the ways of men, but there has always been a kind of twisted logic to his violence. The things he desired and struggled for made a kind of sense. Revenge, avarice, a thirst for power. The things only dreamed by normal men. Their own secret dreams made carnate and ambulatory. Silver threads, thin and frayed though they be, hold him yet to the ways of the world. Here in the night they part and the ties give one by one and he falls away like some winged predator into another country, dark and unmapped and turbulent, so that he is finally free from all restraint, lost." (T*wilight*, pg. 139)

Interesting note: I could not find the word "carnate" in any of my dictionaries. Going online, I discovered that the word can only be found in the Merriam-Webster Unabridged Dictionary and is compatible with "incarnate." Reading Gay is also a fun and fascinating study of words.

RANDY MACKIN: While his novels are outstanding, I think William was at his best when composing short stories. We talked about short fiction a great deal in our literary conversations, he equated short stories with poetry in that both genres try to take a lifetime of experience and compress it into a few lines or a few pages. William believed that short stories were more difficult to write than novels because every word is important and there's none of the wiggle room that a novel might provide the writer. Story endings were important to William, he told me that he worked diligently on the closings of stories, trying to get the endings exactly right. When "I Hate to See That Evening Sun Go Down" was adapted into the film *That Evening Sun*, William told me he felt the filmmaker did an excellent job taking his short story and expanding it into a full-length feature—except for the ending which William referred to as a "big group hug." He acknowledged and understood that filmmakers have different audience concerns than writers, but I remember him talking about how hard he worked on that story's ending. Because of that revelation, I tend to look at the endings of William's stories because they garnered so much of his attention. The closing lines of "I Hate to See That Evening Sun Go Down" are among my favorites:

"Why I believe we've crossed over into Alabama, Meecham told himself in wonder, and in truth the ice-locked world was evolving into a landscape sculpted by memory. The ambulance swayed on past curving lazy creeks he had fished and waded as a boy, winding roads dusted white as mica in the moonlight. // He pressed his face to the glass as a child might and watched the irrevocable slide of scenery—tree and field and sleeping farmhouse. He studied each object as it hove into view and went slipstreaming off the dark glass to see if it might have something to tell him, some intimation of his destination."

We have brought out four posthumous novels and this collection of short stories. Now that we can see the full extent of William's lifetime of literary effort, what insights about his work have you gained from working on these books?

MATT SNOPE: I know I'm biased but I am so thankful that the team has worked on, literally rescued, these posthumous works. I mean, it's tragic to imagine these works sitting in dusty obscurity in an attic somewhere. Also, although similarities galore exist between Cormac McCarthy and William, I'd put William at his best up against Cormac any day. Don't get me wrong—Cormac writes like a motherfucker—but William has a sense of compassion and a sense of humor that's often missing in Cormac, even though both have similar backgrounds and write about some similar things. Where Cormac is jaded and bleak, William brings an innocence and curiosity about the world that is very touching.

RANDY MACKIN: As an academic, posthumous works have sometimes been difficult for me to accept. I've had something of a change of heart, though, while helping edit this collection. We'll have very little unpublished material from William after these words are in print. Like true addicts, we'll crave another fix. I'm glad to see all these final words—fully formed short stories, fragments, meanderings, whatever they might be—finding a home between the covers of a book. Are these posthumous works in their entirety as good as the books published during William's life? Some, yes; others, no. But they are essential and need to be published because these words are all we have. Here, the concern of editors is the reading public, those out there who won't be sated until they have access to all of William's words. It is for them, I think, these remaining pages need to be in print.

GEORGE DILWORTH: Gay has been fairly criticized at times for redundancy. I, too, have seen what the critics saw…only differently. Earlier in his life, we know that Cormac McCarthy pointed this out to him, and I think William took it to heart. Afterwards, when he was redundant, he did it deliberately. Usually, repetition calls for attention, a closer look, a second thought. I believe he used it that way to make you recall a scene or image and because he liked the way it sounded and what it said to him and he chose to keep it. (Might he have said, "Who's telling this yarn anyway?") With the posthumous works, beginning with the early written *Little Sister Death*, I began to see the way William honored the scribes who had inspired and taught him so much through his own original, authentic language. Michael's afterword in *The Lost Country*, linking the genres with books and authors Gay admired, was fascinating and fit well with my thoughts on the matter. William Gay is something new, a product of all his influences forged in fire. His is a rich, vivid, and haunting voice like no other.

DAWN MAJOR: What pleased me the most from reading/editing the final works was the validation I felt about claiming William was creating a Southern mythology. These works continued to support my theory. There are probably some folks out there who disagree, but for me, he employed the same world-building techniques—painting, mapping, meticulous attention to climate, terrain, plant life and wildlife, and repetitive settings and characters—as famous world-building authors such as J.R.R. Tolkien. I suspect, if he had the education, background, and time that someone like Tolkien had, Ackerman's Field and the Harrikin would have been articulated at a far grander scale.

William was also a master metaphoric writer and he often used poetic tools, the symbol being one of my favorites. Common symbols one should look for from William's work are: black dogs (Faustian connection), clocks, calendars, windows, mirrors or something reflective, hornets (shout out to Stephen King, I believe), and snakes. Many of his classic symbols have to do with his treatment of time. I believe one reason his work is so episodic is because he didn't view time linearly; his plotlines jump around sometimes because time doesn't really exist in this neat chronological manner and that concept ties into William's philosophy.

William published three novels while he was alive, **The Long Home, Provinces of Night,** *and* **Twilight,** *so now we have added an additional four:* **Little Sister Death, Stoneburner, The Lost Country,** *and* **Fugitives of the Heart.** *He also published three collections of short stories,* **I Hate to See that Evening Sun Go Down, Wittgenstein's Lolita and The Iceman,** *and* **Time Done Been Won't Be No More,** *and now we have added this final collection. How would you judge the material that we have published posthumously against the material he published while he was alive?*

MATT SNOPE: This is a great question. I genuinely think William would be overjoyed that his output extended beyond what he published in his lifetime. He probably would have been annoyed by me because one thing I've always been a bit on the fence about his use of the comma splice. But at the same time, it gives his writing a unique character, and having a corpus of writing published while he was alive helped with the posthumous stuff.

SUSAN McDONALD: I believe the posthumous works are as good as those published while he was alive. However, without the meticulous care and concern of James Michael White, none of the posthumous works would have seen the light of day. Having been a witness to the jumbled state of the unordered notebooks and scattered writings discovered in that attic that ultimately became the posthumous writings, it took countless hours, days, and weeks spent out of love and respect for William putting the writings into the order in which William intended so they could be published.

GEORGE DILWORTH: Obviously, I value every piece of composition ever published by this man. Gay was at the peak of his powers long before his death and the work discovered at his home, and in the attic of his former home, contained material both old and new, none of which I consider to be inferior (some unfinished and groping about with ideas perhaps, but not inferior). Therefore, I find the posthumous material equal to (if not surpassing) the material published prior to his death.

Feel free to add any thoughts, observations, memories, etc. if you have anything you want to say.

RANDY MACKIN: Looking back, it seems odd to me that William and I never talked about spiritual matters, or the afterlife, or what notions we had about those issues. A few months after William's death—and just weeks after his youngest daughter Laura's passing—I met William's other daughter, Lee, for lunch at a Hohenwald restaurant. We reminisced, swapped stories, talked about what might happen next with his work. Lee, also now deceased, made a couple of comments that have always stuck with me, and I don't think she would have minded me sharing them here. Lee said,

"Daddy always wanted to see a ghost." She thought her father had questions about the life after this one and seeing a ghost might have proven to him that existence does go on in some form after we have "shuffled off this mortal coil." And she told me this story: the day Lee went to the mortuary to pick up William's ashes, someone's phone rang while she was waiting, and the person had a whippoorwill ringtone. Lee said a sense of calm passed over her, as if her father was sending her a message that everything was okay, that he was where whippoorwills call as they do in many of the quiet moments of his fiction. Wherever William is, I hope it's a place like the one the autobiographical Edgewater found when he waked after a forlorn night in the woods, quoted from a manuscript page William shared from *The Lost Country*:

"But his heart was lifting and his feet felt fleet and light. The day was new and unused and this day was one that had never existed before and he saw it as a footpath that led into a world that was sensual and many faceted and complex beyond his understanding, but for the moment he was comfortable in it and roofs and shelter and ill weathers were things of no moment. He thought the only dwelling he needed was the unconfined and unwalled world itself."

MATT SNOPE: If there is an afterlife, I know William is in a good place. I imagine him with his feet in a cool creek, happily writing longhand on legal pads. I know that his life wasn't always easy, but I am so glad he stuck to his guns and pursued his gift. The world's better for it. I also think he's a good role model for men, in that William was both tough as jerky and also, obviously, very sensitive, observant, and poetic.

DAWN MAJOR: It was a great honor to be part of this process. While this is the "end" of his final works, it's really the beginning of my journey with William because (to the chagrin of my poor husband), I'm never going to stop talking about him. I hope to continue to write, lecture, and advocate for William. In fact, the reason I started blogging and advocating for living Southern authors on my website www. dawnmajor.com was because I saw the need after working with Team Gay to promote Southern authors. I plan to write an article about the supernatural elements in William's work and hopefully expand readership to genre readers by publishing in speculative fiction journals. Also, I (big project) plan to reread the entire oeuvre again paying particular attention to settings so I can map out his fictional landscape more accurately. I'm interested in writing articles about his treatment of time and the road narrative as well. That's the thing about William's work—it's just so rich you can pick and choose and go down different rabbit holes and still find more.

SUSAN McDONALD: It was clear from his works, from his manuscripts and notebooks, that he was unorganized and severely lacking in resources, even enough notebooks so that he did not have to write in margins or on the back of pages. To think of what he could have accomplished by having equipment such as computers on which to compose, edit, and save copy would have increased the number of his works, saved those that we know were lost and added to his legacy, although he may not have ever wanted to write in any other way but longhand.

William was a man of great curiosity in almost every area of literature and music and if he met someone versed in an area in which he had little knowledge, that person had his unwavering attention while he listened and learned. I am most captivated by William's nature to be drawn to the paranormal, occult, and mysterious. This was evident in his desire to personally pursue the Bell Witch legend and the resulting impact it had on him. He felt something unearthly, and it stayed with him after leaving the scene where it all happened. His scenes set in cemeteries, forests, any place in "full dark," and abandoned shacks and cabins created a visceral aura of apprehension, fear, evil and even horror. In *Little Sister Death*, the snake was a metaphorical example of this.

I think of William as personified in *The Lost Country* by Edgewater, a man with great principles who couldn't put up with any bullshit, who guarded his privacy and was always searching. I know he loved his children to a fault and that he was grateful for his friends, but I believe he thrived on being alone to think, write, and create.

About the Author

Born in Tennessee in 1939, William Gay began writing at fifteen and wrote his first novel at twenty-five, but didn't begin publishing until well into his fifties. He worked as a TV salesman, in local factories, did construction, hung sheetrock, and painted houses to support himself. His works include *The Long Home, Provinces of Night, I Hate to See That Evening Sun Go Down, Wittgenstein's Lolita*, and *Twilight*. His work has been adapted for the screen twice, *That Evening Sun* (2009) and *Bloodworth* (2010), with an adaptation of *The Long Home* forthcoming. He died in 2012.